Dr. Olea Nel was born in Cape Town, South Africa. After completing her training as a teacher in Andrew Murray's heartland of Wellington, she relocated to Australia to further her studies. Besides attaining a PhD in Linguistics, she also has qualifications in Information Studies and Theology. Having now retired from her position as a senior librarian at the National Library of Australia, she is able to pursue her passion for research, especially within the fields of church history and biography. Her aim is to share her findings with fellow Christians.

Andrew Murray:
Destined to Win

Book Two in 'Destined' Series

Olea Nel

Clairvaux House

© 2016 by Olea Nel
Published by Clairvaux House
24 Taggerty Street
Ngunnawal ACT 2913
Australia

Cover design by Clive Thompson
Maps and layout by Geoff Alves

Unless otherwise indicated, Bible quotations are taken from the Holy Bible,
King James Version 1611.

ISBN 978-0-9925671-5-6

Contents

Author's Note

This novel is the second in my trilogy on Andrew Murray's life, and covers the years 1850-1856. The first novel covers Andrew Murray's first year in ministry and is titled: *Andrew Murray Destined to Serve: A Biographical Novel.* But although this present book is part of a series, it can quite happily stand on its own.

As with the first novel, this is a dramatized biography told in the first person. Fortunately, Andrew Murray was an avid letter writer, particularly to his father and brother John. In these letters, he would freely discuss his thoughts and feelings, and even bare his soul regarding his spiritual walk. I therefore felt at ease in writing my novel in the first person.

Essentially, my aim with this series is for readers to get to know the real Andrew Murray, and not just the giant of the faith that he later became. In essence, I've set out to trace his spiritual journey within the highs and lows of everyday life. I also wanted readers to realize that there was a 'before' and an 'after' period in his life, and that his devotional works literally pulse with the spiritual lessons learnt during the period covered in this book.

Maps

I've included a few maps to help readers who are not familiar with South Africa. If you are reading this novel on a Kindle device, you may want to refer to the Map Page on my website at: http://www.onandrewmurray.com/maps

Photographs

For those who are interested, I've included a few photographs of places and characters mentioned in this story. They can be viewed on the Photos Page of my website at:
http://www.onandrewmurray.com/photos

Bibliography and Notes

I've included a bibliography and a few notes for historical buffs.

Glossary of Terms

There is a glossary of Dutch terms at the back of the book. While I have kept the use of Dutch to a minimum, there are a few terms that have been consistently used to indicate conversations in Dutch.

Because Andrew Murray was a Dutch Reformed pastor, he would have always been addressed as *Dominee* (Reverend) by his Dutch-speaking parishioners, and Mr. Murray, by his English-speaking ones. He, in turn, would have used the appellation *Meneer* (Mr.) and *Mevrou* (Mrs.) when conversing with members of his Dutch-speaking congregation.

Another Dutch term that needs to be mentioned here is *consulent* (acting minister). I've used it throughout this novel because it had a specific meaning during Andrew Murray's day. A pastor serving in one congregation became a *consulent* to an adjoining congregation if the latter was without a pastor. As part of his duties as *consulent*, he would have been required to conduct a series of services in the adjoining congregation once a quarter.

These would have included: preparation for Holy Communion, the Communion service itself, followed by a thanksgiving service. He would have also needed to conduct marriages, baptize infants, and test communicants on the Heidelberg

Catechism and their biblical knowledge. His visit would have therefore covered several days.

Those with a knowledge of South African history will notice that the term *Voortrekker*—to denote Dutch stock farmers who trekked across the Orange and Vaal Rivers—is never used. This is because that term was not in use during the 1850s.

Acknowledgments

I would like to thank my husband Peter for his unflagging encouragement and support while writing this novel. His regular input has helped to raise the readability of this book. I'm forever grateful.

I'm deeply indebted to Gwenyth Bray, Carolyn Wood, and Attie van Wijk for donating their time to read my manuscript and provide invaluable input. Their generosity in this respect was a godsend.

A special word of recognition goes to the following people who supplied photographs or little-known information for this project. They are Madaleen Welman of Herschel Girls' School in Cape Town, who kindly sent me photographs of the original section of Herschel; Heidi Morgan, who provided photographs of buildings associated with Andrew Murray's time in Bloemfontein; and Malan Schrecker, who sent me information on Dirk van Velden and Ladismith.

I would also like to thank a number of people for their ongoing expressions of support while I was in the throes of writing this novel. They are Marietta van der Merwe, Mariana Nesbitt, Claudia Curtis, Lori Jackson, Margaret de Guara, and Maureen Pettrey. Their encouragement helped to keep me going. I can't thank them enough.

A special word of thanks goes once again to Geoff Alves for making himself available to format this novel.

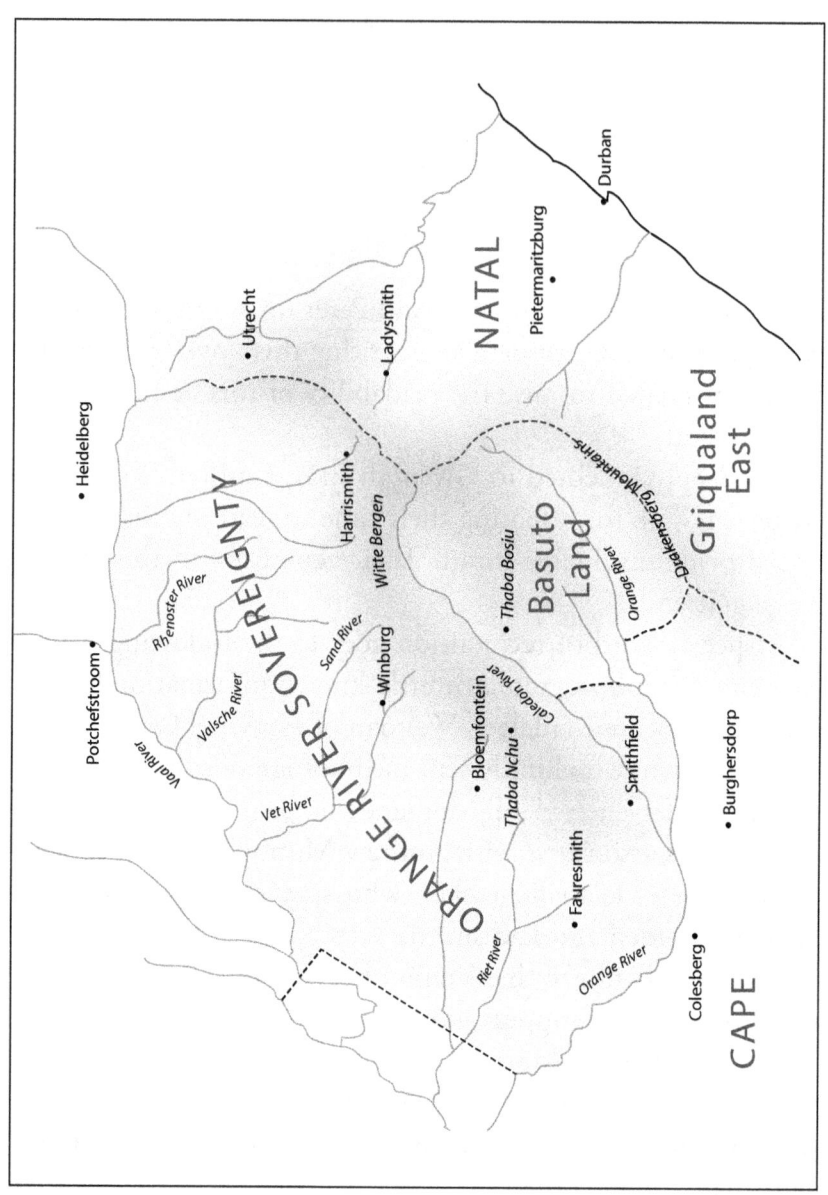

Orange River Sovereignty between 1849 and 1854

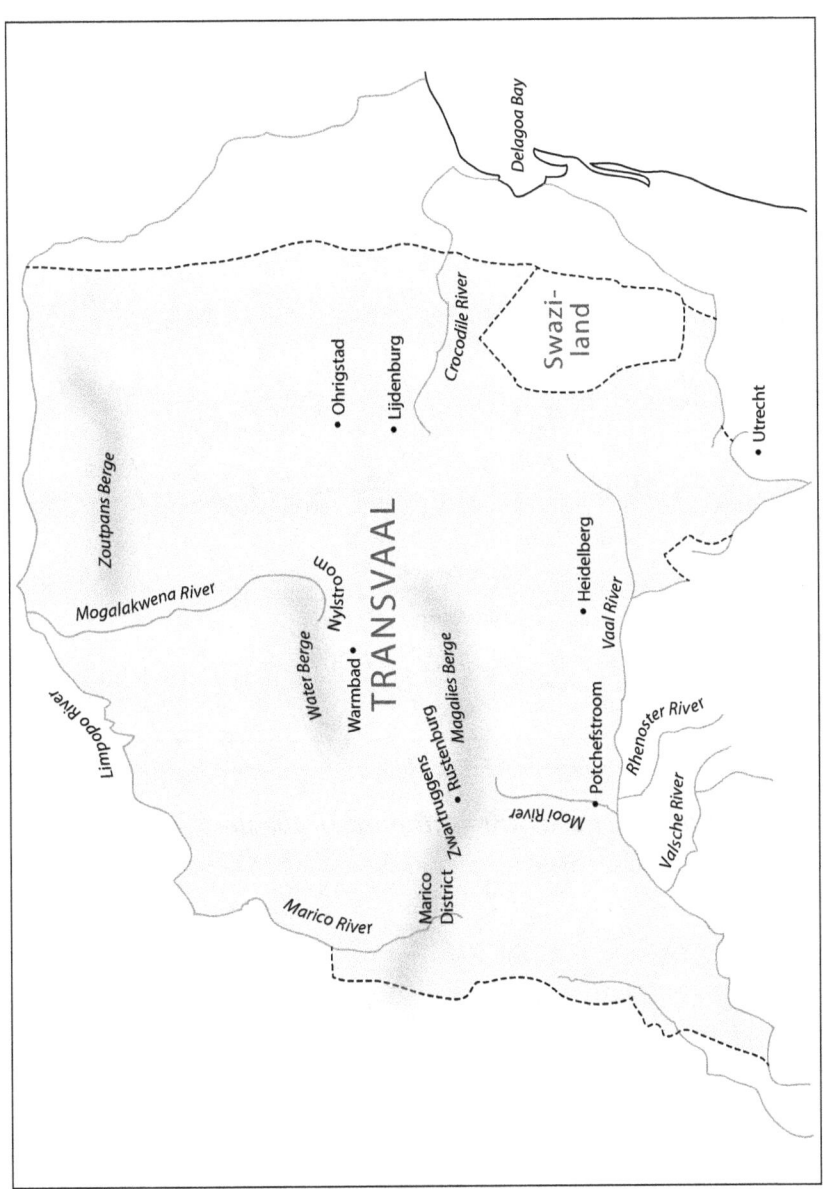

Transvaal between 1849 and 1852

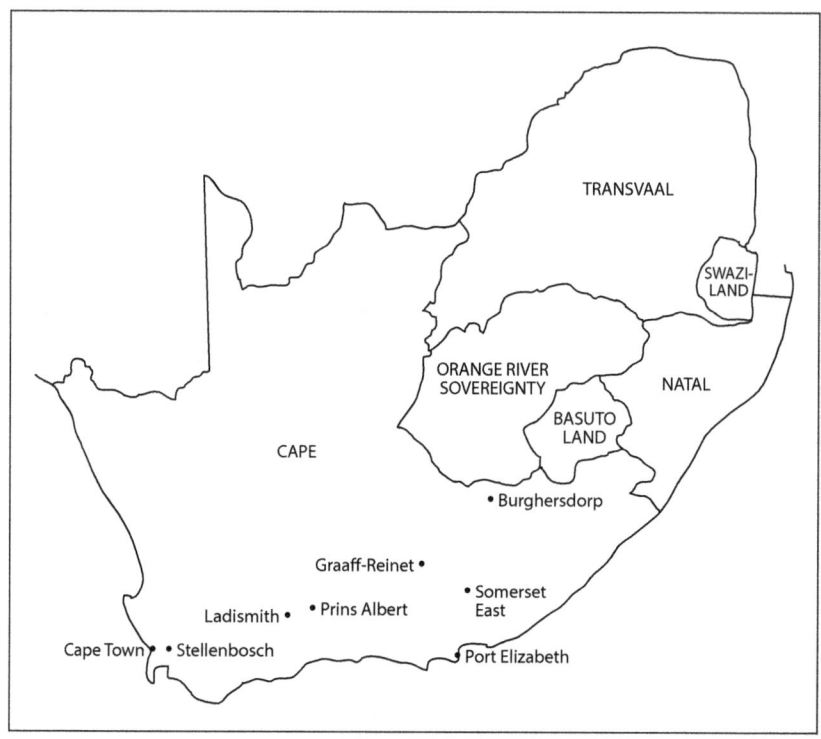

Towns in the Cape that are mentioned in the story

Prologue
Clairvaux, Wellington

July 1915

I drew my collar up against the freezing cold of a July morning in Wellington, and walked along the pebbled pathway leading to Andrew Murray's home, my feet scrunching the pebbles as I went. His modest house fronted a laneway that was scarcely broader than the width of two horse wagons. And except for the tubs containing evergreen shrubs on either side of the front door, the laneway was devoid of all flowers or plants.

I tapped on the chocolate-brown door with the knocker provided, and waited. All appeared still within. I knew I had the correct date for my second interview with Dr. Murray because it was the first day of the mid-year break at Stellenbosch Theological Seminary. And you didn't forget a date like that, especially if you were a professor at that institution. Well, perhaps "break" wasn't the correct term for what I had in mind. Over the next few weeks I intended to embark on Andrew Murray's biography. And my enthusiasm for this project was such that I couldn't think of any pursuit more enjoyable than sitting beside a roaring fire, pen in hand.

I unbuttoned my overcoat and withdrew my gold watch from its pouch. It was twenty-seven minutes to ten, exactly three minutes after the stated time for my arrival. I tapped on the door again—a little louder this time. I wasn't unduly concerned about the wait because I detected smoke pouring out of two chimneys. Perhaps Annie, Andrew Murray's daughter, hadn't heard my initial knock. I knew she acted as her father's amanuensis by writing his correspondence and even the texts of his books he dictated to her. I paused to dwell on this thought a little longer, wondering whether I would be able to dictate my books if painful tingles in my arms and hands hampered me from holding a pen. I thought not.

Shrugging off this thought, I stepped back a few steps to view the façade of the building. Dr. Murray hadn't wasted an inch of land. From the laneway, you couldn't tell that he had positioned his home on a flat ridge overlooking a narrow valley of vines with a low-lying hill beyond. This pleasant outlook had inspired him to name his home Clairvaux after his hero of the faith, St. Bernard of Clairvaux, the French monk who had lived in the twelfth century.

I recalled Dr. Murray's words as he explained the naming of his home with a chuckle and a wink: "Not that the average person around here would know that I've named my home after a monastery in France, Johan. They simply think that I've chosen a French name because most of the farmers in these parts are from French Huguenot stock. So they heartily endorse it."

I walked to the gate a few paces to my left and peered through the opening below the lintel. Beyond was a well-kept side garden with a narrow patch of lawn skirting the edge of an L-shaped *stoep* that wrapped around the back of the house. It was off this back *stoep* with its pleasant views that Andrew Murray had chosen a room for his study.

Still detecting no sign of life, my thoughts turned to Andrew Murray's eighty-fifth birthday party that I had attended on 9 May. I had arrived at the same time as a few first-time guests, and had watched amused as their eyes had scanned the plain exterior of the house only to be beguiled a little later by the old-fashioned charm and warmth of the large sitting room that looked out upon the side *stoep* and manicured lawn.

My reverie was broken when the door suddenly opened and Annie stepped out, looking this way and that. Spying me near the gate, she pressed her hand to her heart in theatrical fashion and blew out a breath in relief.

Although she was in her thirties, she looked much younger on account of her fair hair being arranged in a loose bun at the nape of her neck. I noticed that a few wisps had escaped unheeded and were blowing every which way in the breeze. She looked quite fetching this morning in a dark maroon velvet dress that had obviously been demoted to day wear. But in spite of her plain features, I found that her kind face and intelligent eyes drew one to her. The overall impression was of a young woman with an intellectual bent who had spurned glamour in favor of more academic pursuits.

"Good morning, Professor du Plessis," she said offering her hand. "For a minute there I thought you may have left. I'm so sorry to have kept you waiting. You see, Pa has been dictating Day 31 of his latest pocket book to me. He's titled it: *The Secret of the Faith Life*. Unfortunately, we still have a few paragraphs to go." She offered me an apologetic smile, then continued: "He says that he needs to finish this book before he's able to give you his full attention. So I hope you don't mind waiting a little longer."

She led the way inside and ushered me into the sitting room. I observed that her usual graceful demeanor had given way to jitteriness this morning.

"I've just been helping our maid, Mimi, light the fire in here. It shouldn't take too long to warm up."

Before I could assure her that I didn't mind in the least, and that the time alone would help focus my thoughts, she had already turned to go.

She was about to close the door behind her, when she glanced back at me and said, "I'd better get back. Hopefully Pa hasn't lost his train of thought by now."

But instead of closing the door, I watched in surprise as she shut her eyes and lifted her hand to her forehead. "Oh dear!" she said in breathless fashion, "I've forgotten to take your overcoat. How unmannerly of me!"

To my amusement, she bustled back into the room while I dutifully slipped out of my coat and handed it to her with a flourish.

"I wouldn't worry about your father losing his train of thought, *Juffrou* Murray. He has the uncanny ability to hold what he wants to say until he is ready to convey it. So I'm sure you'll find that his thoughts will flow when you get back.

"I'm sure you are right, Professor du Plessis. You must think me a real nervous Nelly. I'm afraid I take after my Aunt Maria, you see. No doubt Pa has already mentioned her."

"You mean the Spanish doll?"

She lifted a brow in surprise. "So Pa has already told you about her. I dare say he's described her in terms of dancing the flamenco to the accompaniment of castanets when she got upset."

"That he has. And apparently he and your Uncle Willie were of the view that she might have been a throwback to a distant Spanish relative on your maternal grandmother's side. I suppose that's feasible because the Spanish did rule the Low Countries at one time."

"Hmm, I prefer the version that she was a throwback to our French connection. You may not know this, but besides being from German stock, *Ouma* also had French Huguenot ancestors who came out to the Cape in 1688."

"A far more acceptable explanation, I'm sure," I said, with tongue in cheek.

Her lips twitched at the corners while she deftly flicked off a thread of lint from my coat. "In any case, I don't play the castanets—if you know what I mean. I just get nervy when things don't go according to plan, like now."

"Think no more of it. I'd love a moment to myself before the hearth."

I watched as her body released its tension and she broke into a smile. "That's what Pa said. Well, I'd better get back. We shouldn't be too long."

After she had left, I gravitated to the warmth of the hearth where I caught sight of myself in the beveled mirror that hung over the mantelpiece. I wasn't a vain man, but wanting to maintain appearances, I ran a comb through my hair and smoothed my full moustache, of which I was justly proud. I then patted my cheeks to make sure my morning shave passed muster. Despite everyone else sporting a beard at Stellenbosch, I drew the line at growing one, preferring to retain a youthful look.

Having warmed myself adequately at the fire, I went to sit in a winged armchair nearby. I extracted my notebook from my briefcase and proceeded to peruse the notes I'd made during my first interview in May. They were rather sparse, to say the least. I'd obviously been so swept along by the story and intrigued by Dr. Murray's dramatic gesticulations that I'd failed to take notes at certain points. Not to worry, I thought. Fortunately there were letters and documents that Annie had indexed on which I could rely.

I stared at the first page of notes, and shook my head in wonderment. Just three days before Andrew Murray's twenty-first birthday, he had been inducted as pastor of Bloemfontein, the capital of the Orange River Sovereignty. But because he was the only pastor beyond the borders of the Cape at the time, in reality, his congregation consisted of over 12 000 Boers in the Sovereignty and a further 8000 across the Vaal River. And because he was acting minister, or *consulent*, to three other church centers in the Sovereignty, it was expected that he travel to one or other of these centers every second week to conduct a series of services associated with Holy Communion. These usually numbered five: one on Tuesday evening, three on Wednesday, and one on Thursday morning.

During these services he would marry couples, baptize infants, and test young people on their knowledge of the Bible and Heidelberg Catechism. Those who passed—usually about half—would be received into membership on Thursday morning. He would then rush back to Bloemfontein, usually arriving there by late Friday afternoon. This would barely give him enough time to prepare for the usual week-end services. These started on Saturday evening with a service for the Coloreds who made up the Cape Corps. Then on Sundays, there was a service for the Dutch farmers in the morning, followed by a Sunday school class for the English settler children directly after lunch. Barely an hour and a half later, he would have to conduct the English service. To cap it all, the Dutch farmers requested a late afternoon service during the summer months.

My head was in a whirl just thinking of all these services. It was ridiculous in the extreme, especially as the other three church centers of Winburg, Smithfield and Fauresmith were on average a day-and-a-half's journey away. And from what I was led to understand, it was far from a pleasant journey. There were potholes and deep ruts in the road to avoid, and the constant jolts told terribly on the body, even when riding in a well-sprung Cape cart.

I flipped over to the next page of my notes. Huh! I uttered aloud in consternation. For there, scrawled across the top of the page, I had written the heading TRANSVAAL in capitals. Poor fellow! Just six months into his ministry, he'd been persuaded to tour the vast area across the Vaal River during his six-week summer vacation.

I was still shaking my head in disbelief, when I heard a light tap on the door, and saw Annie's head appear around it.

"You'll be relieved to hear that Pa's completed his pocket book, Professor du Plessis. As you surmised, the words flowed. Please come through. He's waiting to greet you."

When I entered the study, Dr. Murray was standing with his back to the hearth while pumping his feet up and down. To my surprise he looked sprightly, and his cheeks were aglow with health.

"Come in, come in, Johan. Sorry to have kept you waiting, but it was essential that I complete my pocket book in order to give you my undivided attention."

"I must say you are looking exceptionally well, Dr. Murray."

He smiled in agreement. "This might come as a surprise to you, but in my old age I've come to like Wellington winters. You see, I rarely leave this room. It enables me to stay well, and my creaky old bones pain free."

"Very sensible, Dr. Murray."

He swept his hand over his balding head then along the back of his grey-streaked hair to their very tips. I noticed that his hair had grown considerably longer since my last visit and was already brushing the tops of his shoulders.

Being an observant man, who had an uncanny ability to read one's thoughts, he said, "The downside of not venturing out is that my hair grows too long, and my beard too bushy. I won't be visiting a barber until spring, you see. And asking Annie to do the honors is out of the question. I did so one year to my regret."

There was still a twinkle in his eye when I shook his hand then went to sit in the seat to which he pointed. He followed closely behind, making his way to his high-backed armchair that had been swiveled to face mine. Because his desk had been placed flush against the window that overlooked the valley of vines, there was a generous space in the center of the study for several chairs.

He watched with amusement as I craned my neck to look out the window to inspect the snow-capped hill beyond. "Quite a different tableau from when you were here in autumn. But not without its own charm, of course."

"That goes without saying, Dr. Murray."

"But while it looks rather dreary now, you should see it in springtime. I love to watch the leaves multiply on the vines, then observe the forming and ripening of the grapes, followed by the bustle of harvest—a perfect parable of the Christian journey, don't you think?"

Before I could answer, we were interrupted by the maid, Mimi, who brought in a pot of coffee. She was followed by Annie carrying a tray of side plates that each contained an array of *boerbeskuit.*

Dr. Murray's eyes sparkled with mirth as he surveyed the assortment of *boerbeskuit*. "Ah, Johan, my coffee wouldn't be the same without a rusk or two to dunk. Please feel free to do the same. This cultural habit that I learnt from the frontier Boer has remained with me all these years. I've even introduced it to English friends from London who resisted the idea at first. But after a while, they joined me with a chuckle and a wink when polite society wasn't present."

"Be assured, Dr. Murray, I have no qualms about dunking *boerbeskuit*. It's par for the course among the students at Stellenbosch."

"And it's par for the course around here too—polite society or no," said Annie, while placing one of the plates on the side table next to me.

I noticed that the selection of rusks ranged from a milky cream to a rich honey color, with one or two containing a smattering of aniseed. I selected the milky one and dunked it in my coffee with more circumspection than usual. Once in my mouth, my taste buds delighted in its creamy texture.

"Now remind me, Johan, where did we get to with my story when you were here last?"

I took another sip of coffee to wash down the rusk, then rattled off the exact point without hesitation: "You were back in Bloemfontein once more after contracting malaria in the Transvaal, and Dr. Drury, who was about to leave for England, stayed back an extra few days to examine you. Both he and Dr. Fraser didn't hold out much hope for you continuing in the ministry."

Dr. Murray lent back in his chair, cup in hand, and donned a far-away look. "Dear Dr. Drury. I can just see him in my mind's eye: tall, angular, and as spiky as the aloe in the veld, but oozing goodness within. He was the only one who could rein me in, you know."

"What about Dr. Fraser?"

"To tell you the truth, I don't think it even dawned on him that I might need reining in. You see, for several years he'd been an assistant army surgeon to the 91st Regiment. And who's ever heard of a soldier who needed persuading to take recuperation leave? But Drury was another matter entirely. He would lay down the law, tell my consistory off for working me too hard, then persuade Elder Willem Pretorius to oversee my recovery."

"It was a miracle," interrupted Annie, who had joined us for morning coffee. "If it hadn't been for Dr. Drury extracting a promise from Pa to convalesce for six weeks, he would probably not be in the ministry today."

Dr. Murray broke into a smile. "Well Johan, it seems as if you should be interviewing Annie instead of me."

I returned his smile. "I fully intend to one day."

Annie blushed, then got up to go. "Don't worry, Pa. I can take a hint. I only hope that you will tell your story warts and all."

I watched amused as he waved her out of the room. He then turned to me and said, "I hope you remember our pact, Johan? I'll share all with you, but please write only that which you deem appropriate. Now where were we?"

"You were about to be issued with a call to the Transvaal."

"Ah yes. And oh, how I wanted to go!"

"So what hampered you, Dr. Murray? Was it because of opposition from the Presbytery of Graaff-Reinet to which you belonged at the time?"

He observed me through hooded eyelids, his lips twitching with mirth. "Let's not get ahead of ourselves here, Johan."

I knew that look, and knew he was ready to begin. And if my last interview was anything to go by, I also knew that he wanted to immerse himself in the story with no interruptions from me. He wanted to relive every moment again—at times using dramatic gestures to emphasize a point, at others, slowing down the pace when describing some moving occasion or a moment of inner reflection. He would then suddenly hasten the tempo once more while relating a challenging circumstance or an exciting event.

It promised, once again, to be an exhilarating journey, and I could hardly wait to accompany him on the ride.

I

On the Road with Elder Willem Pretorius

July 1850

Elder Willem Pretorius and I were in high spirits when we set out for Graaff-Reinet at the beginning of July. We had toyed with the idea of taking the wagon, but had decided against it in favor of his four-seater Cape cart that was comfortably upholstered with an excellent hood and roll-down covers. And because it hadn't been long since my lengthy recuperation after contracting malaria, he had insisted on taking his driver to relieve me from having to take my turn at the reins. So there was every prospect that I'd be looking rested and well when I arrived home.

While stowing my case between the front and box seats, and bundling my bedroll and blankets into the latter, I caught sight of Pretorius's hatbox. Observing my knowing smile, he said, "*Ach*, I get so few opportunities to wear top hat and tails that I couldn't resist bringing them along."

"I notice that you have two cases, *Meneer* Pretorius. I dare say you have packed in a dinner suit as well."

"That goes without saying, *Dominee*. I wouldn't want the

Graaff-Reinetters to think we were all country bumpkins around here, now would I?"

We were still sniggering like school boys when we hopped into the cart. I couldn't help noticing how agile he was for a man approaching fifty. But despite his greying hair and chin beard, he looked at least a decade younger than his forty-eight years. I'd also observed on other visits to Graaff-Reinet that he loved to play the role of a younger man. But it was undoubtedly his penchant for travel and adventure that made him readily agree to take me home for a short recreational spell. Needless to say, my four deacons plus Elder Jacobus van Zyl were only too pleased to let him do it.

We exchanged smiles as the cart pulled off and I helped him pull the knee-rug over our legs. I leaned my head back on the plumped headrest and observed the scattered homes as we passed by. Bloemfontein had almost doubled in size since my arrival last May. There were now about eighty houses plus several stores, not to speak of a market place with a bell to announce the times of the cattle sales.

The growth of the town had prompted Major Warden to employ Andrew Bain to design the street layout and the plots for future homes. And as there were always a number of drunk and disorderly English settlers in the lockup, my closest friend, Charles Stuart, who was also the magistrate, was always assured of a never-ending supply of convicts to clear the vegetation and dig water furrows from the spring in the center of the village.

The thought of the village spring reminded me of the first time I had passed it on my way to the schoolroom to conduct my first church service. It had been a freezing morning, and the spring had been iced over. But by mid-August, it had been surrounded by a profusion of flowers that continued to bloom for about nine months of the year. And although there were different versions as to how the name Bloemfontein—fountain of flowers—came into being, I favored the version that linked the spring to its flowery surrounds.

My train of thought was broken when Queen's Fort came into view with its four, nine-pound cannons. Directly below was the barracks complex that housed about a hundred or so Cape Riflemen plus a further sixty Dutch-speaking Coloreds of the Cape Corps. Yet in spite of this insignificant number, the commanding officer, Major Warden, was hopeful that it would deter Paramount Chief Moshesh of the Basuto from declaring war on the British.

But why, oh why, had Warden drawn that unworkable boundary line between the farmers in the lower Caledon Valley and Moshesh? By all accounts, it was grossly unfair to the Basuto. And to keep on the right side of Moshesh's ire, most of the Boers living near the town of Smithfield had openly declared their support for the chief.

I was still mulling this over in my mind when I heard Pretorius heave a sigh next to me. "I'm sure you're thinking what I'm thinking, *Dominee*. If Major Warden hadn't drawn that unfair boundary line that was sure to cause trouble with Moshesh, he wouldn't have had to use the money earmarked for our church building to purchase extra guns and ammunition now. And because he's overspent on stockpiling those armaments, the Sovereignty is in debt. It's a disgrace!"

"So it is, *Meneer* Pretorius. But at least the consistory is roofed over, so we need to be thankful for small mercies."

"I'm afraid I don't see it that way. The Warden line is all about greed and doing the bidding of Warden's pals. He is stealing land from Moshesh so that those British land speculators can purchase it for a song, then sell it later at a hefty profit."

"To be fair, it's not all Warden's fault that our church building hasn't been completed. He told me just the other day that the Sovereignty's revenue was only half of what it should be to cover civil purposes. So he's had to take out a loan from the Cape treasury."

"That's terrible! When will our church building ever be finished then? The foundation stone was laid in January 1849, and now it's July 1850. That's one and a half years."

Once Pretorius got going on a topic there was no end in sight to his observations and complaints, so I skillfully changed the subject. "To get back to Major Warden, *Meneer* Pretorius, of one thing we can be sure, he's misjudged Moshesh."

"Huh! Not only Moshesh, *Dominee*, but most of the Boers as well. And as I've already told you, those around Smithfield will disobey Major Warden's command to form a commando to fight Moshesh. Of that I'm certain."

I nodded, knowing what Pretorius said was true. But I wanted to leave these problems behind for another day, so I closed my eyes to indicate this fact. All I wanted to do now was to delight in my contemplations of family and home.

My thoughts soon turned to Burghersdorp, a small town in the Eastern Cape that lay just south of the Orange River. It was there that we would be taking a full day's break to visit my newly-married brother John, and my younger brother Charles. John had married Maria-Anna, the daughter of my parents' closest friends, the Ziervogels, in December. But because I'd been on my preaching tour in the Transvaal at the time, I'd been unable to attend his wedding.

I smiled as I remembered the day we'd arrived back in Graaff-Reinet after ten years of absence overseas. There had been a welcome morning tea for us. And it was at that event that John had met Maria-Anna and had fallen in love with her. During their short courtship, I had felt that I was losing him as my best friend and confidante. But now that he was a settled married man, I was hopeful that we could resume our close friendship again.

It was amazing, I thought, how we could be brothers and close friends and still be surprised at the actions of the other. Although newly married, John was still prepared to instruct our seventeen-year-old brother Charles in Latin and other subjects in preparation for theological studies in Utrecht.

I sighed at the thought of the extra expense that Dutch families had to fork out for Latin tuition if they wanted their sons to study overseas. The problem was that unlike English and Scottish universities, where the medium of instruction was in English, in Holland, it was still in Latin. And to employ a skilled Latin teacher at the Cape was a significant drain on the family purse. Charles was therefore one of the fortunate ones in having an older brother to instruct him. And as he was only due to leave for Utrecht when our other brother Willie returned, he still had three years up his sleeve to gain the competence required.

My thoughts lingered on each brother in turn and then on my saintly father. How proud he must be that four of his sons had decided to be pastors!

The steady pace of the cart and the hypnotic sound of the horses' hooves had lulled Pretorius to sleep. I, on the other hand, was still too excited at the thought of spending a full day with John and Charles in Burghersdorp to succumb so early in the piece. The more my thoughts took flight, the greater my expectation that this would probably be one of my best holidays ever.

I had miraculously recovered from contracting malaria. My first year of ministry with its inevitable bungling was over. And I had made a breakthrough with my sermons while on tour in the Transvaal. Then there was the wonderful news of the appointment of *Dominee* Dirk van Velden to Winburg. From my perspective, his coming would leave me free to accept the call to the Transvaal. While I hadn't actually received the official letter yet, I knew that the combined consistories of Potchefstroom and Rustenburg were waiting for my complete recovery before issuing it. All I had to do now was persuade my father that accepting this call was indeed God's will for my life. And with Dirk van Velden's appointment to Winburg, I couldn't foresee any complications.

While all looked bright on the horizon at that moment, life has a way of thwarting our best laid plans. For as the saying goes: "Man proposes but God disposes."

2

Within the Bosom of the Family Again

July 1850

With our two-night stop-over in Burghersdorp, plus a rest day on Sunday, the journey to Graaff-Reinet took us around nine days. The last section of our journey through the Great Karoo with its endless horizons of low shrubs and scattered *kopjes* seemed interminable. But now in the late afternoon, the setting sun had begun to highlight the reds and oranges of the rocky outcrops that dotted our route, thus making this boring terrain come alive with glorious tinctures of color.

My heart lurched with delight as I caught a glimpse of Spandau Kop, the pyramid-type hill that overlooked Graaff-Reinet. As we journeyed closer, the church steeple came into view. It seemed to shoot up skyward from a lush canopy of green trees that I knew was being watered by the Sundays River that looped around the town in the shape of a horseshoe.

Whenever I neared Graaff-Reinet, I always got the impression of arriving home after a long trek through the wilderness. And I knew that Pretorius thought so too. At that moment, he couldn't take his eyes off the church steeple that was such a powerful symbol of God's presence in the town.

"I wonder when Bloemfontein will be able to boast a steeple like that, *Dominee?*"

I let the question hang unanswered between us. I would soon be home in the bosom of the family, and who wanted to think of Bloemfontein at a moment like this. Besides, I needed to refresh my memory regarding the ages and birthdays of my siblings. When I had commented on their ages and how they had grown the last time I was home, they had giggled with delight.

I fished in my inside pocket for my birthday book, and opened it to the first page. A curious Pretorius leaned over to see what I was reading.

"Just acquainting myself with everyone's birthdays, *Meneer* Pretorius."

"*Ja*, you'd better fill me in as well. Young children love it when you remember their names and guess their ages. I always add on an extra year because it makes them feel important."

"Unfortunately, I'm expected to get it right."

"Start with your eldest sister first—you know, the capable one who speaks English and Dutch equally well. I always feel that I have to rehearse what I want to say before addressing her."

"That's Maria. My brother Willie and I like to refer to her as our Spanish doll because she wears her dark hair parted in the middle and drawn back into a bun, just like the Spanish doll in my mother's Delft cabinet. She's also highly strung and tends to be flamboyant when she gets upset. Nevertheless, she's solid gold beneath."

"How old is she now?"

"She's just had her nineteenth birthday in June."

"Who's next?"

"Jemima. She's my little German fräulein who favors wearing her blond hair in plaits. You won't be able to miss her because she likes to arrange them like a band over the top of her head. She's fourteen already and spends a great deal of time in the kitchen baking cake."

I knew Pretorius had a sweet tooth like mine, so I looked his way and winked. "Her specialty is melktert and koeksisters."

"Hmm! I can't wait." He looked pensive for a moment then asked, "Who's the sickly one who had rheumatic fever?"

"That's James. He's a year and a half younger than Jemima, and will be thirteen in October."

"If I remember correctly, the next one in line is a girl."

"That's Isabella. She's eleven, and the organizer par excellence of the family. She doesn't like wearing her hair in buns or plaits, and, given half the chance, would wear it loose. But Ma insists that it's properly turned under on Sundays."

"Yes, I remember her well. She's the talkative one who loves to converse with visitors."

I nodded, recalling how difficult it sometimes was to get away once she'd engaged one in conversation.

"There's yet another girl, isn't there?"

"Yes, pretty little Kitty. She's very playful and has fair hair like Jemima. As she is nine, and therefore close in age to Isabella, the two of them do everything together."

Pretorius broke into a chuckle. "You don't have to remind me who's next. It's none other than boisterous little George. When we were here for the Presbytery meeting in September, your father told me that he was at his wits' end over his lively behavior. Apparently, after your departure for Bloemfontein, he had begun to play up. How old is he now?"

I didn't have to look at Georgie's entry, nor that of baby Helen's. So I snapped the birthday book shut, and returned it to my inside pocket.

"He'll be five next month, *Meneer* Pretorius. And if the truth be known, he's just a normal little boy who's rebelling against the continuous discipline exerted by Maria and the girls. At the other end of the spectrum, he's being fawned over by my doting mother. But when he's with me, he settles down nicely."

"*Ja*, your father said the same thing. He also asked for my advice on the subject. One thing I couldn't help noticing is that Georgie was on his best behavior with your father's driver, Amos. I believe he has grandsons around Georgie's age?"

"That's true."

"Well, you might be pleased to know that I advised your father to employ a younger driver and promote Amos to general manager of the servants and outside area. That way, when your father's away from home, he'll know that Amos is there to supervise Georgie when he's playing outside. As part of his duties, he can teach him to ride as well as take him on visits to his little friends on nearby farms."

I raised an appreciative brow, while wondering why I hadn't thought of that solution. Having been on the receiving end of Amos's no-nonsense approach when I was young, I was fairly certain that Pretorius's plan would work.

We had just turned into Parsonage Street, and there in the distance stood my childhood home, its Cape Dutch gable glistening in the setting sun. The vista of this beautiful building plus the long avenue of trees, with equally impressive buildings behind, caused us both to fall silent.

As the cart drew nearer, I caught a glimpse of the rounded windows of the cellars beneath the main house. As a child, I loved to play hide and seek there with John and my younger brother Willie. But as Isabella and Kitty had now outgrown the hide-and-seek stage, it was unfortunate that poor Georgie would have to forfeit that delight. Hmm, perhaps not, I thought. I'd make it my business to play with him there one day.

At last we were turning right into Murray Street, then left into the side street that led to the wagon entrance behind the parsonage. In my mind's eye, I could see my siblings rushing down the back steps to greet me, just as they had done when John and I had arrived home two years before. How wonderful it would be to see them all again!

The gate was standing open, and there was Amos giving us his usual salute. But what was different this time was that Georgie was standing next to him, a broad grin lighting up his face as he too saluted us.

The cart had barely come to a stop, when Georgie came bounding up. "I escaped, I escaped," he yelled, while hopping up and down.

I exchanged amused glances with Pretorius. "Where did you escape from?" I asked.

"From Papa's study. Isabella was teaching me to read there when we saw the cart come up Parsonage Street. So Papa got up to tell Mama, and that's when I escaped."

"Why didn't Isabella follow you?"

"Because it's cold outside and she gets the sniffles."

"I see. So where is everyone else?"

"They all have influenza except for Mama, who's looking after little Helen, and Jemima, who's baking cake in the kitchen."

"So who's supposed to be looking after you?"

Georgie puckered his nose as he pondered this question. "Jemima. She's now in charge. But she's not so strict as Maria 'cause she allows me to play outside."

I noticed that without Maria to supervise him, Georgie looked more like an urchin than a lad from a respectable family. He was dressed in a pair of old pants and a creased shirt. And although the cold had descended along with the setting sun, his shirt sleeves were rolled up to the elbows. His shock of auburn hair also seemed more unruly than usual, and there was a crusted smear across his left cheek.

I became aware that he was still keeping his distance and eyeing me with a questioning look. "Aren't you going to greet *Meneer* Pretorius and me?"

"Your beard looks funny because it's all patchy. Is it because you're sick? I don't want to catch it."

I heard Amos snigger behind me and Pretorius make a quip under his breath. The fact of the matter was that although I was twenty-two, my beard was still stringy and not up to being seen in public. I had used the long journey home as a test case to see whether it could pass muster. But by virtue of Georgie's comments, it had obviously failed the test miserably.

"Yes, I was very sick, but I'm feeling much better now. And no, you can't catch it."

I'd barely uttered these words, when he catapulted himself into my arms, nearly bowling me over. I set him down quickly while reminding him to greet *Meneer* Pretorius. It was during their friendly banter that I caught sight of Jemima tripping across the yard to greet us, a woolen shawl tightly wrapped around her shoulders. Her cheeks were aglow with health, and as expected, her plaited hair was looped round her head in the style she favored most. Although only fourteen, she looked the epitome of a young lady of seventeen or thereabouts.

Pretorius obviously thought so too because he addressed her as *Juffrou* Murray, an appellation usually reserved for the eldest daughter of the family once she had reached marriageable age. I marveled at her composure as she explained that it was Maria who was the eldest daughter, and that he should call her Jemima.

She then pecked me on the lips and said, "I hope ragamuffin Georgie here has been able to make up for the rest of the family not being present to greet you. But hopefully they'll be well enough tomorrow to make an appearance."

"Not to worry, Jemima. I'll poke my head around their bedroom doors and wave a hello."

"No, you can't," said Georgie, looking stricken and shaking his head. "Mama said that the sick rooms are out of bounds. So you're not allowed to do that."

Jemima ruffled Georgie's hair while smiling down at him. "Quite right, Georgie. In any case, Maria and Kitty wouldn't want to be seen at their worst, now would they? They would like to be wearing pretty frocks with their hair neatly arranged when greeting Andrew. And I'm sure he would want to look his best as well. That's why I've asked cook to place a jug of warm water in both his and *Meneer* Pretorius's rooms. And guess what? There's one in your room as well."

I combed my fingers through my dry and dust-caked hair, realizing that it must look a fright. Recalling that Amos was waiting patiently a few paces behind, I turned to greet him. He grasped my hand in his and pumped it up and down in silence, his eyes managing to convey unsaid words of thankfulness that I was home again. When he eventually spoke, his words were down to earth, yet nevertheless profound.

"*Ach Kleinbaas*, when one has been near death and back again, buttons, bows and beards don't count for much, do they?" Tapping my arm playfully he added, "You have my permission to become your boyish self again."

Before I could answer, he raced on. "Now leave everything to me and Joel, who's your father's new driver. I'll introduce *Kleinbaas* to him later."

I gave Joel a nod by way of greeting, and handed my shoulder bag to Georgie to carry. Taking his free hand, we followed Jemima and Pretorius across the yard then up the flight of back steps. I was home again, and as Amos had suggested, free to be my playful self. As for the sick rooms being out of bounds, well, rules were there to be broken. But first—my beard had to come off.

3

Unwelcome Advice

The next morning at breakfast, I put my plan into action. If I could get my parents to agree to letting me go on a second tour of the Transvaal in September, I was certain they would also agree to me accepting the call to be pastor there as well. To win them over to endorsing the tour, I explained that I needed to stop the Jerusalem Pilgrims from going on trek through a disease-ridden Africa to Palestine.

I was in such high spirits at being in the bosom of the family again that one and all agreed that I appeared well enough to go on tour. Even my father, who had been unwilling to commit himself so early in the piece, finally gave his approval. The only dampener was my mother's hesitation. But on hearing that *Dominee* Dirk van Velden—the pastor designate of Winburg— would be available to accompany me, she too gave her consent, albeit with a wan smile.

Although one hurdle had now been cleared, the all-important one still remained. I was yet to discover my father's views concerning my call to the Transvaal. And because it wasn't appropriate to discuss the matter in front of the family, I requested to see him in his study on the second day of my visit. The sooner I got it over with, the better.

⁂

It was just after lunch, and we were making our way there, when he turned to me and said, "I hope this isn't about that call to the Transvaal you wrote to me about."

"Actually, it is, Pa."

"Well, in that case, your mother needs to be present. I'll fetch her while you take a seat at the table."

There were no armchairs in my father's study, or any chairs that were remotely comfortable. Instead, he favored a six-seater oblong table with rounded edges that could seat eight men at a push. It had been placed against the wall at the far end of the room, leaving a large space between it and the desk, which had, in turn, been placed immediately in front of glass-encased bookshelves on the opposite wall.

I sat down with my back to the wall, leaving the head of the table free for my father, and the seat opposite for my mother. After considering why he should want my mother present, I decided that his desire was quite reasonable, given what had happened when I had received the call to Bloemfontein.

It had been during the visit of Drs. William Robertson and Philip Faure in February the previous year that I had been persuaded to accept the call. They had stopped over in Graaff-Reinet on their return journey after an extensive tour through the Orange River Sovereignty and the Transvaal. And at every place they had visited, they'd been inundated with requests for a pastor.

The long and the short of it was that although, according to church law, I was legally underage, I had felt obliged to accept the call. In a persuasive manner, for which he was renowned, William Robertson had assured me that Governor Sir Harry Smith would be more than happy to consent to my appointment, especially if I were willing to conduct services for the English settlers and the garrison stationed there.

All the while, my mother had been kept in the dark about the matter until it was due to be announced at dinner. She had been furious, and had expressed her opposition to the call in no uncertain terms. Her main argument was that I was too young and immature. She was also against disobeying church law. But she had been outflanked in her arguments by both Robertson and Faure, not to speak of Elder Willem Pretorius, who had also been present at the dinner.

So understandably, my father was now being careful to include her in our discussions.

From my perspective, I was fairly confident that my parents would agree. After all, I was now twenty-two, and most of my mother's previous objections no longer applied. I was also on the mend health-wise, and by the time the official letter arrived, I was sure to be back to normal.

Having persuaded myself that this was how matters would turn out, I shrugged off the vestiges of doubt, and turned my attention to the family photographs that hung on the side wall. There was a photograph of each sibling as well as several portraits of my mother and father during the early days of their marriage. I decided that this was as good an opportunity as any to take a closer look.

There was one of my father that had been painted just before he had left Scotland. He had come to the Cape in 1822 with a group of other Scots in order to fill some of the vacant positions in the Dutch Reformed Church. How young and handsome he looked! I couldn't help admiring his broad shoulders, high forehead, and dark hair that was neatly combed to one side. It covered his ears and turned under neatly at the nape of his neck. His figure was firm and trim, and as was his habit even now, he was clean shaven. In fact, except for a few rings under his eyes and his wonky knee, he hadn't changed much over the years. He still had a full crop of hair and could probably fit into the same suit at a pinch.

As I studied his photograph, I couldn't help recalling how he'd met my mother, who was then Maria Stegmann. It was while being billeted with her family in Cape Town during his attendance of the Dutch Reformed Synod of 1824 that he had come to know her. And while still attending the Synod, he had asked for her hand in marriage. But because she was only fifteen, he was forced to wait another year until after her confirmation to tie the knot. He was thirty-one when they married, and she, only sixteen.

I now studied their wedding photo. How young and pretty my mother looked. And how brave she must have been to leave her family and friends at that young age to move to what was then the wilds of Graaff-Reinet on the Eastern Frontier. While she was certainly a pretty young girl in the photograph, she was now a beauty, even at forty-one. Her skin was still smooth, and her blue eyes shone with life. Added to this was her brilliant smile and shiny fair hair that she twisted into a long finger curl above each ear.

In fact, she looked to be in her twenties. And that was no exaggeration. At John's induction service at Burghersdorp the previous year, he had led her into church on his arm just before the service was due to begin. At the close of the service, several older couples had come up to welcome her, thinking she was John's wife. You should have seen the look of surprise on their faces when she informed them that she was actually his mother!

I was still smiling at this incident when my parents entered the study. They had obviously been discussing the question of my call, because I could tell from my mother's expression that she was far from happy. When we were all seated, she began to finger her lace-fringed handkerchief that was neatly folded beneath her bracelet—a sure sign that she was troubled.

"This won't take long, my dear," said my father, giving her right hand a quick squeeze. "I'm only sorry that this topic has arisen in the first place."

Turning to address me, he said, "Now Andrew, exactly how long have you been the pastor of Bloemfontein?"

"Just over a year, Pa."

"And you want to resign and accept a call to the Transvaal—a call, I might add, that has not yet eventuated."

"Never fear, it will, Pa. They're probably waiting for me to recover from my illness first."

"Understandably. But what about Bloemfontein? How do you think your parishioners will feel if you up and left them just a few years after your arrival? And more to the point, what about your acknowledgment that you were obeying God's call to go there in the first place?"

I glanced across at my mother, and noticed her arched brow. I suspected that she was thinking exactly what I was.

"You must admit, Pa, it would have been nigh on impossible for me to say no, especially with you and Dr. Robertson egging me on."

"That's not true, Andrew. You could have declined at any time."

"Possibly, but I would have felt a heel. In any case, there was no other choice available to me because I was underage. The truth is, that if I'd stayed here as your ministry apprentice, I would now be free to choose for myself without any coercion."

"The fact remains, Andrew, that you accepted the call, and should therefore see it through for a number of years. You owe it to your congregation. That's my firm opinion on the matter."

An uncomfortable silence followed. Why couldn't he see the big picture, I thought? And why couldn't he let me decide for myself for a change. Not ready to give way, I decided to dig my heels in and put forward the plan I'd devised.

"I understand what you are saying, Pa, but you're adhering to a principle of your own making, while I am viewing the question from another perspective. What about the ten thousand or so Boers in the Transvaal who are spiritually destitute? I just can't see why the Presbytery couldn't redistribute the work in the Sovereignty. Dirk Van Velden could go to Bloemfontein every second month, while John could take Smithfield. And when Colesberg gets their new minister, he could help out at Fauresmith. I'm prepared to vouch that the position in Bloemfontein would be filled before long. It's far too important not to be."

"And I suppose you haven't stopped to think what these men might have to say about these arrangements?"

"I'm sure they'd understand what I'm about, and do their best to help out."

My father shook his head as if to imply that my plan was completely unworkable. My mother, meanwhile, sat with eyes lowered, her hands folded on the table before her. I knew she would have her say once my father had had his.

He regarded me steadily before beginning to speak. "I'm afraid these men might beg to differ with you, Andrew. John, for one, will need to become *consulent* for a small group of newly-formed congregations in the near future, and so will the minister of Colesberg. As for Van Velden, well, he'll have enough on his plate. He's already been appointed as *consulent* for Harrismith as well as Pietermaritzburg in Natal. And then there's a host of other issues to consider."

"Like what, Pa?"

"For one thing there's no Presbytery across the Orange and Vaal Rivers. There would need to be three pastors in those parts before a Presbytery can be formed. That means you will be left to your own devices in the Transvaal without peer support or guidance. And for a bold, impulsive, and independent thinker like you, that's a very dangerous position to be in spiritually, and a situation I can't support."

So there it was—the true reason why he wanted me to stay in Bloemfontein: I couldn't be trusted. What a ridiculous notion! If I could be trusted to serve in the Sovereignty, which was miles away from Graaff-Reinet, why not in the Transvaal? And as for being bold, to my mind I needed to be even more so.

As I thought the matter through, I couldn't help blurting out, "I'm not *that* bold, Pa."

Quite unexpectedly, my father's lips began to twitch. "No?" he said. "Well that's not what I heard. According to Dr. Abraham Faure in Cape Town, Sir Harry Smith was quite taken aback by your audacity to tick him off for changing Dirk van Velden's appointment from Winburg to Harrismith."

"Yes, and who can blame me? I just couldn't abide his carrot and stick mentality. Do you know, just because the pro-republican Boers in Winburg voiced their opposition to something Major Warden had done, Sir Harry decided to punish them by taking away their appointed pastor. His motivation went against every godly principle. This action would have also broken his promise to them, and I told him so. Just think about it, Pa! Winburg, has more than three thousand Boers, while Harrismith has less than three hundred souls—most of them English settlers."

My father held up his hand to halt my tirade. "I'm sure one and all would agree with you, Andrew. I, for one, consider his conduct unconscionable. Nevertheless, such men are dangerous, and more so Sir Harry. He's an eccentric who often acts on a whim. He can be generous to a fault as well as mean-spirited and petty. You therefore never know where you stand with him. And I fear that he will one day try to get back at you."

"So what should I have done?"

"The best solution, and the correct one, would have been for you to have contacted Dr. Abraham Faure in Cape Town. As the actuary of the Synod, and therefore the official representative of our church with the government, he would have spoken on your behalf. He's arguably the most influential man in the Colony after the Governor. And he's gained this influence because of his tact and godly approach—something you have yet to learn. Moderators have come and gone, but Dr. Abraham Faure has remained."

I nodded to indicate that I would keep his advice in mind for next time. But as matters stood, I felt that my approach had won the day.

As if reading my mind, my father regarded me closely before continuing, "I'm afraid a similar type of situation might occur in the Transvaal, Andrew. And without a Presbytery to keep you in check, you are liable to become proud and autocratic. That's why I'm against you accepting a call to the Transvaal."

I could tell that my father had had his final say, while I, on the other hand, still had an ace up my sleeve. And he had just given me the opening to present it.

"Pa, before we close this topic, I think I have the answer to the Presbytery problem you referred to a moment ago. My best friend, Jan Neethling is due back from Utrecht at the end of this year. And as we are very much alike in approach, I'm sure he'd be open to taking my place in Bloemfontein, while I accept the call to the Transvaal."

My father exchanged an exasperated glance with my mother before regarding me with an expression that suggested heightened annoyance.

"Listen Andrew," he said, trying to keep his tone even. "Why not let Jan Neethling go to the Transvaal? I've heard from other members of the Synodical Committee that he'd make an excellent candidate for that region. He also has family ties there. I believe his cousin is married to the Hollander Bührmann. And as far as I'm aware, no other call has yet been issued to him because he's touring Europe at present. By all accounts, he'll only be back towards the end of next year."

"Next year? But he told me he'd be back *this* year."

"Well, you're wrong on that score. He's using part of his inheritance to spend an extra year in Europe. So when you visit the Transvaal in September, it will be an ideal time to let them know that he's available."

I sat there deflated. I'd had it all worked out. And now every one of my ideas had been knocked on the head. I glanced over at my mother who was observing me with compassion in her eyes. She stretched out her hand to cover mine.

"Look here, my *liefling*," she said. "You can't go to the Transvaal. The Lord has made that clear to me. It's obvious that He is granting you healing for a purpose. And His mercy is not to be abused. You should be slowing down so that you can be spending more time with Him. And if you go to the Transvaal, that will be impossible. The huge distances you'll need to travel will sap your strength to such an extent that you won't be able to continue in the ministry. Dr. Drury was adamant about that when he was here. He told us that it would take a couple of years before you'd be completely well."

"But you and Pa consented to my going on tour there in September. So what is the difference?"

She hesitated a moment before replying. "I agreed because no one else is available to dissuade those Jerusalem Pilgrims from going on that ridiculous trek. And if they did, and died of some tropical disease on the way, it would forever be on my conscience. And because this is a critical issue, I know that the Lord will ensure journeying mercies, especially if *Dominee* Dirk van Velden accompanies you."

During the silence that followed, I considered her arguments. They just didn't make sense. If God could give me journeying mercies during my visit in September, He could also hasten my full recovery so that I could accept the call. With this in mind, I sensed that my mother's faith in God's ability to do just that was lacking. And because of that, I felt justified in ignoring her advice.

As if reading my thoughts, she patted my hand and said, "You see, my *liefling*, it shouldn't be solely about the needs of the Transvaal, or whether there'll be someone to take your place in Bloemfontein. It's about what God wants for you and *your* ministry. Your problem is that you haven't sought the Lord enough regarding this matter. So why don't we do so now?"

We bowed our heads there and then in my father's study, and although my lips said amen to my parents' prayers, I still felt a yearning to accept the call. Worse still, there existed within me an inexplicable urge to disobey my parents' wishes, or at least, not to give them the credence they were due.

4

Jumping Hurdles

August 1850

My desire to be my own man came to the fore in a big way a few weeks later. Out of the blue, two major hurdles blocked my path to going on tour to the Transvaal. The first came in the form of a letter from *Dominee* Dirk Van Velden. In it he told me that he wouldn't be able to take up the ministry in Winburg until after 15 October. This meant that if I were to avoid the unhealthy season in the Transvaal, I'd have to travel alone.

A few days later, the second hurdle made an unwelcome appearance.

I had just arrived home on Friday afternoon from conducting the quarterly communion services at Fauresmith. Anxious to see if I'd received any letters, I made my way to the sideboard in the parlor. As it so happened, a pile had been placed there by my good friend Charles Stuart, who was sharing my home. He had moved in after the departure of his former housemate, Dr. Drury, in February, and had been a wonderful support while I was recuperating from malaria. But just before I'd left for Graaff-Reinet, he'd informed me that he was having his own home built and would be moving out sometime in October.

As I shuffled my letters, I realized that I'd miss his companionship as well as his little acts of kindness, like collecting my post. And although he was double my age, I counted him as my best friend and Christian confidante. To my mind, he was one of those salt-of-the-earth Scots who was always positive and bright. He was also one of the few settlers who actually loved living in the Sovereignty. As he explained, it gave him great pleasure to be able to ride out each day to view the plentiful game and wildlife in the vicinity of Bloemfontein.

My drifting thoughts were cut short when I spied an official-looking letter from Dr. Abraham Faure. Not expecting any correspondence from him, I opened it immediately. What I read there, shocked me to the core.

"I don't believe this! I just don't believe this!" I said out loud, my voice strident with indignation.

"What don't you believe?" came the response from an amused Stuart who had just entered the room.

"Dr. Abraham Faure, the *actuarius* of the Synod, and arguably the most influential man in the Cape Colony after the Governor, has just written to say that Sir Harry Smith has ordered me to postpone my tour of the Transvaal indefinitely."

"I thought it was a settled matter," said Stuart, looking perturbed. "Why the sudden change of mind?"

"It says here: 'Because of the disturbed state across the Vaal.' In other words, Sir Harry is once again applying his abominable starvation principle."

I jerked out a dining room chair, placed the letter on the table with an exaggerated flourish, and sat down while eyeing the letter before me as if it were some deadly reptile threatening to strike.

"Fancy depriving the whole of the Transvaal from hearing the Gospel because of the political offences of a few!"

Stuart, who was a seasoned magistrate and able to keep his indignation in check, joined me at the table. I watched as he ran his hand through his auburn hair while considering the situation.

"You have to realize, Mr. Murray, that you are dealing with a whimsical and erratic Governor here."

"A rogue one, more like it."

"Undoubtedly. From what I hear, he's also theatrical in the extreme, and can trump the eccentricities of any Englishman of his generation."

Stuart's facial expression suddenly changed, and with it his formal manner. He leant back in his chair, folded his arms, and looked across the table at me with a supercilious grin. He'd obviously recalled some story or other he'd heard about Sir Harry.

"Have you heard what happened when Sir Harry landed in Port Elizabeth to confront the Xhosa chief Maqoma?"

"No, but I'm all ears," I said, not really feeling in the mood to learn of Sir Harry's eccentricities. But I felt that I needed to humor Stuart.

"Well, after landing at Algoa Bay, he set off up the beach to the local hotel, where he spotted Maqoma in the crowd. Calling him forward and ordering him to kneel, he placed his foot on Maqoma's neck and said, "This is to teach you that I am the chief and master here, and this is the way I shall treat the enemies of the Queen.""

"Unbelievable! Has the man no commonsense? Doesn't he know that dishonoring the chief in front of his people in that way is sure to provoke the anger of the Xhosa?"

"But that's not all," continued Stuart. "When he reached King Williamstown, he put on another of his theatrical masterpieces. He arranged for a brass doorknob on the end of a wooden tent pole to be brought to him along with an ornamental pike. The brass doorknob he named the Stave of Peace, and the pike, the Stave of War. Sitting astride his horse, he ordered the chiefs to come forward to touch the Stave of Peace. Then, after reading a proclamation to them, he ordered each chief to kiss his boot to demonstrate their submission. Once they had complied with this order, he then threw the so-called Stave of War down, shouting, "This is the end of war!"

"My goodness, Mr. Stuart, I cringe at the thought of what went through the minds of those Xhosa chiefs. And although I'm not prophetically inclined, I'm prepared to put my head on a block that war will be looming on the Eastern Frontier before long."

During the silence that followed, I thought of my father's words about the likelihood of Sir Harry wanting to get back at me for daring to question his authority. At the time I hadn't believed that possible. But now I believed that anything were possible as far as Sir Harry was concerned. And yet I knew there was another side to him as well.

I began to snigger as I recalled a story that the Boers of Winburg had told me about him. Stuart, realizing that I was about to recall another of Sir Harry's theatrical antics, looked my way with eager anticipation.

"Have you heard what happened when Sir Harry arrived in Winburg shortly before declaring the territory between the Orange and Vaal Rivers to be British?" I asked.

"No, but I'm all ears," said Stuart, echoing my words.

"Well, it occurred like this: When Sir Harry drew near to Winburg, a large party of Boers, as well as the Basuto chief Moshesh with his entourage, rode out to welcome him."

"Just stop there a moment, Mr. Murray. Are you saying that the Boers actually went out to welcome him?"

"Certainly. The reason is that many of them had fought under him during the Frontier Wars before he became Governor. So he was somewhat of a hero to them."

Stuart showed his surprise via a raised brow, then nodded that I should continue.

"Well, shortly after lunch, he leaped onto the table to address the Boers and the Basuto. Half way through his speech, he paused before declaring in a loud voice cracked with emotion: 'We must get to work to build a church.' Fishing in his pocket in theatrical fashion, he extracted his purse, and counted out £25 as a donation to the building fund. He then called upon Moshesh's missionary, Eugène Casalis, to lead in prayer while he knelt on the table. To everyone's astonishment, he was so overcome by emotion that tears started to pour down his cheeks. As he was unable to halt the flow, he was obliged to cover his face with his handkerchief for the rest of the prayer."

Stuart shook his head in disbelief, while I heaved a sigh followed by a gravelly groan. While these stories had taken the edge off my anger, I had still to decide what to do. Should I just roll over and capitulate, or was there a way to bypass this unfair boycott of my preaching the Gospel? One thing was certain, Sir Harry was flexing his political muscle. And in a proverbial way, he probably fancied that his boot was on my neck. Well, I wasn't having it. I would try to go anyway and show him what I was made of.

My ire was up again, prompting me to say, "You know, Mr. Stuart, some of those Boers across the Vaal already think that the English are the Antichrist, or at least one of the horns of the beast mentioned in the Book of Revelation. So you can imagine what they would say if they heard that Sir Harry had forbidden me to preach to them indefinitely."

Stuart looked at me with mouth agape. "You don't mean to say that they really believe that drivel about England being one of the horns of the beast?"

"I'm afraid so, Mr. Stuart. There's a group in the Marico District east of Rustenburg who seriously believe that."

"But that's not based on Scripture. It's pure speculation. I'm sure you wouldn't have trouble pointing that out. After all, England's not actually mentioned in the Bible."

I swallowed hard before replying. "She is in the marginal notes of the Dutch Bible of 1618. And that's the old Bible some of the Boers took with them on trek."

Stuart sat there speechless for several moments. "Do you mean to tell me that the translators included their speculations in the marginal notes?"

I nodded.

"Which other countries do they mention?"

"Naples, Portugal, Spain—"

"Naples?"

Stuart puckered his brow while obviously searching his memory for the history of this city state. "How interesting!" he said, a few moments later. "If my recollection of European history proves correct, the Duchy was taken over by Spain in the 16th century and ruled by viceroys. So it's understandable, I suppose, that it was regarded along with Spain and Portugal as one of the horns of the beast. But who owns it now?"

"It was conquered by Napoleon earlier this century, but I believe it's now back in Spanish hands."

"Oh dear! But please continue, Mr. Murray. I'd like to know the others on the list."

"They are: Naples, Portugal, Spain, France, England, Denmark, Sweden, Poland, Hungary, and Bavaria."

"You poor fellow! You'll certainly have your work cut out in persuading them that the marginal notes aren't true."

"And that's not all, Mr. Stuart. This group is intent on trekking to Jerusalem."

Stuart gave me an incredulous look, then threw back his head and chortled a laugh. "Well, that trumps them all."

I waited for him to gather his thoughts and to grasp the consequences.

"But they'll die of tropical diseases, Mr. Murray! For all we know, they don't have a clue of cartographical distances."

"Exactly, Mr. Stuart."

"Well, given the information you've just told me, you simply have to think of a way to go."

I was about to suggest a viable option, when he continued. "My wife died of an obscure tropical disease while we were living in India, you know. I contracted it as well, but managed to pull through like you did with malaria. When I eventually did, she had already passed away. It was a terrible shock. So I sold my coffee plantation and came out here."

He forced a smile then added, "I'm pleased I did, because the wilds of Africa have helped to heal my broken heart."

This was the first time Stuart had shared something of his past. I now understood a great deal about the man and why he had been loath to live alone. Fortunately, it only took him a few moments to snap out of his melancholy and to revert to considering what I should do.

After a time of prayer and throwing a few ideas into the ring, we finally decided that I should write to Dr. Abraham Faure to request ten weeks' leave. A firm endorsement of this move came a few days later when I received a letter from Bührmann requesting me to come to the Transvaal around the time of the *Volksraad* sitting in October. This was followed by a letter from Faure a few weeks later granting my request. The only downside was that I wouldn't be able to go home for Christmas. But I could live with that.

The evening after I had received Faure's letter, Stuart fired off a cannon ball.

"It's a crying shame that you won't be able to enjoy your Christmas break in Graaff-Reinet," he said. "I was actually banking on it before this matter with Sir Harry raised its head. You see, I was planning on asking you to be best man at my wedding in Colesberg on 10 December. I'd even arranged the date so that you would be on vacation then."

Because I was too overcome by surprise to speak, Stuart continued. "I'll be marrying a lovely Christian lady named Emily Helmore. She's the sister of the Rev. Holloway Helmore, a missionary from the Kuruman district where Dr. Robert Moffat is serving. She's still young—only twenty-eight—and is presently running a school for young ladies in Colesberg. As you know I go there regularly for vacations to enjoy my favorite pastime of galloping in the midst of migrating game. Well, last time I was in that vicinity, I popped the question."

"Goodness me! You are a dark horse, Mr. Stuart. It must have taken every ounce of self-control to keep this news from me. A hearty congratulations to you, sir! I hope you'll be very happy."

After pumping his hand and giving him the obligatory slap on the back, his mask of privacy finally slipped. Overjoyed that he was getting married again, he shared every detail of his domestic arrangements, down to the color of the new sitting room suite he'd ordered from Port Elizabeth through Mr. Adolph Coqui, the Jewish shopkeeper.

Almost as an afterthought, he finally said, "I know I look a trifle weatherworn from my time in India, but I'm only forty-one, you know. It was therefore high time I tied the knot again."

He got up to indicate that he was about to retire, then stopped in his tracks as if wondering whether to stay or go.

I was waiting for him to make a move, when he said, "A word of advice, Mr. Murray. Don't leave it much longer before you start looking for the lady of your dreams. We fellows living out here in the wilds of Africa tend to become too self-focused and set in our ways for our own good. Don't let that happen to you."

I shrugged off his advice as being the usual type of statement a future groom might make to a bachelor friend. Little did I know then that his words would come back to haunt me.

5

Ambushed by the Jerusalem Pilgrims

October–December 1850

I had two main objectives in mind with my second tour across the Vaal. The first was to conduct services for the Potgieter people of the Zoutpansberg district, and the second was to spend time with the Jerusalem Pilgrims. Unfortunately, both visits presented scheduling problems.

In relation to visiting the Potgieter people who lived in the north-east corner of the Transvaal, it was simply not feasible for me to travel the entire distance. So I scheduled a service for them at a place called Warmbad—a natural warm-water spring about nine *schoften* south of their district.

When it came to scheduling a visit to the Jerusalem Pilgrims of the Marico District, I decided it was best to travel there on my homeward leg. Although I was heartened by the fact that many within that district had intimated that they wanted to hear the Gospel message, I was nevertheless aware that a few of the diehards might stop me from proceeding to the scheduled church place.

On 9 October, I duly set out for the Transvaal, arriving at Potchefstroom on Friday, 18 October. After conducting the usual set of services, followed by a few days of rest, I continued on to Rustenburg. To my amazement, there, in the center of the village, stood a roomy cruciform church nearly ready to be roofed over.

The speed at which this church was being built, reminded me of the church situation in Bloemfontein, where we were still waiting for the Government to provide the promised funds so that our church could be completed. By contrast, it was projected that this church would be completed by the second quarter of 1851. With an inward groan, I braced myself for the invitation from the wardens to consecrate it.

As if reading my thoughts, one of the wardens, who was showing me around the building site, did just that. "You will have to return next year to consecrate our church, *Dominee*. Perhaps we could set a date now, otherwise the builders might be tempted to slow down over the summer months."

He looked at me expectantly while I racked my brain trying to think of another pastor who might be prepared to take my place. It was a hopeless exercise, and I knew it.

"When would you like someone to come?" I asked.

"Perhaps May would be the best time. And I'm afraid it will have to be you because you might even be our pastor by then. Just you wait and see!"

Over the next few weeks, the same refrain was uttered at every church place I visited. And at every place, my response was always the same: "*Ach*, as much as I would love to accept the call, I owe it to my Bloemfontein congregation to remain with them for the next few years."

I would then go on to add that they should call Jan Neethling, who was free to accept. But my words always seemed to fall on deaf ears. The people would either smile knowingly, or would respond that Bloemfontein would understand. And the more I listened to their pleas, the more I wanted to accept.

When I reached Rustenburg on my return journey from Warmbad, the church wardens offered to accompany me on my visit to the Jerusalem Pilgrims.

"You can't go there alone, *Dominee,*" said one. "The thing is, we've heard rumors that a group of the Pilgrims intend to stop you from entering their district."

As it turned out, that's exactly what happened. We were an hour from the farm where the church services were due to take place, when we were stopped by a group of men who demanded that I give an account of my beliefs. Because they'd set my cross-examination for the next morning, we were forced to set up camp at a nearby farm.

Fortunately, Commandant Adriaan Stander arrived that evening with a large party of men. My wardens were relieved to see him because, as they explained, he wasn't really one of the Jerusalem Pilgrims. After fighting the British at the Battle of Boomplaats in 1848, he had fled to the Transvaal, where Commandant-General Andries Pretorius had helped him acquire a farm in the Marico District. And from what I could gather, he was keen on returning to the Sovereignty, but was unable to as long as there was still a bounty of £500 on his head.

While he apologized for my having been detained, he nevertheless requested that I agree to the cross-examination that would take place the next morning.

Having no other option but to stay there for the night, the wardens and I retired to a small tent where we prayed furiously that we would be let through. Our prayer time proved to be one of those special occasions when we were profoundly conscious of the Lord's presence.

As I lay in bed afterwards, I rehearsed what I would say. I knew I was well prepared, and that the Lord was about to demonstrate His mighty power by laying bare the deceptions of Satan.

My thoughts turned to my previous tour of the Transvaal when I'd met with one of their number. I'd been so amused by his ridiculous arguments that I'd foundered in my replies. I'd also failed miserably to convince him that the north-flowing stream that the group had named *Nylstroom* was not in fact the Nile, but a tributary that flowed northwards into the mighty Limpopo River.

I consoled myself with the thought that this time I'd give them a geography lesson. I'd brought a map of Africa and Palestine with me that I'd drawn on a large sheet of paper. I'd been fortunate enough to obtain it from the printing division of our Bloemfontein newspaper, *The Friend*. It was now rolled up in a dispatch tube that I'd managed to wheedle out of Joseph Allison, Major Warden's clerk. I intended to show them just how many ox-wagon *schoften* it would take to travel through Africa to Jerusalem. All I had to do was convince a few of the leaders that such a trek wasn't viable, and I knew that the rest would fall into line with their decision.

Feeling assured that the Lord would anoint my lips, I rolled over and entered dreamland.

When the time for my cross-examination arrived, I took my seat on the wagon box while forty-or-so Boers put me on trial. It goes without saying that they spoke a great deal of nonsense when trying to prove that I was not a true minister of the Word.

"Who sent you?" called out one.

"Was it the Governor?" shouted another.

"I'm on vacation gentlemen," I said. "No one has sent me. I came because I was invited by some of your group to preach the Gospel to you, just as I have been doing throughout the Transvaal. The wardens will tell you how many places I've been to."

"That may be so," said the first Boer. "But for us, you're not a true minister of the Word. We've heard that you were trained in England. We also know that you are receiving your pay from the Governor. And he's an official of the Queen of England, whom we know to be the Antichrist."

"Let me correct you, *Meneer.* I went to school in Scotland, not England, and was trained for the ministry in Utrecht, Holland. And as for receiving my pay from the Governor, that is true. But let me ask you this: Do you have a penny in your purse? Don't worry, I'll give it back to you. I just want to demonstrate a point."

He put his hand into his pocket, but on hearing a few whispers from the crowd, hastily withdrew it.

"Perhaps someone else has a penny or some other coin with the Queen's head on it?" I asked.

No one budged, because it was now obvious why I had made the request.

"Well let me show you one of my pennies then."

I was careful not to be too theatrical. I simply opened my purse and took out a penny.

"As you can see, gentlemen, it has Queen Victoria's head on it. And yes, I earned it for my work as a pastor. But if you say that she's the Antichrist, why do you then use her money to buy goods? And why do you trade with the Orange River Sovereignty and Natal when those territories have been annexed by her officials? I also happen to know that you purchase your ammunition from *Meneer* Adolph Coqui, the Jewish shopkeeper from Harrismith. And when purchasing your goods, he pays you in pounds, shillings and pence."

Eager to move on from this topic, I forged ahead. "But I haven't come here to speak of these matters. I've come to present you with a large map of Africa and Palestine—like the one at the back of the *Statenbijbel*."

I grabbed the dispatch tube at my feet, and extracted the map which I then handed to one of the wardens to hold up for everyone to see. The relief that I had moved on from the topic of the Queen's money was palpable. All eyes were now glued on the map.

I didn't utter a word about the dangers of trekking to Jerusalem. Instead, I showed them places on the map that they knew, or had heard of, like Bloemfontein and Cape Town. I then told them how many *schoften* it usually took from Cape Town to Bloemfontein. I measured the distance with my thumb and forefinger, and keeping the fingers taut at that distance, proceeded to estimate the number of ox-wagon *schoften* from the Marico District to Jerusalem. It became clear to all that their quest was an impossible one.

"Please tell us *Dominee*," said Adriaan Stander, "what place would we reach if we traveled due East."

I had an inkling from his demeanor that he already knew the answer, but wanted the others to hear it from my mouth.

"It would be Delagoa Bay, which is administered by Portugal."

There were grimaces and frowns all round. And little wonder! Malaria, or Delagoa Bay fever, as it was known in those parts, had taken many a family member. In addition, this group also considered Portugal to be one of the horns of the beast.

I had barely answered this question, when Adriaan Stander thanked me for my explanation, and welcomed me to the district. "We are looking forward to hearing you preach. It's been years since most of us have heard a sermon."

I was overjoyed to note that upwards of 200 were present at each service. But then on the Monday, just after my final prayer of thanksgiving, another dispute erupted with the diehards. The upshot was that I was again requested to hold a special meeting with the whole congregation in attendance. The reason given was that the moderates wanted to consider my arguments against those of the diehards. I was naturally against such a debate, but finally relented in order to quell the concerns of the majority.

During the meeting, Paul Roos, Stoffel de Wet, and Jacob Erasmus regaled me with the contention that the Queen of England was one of the horns of the beast. Roos had brought his copy of the *Statenbijbel* with him, and had insisted on reading the marginal gloss relating to Revelation 17:3.

"*Meneer* Roos," I said, "could you tell the congregation in which year the *Statenbijbel* was published. You'll find the date on the title page at the beginning."

De Wet and Erasmus helped him find the place, after which he looked up and said, "1637, *Dominee*."

"I don't suppose you know who the King of England was at that time, do you?"

He shook his head.

"Well, let me tell you. It was Charles I, the king that the Reformed Church and other Calvinists despised. The English Parliament thought him to be a bad king as well, so they tried him for treason and then beheaded him."

Everyone was listening with rapt attention. So I knew that I had to be careful how I drove my main point home.

"It appears to me, brothers and sisters, that the translators of the Dutch Bible must have speculated that a such a bad king as Charles I was likely to be one of the horns of the beast. This type of speculation was rife at the time, and the translators hint at it in their marginal note. Could you please read the introduction to the list of kings again, *Meneer* Roos? Now listen carefully to what it says."

After paging to Revelation 17:3 again, Roos read the marginal note associated with it: "And these ten kings have for a long time been reckoned and described in this manner: the King of Naples—"

"Just stop there please. Did you hear what the note said? These ten kings have for a long time been *reckoned* or *thought* to be the horns of the Beast. It didn't say that they *were* these kings, only that they were *thought* to be these kings. In other words, the list was pure speculation on the part of the translators. And now with hindsight, we know that many English kings have reigned over the past two hundred years. But neither they, nor King Charles I, nor any of the other kings mentioned were the horns of the beast. The Bible tells us that the Antichrist will appear at the end of the age, and that it is only God who knows the time and the hour. For all we know, a countless number of kings and queens will be crowned before that day arrives."

By the close of the meeting, all but the diehard party were satisfied with my explanation. Nevertheless, it was sad to observe how this small group was literally seeking salvation through opposition to the Antichrist. I prayed that the Lord would have mercy on them. And even though I had disapproved of such a meeting in the first place, God had used it to break down the last vestige of opposition to my being there. To my utter amazement, the leaders of the moderate group visited me on the following day to beg me to come and work amongst them.

As I considered the amazing unanimity of the call across all the districts of the Transvaal, I could not but help question my parents' advice to decline all invitations. What if God were really calling me there? And what if my parents were wrong?

When I arrived in Winburg on my way back from the Transvaal, I had the pleasant task of inducting *Dominee* Dirk van Velden on Monday, 9 December 1850. He was an aristocratic-looking man with sharp features and neatly groomed hair that was parted to one side. I judged him to be in his early thirties. Besides Dutch, he was also fluent in French and Flemish, having been the pastor of a small parish in Belgium for six years.

We hit it off straight away, both of us looking forward to forging a close friendship. It was just such a pity that he was an inveterate pipe and cigar smoker, often alternating between the two.

In the course of one of our conversations, I asked the usual question that one poses to newcomers from Europe: "Tell me *Meneer* Van Velden, what prompted you to accept the call to South Africa?"

"It was mainly because of my wife and children, *Meneer* Murray. They were forever coughing and wheezing in Belgium. And although my pastorate was situated in a picturesque area of that country, it tends to be rather dank and bleak there, giving rise to colds and influenza. So here we are."

"And do you think the weather has been beneficial for their health thus far?"

He gave me a skew smile while stubbing out his cigar. "They're now complaining of the heat and dust. But despite their moans and groans, I'm hopeful that their health will improve in due course."

Being tired from my tour, and not being able to cope with the pipe and cigar smoke that continually drifted my way, I declined his offer to enjoy my rest day with the family on Tuesday. This turned out to be a wise decision because both he and his wife were exhausted from having to greet the thousands of Boers who had descended on Winburg for his induction.

When Tuesday morning arrived, and I was ready to leave, a rather concerned-looking Van Velden accompanied me to my cart. "I feel overwhelmed," he said. "This vast congregation of Boers is a daunting prospect in comparison with what I was used to in Belgium. And what is particularly worrying are their bitter complaints about the political situation and the constant warmongering between the African chiefs. I had no idea this area was so fraught with danger. Please pray that I will cope, *Meneer* Murray. From what I've heard, I don't think I'll be able to match your exemplary service to these people."

"The answer to that, *Meneer* Van Velden, is to set your own agenda and to only do what you can cope with. I'm afraid, I'm only now beginning to learn that lesson myself."

He flashed a knowing smile. "Thank you for that advice. I'll be taking it to heart, I assure you."

I drove away feeling reassured that the congregation of Winburg was in good hands. I thought of Charles Stuart who was getting married on that very day, and wondered when my turn would come. I contemplated my lonely Christmas in hot and dusty Bloemfontein, but even that thought couldn't dampen my soaring spirits. I had made a new friend, and had been God's messenger in the Transvaal. My only concern was the painful tingles in my hands, arms and back that I'd become increasingly aware of towards the end of my tour. They were obvious warning signs that I needed to rest.

6

In the Valley of Decision

January-March 1851

The long-awaited call to the Transvaal came at the end of January. Accompanying this letter was an invitation to consecrate the church building in Rustenburg in mid-May. What was I to do? How could I accept this call against my parents' wishes? I went into the front parlor and sat down in Drury's favorite armchair that he had given me along with the rest of his sitting room suite before departing the Sovereignty. I read one letter, and then the other—again and again—as if there were some secret code hidden within the words that would help me decide.

After committing both matters to the Lord in prayer, it became clear that I needed to seek the advice of others besides my parents. Dirk Van Velden was top of my list because he would be effected most were I to accept the call. I would also invite him to accompany me to the Transvaal to dedicate the Rustenburg church in May. It was the right thing to do, although his short time in the Sovereignty would probably prevent him from accepting.

The others on my list were Mr. Wuras, the German missionary of Bethany, Dr. Robert Moffat, who was visiting his son on a farm north of Winburg, and last, but not least, Charles Stuart. Having thus compiled my would-be advisers, I departed for Winburg the following Monday.

I was heartily welcomed by Van Velden and his family when I arrived at his parsonage on Tuesday. As expected, he declined my invitation to accompany me to the Transvaal. I was about to broach the topic of my call, when he beat me to it.

"I think I know why you are really here, *Meneer* Murray. The news is being broadcast far and wide: You've accepted a call to Potchefstroom in the Transvaal. Is that not so?"

He regarded me with a broad smile, his eyes dancing with amusement.

"How do you know that?" I asked. "Surely Potchefstroom hasn't announced this fact. In any case, I've only just received their letter of call."

"So you haven't read the latest edition of the *Kerkbode* yet?"

The question stopped me in my tracks. What on earth did our church periodical have to do with this?

"No, as it happens, I haven't got round to it yet."

Van Velden rose from the dining room table at which we were seated, and with a deft movement located his *Kerkbode* on the sideboard. He then flipped open a cigar box that lay alongside, grabbed a cigar, and was seated again within a few seconds. Still holding the unlit cigar between two fingers, he flicked through the pages of the *Kerkbode* in quick succession until he located the article he wanted me to read. Upon smoothing the pages flat, he swiveled the open booklet around, and slid it in my direction. He then proceeded to light his cigar. Besides the report I had written on my visit to the Transvaal, I couldn't see any article that was remotely of relevance.

"What exactly am I looking for, *Meneer* Van Velden?"

"There's a telling statement towards the end of your report that you obviously didn't write. It bears the stamp of Dr. Abraham Faure."

Van Velden drew on his cigar while watching me beneath hooded eyelids.

"*Ach* no!" I said, having just located the paragraph in question. "How could Faure have done this to me! It says here that Potchefstroom has presented me with a unanimous call after laying a petition of eleven hundred signatures before the Synodical Committee, begging them to use their influence to secure my acceptance. And then Faure writes: 'It is not improbable that Bloemfontein will soon be vacant, seeing that the desire for this young pastor is so urgent.'"

I read it through again in disbelief.

"I think you should accept, you know," said Van Velden.

"But that would leave you as the sole pastor in the Sovereignty. And there's also Bloemfontein to consider."

"*Ja*, that's true, but let's think this through from a strategic angle. When you leave Bloemfontein, I'll decline any invitation to be *consulent* there because I have enough on my plate looking after Harrismith and Pietermaritzburg in Natal. So with no pastor to shepherd the congregations of Bloemfontein, Smithfield and Fauresmith, I'm certain Sir Harry Smith will ensure that your position is filled quickly. So you needn't worry on that score."

"I'm aware of that, *Meneer* Van Velden, but it's not Bloemfontein that concerns me most. It's the opinions of my parents. They are set against my accepting this call. My mother is concerned about my health, while my father argues that I owe it to Bloemfontein to stay a few more years."

"But they obviously don't mind you going on tour to the Transvaal every year, do they?"

"No, they have no problems with that."

Van Velden balanced his cigar on the lip of the ashtray before him, folded his hands, then gave me his full attention.

"You know *Meneer* Murray, it's unrealistic to expect you to travel on a yearly basis to the Transvaal just because you happen to be a pastor living in the Sovereignty. I certainly have no intention of doing so. The whole notion is ridiculous, because neither Bloemfontein, Smithfield nor Fauresmith—not to speak of the Vaal River people—can be effectively served by a pastor who is constantly touring the country. So it's better for all concerned if you accept the call to the Transvaal. It would mean that you could focus solely on their spiritual needs. As for Bloemfontein, I dare say you'd agree with my assessment that they've hardly had you for their pastor in any case."

Van Velden's arguments in favor of my accepting the call caused me much mental wrestling and sleepless nights. My anguish was heightened when Stuart, Wuras and Moffat also urged me to go. By contrast, my parents stuck doggedly to their original opinions. In a letter I received from them in the next post, my father once again outlined his objections. But as they were simply a reiteration of what he had said before, I skimmed through his part of the letter, feeling frustrated that he hadn't supplied any further arguments to help me decide.

When it came to my mother's note at the end, I read it through carefully, and submitted every one of her thoughts to the Lord in prayer.

"My dearest Andrew," it read. *"Take time to listen to what God is saying to you, especially through your body. The ministry is not about rushing hither and thither, but about going deeper with the Lord and taking your congregation with you. The Transvaal needs*

a mature pastor who is able to set firm boundaries to the extent of his ministry. You are still too immature to do that. And even if this were not so, your personality is such that you will not allow yourself to be reined in. So I fear that before long, you will experience a physical breakdown that could lead to the end of your ministry. Surely that is not the path the Lord has planned for you. Leave the Transvaal to the Lord. The people there are His responsibility. Then listen to what He is saying to you through your body. You'll find your answer there, my liefling."

As I read her note again, I knew her advice to be sound and true. Over the past few weeks, the tingling sensations in my arms and hands had increased. To my frustration, I found that they would only subside with extended rest. And given my demanding travel schedule to Fauresmith and Smithfield, a rest was a luxury I could ill afford. Furthermore, because I had just arrived home from a tiring trip to Winburg, including side trips to see Wuras and Moffat, my tingles had returned with a vengeance—so much so, that it hurt to hold a pen.

I stretched out my hand, then clenched it. I did this a few times, and with each action I could feel the tingles increase. I knew then, without a doubt, that the Lord was speaking to me through my body.

I was also forced to concede that I found it difficult to say no. Even Dr. Drury had been aware of this weakness. And if I were to be honest with myself, and he were still in Bloemfontein, I knew he would counsel against my going, as would Dr. Fraser. It was probably for this reason that I'd been avoiding him lately. But even without his medical opinion, I knew that God was telling me to stay.

I lifted my pen, and despite the pain, began to write my reply. My parents would be the first to know of my decision, followed by Potchefstroom. I waited until Sunday, 9 March 1851 to announce it to my Bloemfontein congregation. As expected, it was met by rapturous applause, followed by the singing of psalms of thanksgiving. When the excitement had subsided and all was still, I offered up an earnest prayer for the Transvaal.

I was now left with the daunting prospect of having to face the people across the Vaal alone when I went to consecrate the Rustenburg church in May. Fortunately, John took pity on my plight, and agreed to accompany me together with his wife, Maria-Anna.

As he explained in his letter, taking Maria-Anna would ensure that we would enjoy a leisurely trip. She would also be a decided asset by way of explaining the issues surrounding my poor health to the women across the Vaal. John promised to do likewise with the men—with a good dollop of embellishment, no doubt.

When we arrived in Potchefstroom, we were met by Elder Frederik Wolmarans. For all intents and purposes, he was regarded as the pre-eminent elder in the Transvaal, and was also acknowledged as such by Commandant-General Andries Pretorius.

He was a tall, well-set man with receding white hair that was neatly combed back. I noticed that his upright deportment and stately bearing never failed to overawe those with whom he came into contact. And on this occasion, it was no different. I noticed that John and Maria-Anna accepted his warm welcome with due deference. With me, however, it was a different matter. He lost no time in tackling me head-on about my rejection of their call.

"You have no idea, *Dominee*, how disappointed we Transvaalers are that you didn't see your way clear to becoming our pastor. Our call was unanimous, you know. And from our feedback from the Boers in Bloemfontein, we were led to understand that they were already reconciled to you going."

I took a deep breath before trying to explain. I had to make him see that my decision was the correct one for both the Transvaal and myself.

"I would just like to say how much it pained me to decline this call, *Meneer* Wolmarans. I wanted to come. I really did. You'll also be surprised to hear that *Dominee* Van Velden as well as a few friends encouraged me to accept. But contrary to what you might think, my non-acceptance had little to do with Bloemfontein."

"So what was the reason then? It's important that I know."

"In a word, my health, *Meneer* Wolmarans. Ever since contracting Delagoa Bay fever, I've struggled with it. You see, I contracted this fever at a time when my body was at a low ebb from too much travel and overwork. So now my whole system is worn out. Two doctors in Bloemfontein advised me that it could take a couple of years before I'd be completely well again. One even wanted me to resign from the ministry. But because my initial recuperation was so swift, I didn't observe the danger signs until now."

I could tell from Wolmarans's expression that comprehension was dawning. "Yes, I must say that the last time you were here, I couldn't help noticing that you were just skin and bone. But as there was color in your cheeks, I thought no more of it. I'm also aware that bouts of Delagoa Bay fever are apt to return."

"Those are not my only symptoms, *Meneer* Wolmarans. What worries me are the painful tingles in my arms, hands, and back that occur whenever I don't get enough rest. I fear that in order to continue in the ministry, I might be forced to take several months' leave down the track. And that wouldn't be fair on the Transvaal. I couldn't in good faith accept a call under these circumstances."

Wolmarans tapped my arm lightly and smiled. "Thank you for explaining the situation. Now, you'll have to do so from the pulpit in both Potchefstroom and Rustenburg."

I heaved a sigh to indicate how unpalatable this was to me. But before I could object, Wolmarans laid down the law. "There are no ifs or buts about it, *Dominee*. You owe it to the congregations across the Vaal to explain why you declined their unanimous call. I assure you, once they are made aware of your health problems, they'll understand and even endorse your decision."

Unfortunately, this did not turn out to be the case. While they may have understood my reason for declining, it did not stop them from voicing their complaints. Wherever I turned, the following lament would arise, "Are we to be always pastorless?" All I could say in reply was that the Lord would provide. But these words proved to be cold comfort to people who had been waiting years for their own pastor. It just pained me to think that God had set an open door for the preaching of the Gospel across the Vaal, yet no one was willing to go.

On our return journey to Bloemfontein, John and I sat on the box seat of the cart where we could natter without boring Maria-Anna. It was John's turn to take the reins, and I couldn't help noticing how much he had filled out since his marriage.

He had also matured, and had become less concerned with what people might think of him—probably a direct result of being well-accepted by his congregation in Burghersdorp.

Being much like my father in looks, build, and temperament, he was one of those sensible souls who always trod carefully and took pains not to rock the boat. With me, however, it was a different story. He couldn't help becoming the elder brother who was a little too free with his advice.

By contrast, I had lost a great deal of weight during my bout of malaria, and had failed to put most of it on again. And from my perspective, I didn't think my ministry in the Sovereignty was as successful as his in Burghersdorp. The Transvaal, however, was another matter altogether. That's where my heart was. And as I contemplated their situation, I ached to do something for them.

"I have a feeling that this open door in the Transvaal could soon close," I said to John.

"I hope not, Andrew. But then the congregations across the Vaal need to do their part as well. On the one hand, they want the Synodical Committee to find them a pastor, while on the other, they do nothing but criticize the Committee's efforts, accusing them of being a lackey to the Government. To top it off, they don't even want to resume formal ties with the Synod. Well, they simply can't have it both ways."

"To be fair, John, they are more positively disposed to the Synod these days. They have also come to realize that they have to do their bit."

"But not in relation to extending a call. They want the Synodical Committee to do even that on their behalf. That's not how it works. To be perfectly candid, Andrew, I can't understand their thought processes in this respect. Take Jan Neethling, for example. He would be eminently suitable as their pastor. But no, the elders I spoke to said that they were hesitant about calling him because they were not sure of his leadership skills. They didn't know if he had the right personality to deal with the challenges that he'd be facing. And in any case, he was from Stellenbosch in the Western Cape, and everyone knew that the Afrikaners from there were not Dutch enough and had little understanding of the frontier Boer. On and on it went in the same vein."

"Hmm. I'm afraid their arguments don't always add up."

"Not only that, Andrew, they told me that now that you've declined their call, their preference is for a Dutch pastor with some ministry experience. How on earth can they bypass one of their own sons in favor of someone from Holland who knows nothing about the people or conditions in this part of the world? It doesn't make sense."

"I suppose that's why they were so upset when they heard that Dirk van Velden was being appointed to Winburg. From their perspective, it gave the Sovereignty two pastors, while they had none."

"Yes, but who requested that a Dutch pastor be head-hunted for the Sovereignty? And who appointed Van Velden once he agreed to come? And who paid for his voyage aboard an expensive steamship? And who is paying his stipend now?"

John looked my way and waited for an answer.

"Sir Harry Smith, of course."

"Exactly! And look how difficult it was for the Synodical Committee to find Van Velden in the first place. According to you, he only came because of health issues in his family. Besides, I've heard that he's of a slightly liberal hue. Pa says the Synodical Committee gave him the benefit of the doubt in order to get him appointed. So besides calling an outright liberal pastor, where on earth is the Synodical Committee going to find an orthodox one with a few years' experience? They hardly exist in the Low Countries."

I didn't reply, knowing that what he said was true. If only I could wish away the Transvaal's predisposition for all things Dutch. I leant back and listened to the hypnotic rhythm of the horses' hooves. I prayed that the Lord would soon open the door for an orthodox pastor to be appointed across the Vaal. But how could *I* help in that respect? What were the hurdles?

As far as I could tell, a major one from the Synod's point of view was that the congregations across the Vaal did not want to establish formal ties with it. The Synodical Committee was therefore reluctant to send them a pastor who would not be able to enjoy the support of a local presbytery. I knew my father was thinking along these lines when he'd advised me not to accept the call.

But what if I could persuade the Transvaal congregations to join the Cape Synod? It was a long shot, of course, but all things were possible with God.

"John, I have an idea. I'm going to try to persuade the Transvaal congregations to join the Cape Synod. Surely that would help to facilitate a ministry appointment?"

John looked my way with a skeptical brow. "And when do you propose to do that?"

"Next year. I'll go on another tour. I'll write to the Synodical Committee and let them know of my plan. I might even persuade them to let Jan Neethling go with me in an official capacity."

"You are letting your ideas run away with you, Andrew. By then, Jan will have already been called to a pastorate. So I don't think you should assume that he would want to go."

"Jan? He'll jump at the opportunity, especially if the tour is scheduled before his induction."

John looked thoughtful for a moment. "Well, if you can pull this off, I'll doff my hat to you."

I grinned by way of reply. At last there was a glimmer of hope for the appointment of a permanent pastor across the Vaal.

7
Rumors of War

June 1851

When we arrived in Bloemfontein, the town was bustling with activity. The outspan places were filled with wagons, tents and horses, and I could also discern, Rolong, Fingo, Griqua and Koranna tribesmen loyal to the British chatting in groups around open fires.

"I don't like the look of this," I said. "Warden seems to be preparing for war with the Basuto chief Moshesh."

"Why now?" said John. "It's absolute foolishness. Doesn't he realize that another Frontier War with the Xhosa has broken out in the Cape? So how will he be able to call upon reinforcements? By the looks of things, he doesn't have enough men."

"I don't want to sound critical, John, but Warden's a hopeless strategist. He'll also have to face the fact that the vast majority of Boers will refuse to go on commando duty. To tell you the truth, I can't blame them because he's been ignoring their concerns as well as the advice of the commandants."

"So where does he get his advice from?"

"Well, to call a spade a spade, it's from the British land speculators who are hell bent on dispossessing Moshesh of much of his land. And it's more than likely that this military campaign has something to do with punishing Moshesh for not adhering to the boundary rules that he has drawn up. We'll find out soon enough, I dare say."

The following morning, just before we were about to sit down to breakfast, Major Warden's clerk, Joseph Allison, appeared at the parsonage door dressed in full Cape Mountain Rifles' regalia consisting of a gold-trimmed, navy shell jacket with scarlet collar and a white sash-belt across the chest.

Although in his early thirties, Allison's short, blond hair and spattering of freckles made him appear at least five years younger than he was. And unlike the other British settlers in these parts, he was the only one to have been born in the Sovereignty, or rather at Thaba 'Nchu, where his father had been a Methodist missionary to the Rolong tribe for several years. Being on bantering terms with him of late, I invited him to join us for breakfast.

"I gladly accept, Mr. Murray. It will be a pleasure being able to talk to normal citizens for a change."

"You look rather tired and despondent, Mr. Allison," I said.

"So would you be in my shoes. I dare say you've guessed that we're preparing for an ill-advised military campaign against Moshesh. Unfortunately, we have no other option. Our authority is at stake, and so is that of the Sovereignty."

"Why the urgency, Mr. Allison?" asked John. "Surely Warden can wait for a more opportune time?"

"I'm afraid not, sir. Moshesh knows that a war with him is inevitable, so he's been amassing his combined forces. He also seems to be champing at the bit to get this war started. For a few months now, he's been subjecting both English and Boer loyalists near Smithfield to a systematic campaign of plunder.

They've had to leave their farms and retreat with all their worldly goods to a huge laager they've formed for personal safety."

I noticed the color drain from Maria-Anna's face. She had finally grasped what Allison's visit was all about. John, to his credit, pretended not to be concerned, and continued to press Allison for more details.

"What about the non-loyalist Boers? Are they being attacked as well?"

"I'm sure you know the answer to that better than I do, sir. For as you are surely aware, the wagons from Burghersdorp are still plying the road to Basutoland to trade with Moshesh. And it's not just merchandise they are trading, but also arms and ammunition. Magistrate Vowe of Smithfield has it on good authority that they are paying for sorghum with gunpowder and lead."

"So why don't your officials simply stop the trade?"

"A very good question. It also happens to be the one that's uppermost on Major Warden's mind. And without wanting to sound disloyal, I would like to add that since I have considerable competency in Dutch, I've come to realize that it should have received due attention long before now."

"Well, let's face it, Mr. Allison, the Boers are in the majority in the Sovereignty."

"Quite so, sir. But there are those, I'm afraid, who are only now coming to terms with this fact. So to answer your question, most of the Boers in the Caledon Valley are in favor of peace with Moshesh. For this reason, Commandant Snyman, there, turns a blind eye to the ongoing trade between Burghersdorp and Moshesh."

"I see. But to get back to this punitive expedition against Moshesh. When is it likely to take place?"

"Soon, sir. We're just waiting on the Boers from the various districts to arrive so that a commando can be formed. We were hoping for a turnout of at least 300, but the present estimate is about 120. So I fear we are looking down the barrel of a gun."

Allison turned towards Maria-Anna. Acting the part of the gallant officer, he smiled and bowed his head slightly in her direction. "Don't be concerned about your safety when travelling home, Mrs. Murray. Our troops won't be going south to Smithfield, but north-east to Platberg near Harrismith. It's a safe place to set up camp. From what I understand, Major Warden intends to attack Chief Moletsane, an ally of Moshesh, at Viervoet. That's where the battle will take place. But while there's nothing to fear, Major Warden has nevertheless requested that you leave for Burghersdorp as soon as possible."

Maria-Anna didn't need further prompting. She hurriedly shifted back her chair and rose from the table, forcing us men to do likewise. "Please convey our thanks to Major Warden for sending you over to warn us of this impending danger. And now you'll have to excuse me, Mr. Allison. I think I'll heed his advice and collect our belongings for a speedy departure."

She hurried from the room, leaving the three of us still standing.

Allison took his cue and made to leave. Before going, he turned to John and whispered, "I would try to avoid the Smithfield road if I were you. The Basuto are plundering the farms there on a regular basis. And although they studiously avoid the Boer households who favor Moshesh, one never knows."

An hour later, John and Maria-Anna were ready to leave. But instead of the usual happy smiles and fond goodbyes, Maria-Anna was a bundle of nerves, while John wore a worried frown, and I was naturally despondent by their need to rush home. What was worse, I was feeling torn between two opposing views. On the one hand, I wanted to support the troops who would be obeying Warden's foolhardy command. On the other, I could understand the reasons why the majority of Boers refused to fight. At the same time, my heart went out to the missionaries on both sides of this conflict. Then there was Joseph Allison, a disillusioned man as ever I'd come across. It wouldn't surprise me if he decided to resign his commission one day soon.

What a mess!

8

The Battle of Viervoet

June–July 1851

Warden didn't set out for Platberg until the last week of June. He'd chosen Platberg for his camp because this flat, table-top hill that overlooked Harrismith would ensure the safety of the troops without having to post too many guards around its perimeter.

Just before he departed, I went to the outspan place where the troops had gathered. There they sat on their horses—a mere 160 Cape Riflemen, 120 Boers, and about a 1000 or so African tribesmen loyal to the British. Apparently several hundred more were to join this rag-tag army en route. Although I was only requested to say a prayer, I felt I couldn't let them go without urging each man to hand his life over to the Lord.

As they rode off, I quaked in my boots.

Over the next few days I couldn't concentrate on anything much, not even my sermon preparation. Instead, I would walk up and down the parlor, lifting both sides up to the Lord in prayer. Then I'd stride to a nearby hill and pray some more. On my way back, I'd enter the consistory and do the same.

It was still the only part of the church that had been roofed over on account of the church building fund being siphoned off for ammunition and provisions. As I walked through the unfinished sanctuary, I wondered if I'd ever have the privilege of consecrating it.

The time seemed to drag achingly slowly as a dreary and seemingly deserted Bloemfontein waited to hear the outcome of the battle. Unfortunately, no one knew exactly when it would take place. So all we could do was wait and pray.

It was on Wednesday afternoon, 2 July, that I received my first inkling of the outcome. I was preparing a sermon at the dining room table in the parlor, when Dr. Fraser rode up. I watched him hop off his horse, then bound up to the front door. Realizing that something was amiss, I opened it just as he was about to knock.

"What can I do for you, Dr. Fraser? Please come in."

"There's been a terrible bloodbath at Viervoet, Mr. Murray—a terrible bloodbath."

"Our troops or theirs?" I asked, before he could continue.

"Ours, unfortunately. One of Field-Cornet Fick's men arrived an hour ago to request my help with the wounded. I'd offered my services to Major Warden before he'd left, but he thought that it wouldn't be required."

"So what can I do for you?"

"Apparently the troops will be retreating shortly to Thaba 'Nchu, and as I won't make it there tonight, Fick's man suggested that I obtain a letter of introduction to a Boer farmer along the way. He warned me that it would prove difficult to find a place for the night on account that most Boers were against this attempt by Major Warden to bring Moshesh to heel."

I looked across the front garden to where Fraser's horse stood, and spied a full saddlebag as well as a bedroll tied to his horse's neck.

"I'll certainly be able to help out with a letter, Dr. Fraser. Please follow me. The maps of the various farming districts are hanging on my bedroom wall. They will help us pinpoint the best farm for you to stop at overnight."

I led the way, with Fraser following close behind.

Besides being my doctor, most of what I knew about him came from Charles Stuart. After resigning his commission as assistant army surgeon to the 91st Regiment in the Cape, he'd arrived in the Sovereignty at the beginning of 1850, and hadn't looked back.

The rumors had it that he'd come to the Sovereignty to realize his boyhood dream of becoming a big-game hunter. But according to Stuart, he was using it as a cover for land speculation. He'd not only bought a farm a few miles outside Bloemfontein, but also several others just south of the Vaal River. Nevertheless, it appeared that he had no intention of doing much farming. The extent of his husbandry was five acres under cultivation, twenty sheep to keep the grass down, and a number of horses for his wagon. Most of the time he lived in town, where he offered his medical services—that is, when he wasn't away on hunting trips.

As I wrote his letter of introduction, I couldn't help smiling at the difference in his appearance from when I'd first met him. I'd just arrived back in Bloemfontein from my first tour of the Transvaal, when Dr. Drury had asked him to offer a second opinion on my physical condition after my near-death experience with malaria. At the time, he'd looked completely out of place with his ruffled cream shirt and green velvet waistcoat.

Now, he looked no different from the average Boer. He was dressed in old hunting clothes that smelt of the veld, and sported a full beard that suited him down to the ground. He also wore his auburn hair much longer these days. It curled over his ears and hung well below his jacket collar. The only link with Scotland, or perhaps his time in the army, was his leather riding boots that showed evidence of spit and polish.

As I handed him the letter together with several Gospel tracts that had been written in simple Dutch, I couldn't help remarking on his appearance.

"You'll pass for a Boer any day, Dr. Fraser."

"That's the general idea, Mr. Murray. I've discovered that having a beard together with my ability to sound the back 'g' in *nag*—which the English can't do—has opened up many a door to me in the Boer community."

"Well hopefully, these Gospel tracts will do the same. They're like gold-dust in these parts. But before you go, please allow me to say a prayer for both you and those you'll be treating."

I didn't inquire what he had learnt of the battle. This was not the time for that. All I did was ask for God's blessing on his labors, together with travel mercies and an open door at the farmhouse where he would be staying en route.

After watching him gallop off, I found it difficult to concentrate on my sermon preparation. My mind was continuously occupied with questions concerning the battle and why the troops had needed to retreat to Thaba 'Nchu, the headquarters of the Rolong tribe. It didn't make sense.

But as the hours turned into days, I put these speculations behind me. I would surely hear every detail soon enough.

9
Johan Fick:
The Purveyor of Bad News

8 July 1851

O n 8 July, a few of the troops began to drift back—their slumped shoulders a sure indication of their embarrassing defeat.

"Our prestige as British soldiers has been trampled in the dust," said one.

"We either have to regain our authority or retreat from the Sovereignty altogether," said another.

Among the returned soldiers were two disillusioned Boers. I caught sight of them sitting in silence around an open fire, their despondency etched on their mud-flecked faces. As I drew closer, I recognized Field Cornet Johan Fick and Cornelis de Villiers from Winburg. They got up to greet me, and observing that I was carrying a veld stool, invited me to join them.

I didn't speak or inquire about the battle. I just sat there sharing their dejection, although I knew that I didn't have the faintest conception of what they'd been through.

After what seemed an age, Fick shook his head and said, "It was terrible, *Dominee*—terrible. Commandant Erasmus from the Bloemfontein district was in command of our commando of 120 Boers, while I was second in command. But to grasp the full picture, I will need to tell you about the preliminary actions as well.

"Please go ahead, I'd like to hear every detail."

"Well, just before we were about to leave Bloemfontein, Major Warden sent Chief Sekonyela of the Tlokoa tribe ahead with a small escort to gather his warriors on the way. To us Boers, this was utter madness, because the chief had to travel for a short distance through Basuto territory, and was bound to be attacked."

"*Ja*, and that's exactly what happened," said De Villiers. "A large band of Basuto and Bataung warriors drove Sekonyela into the hills. And there he was left for a whole day to defend himself."

"By the time we reached Platberg," continued Fick, "Warden's anger knew no bounds. And while he was still in this frame of mind, he sent a message to Moshesh to meet him at our camp."

"And naturally enough," butted in De Villiers, "Moshesh wouldn't come—not with all his tribal enemies there. So he sent his missionaries Casalis and Dyke instead. They tried to negotiate a few concessions, but to no avail."

"Do you know what Warden's demands were, *Meneer* De Villiers?"

He looked across at Fick who rattled off the numbers: "Six thousand head of cattle and three hundred horses to be delivered by 4 July. Both Erasmus and I thought this a realistic demand. We also persuaded Warden to stick to his original strategy of attacking Chief Moletsane at Viervoet. We argued that he and his Bataung warriors would be tired after having followed Sekonyela into the hills, and would therefore not be able to put up much of a fight. In addition, he hadn't been party to any pre-battle negotiations."

De Villiers heaved a sigh, then shook his head a number of times. "This strategy would have worked wonderfully if it hadn't been for Kaffir beer."

I searched his face, not comprehending.

"Meneer Fick will explain in due time, *Dominee."*

I nodded, giving Fick the eye that he should continue.

"After taking our advice, Major Warden issued a command for Major Donavan to storm Viervoet with a large force of Rolong and Fingo tribesmen. As you may be aware, Viervoet is very similar to Platberg with its flat top with steep precipices. When the Bataung under Moletsane saw our men approaching, they abandoned their villages and fled via pathways on the other side of the hill, leaving their cattle for us to capture. And as the cattle were what we had come for, our main aim was now to herd them down the hill."

"That must have been an exacting task, given the terrain?"

"Certainly," said Fick. "But there were several well-worn tracks for that purpose. The Rolong and Fingo tribesmen, who were already at the top of the hill, were given the task of rounding them up, while the Korannas and some of the petty chiefs were responsible for herding them down the hill. It was then the turn of my men together with some smaller clans to drive them away from Viervoet—all straight forward up to this point."

Fick fell silent and dropped his gaze. He stared at the ground as if seeing the battle being replayed there before him. When he spoke again, it was in a measured tone.

"When the Rolong and Fingos had completed their task, Major Donavan allowed them to plunder the huts. Unfortunately, the Rolong helped themselves to the newly brewed Kaffir beer that they found there. And, from what happened next, they must have done so with free abandon. Major Donavan's men plus most of the Fingos had already started to descend the hill, when they realized that Moletsane and his warriors had returned accompanied by three Basuto divisions. The Rolong were now surrounded by these warriors and cut off from the rest of the allies, while Major Donavan was prevented from going to their aid by the relentless attack of the enemy from above."

Fick paused to master his emotions, while I clenched my fists in preparation for what he was about to describe next.

"We Boers only realized that Moletsane and the Basuto were on the summit when we heard the screams of the Rolong being butchered to death or hurled off the cliffs. We naturally abandoned the cattle and hurried to the aid of Major Donavan. Fortunately, Commandant Erasmus, who had been guarding the drift on the Caledon River, was aware of Moletsane's return, and arrived with the rest of the Boers and a division of African warriors in the nick of time. If he hadn't done so, the Rolong would have been wiped out."

After a lengthy pause, De Villiers took up the story. "You know, *Dominee*, I've been in several battles before, but nothing like this one. We were outnumbered seven to one, yet we were able to keep the enemy at bay long enough to rescue the wounded. Fortunately, our rescue mission became easier when the Bataung and some of the Basuto left the battlefield to round up their cattle."

"Have you any idea of numbers, *Meneer* De Villiers?"

"The last count was a hundred and fifty-two dead and several hundred wounded. We have no idea how many. As for the Bataung and Basuto, I would hazard a guess that it would be little more than fifteen or sixteen dead."

Fick raised his gaze to meet mine. "Unfortunately *Dominee*, the dead and wounded were mostly Rolong tribesmen. That's why we were forced to retreat to Thaba 'Nchu, where their women folk could look after them."

"So what happens now," I asked, my head in a whirl as I tried to think through the implications.

"Now the Sovereignty will descend into anarchy," said Fick. "The Basuto will be raiding whenever and whoever they please, and Warden won't be able to do a thing about it. And as the Rolong and Fingos, plus some of the minor bands, won't be able to protect themselves, they'll have to come to Bloemfontein."

The vision of all these tribal people descending on our little village with their cattle and other livestock didn't bear thinking about.

"You can't be serious, *Meneer* Fick. How will they be able to feed themselves without having access to mielie-meal and other staple foods?"

"Major Warden will just have to issue them with supplies. He's got them into this mess, so he's responsible for their well-being."

Fick grasped a nearby stick and poked the dying embers of the fire with undue force. "The more I think about it," he said, "the more I realize that it was utter madness taking on Moletsane and Moshesh. What if we'd been attacked by six divisions of Basuto, instead of three?"

De Villiers nodded in agreement. "I cringe every time I think of it. We should have listened to Commandant Senekal, who warned us of the consequences."

Both men were observing me closely to see if I would put two and two together.

"So Senekal didn't join the commando, then?"

"He flatly refused," said Fick. "And because he's a commandant, most of the men in the Winburg district followed his
lead."

"But he's an appointed official of the Government." I said.
"He can't just disobey an order."

"I'm afraid he did, *Dominee*. And because he rebelled, he's
likely to receive the death sentence."

I looked at them aghast. "But can't he plead that his judg-
ment was correct in this matter?"

"Undoubtedly. Nevertheless, we want to make sure that he
doesn't have to face a military court in the first place. That's
why we're here. We want to persuade Major Warden to com-
mute all death sentences to fines."

Fick paused, then leant towards me, his forefinger raised. "I tell
you this, *Dominee*, if Warden wants to proceed with a court-mar-
tial, he'll have a Boer rebellion on his hands. And the last thing
he needs at this moment is for the Boer rebels to join forces with
Moshesh. As it is, most of the Boers in the Caledon Valley are already siding with him. And I wouldn't be surprised if the Winburg
rebels decide to sign a peace treaty with him as well."

"*Ach*, if only I could be of help in some way," I said. "But
being a pastor to both Boer and Brit, I have to remain neutral
in these matters."

De Villiers raised a brow to indicate that he wasn't convinced. "*Ja*, I understand what you're saying, but that doesn't
exclude you from pointing out the obvious to Major Warden.
After all, you are party to the opinions of both sides and know
what's going on in all districts. He needs your help. He's not
only feeling humiliated at the moment, but also desperate to
gain a future victory over Moshesh. He'll listen to you. Be assured of that."

❧

I noticed that the fire was almost out, and that a cold breeze had started to blow off the surrounding hills. This prompted me to invite the men to the parsonage where they could wait until their audience with Major Warden was due.

As we made our way there, I couldn't help visualizing the battle as they had described it to me. But what was just as distressing, was Fick's prediction that the Sovereignty would now descend into anarchy.

As it turned out, his reading of the situation was remarkably close to the mark.

10

A Time of Turmoil

July–September 1851

Over the following months, I was to observe Warden's desperation at first hand. After hearing from the field cornets that no Boer would obey the call to serve in a future commando, he sent out a circular letter that displayed his complete lack of understanding of the Boer character. On the one hand, he promised them a third of all captured live-stock, while on the other, he warned that they would forfeit their farms if they didn't report for commando duty.

The result, of course, was that every Boer resisted his sum-mons, including those who had accompanied him to Viervoet. Unfortunately, the latter were now being ostracized by the rest of the Boer community, and to make matters worse, some of the rebel Boers had persuaded chief Moletsane to steal their livestock. As a result, Warden was forced to apply to Lieutenant Governor Pine of Natal for reinforcements to protect the loyal Boers.

In the meantime, bands of Fingo and Koranna tribesmen had flooded into Bloemfontein where they had taken over the outspan places. As Johan Fick had predicted, Warden was forced to issue them with rations. I also heard from Charles

Stuart that they were clamoring for compensation. But as the revenue raised in the Sovereignty barely covered its civil requirements, there was no hope of them receiving anything.

A few weeks later, the Rolong tribe was forced to leave Thaba 'Nchu when the Cape Rifles were recalled to Bloemfontein. As a result, they were given unoccupied land outside the town.

Warden did the same for the petty chief Carolus Baatje and his band of half-castes when they arrived from Platberg. Joseph Allison told me that it was the least Warden could do for Baatje, considering that the allied troops had used his headquarters to set up camp just prior to the Battle of Viervoet. Apparently, the constant threat from Moletsane and his hundreds of Bataung warriors was too much of a war of nerves for Baatje.

Naturally, this situation couldn't continue indefinitely, especially when it became known that the Basuto had moved into the lands of the Rolong and Koranna and had destroyed their kraals and seized their remaining cattle. Fortunately, the reinforcements from Natal arrived shortly afterwards. Among their number were 590 Zulus who were able to take back Thaba 'Nchu for the Rolong and be stationed there to act as a shield from further raids by the Basuto.

The rest of the reinforcements, consisting of 172 infantry and 17 Cape Mounted Rifles, were sent to the Winburg District to protect the loyalist farmers from similar raids. But it soon became apparent that their number was far too few for the task at hand.

As if all this turmoil weren't bad enough, it soon came to Warden's notice that the Fingos and the half-castes under Carolus Baatje were raiding some of the exposed Basuto kraals. As the prospect of counter raids was too close to home for Warden's liking, he immediately stopped supplying these groups with rations and ammunition, thus leaving them to fend for themselves. Carolus Baatje was forced to return to Platberg, while the Fingos settled on freehold land outside Bloemfontein.

If the truth be told, Warden's authority was now restricted to Bloemfontein. And the only hope of regaining it across the rest of the Sovereignty was a timely message from Sir Harry Smith to say that reinforcements were being sent from England. But as Stuart so pointedly remarked, these English troops would be a long time in coming. And in the meantime, anarchy would continue to prevail.

Nevertheless, from the perspective of Allison, who was at the beck and call of Warden, the news was a godsend because it had given Warden a new lease of life. His mood had apparently improved even further on hearing that funds had been released from the Cape Treasury to enable him to start stockpiling armaments and provisions for an extra 1500 men and 500 horses.

Despite Johan Fick's promptings, I was at a loss to know how I could help ease the present situation—that is until Saturday morning, 27 September—to be precise.

I was sitting, yet again, at the dining room table in the parlor preparing a sermon, when I looked up during a moment of reflection. There, through the window, I caught a glimpse of Joseph Allison walking towards the parsonage. What now, I thought, observing his frown and purposeful stride. He was obviously on an official errand.

"Please come in," I said after opening the door to him. "Before you tell me what this is about, let's adjourn to the kitchen. I have some coffee brewing there."

"Any rusks?"

"A tin full, I'm happy to say."

He threw his officer's cap with its decorative feather on the couch and followed me into the kitchen. Standing alongside the table, he swept off a few crumbs, then extracted a letter from his inside pocket. After unfolding it carefully, he placed it on the table at my assumed seat.

"Please read it first before you start dunking your rusk, Mr. Murray. I don't want any inadvertent coffee splashes to land on it."

"Perhaps you can give me an indication of what it's about."

"The letter's from Commandant-General Andries Pretorius. He says that Moshesh as well as most of the inhabitants of the Sovereignty have invited him to come here to act as mediator, and that he intends to come with peaceful intentions."

"*Ach* no!" I said, looking up from pouring the coffee.

"That's more or less what Major Warden said—without his expletives of course. He's convinced that Pretorius is coming with a commando. And after it has joined forces with the Winburg rebels, the combined force will proceed to Bloemfontein. Major Donavan, by the way, has heard a similar rumor."

In my agitation over this news, I'd spilt some coffee on the table, thankfully well away from the letter. I grabbed a cloth and was busily wiping up the spill, when Allison fired off the next cannon ball.

"Warden is livid, of course. And even though Pretorius may have peaceful intentions, Warden is totally opposed to a peace treaty with Moshesh. He also intends to capture Pretorius when he comes. He is therefore withdrawing the troops from Winburg, and wants you to acquire wagons to fetch Mr. Van Velden."

I looked at him aghast. "But that's utter madness. It's tantamount to a declaration of war even before Pretorius has set foot in the Sovereignty. It will also result in a state of confusion for one and all. In any case, why would Van Velden need to leave? But more to the point, what about those poor Boers who are being subjected to raids by Moletsane because they obeyed Warden's call to join the commando?"

A trace of a smile appeared at the edge of Allison's lips. My statement had obviously mirrored his own thoughts on the matter.

"The plan is for them to come to Bloemfontein as well," he said, while studying me closely.

"But that's ridiculous. Where would they stay? There are wives and children involved. And Queen's Fort wouldn't be able to hold them all. And what about their livestock and servants?"

"Well, you'd better pose those questions to Warden yourself. You're the only one around here he might listen to. After all, you can see the implications from the Boer perspective."

I passed one of the mugs of coffee to him and offered him a rusk from the open biscuit tin that I'd laid on the table. I then sat down to read the letter for myself.

"As you are aware, Mr. Allison, I've never interfered in political matters before, but I consider it my duty to do so now. So as soon as we have finished our coffee, I'll accompany you back to see Warden."

"How will you broach the subject? You have to realize that he's hopping mad at the moment."

"I'll simply argue that it wouldn't be wise to show his hand on the basis of a letter that Pretorius has clearly written to ascertain his response. In any case, if Pretorius was on the warpath, why let Warden know he was coming? No, I'm sure he's intentions are honorable. As for those rumors, I wouldn't be a bit surprised if they stemmed from the Winburg rebels."

"So what would you suggest?"

"A better strategy would be to wait and see how events unfold. I'll argue that if the troops are withdrawn from Winburg without explanation, the more rebellious Boers are likely to read into it what they will. And who knows where that could lead."

Allison nodded. "That might work. I only hope that your reading of this situation is correct."

I handed the letter back to him, then joined him in the companionable activity of dunking *boerbeskuit*. It afforded me the time to reflect on my decision. As I did so, the thought struck home that strategizing with Allison in my kitchen was quite a different matter from fronting up before Warden and offering him advice. It would have to be done in such a way that he wouldn't lose face. I'd also have to appear to be an ally rather than an opponent.

I grabbed another portion of *boerbeskuit,* and told Allison to do the same.

"Just formulating my opening lines," I said, holding the rusk aloft in theatrical fashion before dunking it and then bending over to catch the softened portion in my mouth before it plopped into my coffee.

Allison smirked as he watched me. "You'd better leave the Boer side of yourself behind when you step into Warden's office. You'll need to metamorphose into the perfect Scottish gentleman. An Englishman would be better, but I suppose a Scot will just have to do."

II

Problems Escalate

27 September 1851

My interview with Major Warden went exceptionally well. He seemed to be relieved to have someone with whom he could discuss the critical issues facing the Sovereignty.

"Your arguments have merit, Mr. Murray," he said. "There-fore I'll refrain from ordering the troops back to Bloemfontein for the time being. But at the slightest indication that Pretorius is planning to cross the Vaal, I'll be revisiting my original plan. I hope I've made myself clear." He favored me with a tight smile as I got up to leave.

I walked home rejoicing that I'd managed to stay his hand—that is for the time-being at least. I entered the parsonage and sat down at the dining room table to continue my sermon preparation. I'd hardly been there five minutes, when I heard the sound of horses' hooves followed by muffled voices. Not another interruption, I thought. I should have gone to the consistory this morning.

Peering through the window, I saw two Boers leading their horses along the side path to the back of the house. What on earth do they want? I hastily made my way through the kitchen to the back door. I opened the top half, and was pleased to note that my houseboy, Godfrey, was already taking care of their horses.

With their hats off, I recognized one of the men to be Frederik Linde who resided on a farm just within the boundaries of the Bloemfontein district. The other Boer looked familiar, but because most farmers sported full beards that covered half their faces, it was often difficult to tell them apart if one didn't know them well. He introduced himself as Jan Vermaak, and said he was from Winburg. I invited them to proceed to the front parlor, but they declined, saying that they preferred to sit at the kitchen table.

They had obviously ridden far, so I served them a drink of cool water with a sprig of mint. And because it was only mid-morning, I then went about brewing a fresh pot of coffee. That done, I retrieved my trusty tin of *boerbeskuit* from the padlocked chest nearby and placed it in the middle of the table, being certain that they wouldn't care about table settings or serving niceties. I then sat down to face them, noting their worried expressions.

Linde spoke first. "Matters are going from bad to worse in Winburg, *Dominee*. The situation there is descending into chaos, and the troops are far too few to keep law and order."

"So what's been happening?"

"It started just before the Battle of Viervoet when we Boers found ourselves in three opposing camps. There were those who felt we should do the right thing by the Government and obey the call to form a commando. Then there were others who formed a rebel group that was totally opposed to such an action. So in order to punish the commando group, they persuaded Chief Moletsane, to steal cattle from them. Our group, on the other hand, was against this action because we did not want the African tribes involved in our affairs. Nor did we want to get involved in their tribal disputes. All we desire is for peace to return.

"So what is the situation like now?"

Linde exchanged glances with Vermaak who indicated that Linde should continue. "I'm afraid the Viervoet commando group has retaliated, *Dominee*. Being at their wits' end and not knowing how to stop the raids, their leaders have persuaded Chief Sekonyela, who's an ally of the Government, to steal the cattle of the rebel group. But because Sekonyela regards our peace group as also anti-government, he's given the command for his warriors to steal our cattle as well. In fact, both our farms have been targeted and all our cattle stolen. We have therefore been forced to seek a way to put a halt to this dreadful situation."

At a loss what to say, I simply uttered the obvious: "That's terrible news! I just don't understand how fellow Boers, who are supposedly Christian, can act in this way towards one another. So what have you decided to do?"

"We've already acted, *Dominee*. We signed a peace-treaty with Moshesh on 3 September. While we were there, we asked him if he would be in favor of us inviting Commandant-General Andries Pretorius to broker a peace deal between the Winburg groups as well as the Government. We were greatly relieved when he said yes. So we immediately invited Pretorius to come to the Sovereignty for this purpose."

"I see," I said, keeping my expression in check. "Do you think he'll come?"

"We've been to fetch him on five different occasions, but each time he's refused, saying that he still had to get permission from the *Krygsraad*."

"Hmm, that's understandable. As you are aware, there's still a bounty of £2000 on his head because he led a commando against Sir Harry Smith at Boomplaats."

"*Ja*, we know all that, *Dominee*. But we also know that a bounty wouldn't deter him. You see, last week we received a letter from him saying that the *Krygsraad* had finally agreed to our proposal. He's now in Potchefstroom preparing to come. Apparently, he's still having discussions with a few of the leaders there."

"I see," I said again, while hoping that my disquiet didn't show.

Reading between the lines, it seemed that not everyone on the War Council was in favor of him poking his nose into Sovereignty affairs. I couldn't imagine Commandant-General Hendrik Potgieter of the Zoutpansberg giving his approval—that is if he even knew about this venture—nor Commandant-General Enslin of the Marico District, for that matter. And come to think of it, I was certain that Commandant Gert Kruger would be opposed to it as well. Then there was Elder Wolmarans, one of Andries Pretorius's main supporters. I couldn't help wondering what he thought of this venture.

I looked from one man to the other, and knew they were holding something back. Linde hesitated a moment and then ploughed ahead. "The thing is *Dominee*, Pretorius may want to come in peace, but the rebel Boers may have other ideas. That's why we've come to see you."

"What other ideas? If you want me to help in any way, you need to tell me the truth. Come now gentlemen . . . out with it!"

Linde gulped down the rest of his water and placed his glass firmly on the table. He then met my gaze with resolve.

"The situation is like this: On 25 August, a rebel group of about a hundred and thirty-nine Boers held a meeting at which they signed a memorandum requesting Andries Pretorius to forcefully intervene in Sovereignty affairs. That's why he's been having discussions with the *Krygsraad*. But thankfully, its members have refused to sanction any forced intervention."

"So why are you worried then?"

"It's the rebel party. We're afraid they might persuade Pretorius to change his mind once he's here. It's a possibility, you know. All that's required is for them to convince him that the majority of Boers in the Sovereignty will support an armed action."

I felt exasperated by this news, knowing that if Pretorius entered the Sovereignty, no word of mine would be able to stay Warden's hand. I desperately needed time to think.

"Before you continue, *Menee*r Linde, I think we need to perk ourselves up with a cup of coffee."

They chuckled at my response, and appeared relieved at my interest in the Winburg situation. While acting as host and offering them *boerbeskuit*, I braced myself for what they would tell me next. After all, this situation had a bearing upon everyone in the Sovereignty. And from where I stood, war clouds seemed to be gathering at an alarming pace.

"By the way, gentlemen, you appear to be travel worn. Where have you come from today?"

"We've been on the road since yesterday," said Vermaak. We visited Moshesh to let him know that Pretorius has agreed to come. But we weren't the only Boers there. Just ahead of us were a group of rebel Boers."

"I see. But from what I know, many go there to trade with him."

"That's true," said Vermaak, joining in the conversation. "But not this group. Their leader was Adriaan van der Kolff, the well-known criminal and escapee from the Potchefstroom prison. He's been leading the raids against the Boers who joined the Viervoet commando. He's also one of Moshesh's agents, whereas we have only met Moshesh once before.

He paused for a lengthy interval while looking into the distance—not an uncommon occurrence amongst Boers living on farms far removed from their neighbors. I decided he needed a prompt.

"Were you able to hear what he had to say, *Meneer* Vermaak?"

"Oh yes. He made sure we did. To our utter dismay, we heard him beg Moshesh to attack the extra reinforcements that were on their way here from Natal. He argued that it was a better option to ambush them along the road than to have to face a combined force in battle once the troops were here."

"I don't believe I'm hearing this, *Meneer.*"

"But that's not all," interjected Linde, who had the gift of the gab. "He then presented Moshesh with a letter from Pretorius, saying that he was seeking the great chief's help to oust the British from the Sovereignty."

I looked from one man to the other, trying to digest what I'd just heard.

"It's a forgery, *Dominee,*" said Linde with conviction. "Pretorius would never call upon African help to fight his battles."

I nodded in agreement. I was also sure Moshesh would know enough about Adriaan van der Kolff to see through his machinations. What worried me, however, was why Pretorius was still having discussions with the leaders in Potchefstroom when the *Krygsraad* had supposedly given him the nod to proceed to the Sovereignty."

I put this question aside for the moment while I asked another of Linde. "What did Moshesh say to Van der Kolff? Do you think he believed him?"

"*Ach* man, I'm afraid it was impossible to read his expression. He simply thanked Van der Kolff and his group for coming, and said he would consider Pretorius's request. When it came to my turn to present Pretorius's letter, I was so upset that I'm afraid I foundered in my speech. All I could say was that peace was better than war, and that my letter from Pretorius was the genuine one."

No one spoke for a while. In true Boer fashion, we simply sat there dunking our *boerbeskuit* and thinking our own thoughts. As I went over their description of events, something that Vermaak had said struck me as odd. I was about to ask him about it, when Linde broke the silence.

"You see, *Dominee*, if Moshesh goes ahead and ambushes those troops, then Warden will think that Pretorius has come to make war instead of peace. And that might draw the rest of the Boer population into a drawn out conflict with the Government. And I tell you this . . . the way most Boers feel at present, there won't be any hesitation on their part."

"But what troops are you talking about here, *Meneer* Linde? I haven't heard of any extra reinforcements coming. And as the troops from Natal have just arrived, they won't be replaced for several months."

Linde glanced at Vermaak then back at me, his forehead a line of furrows. "But everyone knows that Major Warden is stockpiling provisions, *Dominee*. It even said so in *The Friend*. And the rumor doing the rounds is that Major Donavan has warned the rebel Boers in Winburg that reinforcements are on their way."

"And so they are," I said. "But they're coming from England, not Natal. They'll take months to get here, and will probably not arrive before next year. Besides, I happen to know that Lieutenant-Governor Pine has sent the maximum number of troops he can spare."

"Are you sure of this, *Dominee*?

"Absolutely certain. That warning by Donavan is a ploy to keep the rebel Boers in line. And it's obviously working."

Linde turned to Vermaak with a broad smile and said, "I told you *Dominee* would know what was going on."

Vermaak nodded then rose to go. "You have no idea how much this visit has quelled our fears, *Dominee*. But as we have taken up enough of your time, we had better be off. Elder Willem Pretorius has asked us to pop around on our way home. And if we leave now, we'll be able to get to his farm in time for lunch."

At the mention of Willem Pretorius, alarm bells rang in my head. I said nothing at that point, but decided to do so as an apparent afterthought just before they mounted their horses.

I accompanied them into the yard, where I gave each man a hearty handshake. While doing so, I said in a casual manner, "I'm sure you realize that Elder Willem Pretorius is a cousin of Commandant-General Andries Pretorius."

"Of course we do," said Vermaak. "What of it *Dominee*?"

"Well, I'd strongly advise you to say nothing about Adriaan van der Kolff's mistake regarding the imminent arrival of reinforcements from Natal."

"But Willem Pretorius is a man of peace, like us, *Dominee*."

"To be sure. But he's also in constant contact with his cousin. And if Willem Pretorius lets slip that the reinforcements are coming from England and not Natal, then Andries Pretorius might be tempted to join the rebels once he crosses the Vaal."

Linde flicked back his hat slightly to view me better. "*Ja-Nee*, that's a thought."

I smiled, feigning the confidence I didn't feel. "Just bear with me a moment, gentlemen, while we look at this issue from Andries Pretorius's point of view. If he thinks that extra reinforcements could be on their way, he'll know that he does not have the numbers to defeat the British. And reading between the lines, he has probably informed the rebel Boers of that fact. That's why they were trying to persuade Moshesh to attack the troops while on their way from Natal. It is also obvious that the *Krygsraad* has decided that an armed intervention in the Sovereignty could have catastrophic implications for the Transvaal. And I dare say, those implications will be uppermost in his mind when he crosses the Vaal. So gentlemen, as long as Andries Pretorius thinks that extra troops are on their way from Natal, there's naught to fear."

I'd almost persuaded myself that my rhetoric was true. At least it had the desired effect on Linde and Vermaak. To my relief, they left in a far better frame of mind than when they'd arrived. They were not to know, of course, that Warden knew of Pretorius's intention to cross the Vaal, and that he would do his level best to capture Pretorius if he so much as set foot in the Sovereignty. I was also under no illusion that all hell would break loose between Boer and Brit if Warden acted upon his threat. The only solution was to stop Pretorius in his tracks.

After watching Linde and Vermaak disappear into the distance, I returned to the front parlor to spend time in concerted prayer. To keep my mind focused, I decided to follow my father's tactic of walking up and down. I was still in pace mode when Charles Stuart poked his head in at the front door.

"What has brought this on?" he said. "It must be serious."

"It is, Mr. Stuart. If you have a minute, I'd really appreciate your advice."

"In that case, we'd better confer at the table."

He led the way to the opposite end from where my sermon materials were spread out, and sat down. I repeated the conversations I'd held with Warden as well as Linde and Vermaak, ending with the conviction that I needed to persuade Pretorius to stay put."

Stuart nodded. "I heartily agree, Mr. Murray."

"The problem is I need a wagon and a team of horses to be able to travel to Potchefstroom."

"Surely that won't prove a problem?"

"On the contrary, Mr. Stuart, it poses a huge problem, especially in the present political climate. Out of expediency, I was forced to be less than honest with Linde and Vermaak. One has to remember that they've been doing their utmost to persuade Pretorius to come. And here I am wanting to embark on a mission to persuade him to stay. If they so much as get a whiff of what I'm about, they'll never trust me again."

"That's not the issue here, Mr. Murray. You have weighed up the situation and have decided on a course of action that's best for both Pretorius and the Sovereignty."

"That's my view exactly. But where do I get horses from?"

Stuart didn't appear to be listening. By what he said next, he seemed to be on another track altogether. "In relation to Pretorius, I've just come upon some news that might persuade him to stay."

Stuart leant forward and started to speak in conspiratorial tones. "The word is out that Sir Harry might be recalled. And if so, it would be the perfect time for Pretorius to seek a pardon."

I must have looked skeptical because Stuart added, "I think this is more than a rumor, Mr. Murray. Yesterday while I was visiting Dr. Fraser, he received a surprise visit from Adolph Coqui, the Jewish storekeeper from Harrismith. He came personally to deliver a consignment of medicines. He also brought a fairly recent copy of the *London Times* with him—recent, as in two months' old, you understand. And in a lead article we learnt that the Colonial Secretary, Earl Grey, had blasted Sir Harry Smith for incompetence and for his foolhardy expansionist policy that was proving a drain on the Colonial purse. The article also intimated that two Commissioners have already set sail for the Cape to look into the matter."

"Well, that will set the Sovereignty tongues wagging."

Stuart didn't comment, but to my amusement sat bolt upright and slapped the table with the flat of his hand. "Of course," he said, his voice pitched high with excitement. "I forgot all about Adolph Coqui. He's on his way to the Transvaal with a consignment of goods from Port Elizabeth. Now there's a swift answer from the Lord to your prayer!¹"

"But surely he'll be returning to Harrismith first to offload what he needs for his own store? In any case, he'll have to rest his horses for a few weeks before setting out on another lengthy journey."

Stuart greeted my misgivings with a broad smile. "O ye of little faith," he said. "Believe it or not, he's travelling directly from here to Potchefstroom."

"Are you sure, Mr. Stuart?"

"Positive. You see, his son went to fetch the consignment from Port Elizabeth. Coqui was supposed to meet him in Winburg, because it's apparently there that they usually transfer the goods earmarked for the Transvaal into Coqui's wagon. But because of the raids and counter raids in the Winburg district at the moment, Coqui feared that both teams of horses might be stolen. So he's chosen to rendezvous with his son here in Bloemfontein instead."

"But I haven't seen any wagons in our outspan place."

"No, because they're in the overflow one at the edge of town."

I was already out of my seat and making my way to the door when Stuart called after me, "Relax, Mr. Murray. It's Saturday, and their *Shabbat*. So they're not going anywhere. And tomorrow they'll be working through their inventory, I believe."

I had already opened the door when I had a thought. "I must apologize for rushing off like this, Mr. Stuart, but I think I'll invite Coqui and his son over for an evening meal. Would you be so kind as to order in three dinners on my behalf? There's some notepaper on the table over there. Just give it to Godfrey to deliver."

Stuart chuckled while rising from the table. "I've actually come over to invite you to dinner. But I'm sure Emily won't mind two more guests, especially interesting ones like Adolph Coqui and his son."

"Are you sure?"

"Perfectly. Now be off with you," he said, waving me out the door.

12

All about Strategy

October–December 1851

During our journey to Potchefstroom, Adolph Coqui showed himself to be an able strategist.

"I don't think you should advise Andries Pretorius to seek a pardon, *Meneer* Murray. Sir Harry Smith might just dig his heels in. A far better option is for Pretorius to write a letter to Major Warden on behalf of the Transvaal expressing the desire to enter into a permanent peace treaty with the British Government."

"A letter to Warden, you say?"

"Yes. It must be addressed to Warden. Tell Pretorius not to pass him over, but to make him an ally. I'm prepared to vouch that a letter of this sort will come as such a relief to Warden, that he'll probably put in a good word for him with Sir Harry. In any case, with the new direction in policy from London, Sir Harry is bound to accept Pretorius's proposal. And if he does, he'll be forced to grant him a pardon as well."

"I think you might be on to something there, *Meneer* Coqui."

"I'm sure I am. You see, it's all about strategy. So it's vital that you help Pretorius play his cards right. And with the good Lord on your side, and you crafting the letter, I'm sure the outcome is already done and dusted."

Coqui laughed raucously, obviously delighted with the opportunity to manipulate those in power. I smiled back, hoping that his predictions would prove correct.

We reached Potchefstroom on Saturday, 4 October. To my amusement, Pretorius greeted me with open-mouthed astonishment. When he heard the reason for my mission, he didn't hesitate to change his mind about going to the Sovereignty. In fact, he embraced Coqui's suggestion with such enthusiasm that he insisted upon us crafting a letter to Warden there and then.

After a few days' rest, Pretorius instructed his eldest son, Marthinus, and a friend, Daniel Botha, to take me back to Bloemfontein. The plan was for me to present his letter to Major Warden, and for them to return with Warden's reply.

When I arrived back in Bloemfontein on 10 October, I didn't have to wait to be ushered into Warden's office. On seeing me enter the vestibule, Allison indicated that I could walk through. To my surprise, Warden was in high spirits.

"Well, well, Mr. Murray. What a relief to know that you're back safe and sound. Your elder, Willem Pretorius, was at his wits-end wondering what had become of you. He even speculated that you might have been eaten by lions. To calm him down, Mr. Stuart had to give the game away. And because no one can keep a secret around these parts, I got to hear about it too."

"In that case, you probably know why I'm here, Major Warden."

"Well, judging from your relaxed demeanor, I take it that you've persuaded Pretorius to stay put."

"With no difficulty at all, I might add. He did, however, request that I present you with this letter."

"Well, seeing he's decided not to cross the Vaal, I dare say he deserves a reply. So I might prevail upon you to translate it for me."

He scanned Pretorius's letter, then said, "Of course, it lies beyond my province to arrange such a treaty with Pretorius, but I'll certainly transmit the contents to Sir Harry. You never know. He might be in favor of such an agreement, particularly at the moment when he has more than enough to deal with on the Cape frontier."

He hastily scribbled a reply, which he then invited me to translate. He slipped both into an official envelope, sealed it, then sat there tapping the underside with the tips of his fingers while considering what to do next.

"Would I be correct in saying that two of Pretorius's men are standing at the ready to take this letter back with them?"

"Just so, Major Warden. One of them is his eldest son, Marthinus."

"Hmm, in that case, I think I'll hand it to him personally— as a display of my positive response to this new direction in Transvaal diplomacy. Please invite them to come in."

I had already turned to go, when he called after me: "Mr. Murray . . . I'm much obliged to you, sir. Young as you are, you're already proving to be an able leader."

I walked—or rather swaggered—out of his office with head held high. Fortunately, I didn't have time to stroke my inflated ego, because once I had farewelled the men, I'd have sermons to prepare.

It was during the second week of November that Allison arrived at my door again with a request to pay a visit to Major Warden.

"He's just received a dispatch from Sir Harry Smith," said Allison.

"Good news or bad?"

Allison tapped his nose with his forefinger, then said, "I'll leave that to Major Warden to convey. But what I can tell you is that his mood changed for the better once he'd read the portion pertaining to Pretorius."

Warden was still poring over the dispatch when I entered his office. He had obviously been reading a section not to his liking because he heaved a sigh before looking up to greet me.

"Wonders will never cease, Mr. Murray. Matters have moved far more swiftly than I'd ever thought possible. Sir Harry is sending Assistant Commissioners Major William Hogge and Charles Mostyn Owen to finalize a peace treaty with the Transvaal. According to his dispatch, they should be here by the end of the month."

"That's wonderful news, Major Warden!"

"Certainly. But before you start cooing, wait until you hear the rest. Sir Harry would like you to be available to discuss all matters pertaining to the Transvaal and the Boers with them."

"Oh well, I can't foresee any difficulty there. I'll gladly make myself available."

"I'm pleased to hear it, because you'll be expected to remain in Bloemfontein over Christmas."

It took a few moments for this statement to register. "Surely not, Major Warden. That will make it the third Christmas in a row away from home."

"I realize that. But just to put this request into perspective, give a thought to Sir Harry. For if Christmas in Bloemfontein appears to be a bleak prospect to you, how much bleaker this Christmas must appear to him. I fear he's being recalled at the end of March. This will account for the rush to have a treaty signed. I suspect it will be one of his final legacies before he departs the Cape."

"So where does that leave you, Major Warden?"

"You may well ask. I'll probably be booted out once he's gone. I'm not sure if Allison has told you, but he's decided to resign his commission in December to escape this ignominy. As for me, I'll be staying on to see this through with Sir Harry. That's what we soldier chappies do."

I would have liked to have offered a word of comfort, but anything I would have said would have fallen short of the mark. This was not the time for words, only a compassionate silence. So I gave a slight nod and slipped out of his office.

While walking home, I couldn't help reflecting on the mistakes we all make. If only Warden had been prepared to put himself in the shoes of the Boers and Moshesh once in a while, his position as Resident of the Sovereignty would not now be under threat. But for all his incompetence and ill-advised actions, he was still a good man at heart. And at that moment, I couldn't help feeling sorry for him.

What promised to be a lonely summer, unexpectedly turned out to be a pleasant one. When my parents heard that I wouldn't be coming home for Christmas, my father wrote to say that my brother Charles would be bringing my sister Maria to keep me company. Poor Maria, I thought. Fancy having to spend Christmas in hot and dusty Bloemfontein. But I needn't have worried. It turned out that she was more than enthusiastic about the idea.

An hour or so after Charles' and Maria's arrival, we were sitting in the parlor enjoying a chin-wag, when I said to Maria, "I'm so sorry that you were delegated to spend Christmas here with me. It's going to be deathly boring you know."

"It might surprise you to know, Andrew, that *I* was the one to volunteer. Ask Charles, here."

Without warning, she catapulted out of her seat and pirouetted around the room.

In a sing-song voice, she said, "Contrary to what you might think, being here is going to be wonderful. No servants to supervise, no children to care for, no Georgie to scold, and no mending to catch up on every afternoon. I'm free, *free*, FREE! You have no idea how that feels!"

I tried to keep a straight face while observing this demonstration of joy. I couldn't help recalling how my brother Willie and I had joked that Maria reminded us of a Spanish flamenco dancer with her high cheekbones and severe hairstyle, which mirrored the Spanish doll in my mother's Delft cabinet. What completed the picture was her penchant for becoming easily upset.

I glanced across at Charles who was chuckling loudly. He was the sibling who most resembled my father in personality. And although only two months short of nineteen, he was mature beyond his years. He always seemed to be in a good humor, and nothing was too much trouble for him, not even carting Maria to and fro from Burghersdorp to visit John and Maria-Anna.

He was lounging contentedly in one of my winged armchairs while watching Maria with a thoughtful gaze. I think both of us had just realized how demanding Maria's life must be in Graaff-Reinet, and how little spare time she had for reading and visiting friends.

Coming to an abrupt halt, Maria tapped the earthen floor with her toe, then inspected it more closely. "Your floors need to be treated regularly, you know, Andrew. Never mind. I'll see to it. I also notice that your wallpaper is dusty. And this room definitely needs rearranging. You don't mind if I put my design skills to good use, do you?"

I kept the temptation to chuckle in check, and donning a serious expression to match hers, I said, "My dearest Maria, I'm so bowled over by your unexpected enthusiasm for wanting to keep me company over Christmas that I grant you complete control over my entire domain."

She exhaled loudly and sat down on the edge of the settee, back erect, and hands clasped in her lap. She had now donned the serene pose of the perfect hostess, ready for all contingencies.

I was amazed at how quickly Maria settled into Bloemfontein life. It did not take much to keep her happy. She baked and cooked, and in her spare time set up a visitation roster for the whole of Bloemfontein. In fact, she seemed a different person from the highly strung girl I'd first encountered when arriving home from Utrecht. She had matured and, hopefully, so had I.

While Maria was keeping house and paying visits, I was kept busy with pastoral duties and making myself available to Assistant Commissioners Hogge and Owen who'd arrived in Bloemfontein on 27 November. My task was to translate their letters to Pretorius, and to facilitate a meeting between them and the representatives from across the Vaal once Pretorius had been pardoned.

Feeling chuffed that Owen and Hogge were planning to recognize the independence of the Transvaal, I wrote to Dr. Abraham Faure to inform him of this news. It gave me the excuse to raise the question of another tour to the Transvaal in March. It would be during this tour that I wanted to pursue the issue of the Transvaal joining the Cape Synod. It was the optimum time to do so, especially if the independence of the Transvaal was granted.

In my letter, I also requested permission for my friend Jan Neethling to accompany me. A few days earlier, I'd received a letter from Jan informing me that he'd accepted a call to Prins Albert in the Cape, but would not begin his ministry there until August. As he explained, he needed the opportunity to acquire some ministerial experience as well as become acquainted with the expectations of the Boers living in remote areas. With this in mind, he was hoping to visit my father in Graaff-Reinet, followed by John in Burghersdorp, and me in the Sovereignty.

I'd immediately dashed off a reply informing him of my planned three-month tour of the Transvaal, leaving Bloemfontein on Monday, 1 March 1852, and returning on Tuesday, 1 June, or thereabouts. I'd naturally egged him on to accompany me and to use his persuasive powers to obtain official permission from Dr. Abraham Faure.

While I still had to wait for both to reply, I was quietly confident that my tour would eventuate, and that Jan would jump at the opportunity to visit the Transvaal.

The weeks leading up to Christmas had flown by, and at last I was free to take a well-deserved break. It was Tuesday, 23 December, and the start of my official holiday. I had spent the morning writing letters to family and friends, and had just returned home from posting them. As it was an hour or so before lunch, I made a bee line for the couch in the front parlor. I couldn't help thinking how pleasant it would be to lie there while listening to the homely sounds of clanging pots and pans while Maria prepared our midday meal.

I hadn't been there long, when Charles Stuart made an appearance at the front door. He opened it in his usual gingerly fashion, and poked his head inside. Given the hour of the day, I assumed this was a quick visit on Emily's behalf to invite Maria to afternoon tea. Little did I expect that the news he had come to convey was way out of the ordinary.

13
A Lesson in Brinkmanship

22 December 1851

I raised my body slowly upright and swung my feet to the floor. In the meantime, Stuart had gone to sit in the armchair opposite. I was expecting to encounter his usual smile plus an offhand quip about napping mid-morning, when a glance at his flushed face made me realize that this was no social call.

"I must say you look rather flushed, Mr. Stuart. Has your tropical fever come on again? Would you like me to fetch Dr. Fraser?"

"That won't be necessary. This has nothing to do with fever, Mr. Murray. This has to do with righteous anger."

He took out a neatly folded handkerchief and began to dab the perspiration off his forehead.

"I'll get some water and ask Maria to make some tea while you compose yourself."

I was back in a jiffy, placing a tall glass of minted water before him. I watched him down it in one go, then sit back breathing heavily.

"Major Hogg has just given me the sack, Mr. Murray. But I didn't go without a fight—I can tell you that."

I looked at him in disbelief. "Whatever for? What were you supposed to have done?"

"To tell you the truth, I probably deserved it—legally speaking, you understand—but certainly not ethically."

He sniffed the air in consternation while I was forced to wait for him to explain. "As you know, I'm not only magistrate of the Bloemfontein district, but also civil commissioner. My role in that capacity requires me to register land ownership as well as collect fees, quitrents, and transfer dues. These, as you may know, make up the Sovereignty's main source of revenue. Well, earlier this year, when it looked as if we'd be well and truly in the black, I transferred a considerable amount from the sale of town plots into the church building fund instead of general revenue."

"You didn't! I can't believe I'm hearing this, Mr. Stuart!"

"I certainly did, and felt justified in doing so on the back of Sir Harry Smith's promise to provide £325 for the church building. And as you know, less than half of that amount has been forthcoming, the rest being denied on the grounds that the funds need to come out of Sovereignty revenue. So I simply made up the shortfall from land sales here in Bloemfontein."[2]

"But didn't you explain this to Major Hogge?"

"I did, but he has no conception of the importance of the church to the Boers. I went on to explain that it has been a hundred-year-old tradition in their society for the revenue from the sale of town plots to go towards the building of a church and parsonage. I even pointed to Fauresmith and Smithfield as examples of this tradition."

"So what did he say to that?"

"He remained unmoved, and said that my arguments didn't apply to Bloemfontein on account of it being an English town. He also went on to say that it didn't matter from which angle

I approached the case, the fact still remained that I had misapplied funds."

"I'm really sorry to hear that."

"Don't be, because you haven't heard the end of the story yet."

Stuart smiled across at me, his breathing becoming more regular. "Without further ado, Hogge dismissed me. I got up to go, and as I did so I had an epiphany. I pulled myself together and in a cool and controlled manner I said, 'I won't be going anywhere you know, Major Hogge. I'll be staying right here in Bloemfontein. And while you may not realize this at the moment, I'm bound to be the hero of the hour when this story hits the press.'"

Stuart's words brought a smile to my lips, but it was short-lived when I realized that the rebel Boers could use his dismissal as a pretext to fan the flames of open rebellion.

"Ha!" continued Stuart. "You should have seen the expression on Warden's face. He knew exactly what my statement could mean. He just sat there staring at me, white faced."

"What was Hogge's reaction?"

"All ears, Mr. Murray. He took one look at Warden and knew he had to pay attention. At that juncture, I knew I had the upper hand."

"Upper hand with regard to what? I'm afraid I'm not with you, Mr. Stuart."

He chuckled on observing my worried frown, then said, "Calm yourself, Mr. Murray. This story has a happy ending."

To me, however, it was becoming more puzzling by the minute, especially as Stuart was now looking decidedly elated.

"I told Hogge that I planned on offering my services to the community as a lawyer and barrister, and that I intended on announcing this fact via a half-page advertisement in the next

edition of *The Friend*. I added that I would word my announcement in such a way that it would leave no doubt as to why I'd
been dismissed."

"Do you really intend to embark on this action, Mr. Stuart?"

"Of course I do. It will force Hogge to release the funds."

"But what if he digs his heels in."

"He won't, not after eyeing Warden's stricken face. He's also
here to keep the peace, not stir it up."

I must have looked doubtful because Stuart then tried to
placate my fears by repeating the rest of the interview.

"You have naught to fear, Mr. Murray. There'll be no rebellion—believe you me. You see, before I left, I planted the
idea of releasing the funds firmly in Hogge's mind. Staring him
down, I said, 'When you list my so-called misdemeanor in the
Gazette, Major Hogge, I challenge you to state exactly where
I've placed the misapplied funds. But before you do, you had
better ask Sir Harry why he found it necessary to back down
from his decision to punish the Winburg Boers by changing
Dominee Van Velden's appointment to Harrismith instead of
Winburg, as promised. You would also do well to ask Magistrate Vowe what happened when he refused to let the church
wardens sell the town plots of Smithfield. Of course, you can
avoid all the kerfuffle that is bound to follow by releasing the
church funds. Believe me, it will go a long way to making your
job easier in the Sovereignty.' I then turned on my heel and
walked out."

It didn't take much imagination on my part to picture the
scene. I glanced across at Stuart who had crossed his legs and
was now looking completely relaxed.

"So what do you think will happen now?" I asked.

"Hogge's no fool, Mr. Murray. He's also a strategist. I imagine that he'll want to play me at my own game. What I think

will happen now is that he'll try and pip me to the post. He'll call for you this afternoon, relay the good news that the church funds will be released, then announce the fact in the Christmas issue of *The Friend* on Wednesday. Meanwhile, I'll see to it that my advertisement is published in that issue as well."

He got up to go, a far more composed man than when he had entered. At the door he turned to me and said, "Emily will be thrilled that I'll be working for myself. We'll be able to go on regular holidays as well as visits to her brother on the mission field."

He lingered at the door a few moments, his eyes scanning the hills in the distance. "Would you believe it! I'm now a free agent, Mr. Murray, and can do exactly as I please. What a thought!"

Maria and I had barely finished lunch, when Allison arrived at the front door to tell me that Major Hogge had requested a meeting with me that afternoon.

"I don't suppose Mr. Stuart has been here today?" he asked.

I smiled, and gave the briefest of nods.

"Well, in that case, you know what Hogge wants to see you about. Pity you weren't a fly on the wall when he and Stuart had their set to. It was brinkmanship at its best. Stuart was absolutely brilliant. Warden is also thrilled that the church will finally be finished. He's hoping to still be around for the dedication service."

"What about you, Mr. Allison? I've heard that you've tendered your resignation."

"It'll be farming for me. I'll tell you about it before I leave."

He extended his hand. "A merry Christmas to you, Mr. Murray, and a hearty congratulations on the release of the church building fund. I believe Warden intends to call a building committee meeting shortly after Christmas. He doesn't want to be caught napping, you see, especially with the Assistant Commissioners around."

On hearing my groan, Allison favored me with a mock salute while chuckling loudly. "Oh yes, I almost forgot. Andries Pretorius has been pardoned—another reason why Hogge and Owen would like to see you. They want your advice concerning a suitable place for a convention with the delegates from across the Vaal."

He tapped my arm playfully, then strode away, whistling as he went. I couldn't help thinking how much I'd miss his friendly banter and regular sharing of what he termed "administrative insights." But life had to go on, and I needed to let him go with a blessing. Fortunately, Maria was there to keep me company over Christmas.

14
Reading Madame Guyon

26 December 1851 – 9 January 1852

After a pleasant Christmas spent with the Stuarts and Dr. Fraser, it was time to give Maria some undivided attention. We awoke bright and early on Friday, 26 December to a glorious morning with not a cloud in the sky.

"What would you like to do today?" I asked Maria at breakfast.

"Let's read a book together. We could walk to that low-lying hill you pointed out the other day, and take a picnic lunch with us."

To comply with her wishes, I invited her to rummage through the trunk of books in my bedroom. Because I'd only opened it a handful of times since arriving in Bloemfontein, the titles there were just as much an unknown to me as they were to her.

She knelt beside the trunk and began to scrutinize each book in turn. I was sitting on the bed opposite, wondering how long this would take, when she finally came across a work that aroused her interest.

"Who's Madame de la Mothe Guyon?" she asked. "I've never heard of her."

"She was a Catholic mystic in the seventeenth century. I believe she was imprisoned in the Bastille by King Louis XIV for her beliefs."

"How interesting. I see the author's name is Thomas C. Upham. Never heard of him either. And the book was published in New York in 1846. How on earth did you come by it, Andrew?"

"I bought it in London. Many American books can be bought there these days, especially if they are best sellers like this one."

"I see that the title also mentions Fénelon, Archbishop of Cambray. Was he Roman Catholic too?"

"I suppose so. I'm afraid I haven't had time to read the book yet."

"So what made you buy it in the first place?"

"I heard about it during our farewell dinner in Scotland. As several of the guests, including Uncle John, had read this work, it served as the main topic of conversation over dinner. I was so intrigued by that discussion, that I went looking for a copy while in London. And then, quite by accident, I came across her work on prayer at a second-hand bookshop as well. It should also be in the trunk."

She scrounged around for a few moments, then said, "Yes, I see it: *A Short and Easy Method of Prayer.*"

She took it up, flicked through the pages, then slapped the book shut. "Both books will do very nicely, thank you. But I think we should begin with *A Short and Easy Method of Prayer.* I don't know about you, but I find prayer rather difficult. So finding a method that claims to be easy is rather appealing. I'd love to read what she has to say on the subject."

She got up and started to pack the rest of the books in the trunk. "Well, don't dilly dally, Andrew. Help me with these books. We'd better be off on our walk before the morning's over."

We set off with a small picnic basket and an old bedspread that doubled as a picnic rug. On finding a cool spot under a tree, we settled down to read. Maria read chapter one, and I, chapter two. And that's as far as we got. We were so intrigued by Madame Guyon's method of communing silently with God that we felt compelled to try it out.

I sat with folded arms on bent knees, my head resting on my arms. After what seemed an age, I lifted my head on hearing the rustle of Maria's petticoats as she got up to stretch her legs and pat down her dress.

"You know what, Andrew," she said, looking down at me, "I'm certain that Madame Guyon is correct when she says that our prayers are often not from the heart but from the head. I, for one, usually try too hard to speak to God in beautiful language. And I know that I'm often not communing with Him at all, or even attempting to come into His presence. Her method is all about meeting God in the center of the heart, isn't it? And when we are there, and aware of God's presence, we can then make our petitions. Do you think Jesus worshiped in this way as well?"

An interesting question, I thought, and one that deserved further consideration. I went over the Lord's Prayer that Jesus had taught His disciples, then, in my mind's eye, observed Him in the Garden of Gethsemane, His sweat like bubbles of blood covering His face, His soul in agony.

"I'm sure He did, Maria. In both the Lord's Prayer and in the Garden of Gethsemane, He begins with 'Father,' or 'Abba'—Daddy. I can just picture Him stopping at that point to commune with God in the Spirit before continuing further. And then, in order to listen to the promptings of the Spirit, He'd wait upon His Father for an answer. Yes, He must have done."

"I think so too," she said, while folding her dress under her and sitting down once more.

"And another thing, Maria, Scripture tells us that Jesus was totally dependent upon the Father and did nothing without hearing from Him first. And how could He do that if He were voicing his prayers from go to whoa without being still before God to receive an answer? After all, look at all those Scripture passages that command us to be still before the Lord and to wait upon Him."

She closed her eyes and seemed lost in thought for several moments. When she opened them again, she said, "I must say, Andrew, I found it quite difficult at first. My thoughts were all over the place, even when I repeated a few words from Scripture to keep them focused. But then I recalled Madame Guyon saying that we shouldn't fight our thoughts. We should just recall them gently. After all, it's not about thoughts or the external, is it? It's about our spirit communing with the Holy Spirit. What about you? Did you experience the same difficulty?"

I searched my memory to try and make sense of what I'd experienced. It hadn't been wandering thoughts so much as focused ones.

"My problem was a little different from yours. You see, I kept receiving wonderful ideas for my sermons. And in an effort to remember them, I was tempted to shunt God aside and write them down. It took every ounce of effort to continue in silent worship. But you know what? I still remember every idea I received."

"So you intend to keep this up, do you?"

"Definitely. In fact, I regard this method as being a godsend. It has come to my notice just at the right time. I'll be able to drop into silent adoration while trotting along on my horse, while resting at a stream, and while travelling on long journeys in the wagon. It will enable me to rest in the Lord spiritually without having to exert myself mentally. Often, I'm so exhausted that I'm unable to pray vocally. Now I can simply commune silently with the Holy Spirit. But what about you? Do you think you'll persist with it as well?"

Maria drew her knees up under her chin and stared into the distance. "Unfortunately, I'll have to make time for it when I return to Graaff-Reinet. As you know, I hardly have a minute to myself there."

What a pity, I thought. She was aching to be a Mary, but forced to be a Martha.

Over the next two weeks, we walked regularly to our spot on the hillside. Each time we'd practice Madame Guyon's method of silent prayer, sometimes finding it easy to still our thoughts, at other times, finding it more difficult. I suspected that it would take considerable practice before we became proficient. But having embarked on this path, I was determined to keep on persevering.[3]

While I didn't agree with everything Madame Guyon had to say, I was nevertheless convinced that her method of being still before the Lord had enabled her to be so infused by the Holy Spirit that she had possessed the strength to surmount unimaginable difficulties. What was even more impressive, was how she'd been able to convey God's love, despite what she had suffered. And the more I read about her life, the more I wanted the same intimate relationship with the Lord that she had enjoyed.

Unfortunately, Saturday, 10 January marked the last day we were able to walk to our favorite spot on the hillside. The reason was that Major Hogge had requested that I act as interpreter at the Sand River Convention.

As our time for reading was to be cut short, we rose early on that Saturday with the expectation of spending the whole morning on the hillside. By now, we were well and truly into Thomas Upham's biography of Madame Guyon.

It was my turn to read, but even before I'd had time to open the book, Maria was tugging on my arm, prompting me to look her way. Her eyes were dancing with excitement, and her words came tumbling out like pearls that had escaped from a broken string.

"What if I stayed here to help you in the ministry? I could start a Sunday school for the Dutch congregation, and help out with the English one as well. I want to do something worthwhile for the Lord, Andrew, and not just stay home and sew and supervise children."

I looked at her eager face, and wondered what my parents would say to this scheme. As far as I was concerned, I'd welcome her assistance with open arms.

"I'd love you to stay, Maria, but this is a serious commitment that needs careful consideration."

"I'm well aware of that, Andrew. I've already discussed ministry options with Pa, and as you know, he's allowed me to start a Sunday school in Graaff-Reinet. You see, I want to tell people about Christ. I also want to write, just like Madam Guyon did. And now that I've spent some time here, I know we would make a perfect team."

"I'm sure we would, Maria. But don't you want to get married?"

"To whom, Andrew? I scare all the men away because I'm educated and speak pucker Dutch. I'm also twenty already, while most girls in Graaff-Reinet get married at eighteen or nineteen. In any case, I want to be able to look up to my husband. He must know more than I do and be able to lead me in spiritual matters. And if such a man happened to make an appearance in Graaff-Reinet, he might not like me. No Andrew, I'm afraid marriage will pass me by. But where do you stand? Do you have someone in mind?"

I slid onto my back and studied the cloud formations as I pondered this question. I'd given it some thought at various times, but knowing that finding a wife in the Sovereignty was nigh on impossible, I hadn't dwelt on the matter.

"I can't see that happening any time soon, Maria. The girls around here can hardly read, let alone converse on a topic. To be honest, I haven't come across anyone who would make a suitable pastor's wife. Besides, I would only consider marrying someone who could be a friend. Someone I could discuss issues with. Someone—dare I say it—like you."

I lifted my head to gauge her response. She was smiling to herself, obviously pleased with my answer.

"Strange that you should say that, Andrew, because I was thinking the exact same thing about you. What a pair we are!"

"You would have to discuss this idea with Ma and Pa."

"Certainly. But I can't see them objecting. When you go on tour to the Transvaal with Jan Neethling in March, Charles can fetch me. And after you return, he can bring me back again. It'll be as simple as that."

"But Ma might want you to return to Graaff-Reinet."

"I'm sure she would, but it wouldn't be fair on Charles. This is his last year of study before he goes to Utrecht. No, I'll stay in Burghersdorp. In any case, Maria-Anna loves having me around. I give the maids cooking and baking lessons, you see."

I was exploring ways to bypass Charles having to transport Maria back to Bloemfontein, when I had an idea. "Come to think of it, John might be able to bring you back."

"Why John? He'll never agree to come. It will take far too much time out of his schedule."

"Perhaps not. You see, at the church building committee meeting the other day, it was estimated that the church would be completed by the time I returned from the Transvaal. So I've set the consecration service for Saturday, 5 June, while Jan is still here. All I have to do now is ask John and Dirk van Velden to take part."

Maria raised a brow while pondering this news. "Hmm! It seems that returning here might prove easier than I thought. But what about your friend, Jan? Does he know about these arrangements?"

"Not entirely. He knows when we're supposed to be setting out, but I couldn't very well inform him of the details until I'd heard from Abraham Faure."

"But you told me that you'd heard from Faure yesterday. Shouldn't you have written to Jan straight away? I'm sure he won't realize how long it takes to travel from the Western Cape to Bloemfontein. And if he wants to drop by Burghersdorp on the way, he'll have to leave within the next two weeks at the latest. So you'd better write to him today, Andrew."

She was getting all hot and bothered, and her breathing was coming in shallow gasps. For the life of me, I couldn't understand why she was becoming upset.

"You needn't worry, Maria. There's plenty of time for that."

"No there isn't. Jan might arrive here late. And according to you, it's nigh on impossible to change your schedule while on tour. I remember you telling me that the wagons assigned to fetch you from the various church places have to be there at a stipulated time."

"So I did."

"And what about the consecration service? Is that date etched in stone as well?"

"Why on earth do you want know, Maria?"

"Just humor me for a moment, Andrew."

"I dare say it is because I'd like Jan to be present."

I was wondering where Maria was going with this, when she jumped up, moved our picnic basket onto the grass, then yanked at the bedspread with all her might in an effort to get me to stand up.

"What on earth are you doing, Maria? We haven't had morning tea yet."

"You need to write that letter, Andrew, otherwise your friend will never arrive here on time. I don't know how you can be so lackadaisical about it when there's no leeway in your schedule."

"My goodness, Maria, come and sit down and stop working yourself up into a lather. Abraham Faure has already written to Jan. And in the recent letter I received from him, he told me that Jan was hoping to reach Bloemfontein by mid-February."

She let the bedspread slip from her hand and lowered her gaze. After a short pause she said with a child-like whimper, "Well, at least Jan seems organized."

"Very much so. He's apparently been appointed to the congregation of Prins Albert, and thought it a good idea to offload his furniture and settle into the parsonage before setting out for Bloemfontein."

"Well, why didn't you tell me?"

"Because it escaped my mind. And besides, you don't need to know everything, silly. Now sit down and stop fussing. I'm dying to try one of your scones."

It was the first time my "Spanish doll" had materialized since she'd arrived in Bloemfontein, and I doubted whether it would be the last. But be that as it may, I was looking forward to Maria joining me in the ministry. From my perspective, we would complement each other perfectly. And as for her wanting to plan and organize to the tenth degree, well, I could cope with that. I would just have to remember to keep her informed. Come to think of it, I could get her to draw up several copies of my next quarterly schedule for members of my consistory. That was sure to keep her happy.

What I didn't expect, however, was that *I* would be the one pounding my feet to the rhythm of the flamenco guitar in fiery arrogance and indignation—the lessons of humility and waiting on God all but forgotten. But this would only happen after my return from the Transvaal. And when it did, it would serve as a mirror in which I could view myself as I truly was: prideful, immature, and focused on self.

15
Strategizing at Sand River

12–15 January 1852

After dropping the charges of outlawry against Andries Pretorius, Hogge and Owen wasted no time in arranging a convention with him. The place that was settled upon was Piet Venter's farm, about eight miles from the confluence of Coal Spruit and Sand River. At this pivotal meeting, the Assistant Commissioners would be acting on behalf of the British Government, while Andries Pretorius, along with a group of fifteen delegates, would be representing the Boers from across the Vaal.

On Monday, 12 January, Maria and I set off for Winburg in Willem Pretorius's cart that he had kindly lent me. The plan was that I'd park it in the yard at Piet Venter's farmhouse, so as to avoid having to choose between staying in a tent provided by the Assistant Commissioners, and sleeping under a wagon in the Transvaal camp. To my mind, it was important that I be seen to be neutral. The operative phrase here, of course, was "be seen," for I couldn't help rejoicing at Hogge's words when he said the following to me before my departure: "If the Transvaal delegates accept the requirement that slavery will be outlawed, and give an undertaking not to interfere in Sovereignty affairs, then Mr. Owen and I will formally recognize their independence on behalf of the British Government."

After dropping Maria off at *Dominee* Van Velden's place, I proceeded to Piet Venter's farm, where I arrived at midday on Thursday, 15 January. I was hoping to enjoy a meal with Venter, then take a nap before introducing the Transvaal delegates to Hogge and Owen around 5.00 p.m.

When I reached Venter's farm, he accompanied me to the edge of the rise on which the farmhouse stood to view the campsites below. There, to my utter amazement, stood a laager of about fifty wagons along with a good number of tents.

"At least 300 supporters have come with Andries Pretorius," Venter said. "And you wouldn't believe it, but a number of shopkeepers have also made an appearance. From what I can tell, they are already making a roaring trade."

I glanced across at the British camp where a handful of small tents had been erected as well as a sizable marquee. "It appears that Hogge and Owen have only brought a small escort with them."

"Five Lancers, to be exact, *Dominee*. They obviously consider a treaty with the Transvaal to be a foregone conclusion."

Venter tapped my arm to draw my attention to a few tents in a fenced off field that was being used as an outspan place for the horses.

"Those tents over there belong to the Basuto observers. Commandant-General Pretorius informed me on arrival that he'd invited Moshesh to attend the convention. But I've since heard that he's sent his principal advisor, Joshua, instead."

I said nothing, but knew that Hogge and Owen would be

far from pleased if they discovered the presence of Basuto observers. The last thing they wanted was for Pretorius to form an alliance with Moshesh, or to arbitrate a peace treaty, for that matter. But I surmised from the large number of African drivers in the outspan area that no one would be any the wiser—for the moment at least.

After lunch I took myself off to the cart for a nap. I was expecting to doze off easily on account of feeling relaxed about the outcome of the convention. In fact, I was expecting it to be a straightforward affair with no real points of contention. It had been well planned, and each side had forwarded their list of stipulations well in advance. But as I was once again to discover, this was the Orange River Sovereignty, where the unexpected happened at every turn, and disorder was par for the course.

I was still dozing in the cart, when I was awakened around mid-afternoon by animated voices approaching the farmhouse. Interested to see who they were, I lifted the side flap and peered out. My host, Piet Venter was escorting two men up the pathway from the laager. Despite the full beards and wide-brimmed hats, I recognized one to be Paul Bester, the magistrate of Harrismith and the Vaal River district, and the other to be Frederik Linde.

I surmised that like me, Linde had also stayed at this farmhouse on his way to and from the Transvaal on the various occasions he'd tried to fetch Pretorius. As for Paul Bester, I'd heard that he had once shared his current position of magistrate with Piet Venter. So he obviously knew my host well.

After Venter had accompanied the men to the farmhouse door, he turned and made straight for the cart that I'd parked under a tree a short distance away. As something was obviously afoot, I sat up in readiness to hear what he had to say.

"I'm pleased to see that you're awake, *Dominee*, because Paul Bester and Frederik Linde are here to confer with you on an important matter."

"Why me? I'm only the interpreter at this convention. I have no say at all."

"*Ja*, they know that. But they also know that you have direct access to Commandant-General Pretorius. You see, the problem is this: That villain Adriaan van der Kolff has just arrived with a group of about a hundred supporters from the Wittebergen and Vaal River districts, and they want him gone."

My groan was all that was needed to convince Venter that I too considered this a disastrous situation that could derail the negotiations. Fortunately, I'd already laid out my Sunday suit and clerical shirt along the box seat, so was able to dress in record time.

I followed Venter to the farmhouse, and then into the parlor, where I was met by the sullen faces of Bester and Linde. Venter pulled out a chair at the dining room table, and invited me sit down.

"This won't take long, *Dominee*," Bester said. "As you have no doubt guessed, both *Meneer* Linde and I have come here to observe this momentous occasion. But what we didn't expect to see was Adriaan van der Kolff riding into camp with all his supporters. His presence here is an affront to every decent Boer, especially after the havoc he's caused by leading his band of Africans to steal cattle from fellow Boers. It can't be tolerated."

"*Ja*, and as you know, *Dominee*," said Linde, putting in his oar, "he's also forged Pretorius's signature and encouraged Moshesh to attack British troops."

I heaved a sigh, thinking I knew where this was headed. "So I take it that you'd like me to inform Pretorius that you are unhappy about Van der Kolff's presence?"

The men exchanged glances, each wanting the other to speak. Finally Bester said, "I've already reported Van der Kolff's presence to Hogge and Owen. They made it plain that there would be no negotiations until Van der Kolff has been arrested."

"So who's supposed to arrest him?"

"Pretorius, of course. After all, Van der Kolff is in his laager. But the problem we are facing is that Pretorius intends to ignore his presence—ask *Meneer* Linde here."

Linde, who'd been looking into the distance glum-faced, now turned to address me. "While *Meneer* Bester was visiting Hogge and Owen, I was visiting Pretorius. He told me that arresting Van der Kolff was out of the question."

"How so? Did he give any reasons?"

"He argued that Van der Kolff's supporters were bound to attempt to free him, and the resulting melee could lead to his men being shot at. He also said that the situation would be worse if Hogge and Owen decided to arrest him. In Pretorius's view, some of Van der Kolff's supporters wouldn't think twice of shooting the lancers. And if that were to happen, it could provoke a war with Britain."

"*Ja-Nee,*" said Bester, "it goes without saying that an arrest could result in unforeseen consequences."

Like them, I had to agree. But that was not the only problem I could foresee. It was obvious that the Boers who'd arrived with Van der Kolff were expecting Pretorius to include the Winburg and the Vaal River districts within the Transvaal's bid for independence. And their expectations were bound to be causing a headache for Pretorius.

At the same time, I knew that Hogge would reject any such proposal out of hand. In fact, he was inclined to view the problem with the rebel Boers from a different angle altogether. As he'd said to me at one of our meetings, "As soon as those rebel Boers know that they can no longer call upon Pretorius to help them oust the British, law and order will return to the Sovereignty."

I was jerked into the present when Venter broke the silence. "The fact is, *Dominee*, despite the ructions that an arrest may cause, we three agree that Van der Kolff has to go. So we've put our heads together and have come up with a plan. Simply put, we intend to help Van der Kolff escape *before* he is arrested. And we would like you to inform Pretorius of what we have in mind."

Well, this was certainly one for the books, I thought—so much so, that I wasn't sure if I should be part of it. But after a moment's reflection, I too could see its appeal.

"Firstly," said Bester, "I would like you to inform Pretorius that Hogge and Owen are expecting him to arrest Van der Kolff before they are prepared to start with the negotiations. As it stands, Pretorius has no idea that Hogge and Owen know that Van der Kolff has arrived in camp. He's going to be furious with me for telling them, but that's water under the bridge now."

"So what do you have in mind, *Meneer* Bester?"

"I'll let *Meneer* Venter fill you in because he's central to the plan."

"It's dead simple," Venter said. "While you are introducing Pretorius and the rest of the Transvaal delegates to Hogge and Owen, I'll ride down to the laager on one of my good horses. I'll tie him up outside the laager near to where Van der Kolff and his men are sitting. What we need to ensure is that there's an opening nearby. The field cornet who's in charge will need to know of our plan, as well as one or two trusted Transvaalers who can encourage Van der Kolff to flee as soon as Pretorius approaches."

I nodded, then rose to go. Venter had described enough for me to fill in the details. I would have liked to have said a prayer with them, but there was no time for that. I would have to pray on the way.

I hastened back to the cart to collect my shoulder bag and a veld stool. I then proceeded to make my way down the path to the laager. I was still only halfway, when a thought struck.

Just a minute, Murray, I said to myself, while stopping in my tracks. How can Hogge expect Pretorius to arrest van der Kolff when Pretorius has no authority in the Sovereignty? I'll have to point that out to Pretorius.

Highly pleased with this realization, I proceeded down the track. I was almost level with the laager, when another thought assailed me. But Hogge could use the same argument against Pretorius. And given the present situation with the rebel Boers breathing down Pretorius's neck, the latter was bound to request the inclusion of the Winburg and Vaal River districts in the negotiations. And if he did, Hogge was equally bound to throw the "no authority" argument in Pretorius's face.

As I conjured up the various scenarios in my mind's eye, I couldn't help contemplating what the rebel Boers would think of being shunted aside. After all, it wouldn't take them long to realize that these negotiations were solely about the Transvaal.

I closed my eyes and took a few deep breaths to steady my nerves. I knew I was not cut out for this type of caper, but circumstances being what they were, I needed to do all in my power to ensure that these negotiations remained on track.

16

As Wise as Serpents

15 January 1852

I was still standing on the track with eyes closed, when a hand grasped my arm and a familiar voice said, "*Dominee* . . . are you alright?"

I opened my eyes and looked into the concerned face of Paul Kruger, the nephew of my father's friend Commandant Gert Kruger. I'd got to know him on my first tour of the Transvaal when he'd accompanied his uncle and me to Rustenburg. And as far as I could tell, Paul was following in his uncle's footsteps, both as a believer and a leader.

Observing him now at close quarters with the brims of our hats almost touching, he looked to be all beard and moustache with dark eyebrows to match. But unlike other Boers, I knew that his family favored keeping their hair cropped short at the back and sides. And Paul was no exception. Nevertheless, as I recalled, he liked to keep a thick sweep of hair over the top.

"I saw *Dominee* stop on the path a few times, and thought you might be feeling unwell."

"No, I'm fine, *Meneer* Kruger, I was just doing a little thinking and praying. But tell me, what are you doing outside the laager?"

"*Ach* man, I was about to climb the rise to see if Commandant Adriaan Stander and a few others from the Marico District were on their way. There's been a bad outbreak of Delagoa Bay Fever there, so we are not sure if they'll be coming or not. I left a few wagon spaces open for them, but now the Wittebergen Boers have parked their wagons there. So I have to decide whether to create more spaces or not."

"Isn't that the job of the field cornet?"

Kruger stood astride and stuck out his chest. "Believe it or not, I was promoted to field cornet before leaving the Transvaal. In other words, I'm now the general dogs-body around here because the other field cornets are delegates."[4]

My relief on hearing this news was such that I closed my eyes and uttered: "Thank you Lord!" When I opened them again, Kruger was looking perplexed. "Am I able to help in any way, *Dominee*?"

"As a matter of fact, I'm banking on your assistance. You see, there's an evil influence in the laager who goes by the name of Adriaan van der Kolff. And as the Word tells us to be as wise as serpents and as harmless as doves, a few of us have decided that the best option is to allow him to escape."

Kruger broke into a broad smile, his expression eager. "I'm good at escape. So what's the plan?"

I explained the main points in a sentence or two, and was about to inquire whether I should let Pretorius know, when he started to move off.

"*Meneer* Kruger?" I called after him. "Don't you need permission?"

"Not if you are giving the order, *Dominee*."

I wanted to object, but was left standing there. I knew that my clerical garb and the authoritative voice I was trying to foster might have given the impression that I was issuing a command, much like the commandants in those parts. I'd have to be more careful, I thought. But knowing Paul Kruger, I was fairly certain that he wouldn't act upon any plan he didn't think viable.

After gathering my thoughts, I made my way into the laager, feeling concerned about what Pretorius would say to Venter's plan, not to speak of my presumption to discuss it with Kruger first. But I needn't have worried. On hearing that Paul Kruger had everything in hand, both he and the other delegates seemed relieved that something was being done to oust Van der Kolff. Nevertheless, while listening to their opinions, it struck me that most of the delegates did not have the same attachment to the pro-republican Boers in the Sovereignty as Pretorius had. For them, it was all about obtaining independence for the Transvaal. For Pretorius, it was a case of letting the Sovereignty Boers down.

He heaved a deep sigh, then favored me with a tight smile. "I'm indebted to you, for helping to get rid of one headache, *Dominee*, but I fear that the other still remains. What on earth am I going to say to those pro-republican Boers?"

"Whatever it is, *Meneer* Pretorius, it will be much easier with Van der Kolff expelled from the laager."

"*Ja-Nee*, that's true."

I watched him fold up his veld stool and lean it against his wagon. Then, with a wave of his hand, he indicated that I should lead the way.

Once each delegate had been formally introduced to Hogge and Owen, Hogge requested that they take a seat around the trestle table. After expressing a few thoughts on the opportunities an alliance with Britain presented, he came straight to the point regarding Van der Kolff.

"I believe that a large number of rebel Boers have arrived at your laager led by that criminal Van der Kolff. I would like to remind you, Mr. Pretorius, that you have no jurisdiction in the Sovereignty to negotiate on their behalf. Secondly, considering the mayhem Van der Kolff has caused in the Sovereignty, I deem it essential that you arrest him before I'm prepared to commence with these deliberations."

Pretorius took his time before replying. And although I knew what he would say, I waited with baited breath.

"But Major Hogge," he finally said, "if I don't have any authority in the Sovereignty, how am I supposed to arrest Van der Kolff?"

Hogge had been trumped. But not wanting to be outdone, replied, "Don't worry, Mr. Pretorius, I'll grant you that authority."

Pretorius arched his brow with just the right nuance. "While I acknowledge that you are well able to grant it, sir, I would advise that I be accompanied by a few lancers. After all, if I can be granted the authority to make an arrest, the Boers from around these parts might consider it a foregone conclusion that you have extended my authority to negotiate on their behalf as well."

I knew that this was the last thing Hogge wanted to hear. Without missing a beat, he said, "All things considered, I'll accede to your request, Mr. Pretorius. Mr. Owen and two lancers will accompany you."

Pretorius led the way flanked by Commandant-General Joubert from Lijdenburg on one side, and Commandant Gert Kruger from Rustenburg, on the other. I followed immediately behind with Owen and the Lancers, while the rest of the delegates brought up the rear.

As we approached the main entrance to the laager, I heard a soft, but distinct, bird call, followed by another further on. Paul Kruger had obviously placed scouts on the outside perimeter to signal our arrival. I tried to steady my nerves with the thought that as there would be no arrest, there would also be no threat from the rebel Boers. It was obvious that Pretorius was of the same mind, because he strode confidently in the direction to where the Sovereignty Boers were sitting.

Unlike a laager prepared for war, this one was a loose affair with natural trees, bushes and shrubs left between wagons. And except for some trees that had been left in the center, all scrub had been cleared to create a meeting place for morning and evening devotions plus the church services I had been requested to lead.

While our arrival could easily be observed from all areas of the laager, in actual fact, few saw us come in. My heart started to pound in my ears, and I wanted to scream to the lookout to signal our presence. A split-second later, all hell broke loose.

We were almost half-way to where the rebel Boers were clustered in groups, when those Boers nearest us jumped up and closed ranks to form a barrier, their arms cutting through the air to force us back. Meanwhile, the ones closest to the tents and wagons started to clamber over each other to reach their rifles, liquor kegs being knocked over in their haste.

On observing that they might be tempted to fire on the lancers, a group of Transvaal Boers now ran to our aid, screaming at the rebel Boers not to shoot. Others were trying to calm them down or attempting to wrestle the rifles from their hold.

"Quick, Mr. Owen!" I shouted. "Dismiss the lancers. These Boers have been drinking, and might be tempted to take a pot shot at them."

Fortunately, the lancers needed no further prompt to escape the scene. With them gone, the hubbub soon subsided, enabling Pretorius to shout a rebuke.

"What on earth did you think you were doing? Don't you realize that you've just threatened the guards of the very people I'm trying to negotiate our independence with? How can you now expect me to arbitrate on your behalf? I'll be able to do nothing for you. I'll try, of course, but as you will be regarded as criminals, the chances are slim."

As if by magic, a somber calm descended on the laager. Well played, Pretorius, I thought.

He waited until all was still before he spoke again. "Where is Van der Kolff? He's a criminal who has been forging my name on letters, not to speak of other damnable things he has done. If you hand him over now, there's a chance that I might still be able to negotiate on your behalf."

These words were hardly out of his mouth, when shouts from the entrance drew our attention. "He's escaped, Commandant-General. Come quickly!"

We rushed back to the entrance followed by a mass of men at our rear, some squeezing through openings in the laager, while others crowded outside the wagon-sized gap Van der Kolff had used to make his escape.

By the time we reached the entrance, Van der Kolff was already galloping towards a rise some distance away. On reaching it, he turned his horse to face us. He then whipped his rifle off his shoulder, and in a rebellious move, aimed it at Pretorius.

Unperturbed, Pretorius stepped forward and shouted, "You'll have to come closer to make good your shot, Van der Kolff!"

To everyone's relief, Van der Kolff looked over his shoulder, then lowered his rifle. It was then that we heard the unmistakable rumble of a wagon coming our way.

"Adriaan Stander," said Pretorius aloud.

Van der Kolff didn't budge until the wagon with its accompanying riders had passed below. But to both his surprise and ours, the noise of the wagon and the pounding of the horses hooves had managed to mask the sound of the approaching lancers who now streaked past us on their horses from the direction of the British camp. Taken by surprise, Van der Kolff dashed over the rise, while the lancers attempted to follow, but were forced to swerve to avoid the on-coming wagon, thus slowing their progress. At this point, Stander realized that something was amiss, and came galloping towards us.

Pretorius turned to address Owen who was standing behind him. "I fear that Van der Kolff might be meeting up with his band of Basutos, and will therefore lead your lancers into an ambush. If you agree, Mr. Owen, I'll ask Commandant Stander who's now approaching us to call them back."

Owen nodded, then turned to address me with a worried frown. "Do you think the lancers will overtake Van der Kolff?"

"Not when he's riding my horse, they won't," came the familiar voice of Piet Venter behind us. "He's one of the best. I tied him up near the gap facing the outspan field so I could walk straight through to where my friends were sitting. Now I'll have to make do with Van der Kolff's horse. I hope he's up to the mark."

Pretorius, who had been watching Stander ride off, turned to address Piet Venter over our heads. "All is not lost, Venter. I'll be speaking to the Van der Kolff group directly after devotions, and will appoint a couple of them to deliver his horse to you first thing tomorrow morning."

Without waiting for a reply, he looked my way. "Devotions at seven, *Dominee*." He then offered a smile to a bewildered-looking Owen. "And now you'll have to excuse me, sir.

We'll have to secure the laager as well as appoint scouts and guards in case Van der Kolff decides to return with his band of marauding Basutos. Tell Major Hogge that I'll be appointing men to guard his camp as well."

The men were already moving off, when Pretorius called them to attention and started to issue orders. Owen looked on in wonderment as the laager became a hive of activity. Not being an army man, he stood glued to the spot for some time. Piet Venter, I noticed, had already made himself scarce and was a good way up the track to the farmhouse.

Having seen enough, Owen turned to me with a supercilious grin and said, "Cup of tea, Mr. Murray?"

"Thought you'd never ask," I said, with tongue in cheek.

17
The Sand River Convention

16–17 January 1852

Adriaan Stander and the lancers arrived back a few hours later having given up their search for Van der Kolff. Around the same time, it came to Pretorius's notice that Moshesh's envoy, Joshua, had left. It was surmised that he must have taken fright at seeing the lancers pursue Van der Kolff while Pretorius looked on.

The departure of Joshua proved upsetting for Pretorius. So first thing the next morning, he sent two envoys to Moshesh to explain the situation. Around the same time, Major Hogge sent a lancer to Winburg to request reinforcements. So while the laager and the British camp were on a war footing, I hoped that the Convention itself would prove a tame affair. Nevertheless, I was ever conscious that Pretorius could try to chance his arm with Hogge. And as anticipated, that's exactly what he tried to do.

Before the discussions were due to start, Pretorius proposed that the pre-1848 district of Winburg be included in the discussions, and that a general amnesty be extended to those who had actively opposed the Government. He also offered to act as negotiator between Moshesh and the various Boer factions.

Major Hogge must have expected something of the sort from Pretorius, because he was ready with an answer. With unexpected finesse he pointed to the list of Transvaal stipulations that had been sent to him in advance.

"As far as this Convention is concerned, Mr. Pretorius, these are the mutually agreed upon issues under discussion—no more, and no less. I'd also like to remind you, sir, that by tomorrow morning this time, both the Transvaal and the Orange River Sovereignty will have signed a list of articles that includes non-interference in each other's affairs. We will have also disclaimed all alliances with African and Colored nations in each other's territories."

Not one to be easily put off, Pretorius replied, "Nevertheless, Major Hogge, these articles have not yet been signed. So may I ask how you intend to act towards the more rebellious Sovereignty Boers in our midst?"

"As it happens, sir, I've given it considerable thought. I'd be most obliged if you'd tell them that it would be to their advantage if they came to apologize to Mr. Owen and myself tomorrow afternoon. Fortunately, there's a magistrate present who is able to impose modest fines where applicable. Once this has been done, the matter will be considered dealt with."

I noticed that most of the delegates were nodding their heads. On realizing this, Pretorius had no other option but to fall into line with the majority opinion, especially as their eyes were boring into him.

In a tone that conveyed reluctant resignation, he said, "I'll let them know, sir."

Next morning, which was Saturday, 17 January, the Sand River Convention was duly signed amidst rejoicing on the part of the Transvaal Boers, and a glum acceptance by those from the Sovereignty.[5] That afternoon, I was surprised to see the line-up of rebel Boers outside the marquee. As expected, there were also those who refused to apologize, opting instead to trek to the Transvaal. But whether they apologized or decided to trek, it was an important step towards the resumption of peace in the Winburg and Vaal River districts.

After a moving church service on Sunday morning during which many a tear rolled down a greying beard, I had the opportunity of speaking alone with Pretorius, Elder Wolmarans, and Commandant Gert Kruger.

As I sat down in their midst, I couldn't help being conscious of the huge age difference between us. I noticed that Andries Pretorius had trimmed his jawline beard to a grey shadow. It certainly made him look much younger than his fifty-three years. I hazarded a guess that Wolmarans, with his thick crop of white hair and full beard must now be in his mid-sixties, while Gert Kruger, who was going bald and sported a flecked beard would probably be approaching fifty. And here I was, only twenty-three, and about to be as bold as any ankle-biting lion cub. And because these men were not given to subtlety, I dived straight in.

"I can't help thinking, gentlemen, that now that the Transvaal is independent, it would be most beneficial for your churches to join the Cape Synod."

Pretorius winked at the others, then folded his arms as if to say that I deserved a hearing, although under sufferance. When I hesitated, he said, "Go on, *Dominee*, we're listening."

Although put out, I pressed on. "Well as I was saying, you are now independent, so a pastor's salary will need to be paid by the combined Volksraad. That should allay the fears of the Marico Boers and any others who are concerned about English influences."

"Perhaps so," Pretorius said. "But what about the all-important question of acquiring a pastor?"

"It should be much easier now, especially if the pastor knows that he's able to count on the support of other pastors within the *Transgariep* Presbytery. You see, together with Dirk van Velden and myself, another pastor north of the Orange River would enable us to form our own Presbytery, seeing that we will be three in number."

Pretorius met my serious expression with a chuckle. "We were wondering when you'd raise this issue, *Dominee*. I, for one am tired of listening to the unfulfilled promises of that Dutch envoy, Smellekamp. He assured us that he would try his best to obtain a pastor for us, but nothing has come of it. No, it's high time we looked to the Cape again for help."

Wolmarans leaned forward, his expression serious. "You have to understand, *Dominee*, that a decision of this kind will have to be passed by all four consistories, especially the one in the Zoutpansberg district. We don't foresee any problems with the Jerusalem Pilgrims in the Marico District because Commandant-General Johan Enslin is on his deathbed, and there are no plans to replace him. And of course, Commandant-General Willem Joubert of Lijdenburg is on our side. Unfortunately, it will be the Zoutpansberg district that is likely to oppose such a move."

"*Ja*, and we're facing a major hurdle with Commandant-General Hendrik Potgieter from there at the moment," added Kruger. "He wrote to me accusing *Menee*r Pretorius, here, of wanting to negotiate a treaty without his authority and that of the combined *Volksraad*. He also made a number of other accusations. So now we have to get him on side."

Knowing the fierce competition that existed between Pretorius and Potgieter, I was under no illusion as to the strength of the opposition they would be facing. I was about to say something of the kind, when Kruger spoke first.

"Given the situation, we need your help, *Dominee*. Only God and His Word can soften the hardened heart. So tell us, what are the exact dates when you'll be preaching in Rustenburg?"

I couldn't help smiling. When it came to strategy and timing, these men were without equal. And here they were, miles ahead of me.

I retrieved my Bible from my shoulder bag and located my homemade calendar for the tour. There were three sheets, one for each month. A glance at the first was all I needed to remind me of the dates.

"The first service will be on Thursday evening, 15 March, and the last will be a thanksgiving service on Monday the nineteenth. Johannes Neethling will be interviewing the candidates for confirmation as well as the parents who will be presenting their children for baptism. I'll be doing the preaching."

There were smiles all round plus the expected comments about my needing to take things easy. We then got down to strategizing.

It was decided that Gert Kruger, a once ardent supporter of Potgieter, would invite him to attend the services, but would suggest that he arrive several days beforehand. This would allow Kruger to inform him of what had taken place at the Convention.

Pretorius would also write a personal letter of invitation to the services, but would only arrive just before the first one on the fifteenth. By that time, it was hoped that Potgieter would be willing to be reconciled and to accept the Convention.

"So let me get this straight," I said. "*Meneer* Kruger, here, will inform Hendrik Potgieter of the articles of the Convention during the days prior to the services. But who will try to effect a reconciliation between him and *Meneer* Pretorius, here? We can't just hope that it will take place. He needs to be encouraged to take that step."

"But *Dominee*, you can't force something like that," said Kruger. "It needs to happen naturally and when Potgieter is ready. If he's not willing to greet *Meneer* Pretorius on Thursday evening, or accept the Convention by then, there'll still be other services to soften his heart and help him change his mind."

"But if we follow your argument, *Meneer* Kruger, Potgieter will be sitting in the services creating tension all around. Instead of listening to the Word, people will be wondering: 'Will he or won't he?' 'Will God soften his heart enough today?' 'What if he doesn't accept the Convention?' 'Will there be a civil war?' I can just imagine it. No, that's not how it works. There needs to be a public reconciliation between Potgieter and *Meneer* Pretorius. And it needs to take place on Thursday evening after the first service at the latest."

Kruger heaved a sigh. "I still say you can't force something like that."

"And I can't have two leaders sitting in my services who are not reconciled. That's out of the question. We have to first get the spiritual right, then the political will fall into place. It will be the duty of the elders to remind Potgieter of what God requires of him as a Christian leader."

Wolmarans's white eyebrows shot up almost to his hairline. "I can't see him listening to me, *Dominee*. He's a proud man and tends to be a law unto himself."

"He's not above the Word, *Meneer* Wolmarans, but under it. And as an elder, God has given you and the other elders the authority to try and mediate a reconciliation."

"Where does it say that in the Word?"

"Right here."

I turned to Philippians 4:2, read the verse aloud, then began to expound upon it.

"Here we have two women: Euodia and Syntyche—godly women who have served with St. Paul. But they were always arguing and couldn't get along. St. Paul begs them to be of the same mind. But being a practical man, he knows that they might need help. So he entreats his partner in the Word to help those women reach an understanding. And something similar should happen in this situation as well. And as the battle is in the spiritual realm, it should be the elders who need to speak with Potgieter about unity, forgiveness, and love."

Wolmarans was stroking his beard as if rehearsing what he would say. If anyone could change Potgieter's mind, it would be Wolmarans. He had the uncanny ability to persuade. I couldn't help recalling how I had given in to him during the early hours of one morning. He'd asked me to set out to a farm at 3.00 a.m. to baptize a child who had been born after the baptismal service had taken place. The reason for going had been ridiculous. It was purely because the young mother had been anxious that her baby should not to be left out. I'd only agreed because he'd dangled the irresistible carrot of a much needed horse before my eyes.

Thankfully, Pretorius, who had been leaning on his knees, now looked up and interrupted my train of thought. "Surely the Lord will give us the victory in this matter? And what rejoicing there will be, not to speak of the peace of the Lord that will fill Potgieter's heart."

"I'm pleased you mentioned rejoicing and peace, *Meneer* Pretorius, because that's exactly what is mentioned later in this section. It also tells us not to be anxious, but to present our requests with thanksgiving to God who will give us the peace that transcends all understanding to guard our hearts."

I paused, locking eyes with each man in turn. "Please read this portion of Scripture again, and claim it for the Transvaal and yourselves."

Wolmarans, I noticed, had just extracted a small notebook from his inside pocket and was holding a pencil at the ready. With a glimmer of a smile lighting his face, he said, "Just remind us, again, *Dominee*. Where do we find that portion of Scripture?"[6]

18

My Fourth Tour across the Vaal

February–June 1852

Jan Neethling arrived in Bloemfontein with Charles on 13 February. As he explained, he wanted to arrive early so as to rest up for the long trek north.

He was still the same old Jan as I'd known at Utrecht, except now, at twenty-six, the lines spanning his broad forehead had deepened. But besides that, his light-brown hair was still parted to the side, and curls still licked his earlobes. As always, he sported a well maintained chin beard that I was sure would transmute into a full one by the end of the tour.

After the initial welcome, we adjourned to the parlor for refreshments. Thankfully, Maria was on hand to offer us tea and some delicious biscuits that she'd baked with Jan's arrival in view. She then sat on the couch next to Charles, her back straight and her hands folded tightly in her lap. By contrast. Jan looked as relaxed as ever, with one arm dangling over the side of his armchair.

"Before we start discussing other matters, I'd like to get a few planning issues out of the way," he said. "For your information,

Andrew, I'll be returning to Prins Albert after our tour. I've decided to preach for them until my induction. With that said, I'd like you to be the one to induct me. Please say yes."

I was still trying to recall how far it was to Prins Albert, when Jan anticipated my reluctance by saying, "It'll be no hardship on your part, because you can stop by on your way to the Synod. After the induction, we can travel to Cape Town together."

"There's one small problem with this plan, Jan. Both John and I are scheduled to attend the Presbytery meeting in Graaff-Reinet before we set out for Cape Town."

"*Ja*, John mentioned that. But what I propose to do is visit Graaff-Reinet on my way home. While I'm there, I can persuade your father to let both you and John leave the Presbytery meeting early. I can't see how he could object because, according to John, you'll only be fine-tuning your reports there."

I eyed him with amusement, knowing that he wouldn't give up until I'd said yes. With tongue in cheek I said, "I suppose you're hoping to persuade my father and the rest of the Presbytery to attend your induction as well, are you?"

A broad smile lit his face, his tongue protruding slightly between his teeth. "*Ach*, you know me, Andrew. I try never to miss an opportunity."

I noticed that Maria's lips were twitching at the edges. Well might she smile, I thought, because when it came to the planning stakes, Jan would give her a run for her money.

The arrival of Jan and Charles freed me up to go to Fauresmith to conduct the quarterly communion services there. I was going to take Jan with me, but being fresh from Utrecht, he'd been inundated with invitations from members of my consistory. And as Maria knew the way to their farms, I left the three of them to their own devices until I returned.

Our time as a group together was cut short when Maria and Charles left for Burghersdorp the following week. This gave Jan and me time to make final arrangements for our own departure on Monday, 1 March. With Jan as my companion, and selecting to do all the interviewing while I did the preaching, this tour promised to be the best ever.

After the usual round of services at Potchefstroom, we travelled east to Suikerbosch Rand, a beautiful area known for its proteas. While the original plan had been to make Rustenburg my next port of call after Potchefstroom, I'd changed my mind after further reflection. The reason was that I thought it unwise to hold a week of services there just before the planned people's assembly and the combined *Volksraad* meetings.

While it was usual for the *Volksraad* to hold its meetings at the conclusion of one or other of my services, I deemed the meetings on 16 March to be in a different category. For one thing, there would be too much tension in the air for the people to focus on the Word. For another, I feared that Elder Wolmarans might call upon me to speak with Hendrik Potgieter if he showed no inclination to be reconciled with Andries Pretorius. And the last thing I wanted was to be accused of interfering in Transvaal affairs.

I was therefore greatly relieved when my decision was endorsed in an unexpected way. A few weeks before Jan and I were due to set out for the Transvaal, I heard that Suikerbosch Rand had just established its own congregation at their newly appointed village of Heidelberg. The outcome of this happy event was that they desired me to induct their elder-elect, David Jacobs, at Potchefstroom. We were then to return with him to Suikerbosch Rand to conduct my usual set of services.

So from Potchefstroom, it was to Suikerbosch Rand that we set out, our wagon being pulled by eight oxen travelling at approximately three miles per hour over a hilly terrain with few tracks. Although our tour would take three months, we anticipated that a full month of that time would be spent in either an ox-wagon or on horseback. Fortunately, there was always the kind farmer en route who took pity on us and provided horses as an extra means of conveyance.

From Suikerbosch Rand we travelled north-east to Lijdenburg, where we were surprised to find a church being built. As the walls had already reached the rafters, we were able to hold services there after some makeshift coverings had been spread over the roof beams.

From Lijdenburg we headed due north to Hendrik Potgieter's settlement in the Zoutpansberg district. It proved a marathon ox-wagon journey, taking us no less than eleven days of uninterrupted travel to reach the agreed rendezvous at the ford of the Crocodile River. When we arrived there, nine ox-wagons were waiting to escort us to a small laager of a further fifty wagons nearby.

Unfortunately, just before our arrival, the area had been plunged into mourning due to the deaths from malaria of twenty-four loved-ones. And although every household had been affected by either illness or death, we were received with great joy. In fact, the preaching of the Word proved to be a veritable feast to them. Even the children rejoiced, although they scarcely knew the reason why.

During our stay, we were able to place their congregation on a firm footing by inducting J.L.P. Venter as elder, and P.L. du Preez and C. Grobler as deacons.

Our return journey took us south-west to the hot springs of Warmbad, where we planned to enjoy several days of rest and recreation. Expecting to be the sole visitors at the springs, you can imagine our surprise when we came across several ox-wagons belonging to Hendrik Potgieter and his party. They were on their way home after attending the people's assembly and *Volksraad* meetings at Rustenburg.

Potgieter was overjoyed to meet us, as we him. He was a tall, well-built man, although slightly stooped due to physical weakness and the ravages of age. Nevertheless, he had a full crop of hair with only tinges of grey, and what Jan described as a venerable countenance.

He informed us that he was now reconciled with Andries Pretorius, and had also endorsed the Sand River Convention. My heart quickened when he added that he could see no reason why the Transvaal congregations should not now be allowed to join the Cape Synod.

From Warmbad, our journey took us via Rustenburg and the Marico District back to Potchefstroom. As our ox-wagon rumbled into the village, we were amazed to see the huge crowds awaiting us there. Because the little church could only hold six hundred at a pinch, I was forced to hold the services out of doors and offer two communion services on Sunday morning.

What was particularly striking was the attitude of joyful thanksgiving that marked these services. It seemed to one and all that the Transvaal had finally come of age and was destined to embrace a peaceful future with God at the helm. All that remained now was for them to join hands with their compatriots in the Cape by seeking to be incorporated into the Synod.

Because I wanted this act to be solely of their own volition, I asked Jan Neethling to lead the joint consistory meeting that was due to be held on Saturday, 22 May. I intended to remain in the background by offering to be joint chairman and secretary.

On Saturday morning I noted that only Deacon Jan Schutte was there to represent Rustenburg. At the time, I thought nothing of it because other consistory members from Rustenburg had been signatories to Gert Kruger's letter requesting to join the Cape Synod in 1848. Kruger had given the letter to Drs. Philip Faure and William Robertson while on their preaching tour through the Transvaal. They had then discussed it with my father in Graaff-Reinet on their way home. As both Hendrik Potgieter and Andries Pretorius had also signed that letter, I took it for granted that the Rustenburg consistory had selected Schutte to represent them. But as future events would show, I couldn't have been more wrong.

So besides a full complement of consistory members from Potchefstroom, there was only Schutte representing Rustenburg, and Jan and myself representing Lijdenburg. While the main aim was to obtain an official agreement to join the Cape Synod, this decision needed to be endorsed by the *Volksraad* as well. And therein lay a problem.

During my four tours of the Transvaal, I had noted how difficult it was for people to separate State affairs from issues related to church governance. So Jan and I aimed to stress the importance of a consistory being able to act in accordance with church law without any political interference from the *Volksraad*. We also wanted them to understand that both *Volksraad* and consistory should be able to make independent decisions relevant to their own role in society. This led us to devise four questions that we wanted both the meeting and the *Volksraad* to answer.

After four trestle tables had been set up in the church to form a square, Jan skillfully opened the meeting with the following comment: "I'm afraid, gentlemen, I can only support your move to ask the Cape Synod to search for a pastor on your behalf once I've received satisfactory answers to the four questions I'm about to pose."

He then proceeded to distribute copies to each delegate. Once done, he resumed his central position behind one of the trestle tables and proceeded to read the questions:

"Question One: Will the pastor that you call be able to remain a member of the Dutch Reformed Church of South Africa? And even though a congregation may be physically isolated, will it still endeavor to remain under the spiritual authority of the Cape Synod?"

Jan looked up to ascertain their initial response. But as far as I could tell, there wasn't so much as a raised eyebrow. Obviously relieved, he moved on to the next question, knowing it would find favor with the meeting.

"Question Two: Will the salary of the pastor be guaranteed by the Volksraad?"

This was followed by smiles and nods all round.

"Three: Will the Volksraad agree to leave a pastor free to exercise his duties without influence or coercion?"

More nods.

"Four: Will the *Volksraad* agree to refer any spiritual accusation against a pastor to a Commission of Spiritual Oversight, or to the consistory of the congregation in question?"

A hum now went up around the table. Jan skillfully regained their attention by explaining how matters worked in the Sovereignty and Natal with regard to the relationship between the State and the Dutch Reformed Church.

"You will also be pleased to know," he continued, "that while our stipends are paid by the British, the political authorities never interfere in the internal running of our church. The same should hold for the relationship between church and *Volksraad* in the Transvaal.

After a short discussion on question one, the meeting unanimously agreed to both its requirements. It then adjourned while the questions were handed to the *Volksraad* for ratification. After what the latter termed a "lively discussion," it too affirmed the four questions.

While there were many God-given moments of sheer joy on this tour, they all came second to my farewell with Wolmarans. With a broad smile and a flourish, he presented me with a letter addressed to the Synod.

"All the representatives have signed it," he said. "And with you presenting our case to the Synod, I have no doubt that our request for incorporation will be accepted."

Clasping my hand in a vice-like grip, he continued. "*Ach Dominee*, do your best to persuade the Synodical Committee to find a Dutch pastor for us."

"Believe me, *Meneer* Wolmarans, they'll be so overjoyed to have the Transvaal congregations back in the fold that they'll be doing their utmost on your behalf. It's time to leave it in the Lord's hands now."

I placed the letter in my inside pocket, and gave it a pat. Then with a final nod, I climbed aboard the wagon beside Jan. Little did I know then that it would be twelve years before I'd be back.

As we pulled off, Jan gave me a congratulatory nudge.

"It's all the Lord's doing," I said in response. But despite this claim, my pride and self-satisfaction broke out in alarming proportions. I even pictured John shaking my hand and Maria beaming with pride when I shared this news with them. In addition, there was the long-awaited consecration of our church building to look forward to. But best of all, it would be the first time since arriving in the Sovereignty that there'd be family members to greet me at the end of my journey. What a home-coming it promised to be!

19

The Consecration of the Bloemfontein Church

5 June 1852

We arrived back in Bloemfontein on 3 June—two days later than expected. When we entered the parsonage around sunset on Thursday afternoon, John was already ensconced in the parlor. He was putting the last touches to a sermon at the dining room table, a large picnic basket beside him, and a mug of tea in his hand. To my relief, a fire was already burning in the hearth.

Upon greeting me, he said. "You've cut it fine. What held you up? You told me you'd be back on Tuesday. When we arrived here, there was no water, no milk, no food, and only a few logs for the fire. Thankfully, Charles Stuart came to our rescue by inviting us to dinner and fetching your houseboy, Godfrey."

"I apologize for any inconvenience, John, but we were held up by rain in Winburg."

"Anyway, I have good news to report. You'll be pleased to know that I've brought Daniel Sluiter, with me. He's the new schoolmaster of Burghersdorp, and a wonderful song leader. He'll do a magnificent job in leading the singing during the services. He's visiting your schoolmaster, Van der Meer, at the moment."

"But I asked Dirk van Velden to lead the singing. He's an excellent tenor. And as he's not preaching, I wanted to involve him in some way."

"He's a pastor, Andrew, not a song leader. In any case, the poor man has been overly busy trying to patch up rifts in his congregation. Let him just sit back and enjoy the occasion without having to do anything."

Jan, who was seated next to John, and across the table from me, prodded my toe. He had done so on several occasions at Utrecht when he thought John was overplaying the elder brother card. I decided to take the hint by changing the subject.

"Where's Maria, by the way?"

"In Graaff-Reinet. Ma wanted Charles to come home for a short spell, so he took Maria with him."

"But didn't she tell you that she was keen to return here?"

"She did, but Pa overruled her."

"Why was that?"

"Think, Andrew. Pa surmised that since you had been away so long, you'd be sure to go on a few visitation rounds when you got back. That would mean that Maria would have to remain in Bloemfontein alone, or accompany you in freezing conditions. He naturally declared both options unsuitable. And I heartily agree."

I heaved a sigh as I considered the matter. "But he knows that I usually stay put for the duration of July. It's my sermon preparation time. Besides it's far too cold to travel then. And as for the rest of June, I'll only be doing short visitation trips to the farms in the immediate vicinity. I also plan to make a point of speaking to all the families who live further afield over this weekend. So she could have come. I just wish Pa would allow

Maria to make her own decisions for once. She's old enough now."

"Perhaps so, Andrew, but not sensible enough. Pa wrote to say that since arriving back in Graaff-Reinet, she has fancied herself to be a second Madame Guyon. As a result, he's had to try to redirect her excess enthusiasm—not an easy task, I believe. You really must take care that she doesn't become over emotional regarding spiritual matters."

John was sniffing the air with indignation, while I was nursing my disappointment. Only Jan was smiling to himself in obvious appreciation of Maria's attempt to be active in the ministry. The two men couldn't have been more different.

The consecration of our church building on Saturday, 5 June was a sight to behold. Wagon after wagon came rolling into town filling both outspan places. Little Gideon Radloff and his friends assured me that they'd counted no less than 1440 horses and oxen.

I was also relieved that Dirk Van Velden was given a turn to lead the singing. To the amusement of all, Daniel Sluiter became hoarse and somewhat exhausted during the two days of services, so Van Velden was requested to step into the breach.

Despite the freezing temperatures on Saturday night, people enjoyed the camaraderie of huddling around campfires. They were so numerous, that the fluttering flames and the updraft from the smoke cocooned Bloemfontein in an ethereal mist of light. But it was Sunday morning that proved most special of all. Before the sun had even risen, the fires were flickering brightly, and the aroma of fresh coffee had enveloped the town. Bloemfontein had never experienced the like, and would probably never again.

That morning I renewed my calling to be her pastor, and was thankful that God had placed me in her midst.

20

My Dive into the Slough of Self-pity

June–August 1852

John and Jan Neethling left Bloemfontein on Tuesday, 8 June. After their departure, a tangible emptiness descended on the parsonage. How I missed not having Maria around! As it turned out, Bloemfontein would become a busy little metropolis during the month of June. The very next day, I was jolted out of my lethargy by the sad news that Major Hogge had passed away. No sooner was his funeral over, when we heard that our new Governor, Sir George Cathcart, had requested that a gathering of elected representatives from each field cornetcy be held in Bloemfontein on 21 June.

This caused quite a buzz throughout the Sovereignty. Seventy-nine representatives gathered in the school building for three days of deliberations. During the sitting, Andries Pretorius visited Bloemfontein as an observer. He was received in a most friendly fashion, and even delivered an address to the representatives. How times had changed! Dr. Fraser, who had been elected chairman, informed me of the details a short while later.

It came as no surprise that the delegates were in favor of retaining British authority, but wanted to do away with the existing legislative council in exchange for an elected legislative assembly. I was, however, taken aback on hearing that sixty-nine of them had voted for a commando system, with the proviso that a strict policy of non-interference in African tribal disputes be adhered to. After the meeting had adjourned, we were left to wonder what would become of these decisions.

Life soon returned to normal, and June passed into July. Most of my time was now taken up with sermon preparation, interspersed by short visits to farms in the vicinity to break the monotony.

I had just arrived back from one such visit on Thursday, 22 July, and was about to collect my mail from the post office, when I ran into Major Warden's new clerk, Edward Collins. He'd already been in the job six months, but on account of my tour to the Transvaal, I'd not been able to further our acquaintance. I therefore decided that there was no time like the present to do so.

He was a tall, well-built man, somewhere in his mid-forties. And being able to inspect him now at close quarters, I couldn't help being struck by his deep brown eyes that spoke of intelligence and discernment.

I'd heard that he'd lived in both France and the Low Countries at one time, thus enabling him to speak French and Dutch fairly fluently. He'd also been assistant professor in Classics at the South African College in Cape Town before abandoning lecturing to become a farmer. But only a few weeks after purchasing a farm near Smithfield, he was forced to flee with his wife and son to Bloemfontein on account of the Basuto raids in that district.

Given his background and education, it was little wonder that Major Warden had snapped him up after Joseph Allison's resignation.

He greeted me warmly, but I couldn't help noticing that he looked nervy and upset.

"Have you heard the news, Mr. Murray? Major Warden has been asked to take early retirement from tomorrow. He's just announced it, although he's known since Monday. The town's in an uproar about it because of the way it was done. Sir George Cathcart only gave him a week's notice. Fancy that!"

"Do you know who will take his place?"

"His deputy, Henry Green."

"But he's only in his mid-thirties!"

"Nevertheless, he's supposed to be good at his job."

"So where does that leave you, Mr. Collins?

He looked down, not wanting me to see his eyes brimming with tears. "I'm about to lose my job as well, Mr. Murray. Henry Green has just told me that he wants to retain his own clerk. So guess what? He's appointed me government teacher at about half my present salary. That's why I'm out and about. I've just been to *The Friend*, and thankfully, I've been offered the job of translating all Dutch letters to the editor into English."

"Just be thankful for small mercies, Mr. Collins. It will help you get through this."

Collins nodded. He had already turned to go when I called after him. "Mr. Collins? Would you mind waiting a moment while I collect my mail. I'd like to accompany you back to Major Warden's office to wish him well. I dare say he's feeling demoralized at the moment."

Collins tapped the side of his nose. "Stiff upper lip and all that, you know. Please tread carefully, Mr. Murray."

When I entered Warden's office a short time later, I could tell he was a broken man. It appeared that he was leaving with the new-found knowledge that he had sought advice from the wrong crowd—the British land speculators. And to make matters worse, Sir George Cathcart had rubbed salt into the wound via a scathing attack on them in public.

"He's alienated the British in these parts, Mr. Murray. Now all of them are up in arms. And who can blame them? I'm sure you wouldn't like to be called 'a set of covetous, profligate, unscrupulous land-jobbers,' now would you?"

I did my best to curb my smile in the face of Warden's consternation. But had I been in the company of a few Boers, I would have doubtless chuckled out loud. What a pity that Warden couldn't see that Cathcart had hit the nail on the head.

"Where will you go, Major Warden?"

"Oh, I've seen this coming for some time now. So a year or so ago, I bought a farm on the coast near George in the Western Cape. It's there that I intend spending the rest of my days." He shot me a wan smile, then said, "Just think of me breathing in the cool ocean air, while you are inhaling the choking dust of Bloemfontein."

I'm sure he hadn't intended to make me feel depressed, but his quip only served to remind me of my loneliness and the fact that I was about to return to an empty house.

As soon as I entered the front parlor, I shuffled through my pile of letters to find one from the family. There were a few, including one from Maria that I decided to read first. I slit the envelope open, then plonked myself in my favorite armchair to sit in comfort while I savored every word. I never got past the first two paragraphs, because what I read there shocked me to the core.

"*Dear Andrew*," it read. "*I have wonderful news to share with you. I'm engaged to be married to your best friend Johannes Neethling. We've set the wedding date for 4 December, which is Jan's twenty-seventh birthday. As you'll be on vacation in Graaff-Reinet after travelling back from the Synod, Jan intends to ask you to be his best man.*

I hardly know what to think of this decision. It all happened so quickly. And to think of the closeness of the sweet bond that united our souls, and then to think that I have calmly and deliberately consented to form another bond which can never be broken . . . Andrew comfort me. Tell me it was not I, but Christ who did it."

I sat there speechless, trying to take in her words. How could she be so inconsistent—one minute promising before the Lord to join me in ministry, then the next, agreeing to marry Jan—a man she hardly knew. And how dare Jan not breathe a word of his intentions to me. To think that their relationship was blossoming right under my roof without me even suspecting it! And the fact that he did not stay long at Burghersdorp, but dashed off to Graaff-Reinet, says it all. He already knew then what his intentions were. Talk about grasping every opportunity!

Of course he would want to marry Maria. Who wouldn't? He could see that she was a ready-made pastor's wife—educated, able to teach Sunday school, and at the same time cook, bake and sew, as well as support him in the ministry. It wasn't fair! I was far more deserving than he. Just to think that he would be starting out in the ministry with a wife, while here I was struggling year after year without a close friend my own age or a helpmate.

And as for Maria . . . what a flighty miss she'd turned out to be! And fancy having the effrontery to request that I tell her that it was Christ who made her accept Jan's offer. It was the flesh, more like it.

There was a rush of blood to my head, which can only account for what I did next. I virtually jumped out of the armchair and strode to the desk in my bedroom. I drew out my chair with such force that it nearly toppled over. I located a sheet of writing paper and dipped my pen into the inkwell. My thoughts raced and the words poured onto the paper. I would tell her exactly what I thought of her flippant decision.

The letter done, I strode to the post office to catch the last post. On my return home, my indignation rose to new heights when I read the letters from other members of the family. They couldn't get over the wonder of it all, especially my mother. Of course she would be over the moon. What mother wouldn't want to see her eldest daughter safely married to someone like Jan.

It was at this point that the realization dawned that my uncalled-for response had been due to insane jealousy. Both Jan and Maria would have all their dreams fulfilled, while I would have to endure another year of incessant travel and aching loneliness in the Orange River Sovereignty.

Although I understood the reasons for my ridiculous reaction, the ache in my heart failed to subside. Nor could I rid myself of the thought that God was dealing unfairly with me. And as I was no hypocrite, I could not bring myself to pen an apology while I still clung to the thought that I had been short-changed.

Maria's reply arrived two weeks later. It epitomized the saying that 'less is more.' I'd never really understood its meaning until I read her short note. "*Dear Andrew,*" she wrote. "*I know for certain now that it was Jesus who chose for me. Your outburst spoke only of self. It's time, my brother, to wait upon God and seek His will for your own life.*"[7]

What a putdown! But for all that, she had given me the wake-up call I needed. Over the next few days, all I could do was ponder her words.

As time passed, and my indignation subsided, I felt utterly ashamed of myself. I began to recognize that I had swept God aside to cling to my jealousy and self-pity. It had been all about me and my own needs. Oh, what a sinful man I was! If the truth be known, I hadn't matured spiritually at all since the day I'd been inducted. Yes, I'd grown as a leader and in my role as a pastor, but spiritually—no. For a humble man does not take offense, and is careful not to give it.

I thought back to my arrival in Cape Town when I'd realized for the first time that I was a spiritual pauper. I had set my goal then to be able to preach with power like Uncle William and *Dominee* Helperus van Lier. And the only way that this desire could be attained was through close fellowship with God. I needed to get back on track.

With tears of contrition, I consecrated my life anew to the Lord. I also made a firm decision to make good on my consecration by spending time in silent adoration and waiting upon God during my daily devotions.

I certainly couldn't overcome my outbursts of self and pride in my own strength. So by faith, I would let the Holy Spirit do the work for me.

With that decision made, I sat down to write to Maria to beg her forgiveness. While doing so, the thought struck home that if God could provide a husband for Maria, He could also provide a wife for me. I cringed at the thought that Maria and I had tried to run ahead of Him with our own misguided ideas.

Please forgive me Lord. And thank You for intervening. I'll wait on You in future to send the right person my way. I have no idea how this miracle will take place, but You, oh Lord, are the God of miracles, and know exactly what I need. Amen.

21

A Clutch of Surprises

September–December 1852

The Presbytery meeting in Graaff-Reinet at the end of September was a short affair. We pastors had gathered with our elders to put the final touches to our reports before heading off to the Synod that was due to start on 12 October. We were all seated around the table in the roomy church consistory, when my father, acting as chairman, announced some astonishing news.

"Before we begin this meeting," he said, "I'd like to make some important announcements. As it relates to my son Andrew and *Meneer* Van Velden, it is only fair that I should share this news with you here before you hear it at the Synod."

He broke into a broad smile and looked my way. "It has come to the attention of the Synodical Committee that a Dutch pastor, who is earmarked for the Transvaal, will soon be landing on our shores. By the way, Andrew, what does the Transvaal call itself these days? We'd better refer to it by its correct name at the Synod."

"I think it's still open to negotiation, Pa, but the temporary name is The Holland-African Republic."

There were several chuckles and eye-rolls around the table. Noting this, my father said, "Well, I dare say no one will mind if I continue to call it the Transvaal for the time-being."

"Do we know who this pastor is, Pa?"

"I was just coming to that, Andrew. His name is Dirk van der Hoff, and he's due to land in Cape Town during the sitting of Synod, or just after. Unfortunately, there are a few difficulties related to his arrival that will need to be ironed out. They have to do with him being sent out by a Professor Ulrich Lauts from the School for Mariners at Medemblik in Holland."

"The School for Mariners?" repeated John. "So he's not a Professor of Theology then?"

"No, I'm afraid not."

"*Ja*, I remember reading about him," Willem Pretorius said. "He wrote the book *The Cape Emigrants* in which he took the Cape Synod to task for not supplying the regions beyond the Orange River with pastors. He also claimed that we were being visited by Scottish and English preachers who spoke Dutch imperfectly, or not at all."

"That's the one, *Meneer* Pretorius" said my father. "And as you can guess, he was speaking of me."

"But he has no authority to appoint ministers to our Church," I said. "And in any case, his book is a gross misrepresentation of the truth. Your Dutch is excellent, Pa. If it were not so, you wouldn't have been appointed Moderator a few years ago."

My father held up his hand to silence me. "Let's press on," he said. "It's obvious that Professor Lauts does not have a grip on the church situation here, nor our problems in obtaining pastors."

"Quite so," Pretorius said.

My father acknowledged Pretorius's affirmative comment, then continued. "As the Transvaal will be incorporated within the Cape Synod this sitting, Van der Hoff will have to conform to the rules and regulations of the Cape church. He'll have to sign the formularies, and he'll need to receive a letter of call from one of the congregations beyond the Vaal."

"Well, I can't perceive any difficulties there, Pa. As he's Dutch and from Holland, I dare say they'll grab him. And despite him being sent out by Professor Lauts, this is indeed wonderful news."

"Hear! Hear!" came the chorus from around the table.

Van Velden, who was sitting next to me leant over and whispered, "Take it from me, *Meneer* Murray, Van der Hoff will make sure he passes his legitimation with flying colors."

"I dare say that's true, *Meneer* Van Velden. But even if Dr. Abraham Faure has doubts, he'll know that Elder Wolmarans of Potchefstroom will knock him into shape."

We were still chuckling when my father called us to order.

"I have further good news to report," he said. "This time it has a direct bearing on your duties *Meneer* Van Velden. You'll be pleased to hear that Dr. Abraham Faure's son, Hendrik, has recently arrived back from Utrecht, and has been appointed to the congregation of Pietermaritzburg. So you'll soon be relieved from having to travel there every quarter to conduct communion services."

"Wonders will never cease," said Van Velden. "I couldn't have wished for better news."

My father gave him a peremptory nod, then shifted his gaze to me.

"I have yet another surprise in store for you, Andrew. As you may recall, our previous Governor, Sir Harry Smith, requested that the Synodical Committee obtain two pastors from Holland for the Orange River Sovereignty. And although we approached Professors Royaards and Vinke to help us in our search, only one pastor indicated his willingness to travel to our shores. And that pastor, of course, was our dear colleague *Meneer* van Velden who is with us today. Nevertheless, you may all be surprised to hear that the stipend for the second pastor is still available. This has enabled the Synodical Committee to appoint one of our own local sons to Smithfield. His name is Piet Roux."

It was now my turn to stare at my father with unfeigned surprise. "Where is he from, Pa? I've never heard of him."

"He's originally from Paarl in the Western Cape. He studied at Lutheran Seminaries in both Germany and Holland. But since arriving back at the Cape, he's seen the light, and has requested to become a Dutch Reformed pastor."

My father waited for the chuckles to die down before continuing. "He's presently looking after a small congregation in Knysna, but is delighted to be appointed to the large congregation of Smithfield. And coming from a farming family himself, I'm sure he'll fit in perfectly."

This piece of news caused a buzz around the table. Van Velden gave me a congratulatory nudge, while John pressed my lower arm. Willem Pretorius smiled at me from across the table, as did other members of the Presbytery. As for me, I felt as if I were walking through a door marked "new era." No longer would I need to go on exhausting tours to the Transvaal or conduct quarterly communion services at Smithfield. I could now focus solely on Bloemfontein and Fauresmith.

I was still trying to digest this news, when my father added, "Piet Roux has indicated that he would like to be inducted at the end of May, Andrew. And as you are regarded as the *consulent* for the congregations across the Vaal, you will have to induct Van der Hoff as well. I would pencil in a date in late July, because I can't see an induction service happening in the Transvaal before then. They will need time to discuss this development as well as send a letter of call to Cape Town."

"How about Hendrik Faure?" asked Van Velden. "Do you have any idea when he would like to be inducted?"

"I'd suggest you pencil in the beginning of May, *Meneer* Van Velden. Hendrik Faure would probably like it sooner, but the weather for travel is far better then. It will also ensure a larger turnout."

Noting my father's complicit smile, Van Velden saluted with his pen to indicate that he had understood my father's meaning.

Most of us were now glancing down to see the next item on the agenda, when my father cleared his throat, and said, "Now for the sad news. . . ."

As if by orchestration, we lifted our heads in unison to focus on what my father had to say next.

"As it requires three pastors to form a Presbytery," he said, "the Synodical Committee has decided that a separate one should be formed for the regions beyond the borders of the Cape. It will take in the congregations of the Orange River Sovereignty, Pietermaritzburg in Natal, and the congregations beyond the Vaal. It therefore saddens me to have to say that the representatives here from Bloemfontein and Winburg will no longer be members of this Presbytery in future."

Willem Pretorius exchanged a knowing glance with me, while John heaved a sigh. Both knew how much I looked forward to attending the Presbytery meetings in Graaff-Reinet.

My father, who was putting a brave face on it, smiled across at Van Velden and me before continuing. "We'll naturally miss their presence very much, but it's time for them to step out on their own. I'm sure they'll do so most ably."

It seemed strange to me that God was allowing the strings with my family to be cut one by one at a time I needed the home circle most. I'll just have to try to get home for a week or two in July, I thought. Then I remembered Piet Roux's induction service at the end of May, and Van der Hoff's in Potchefstroom at the end of July. There was always something to stop me from coming home. But at least I'd be in Graaff-Reinet for Maria's wedding in December.

I switched my focus back to the meeting, and straightened my report papers on the table before me. It would be John's and my turn next to present our reports. Directly afterwards, we would be leaving to attend Jan Neethling's induction.

A hail of backslaps and guffaws were the order of the day when we arrived at Prins Albert. If the truth be known, it made me feel like a hypocrite. There, I was wishing Jan well and welcoming him into the family fold, when only a few months before I'd been consumed with jealousy regarding his impending marriage to Maria. Oh, my evil heart! At least the memory of my descent into self-pity had once again made me aware of how much I needed to walk closely with the Lord.

Unfortunately, my resolve not to focus on self was sorely tested when I arrived at the Synod in Cape Town. To my embarrassment, most of my colleagues treated me like a conquering hero. I was the man of the moment whose hand needed to be shaken, arm squeezed, or back slapped in appreciation for bringing the emigrants across the Vaal back into the fold.

In addition, I was also to learn that I had been appointed chairman of the *Transgariep* Presbytery—the name the Synod had given to the area beyond the Orange River. I'm afraid, all this attention and ballyhoo went to my head. And try as I might, I couldn't prick my inflated ego. I feared it was becoming a thorn in my flesh that was keeping me from growing spiritually.

Fortunately, I found the family circle in Graaff-Reinet a great leveler when we arrived back from the Synod. With only two weeks to go before the wedding, everyone's attention was focused on Maria and the endless dress fittings for the younger girls. Then, there were the streams of visitors delivering gifts for which Jan and I had to find place in his rapidly filling wagon. The rest of the time, Maria and Jan were out visiting family and friends. According to Afrikaner custom, it was expected that she introduce Jan to them prior to the wedding.

With all the hustle and bustle, as well as the lengthy absences of the couple from home, there was scarcely an opportunity to exchange a word with Maria. Although I had personally sought her forgiveness while in Graaff-Reinet in September, I now wanted to reestablish the close filial relationship that we had enjoyed before my disastrous reply to her engagement announcement. But unfortunately, no opportunity presented itself. In fact, it seemed that before I could turn around, the wedding day had arrived.

As expected, the church was full to overflowing. Maria bedazzled us in her sheer-white cotton dress with its layered skirts and tight-fitting bodice. Towards the back of her head she wore a frilly tulle cap that she had hand-embroidered herself—or so I was told after the wedding. Attached to the cap was a veil that flowed halfway down her dress.

Pa looked so proud as he walked her down the aisle. Then, after presenting Maria to Jan, he assumed the role of pastor and proceeded to conduct the wedding service.

Thankfully, the lunch that was held at the parsonage afterwards was a homely affair. Besides our family, only close friends were invited. I thought I might be able to say a word or two to Maria then, but it proved impossible. Even when we had all assembled alongside Jan's wagon to say our goodbyes, the only significant exchange between us was her peck on my cheek and her whisper that it would be my turn soon.

I cringed once again at the thought that only four months before I had acted like a self-serving bounder for wanting to deny her marriage and children. My ridiculous behavior had uncovered the state of my heart and my reliance on the creature instead of my Creator.

Lord, may it never happen again!

I turned to observe Georgie who was uncommonly quiet while watching the wagon disappear down Parsonage Street. I guessed that for all Maria's scolding and unrelenting discipline, he would miss her terribly.

I gave him a playful punch and a tickle, then said, "Let's go inside and see what's left of the cakes before the others descend on them."

He responded with a smile and a tickle of his own. I encircled my arm around his waist and lifted him up sideways. I then dashed indoors with him kicking furiously behind.

We were back to normal.

22

The Battle of Berea

20 December 1852

During my absence from the Sovereignty, the new Governor, Sir George Cathcart, had decided to restore the prestige of British arms by attacking Moshesh at Berea Mountain on 20 December. As soon as the news of Cathcart's victory filtered through to us in Graaff-Reinet, both John and I decided to leave immediately for Burghersdorp. This move would enable me to reach Bloemfontein by the end of the year.

By the time I arrived in Smithfield on 29 December, the outcome of the Battle of Berea was on everyone's lips. This was especially true of Jacobus Snyman with whom I was staying overnight. Being a church warden, one of the aims of my visit was to discuss the induction of Piet Roux with him. But Snyman had other ideas.

We were sitting on his *stoep* enjoying the panorama of rolling hills, when he broached the topic of the battle.

"You know what, *Dominee*, the Battle of Berea would make the topic of a wonderful sermon. The reason is that Governor Cathcart lost due to arrogance."

"Cathcart lost, you say? But on my way here I heard that he was claiming victory over Moshesh."

Snyman spluttered with laughter. "That's not what people are saying around here. I'm sure you'll hear more about it when you reach Bloemfontein."

"I dare say I will. But you obviously know more than you're letting on."

"*Ach*, it's no secret amongst us Boers. But as Moshesh is the enemy of the English, I've decided that it's best that they not hear of my involvement for the moment. But feel free to tell this story in Bloemfontein. Only leave my name out of it."

"I'll be the soul of discretion, *Meneer* Snyman."

I waited while he packed his pipe with tobacco, then took his time to light it. It was a process not to be hurried, but borne with patience.

After a few puffs, he said, "While I don't know anything about the battle itself, what I do know is that Moshesh is claiming victory, and that the other chiefs have acknowledged this fact, including Moshesh's missionary, Eugène Casalis."

"Have you spoken to Casalis then?"

"Not only that, but Josias Hoffman and I were invited by Moshesh to attend the thanksgiving service that was conducted by *Dominee* Casalis at Thaba Bosiu on Sunday."

"Well I never!" I said.

Snyman chuckled with delight at my response. "But first we had to attend a traditional ceremony in honor of the ancestors. Casalis explained that it was for those who had not made a decision to become a Christian yet."

"I see. It must have been quite an occasion."

"*Ja*, and a very lengthy one. The warriors waded into a stream nearby, singing and chanting while their diviners threw charms into the water. It was during this ceremony that we were able to discuss the battle with Casalis."

"Did you manage to learn how many head of cattle were

rounded up? You see, I read in the paper that Cathcart was promising to capture 30 000 if Moshesh didn't deliver the 10 000 he was demanding as compensation for the various Basuto raids."

With his pipe still lodged between his teeth, Snyman managed a wry smile. "Only about 5000, or thereabouts. That's why the English around here are so livid. But what's interesting is that Moshesh didn't offer to hand over more when he sued for peace the following day."

Now I was really intrigued. "So it was Moshesh who sued for peace? No wonder Cathcart is claiming victory."

"*Ja*, but to my mind it was a stroke of genius on Moshesh's part—or perhaps the honor should really go to Casalis. He told us that Moshesh dictated the letter of surrender, while he helped Moshesh's son, Nehemiah, translate it into English. But I don't believe a word of it. I'm sure he played a far greater role in deciding its contents. He gave both Hoffman and me a copy. I'll go and fetch it."

He returned a minute later with a small sheet of parchment that appeared to have been inserted between the leaves of the Bible he was carrying. It read:

Your Excellency,

This day you have fought against my people and taken much cattle. As the object for which you have come is to have compensation for the boers, I beg that you will be satisfied with what you have taken. I entreat peace with you. You have shown your power—you have chastised. Let it be enough, I pray you. And let me no longer be considered an enemy of the Queen. I will try all I can to keep my people in order in future. Your humble servant, Moshesh.

"This definitely bears the hallmarks of Eugène Casalis," I said.

"I agree. I've also heard that the French are good at diplomacy. And Moshesh is just as shrewd. Reading between the lines, it appears that Moshesh knew he had won, but didn't want Cathcart to return with a larger army. So he pretended that he was the one who had suffered a defeat."

"In that case, it's diplomacy of the highest order."

Snyman snorted. "I'd rather call it a diplomatic charade of the highest order. I'm also willing to vouch that this letter will be remembered as the most remarkable bluff in South African military history. So prepare to enter a cauldron of discontent when you arrive back in Bloemfontein."

Snyman's predictions turned out to be correct. When I rode into town on New Year's eve, a huge cattle sale was underway, the bell tolling at the close of each sale. I rushed down to the sale yard, bumping into Edward Collins on the way.

"Have you heard the news, Mr. Murray? Cathcart has retreated in defeat, and has left us to our fate. I've just bumped into Assistant Commissioner Owen at the sale yard, and he's furious about it. Apparently, Cathcart has declared that he's satisfied with the 5000 or so cattle captured. It's a disgrace—a blooming disgrace, especially after bragging that if Moshesh didn't deliver the 10 000 demanded, he would collect three times that number."

"Yes, I read something of the sort."

Collins was heaving with indignation. "Owen has delivered a written protest. And I believe that Colonel Eyre begged to be allowed to plant the British ensign on Thaba Bosiu—or perish in the attempt. And according to Owen, other officers have also spoken bitterly of the disgrace of retreating."

Collins prattled on, hardly pausing to take breath. I listened patiently, knowing that his views would be a reflection of what other settlers would be saying.

"Do you know that Cathcart has already broken camp and is on his way to the Cape leaving us with a measly 300 soldiers to guard against any future raids? What on earth has happened to British justice and honor, Mr. Murray?"

I watched him stride off, his posture erect, as if to make up for the perceived shortfall.

At the cattle yard I was assailed by similar forebodings of what Moshesh was likely to get up to next. I was about to return home, when I spied Charles Stuart in the crowd.

"I believe the battle was an absolute fiasco," he said. "Dr. Fraser has offered to tell all at dinner tonight. Emily and I would love you to attend. I've also invited Edward Collins, his wife, and their son William. He's a bright young man of about twenty. Will go far."

"Thank you, Mr. Stuart. It's a relief to know that I won't be spending New Year's eve alone. But tell me, do you know if Fraser witnessed the battle?"

"Part of it I believe. And what he didn't witness himself, he heard about from the officers. So his account should prove most interesting."

After dinner, the ladies retired to another room, leaving the men to listen to Dr. Fraser's account of the battle. Their departure was followed by a seat-swapping exercise. Stuart invited Fraser to sit at the head of the table, while he went to sit opposite Collins, leaving me to sit opposite William.

"You know, gentlemen," Fraser began, "the damnest thing is that the Battle of Berea could have been avoided if Moshesh had delivered the 10 000 head of cattle and the 1000 horses Cathcart had demanded."

"A piddling amount, I assure you," Collins said. "Owen has estimated that the losses due to Basuto raids have amounted to £25,000."

"I wouldn't be a bit surprised," Fraser said. "But what irks most is that Cathcart marched into the Sovereignty with 2500 troops, but foolishly only used less than half in the battle. Would you believe, he left one company to guard the ford at the Caledon, and four companies to guard his Platberg camp. And when Moshesh visited the camp with his missionaries Casalis and Dyke to explain that he needed more time to collect the cattle, Cathcart treated him in a cavalier fashion. Not only that, but he threatened to capture 30 000 if his demands were not met within three days."

"So how many head were actually delivered?" I asked.

"Only 3500 of the most inferior type. And when no more arrived by Sunday, Cathcart gave the order to advance to the ford on the Caledon."

I was trying to recall where the ford was, when Fraser, aware of our lack of knowledge of the area, kindly described the lay of the land.

"For those not familiar with that part of the country, the ford is opposite the Berea Mission Station. From it you can see the outcrop of Berea Mountain with its flat tabletop. And like similar geological formations in that area, it's also long and irregular with precipitous sides."

William, who was looking perplexed, said, "But I thought the battle was to take place at Moshesh's headquarters at Thaba Bosiu?"

"So did Cathcart. But the problem he faced was that Berea Mountain was in the way. So he either had to go around or over the top to reach the Phutiastana Valley in front of Thaba Bosiu."

"I see," William said, his expression indicating that comprehension had dawned.

"Now it gets interesting," Fraser said. "Cathcart decided to divide his 1000 strong army into three columns. One was under his own command, and consisted of about 390 men. It was to march around the southern base of Berea, and then move north until it reached the Phutiastana Valley. The central column was under Colonel Eyre, and consisted of 360 infantry and a small attachment of lancers and Cape Mounted Rifles. It also included a few mounted Fingo tribesmen to herd any cattle found. This column was ordered to cross over the top of Berea and to meet up with Cathcart around noon."

"Just stop there a moment, Dr. Fraser," Collins said. "Do you mean to tell me that Cathcart was expecting infantry to help round up 30 000 head of cattle? Do you have any idea how dangerous such a caper is on foot? In any case, it wouldn't be feasible."

This offhand assertion led to a lively discussion. The conclusion was that Cathcart should have provided Eyre with cavalry, not infantry. All the while, Fraser was listening to our musings with marked interest.

"I couldn't help noting," he said, "that every one of you assumed that Cathcart expected Eyre to round up 30 000 head on account of his threat to Moshesh. Interestingly enough, Eyre assumed the same thing. But according to Cathcart, he only ordered Eyre to round up cattle in his path."

The room exploded with guffaws.

"I put my money on Eyre's interpretation any day," Collins said.

"So do I," said Stuart.

"Well, you'll be interested to know, gentlemen, that Lieutenant-Colonel Napier, who was in command of the third column, also thought that capturing cattle was the order of the day."

"And I'm willing to bet," Collins said, "that Cathcart is now claiming that both men got it wrong. So his orders were either unclear, or he's lying."

William, who was grinning from ear to ear said, "And I'm willing to bet that Napier's column was made up of cavalry."

"So it was, young sir. It consisted of 233 Cape Mountain Rifles and 114 Lancers. Their orders were to ride around the northern shoulder of Berea, then move south along its eastern face until they met up with the other two columns at noon. Apparently, Napier was ordered not to take his men up onto the plateau, and only to round up cattle that happened to be in his path."

"It doesn't take much to guess what happened next," William said.

Fraser nodded. "Even the Boers with farms near Berea thought this battle was all about cattle. So they formed a small commando of about forty men at the rear of Napier's column to guard their livestock.[8] I decided to join them to be close to the action and to help out medically where I could."

"Did you observe much of the action?" asked William.

"Only what happened with Napier's column. I watched as his men neared the northern shoulder of Berea, then stopped at the sight of a large herd on the plateau above. While Napier waited below with a small group of Cape Mounted Rifles, he sent the rest of the cavalry up to take possession of the herd. But just as they were driving the cattle down the hill towards the ford, a Basuto force of about 700 horsemen appeared and charged the scattered troops."

Fraser paused, his cheeks ballooning as he blew out a breath. "Unfortunately, a small band of twenty-seven Lancers and five Riflemen mistook a ravine for the path down, and were soon surrounded by the enemy. If it were not for the quick thinking of a member of the commando who rushed to the ford to request reinforcements, most would have been killed. As it was, the loss of life was considerable. And all for what?—just over 4000 head of cattle, a number of horses, and some sheep and goats."

He paused again to give us time to take in this sobering thought. I couldn't help reflecting on Sir Harry Smith's comment that most of the raids and inter-tribal battles in South Africa were about cattle, and that he felt inclined to shoot the lot. But of course the cattle weren't the problem, it was men's sinful hearts.

"Do you know if Napier managed to meet up with the other columns?" I asked.

"No, he wasn't able to. You see, one group of his men was herding the blooming cattle, and the rest were keeping the enemy at bay while the wounded were being collected."

Stuart, who was sitting alongside me, cupped his forehead with his hand while heaving a sigh. "Hopefully, that was the worst of the engagements."

"Thankfully it was, Mr. Stuart. As you have already surmised, Colonel Eyre found the herd on the plateau to be so huge—apparently thousands upon thousands—that his men were unable to manage them. So with the exception of a small herd of about 1500, he was forced to abandon the rest."

We shook our heads in unison, while Fraser took the opportunity to sip his wine. Putting down his glass, he said, "It was not only the cattle Eyre's foot soldiers had to contend with, but also the constant attacks from the same group of warriors who had killed the Lancers earlier in the day. By the time Eyre was able to reassemble his troops and join Cathcart, it was already 5 o' clock."

"Dearie me," Stuart said. "What a fiasco!"

"But wasn't Eyre supposed to meet up with Cathcart at noon?" asked William.

"That's correct. So you can imagine Cathcart's anguish as he waited for the other columns to arrive. As planned, his column had reached the meeting point in the valley at noon. But instead of meeting up with the other columns, he was met by 6000 Basuto horsemen with European weapons. Their tactic was to constantly circle, wheel, and threaten to charge, causing Cathcart's column to keep up heavy firing throughout the afternoon. Fortunately, a thunderstorm at half past four saved the day when both sides were forced to cease firing."

Fraser dipped his hand into a bowl of nuts and sweetmeats, and popped them into his mouth, taking sips of wine in between. This allowed us to do the same. During the interval, I couldn't help wondering how a short thunderstorm could save the day. I waited for Fraser to down the last of his wine before posing the question.

"Could you please enlighten us about your comment concerning the thunderstorm? It wouldn't have lasted more than an hour—surely? So how could it have saved the day when several hours of daylight were still left for fighting?"

" Ah! I was just coming to that," Fraser said. "You see, Cathcart hadn't expected to meet with serious opposition, so he hadn't issued the troops with spare ammunition. And if it hadn't been for the thunderstorm, they would have run out."

A collective groan went up around the table.

"I shudder to think what could have happened," Collins said. "And to think the man is a seasoned soldier!"

I was still trying to imagine the scene, when a wide-eyed William said, "So what happened next?"

Fraser smiled across at him, thus managing to convey that matters weren't as dire as we'd imagined.

"Well, as soon as Eyre made his belated appearance, the combined force retreated to a stone-walled kraal about two miles away. It was there that they spent the night. The next morning, they simply returned to camp while the Basuto warriors followed their progress from the Berea plateau above."

"If that's not a victory for Moshesh, nothing is," Stuart said, slicing his hand through the air.

"I'm loath to ask this, Dr. Fraser, but how many men did we lose?"

"Thirty-eight, with fifteen wounded, Mr. Murray. It's the highest death toll in any engagement with the native tribes in South Africa to date. The Basuto lost 50 warriors plus several women who were caught in the crossfire when they fled from their kraals."

No one spoke in response to this salutary news. We used the pause to sip our wine, or in my case, the minted water that Emily Stuart had kindly provided.

During the conversation that followed, I realized that Cathcart hadn't made the contents of Moshesh's note public. So at a suitable juncture, I produced the copy I'd made from the one in Snyman's possession, then went on to tell them about the warrior ceremony and thanksgiving service.

They listened transfixed, their comments mirroring their fear—not because Moshesh was claiming victory, but for what Moshesh, as victor, might get up to next.

"So what do you think will happen now?" asked Stuart, to no one in particular.

"Well," said Fraser looking grave, "Cathcart told me while on a visit to the wounded that he did not want to lose more troops in another engagement with Moshesh. The reason he gave was that the British Government was considering abandoning the Sovereignty."

"Well that rumor has been doing the rounds for some time now," Stuart said. "But what do you think *he* meant by that? You see, in India the British often pulled out of certain districts, leaving the people to govern themselves. But they still considered the said territory theirs, and often imposed their will from afar. Is that what he was talking about?"

"It's possible," Fraser said. "But the impression I got was that the British mean to de-annex the Sovereignty, leaving us to our fate."

"I can't believe that," Stuart said. "They would never be so cowardly and dishonorable."

Collins looked Stuart in the eye from across the table. "Come now, Mr. Stuart. You're a Scot after all. My honest opinion is that Cathcart has sown the wind, and now we will reap the whirlwind."

23

A Slap in the Face

May–August 1853

Despite the rumors doing the rounds about a possible British withdrawal, nothing official was said, so tempers soon cooled and settler indignation subsided. Unfortunately, the veneer of normality that descended upon the Sovereignty only proved to be the lull before the storm.

In the meantime, life moved on and winter was drawing near. While Van Velden was inducting Abraham Faure's son, Hendrik, in Pietermaritzburg on 8 May, I was preparing to set out for Smithfield to induct Piet Roux on 21 May. Both these inductions would change our pastoral duties significantly. From now onwards, Dirk van Velden would only have to travel to Harrismith to conduct quarterly communion services, while I would only have to travel to Fauresmith to do the same.

When I arrived home after Piet Roux's induction, an interesting note awaited me from Van Velden. He wrote that while in Ladysmith on his way home after inducting Hendrik Faure, he had met Dirk van der Hoff, the pastor designate for the Transvaal. Van der Hoff had obviously sailed around the Cape and had disembarked in Durban before hiring a wagon to take his goods and family to the Transvaal. Poor Van der

Hoff, I thought. It would be rough going having to travel in an ox-wagon over the rolling hills of Natal. Nevertheless, it would serve as an excellent introduction to the conditions he would have to face in the Transvaal.

I grabbed my Bible with its homemade diary at the back to check when I'd penciled in his induction. It read: 31 July. I cringed at the thought of having to endure the freezing journey in a wagon to Potchefstroom at that time of year. But at least I'd have half of July to prepare my sermons, and half of August to recover from the journey before starting out for Fauresmith. It's now up to Van der Hoff to contact me, I thought.

His letter duly arrived on 15 June. I was expecting his missive to endorse my provisional date for his induction, but was annoyed to find that the date was due to be debated at a meeting to be held on 8 August.

What on earth were they thinking? I can't just scrap my schedule here and travel to the Transvaal at a moment's notice. I read the letter more carefully a second time, and then a third. The part that signaled that something was afoot read:

I am informed that the joint Krijgsraad has resolved together with two members of the Volksraad: Messrs. S. Krieger and M.W. Pretorius, and at the earnest request of Elder Snyman of Rustenburg, to call together a general assembly on the second Monday of August to discuss the question of my induction. They have also requested that the Volksraad should hold its session at the same time.

What on earth did the *Krijgsraad* or War Council have to do with this? And why S. Krieger and Andries Pretorius's son, Marthinus? And come to think of it, why Elder Snyman? Why weren't Andries Pretorius and Elder Wolmarans mentioned? Was this letter a signal that there was a changing of the guard?

And what did Van der Hoff mean by "the *question* of my induction"? So it wasn't just the date he was talking about, but the question. Perhaps he was referring to where it would be held. It was supposed to have been in Potchefstroom, whereas the men mentioned in this letter were all from Rustenburg.

The more I thought about its contents, the more concerned I became. The induction of a pastor was a question for the respective consistory, not the *Krijgsraad* or *Volksraad*, and certainly not a people's assembly. Why didn't Van der Hoff put his foot down? He wasn't a twenty-one year old like I had been when I was inducted. He was a mature man in his thirties, and for all intents and purposes, the chairman of the Potchefstroom consistory.

At that moment, the fog began to lift. Reading between the lines, the letter seemed to indicate a Rustenburg backlash against the decision taken at Potchefstroom. That would account for why Wolmarans wasn't mentioned, even though he was the preeminent church leader across the Vaal. After all, he'd been the one to represent the other elders at the Sand River Convention.

And what had become of Andries Pretorius? Was he part of this about-face? I would have to make it my business to find out.

The more I stewed over the contents of the letter, the sharper the picture of what was happening came into focus. The political leaders of Rustenburg together with Elder Snyman were going to put pressure on the other consistories to rescind the decision to join the Cape Synod. And if the brusque tone of Dirk van der Hoff's letter was anything to go by, they had persuaded Van der Hoff to do their bidding.

First, they needed to have the decision of incorporation into the Cape Synod rescinded. And the only way they could hope to overturn a church decision of that nature was to use the vote of the people's assembly to put pressure on the consistories to do just that. It would mean that church elders such as Wolmarans would be railroaded into accepting the majority view. And if he didn't, he might feel obliged to resign. The more I thought about it, the more certain I became that my postulations were correct.

I went to my desk and flipped out a sheet of writing paper. I scribbled a quick note to Dirk van Velden in Winburg requesting that he put out feelers to discover what was afoot.

When I put my pen down, I was conscious of a painful tingle in my arms and hands. It was strange, I thought, how an emotional heart blow could trigger pain in the body, or at least make it more pronounced. Oh, how I'd wanted to serve in the ministry across the Vaal. The people there were ripe to accept the Word. But now, I could only watch from a distance as leaders of a certain political persuasion were trying to manipulate church affairs to promote their own agendas. It was all about politics, and had nothing to do with God. The only good thing to come out of it was that I was saved from having to travel to Potchefstroom at the end of July. And in my present state of health, it would prove a blessing in disguise.

Because the tingles in my hands and arms failed to subside, I decided to pay an overdue visit to Dr. Fraser. Unfortunately, his prognosis was more sobering than I had bargained for.

"Your whole system is run down," he said. "And nothing but rest will cure the aches and pains."

"But I can't take any more breaks, Dr. Fraser. I was away for almost six months last year."

"My dear Mr. Murray, it's either a case of taking off the needed time now, or having to resign from the ministry down the track when your system has completely broken down. It's as serious as that."

"So what would you suggest?"

He looked at me with a thoughtful expression as though summing me up. And although he spoke with gentle firmness, his words carried as much weight as Dr. Drury's penetrating stares and sharp pronouncements had done.

"I prefer the terms *advise*, or *recommend*, Mr. Murray. But understanding your propensity to overdo things, I shall employ a stronger term to press home the seriousness of your condition. With the objective of healing in mind, I *direct* you to take three months' leave over summer to avoid the worst of the heat in these parts. If you don't, I fear that your strength will be completely sapped and you will be laid low. In the meantime, do not stir from Bloemfontein over the next few weeks. I'm sure you'll find plenty to do, what with catching up on reading and sermon preparation."

"I need no cajoling to do just that, Dr. Fraser. But I'm not so sure others will understand."

"You'll just have to tell them. Let your church council know about your health problems this coming Sunday—not the next, or the following one—but *this* Sunday. And make sure to inform them that you'll be taking three months' leave of absence over summer. I don't want you to be tempted to ignore my instructions. I was advised by Dr. Drury to take this type of action whenever your health threatened to take a dive."

Despite the twinkle in his eye, I knew he was being deadly serious.

At the beginning of August, news filtered through that Andries Pretorius had passed away on 23 July. I knew for certain now that there was a jockeying for power amongst the next generation of leaders in the Transvaal.

So what were they going to do about Van der Hoff's induction? Technically speaking, I was still the *consulent* of all the congregations across the Vaal, and therefore the designated person to officiate at that service. Nevertheless, the wording of Van der Hoff's letter seemed to suggest that they were in two minds about inviting me. They probably feared that I might persuade the people to overturn their decision.

Strange as it may seem, my interest in Transvaal affairs was overshadowed a few days later by an announcement that came as a bolt out of the blue. It came on Monday, 8 August, the same day as the people's assembly was due to be held in Rustenburg.

24
The Arrival of
Sir George Russell Clerk

8 August 1853

Monday, 8 August dawned a perfect spring day. Being my day off, I was able to take a walk to the spring near the schoolroom to admire the wild flowers. But although I tried hard to shrug off the vision of the people's assembly taking place at Rustenburg, I was unable to put it out of my mind.

Even after lunch, while I lay on my bed in the hope of a nap, my mind still refused to abandon the question. I was about to go for another walk, when I heard a rap at the door, and Dr. Fraser call my name. The urgency in his voice told me that there was something seriously amiss.

I bounded off my bed and hurried into the parlor, thinking that he was ill or had hurt himself in some way. He was standing inside the doorway, his chest heaving. I rushed to help, but he waved me aside.

"I'm fine, Mr. Murray. I'm just a little out of breath."

He stood there for a few moments, exhaling little gusts of air. Once his breathing had eased enough, he said, "I've come bringing bad tidings, I'm afraid. The Sovereignty is to be abandoned."

He walked slowly to an armchair and sat down with a plop. I was still standing on the spot staring after him, when he said, "You won't believe who's just arrived in town. It's Sir George Russell Clerk, the former Governor of Bombay."

Realizing that this personage must be overseeing the abandonment, I went to sit on the couch opposite Fraser, eager to hear more.

"He's here in his role as Special Commissioner to facilitate the withdrawal of the British from the Sovereignty. He's just told me so himself. You see, his horse stumbled and fell on his leg on his way here, and I was requested to inspect the wound. It was while I was dressing it that he told me. And in answer to my questions, he did not mince his words. The British mean to withdraw completely."

My mind was brimming over with consternation. "But that will be an act of undeniable scuttle, Dr. Fraser. One minute the British are declaring this territory theirs, then the next they have decided to withdraw without so much as a by your leave. What about the people? Do we have a say in the matter?"

"It appears not, Mr. Murray. Thankfully, I started to sell off my farms after the Battle of Berea, just in case Cathcart's statement about abandonment proved to be true. I still have a few more to get rid of, I fear."

I now understood the reason for his breathlessness. He probably stood to lose a great deal if land values plummeted due to the abandonment.

Between moments of dabbing the perspiration off his forehead, he said, "Fortunately for you, your stipend, together with those of the other Dutch pastors, will still be paid by the Cape. I explained to Cathcart that the Boers around here are too poor to pay their pastors. And believe it or not, he agreed."

Fraser looked across at me with an air of accomplishment. I suspected that he had prodded hard to elicit that concession from Cathcart. And because he was still perspiring, I went to fetch a carafe of minted water. After downing the contents of his glass, and pouring another, he said, "No hope of a dram of whiskey, I suppose?"

I met his wistful expression with a broad smile. "None whatsoever, Dr. Fraser."

"Thought so," he said, heaving a sigh. "In any case this is not a social visit. I've come to tell you that I've nominated you for a task that may not be to your liking, I fear. You see, Sir George Russell Clerk wants to summon all elected delegates of each field cornetcy to a meeting here in Bloemfontein on 5 September."

"But where do I fit in? I refuse to take part in political affairs, you know."

"I'm well aware of that, but just bear with me a moment. This meeting that Russell Clerk is calling for is to get the elected delegates to decide upon the form of self-government they desire."

"Just like that—without any previous discussion? There's going to be an outcry from both Boer and Brit, Dr. Fraser. The present administration can't simply withdraw without fixing some of the problems they've created. To put it bluntly, they need to reduce the chaos to some semblance of order. For a start, they need to settle the boundary question with Moshesh as well as the Griqua question over the leasing of farmland to the Boers in the Fauresmith district."

Fraser loosened his bow tie and undid the top button of his shirt. "Well I'm pleased to note that I'm not the only one getting hot under the collar around here. But let's just stick to the facts for the moment. If we count in the field cornets, there will be ninety-five delegates—seventy-six Dutch and nineteen English. With this in mind, I suggested that we hold the meeting in the church."

I sighed, knowing exactly what he was about to suggest next. At the same time it struck me as ironic that the outcome of the Rustenburg meeting was now the least of my worries. In fact, I suspected that I wouldn't give it much thought for some time.

"As you have already guessed," continued Fraser, "Russell Clerk would like you to do the interpreting. He has also requested that you accompany him into the church as well as introduce him to the delegates."

"Will there be a trumpet fanfare by any chance?"

"Don't be facetious, Mr. Murray. This is a serious matter. He would also like you to translate the Decree of Abandonment as well as read it in the church after he has read the English version."

"But people will think I'm party to this decision."

"No they won't. In any case, the Boers are used to you doing important interpreting work. What I would advise is that you clear the church of all chairs and tables after the evening service on Sunday."

Now I was completely at a loss to know what Fraser had in mind.

Noticing my quizzical expression, he said, "Well, the last thing ninety-five delegates will want to do is stand to hold a meeting. So after the decree has been read, and Russell Clerk has delivered his speech, invite them to leave while the trestle tables are being set up. That way, they can discuss their grievances in groups prior to reassembling in the afternoon. You will find that the meeting will be more focused and your interpreting halved."

☙

After a short visit to Russell Clerk later that day, I rushed home to read the Decree of Abandonment. Strangely enough, the term "abandonment" wasn't mentioned at all in the Decree. I found this rather strange, so invited Mr. Stuart over to discuss the matter.

We were both poring over the document at the dining room table, when he said, "I'll read it aloud, Mr. Murray. I find it helps to focus the mind."

I leant back and closed my eyes while he read.

We do hereby require and enjoin you, Sir George Russell Clerk, as our Special Commissioner in our name and on our behalf, to take all such measures, and to do all such matters and things as can and may lawfully and discreetly be done by you, for settling the internal affairs of the said Orange River Sovereignty, and for determining the disputes which exist among the Natives and other inhabitants to establish peaceable and orderly Government therein; and We do command and require all our Officers, Civil and Military, and all our faithful Subjects and Inhabitants of the said Sovereignty to be aiding and assisting you in carrying this our Will and Pleasure into effect. . . . By Her Majesty's command.

"What do you think, Mr. Stuart?"

"Well first, it says nothing about abandoning the Sovereignty. Second, Russell Clerk's powers are limited to settling our internal affairs and disputes only. In any case, in order for the British to pull out, legal and constitutional issues would need to be dealt with first. For example, what becomes of the Letters Patent that promulgates our constitution? Surely it would need an Act of Parliament to rescind it?"

"One would think so," I said, trying to sound knowledgeable. But if the truth be told, I had no idea that a constitution had already been written for us.

"In the meantime, abandonment or no, you'd better study the Griqua question before you visit Fauresmith again. Make sure their delegates know the provisions stipulated by the Maitland Treaty of 1846, as well as Sir Harry Smith's adjustments to it in January 1850. Copies of both can be sighted at our administrative offices."

I already had enough on my plate besides having to struggle through the legalese of two treaty documents. So I decided to prod Stuart for as much information as possible.

"Can you recall any details, Mr. Stuart?"

He rubbed his chin, seemingly deep in thought. "It's a complex issue. But here is the gist: In 1845, Governor Maitland divided the vast stretches of Griqua land into two sections. The southern section was set aside as the Griqua Reserve, and could not be leased. The northern section, on the other hand, could be leased. The only problem was that eighty-five farms in the Griqua Reserve had already been leased to Boers under an agreement between the Griqua Captain, Adam Kok, and *Meneer* Oberholster in 1840."

"But weren't the British aware of that?"

"Presumably, because Sir Harry Smith amended the treaty to help the Boers. While acknowledging that farms had already been leased to them in the Reserve, he nevertheless stated that they were to vacate them when their leases expired. They still have thirty years to run, but time flies."

I was about to ask a question, when Stuart started to tap the table lightly with his middle finger. Something important had obviously come to mind, so I waited for him to say what it was.

"Unfortunately, the problem doesn't end there, Mr. Murray. You see, some enterprising Griqua under the leadership of Hendrik Hendrikse decided that the best solution was to sell these farms. But now the Griqua Council won't allow the title deeds to be handed over."

"How many farms were sold?"

"Sixty-three."

"But surely the problem could be solved if the Griqua simply paid the money back?"

"Apparently not, because they've already spent it."

The situation was far worse than I had anticipated. It also appeared that there was some skullduggery at play.

I glanced sideways at Stuart who was regarding me with a glint in his eye. "You haven't asked me about the leasable land north of the Reserve yet."

"To tell you the truth, Mr. Stuart, I haven't heard any complaints from the Boers living there. Is there likely to be a problem?"

"Could be. You see Sir Harry favored the Boer farmers there, and in the process antagonized the Griqua Council. He extorted an agreement from them that basically converted all their land north of the Reserve into freehold."

Judging from Stuart's expression, I was in no doubt that Sir Harry must have pulled one of his theatrical stunts again.

"He must have offered them a carrot of sorts—surely?"

"Only £300 per annum to be paid by the Cape."

"My goodness! How did he manage to force the hand of the whole Council for such a piddling amount?"

"He threatened to hang them all."

On observing my expression of disbelief, Stuart said, "What's done is done, Mr. Murray. And let's not forget that Sir Harry has been recalled and is now paying the price of ignominy for his indiscretions."

"But do others know about this?"

"Oh yes. It was discussed in two articles in *The Friend* last year. If I recall, they appeared in March when you were in the Transvaal."

He got up to go, then stopped in his tracks. "Ah, I forgot to say that if the British pull out of the Sovereignty, the amount of £300 per annum may no longer be forthcoming from the Cape. And if that happens, strife between Griqua and Boer is bound to resume."

"What about the sixty-three farms that have been bought in the Reserve?"

"Don't ask me. That's a question for Sir George Russell Clerk to address. But I dare say he will do nothing unless the Fauresmith delegates place pressure on him to amend the Maitland Treaty."

I thanked him for his advice and accompanied him to the door. I groaned inwardly thinking of the reading matter I had to get through. I also needed to visit Fauresmith sooner rather than later.

Before leaving, Stuart adopted a more serious tone. "This threatened abandonment is one of stealth, Mr. Murray. The British Government is adopting the same strategy as it did in parts of India. The modus operandi is to secure British interests in a region, then pull out, leaving the people to govern themselves. It's a type of indirect rule. By relinquishing the said territory informally, the government no longer has to commit to military aid or encumber itself with projects that require continual propping up. At the same time, it's still able to exercise influence from afar. And now it's playing that dirty trick on us."

25

To Stay or To Go?

September 1853

As soon as Sir George Russell Clerk had left the church building after delivering his speech on 5 September, I immediately acted upon Dr. Fraser's suggestion of inviting the delegates to leave the building until trestle tables had been set up. As Fraser had predicted, the delegates were more composed when they returned, and soon settled down to nut out their approach.

Dr. Fraser was elected chairman with sixty votes, while Josias Hoffman, Moshesh's friend and agent, was elected deputy. At first, I stood behind Dr. Fraser to do the interpreting. But as the meeting dragged on, I was invited to sit next to him. In this manner I came to be regarded as part of the executive committee.

The deliberations were far from straightforward. The delegates from Fauresmith were particularly volatile, and not surprisingly, because they had the most to lose if the British withdrew without settling the Griqua question.

The Smithfield delegates were adamant that the boundary issue with Moshesh needed to be settled, while those Boers who had refused to fight against Moshesh, wanted the money they had paid in fines returned. Meanwhile, storekeepers like Adolph Coqui required the necessary assurances that they'd be able to travel freely through the Cape and Natal. Others sought permission to purchase munitions of war, while some wealthy settlers wanted compensation for the inevitable slump in land and property values once the British had pulled out.

After a few days of wrangling over these issues, most of the delegates indicated that they needed to return home to take care of their livestock because of the continuing drought. But before dispersing, they appointed a committee of twenty-five to confer with Sir George Russell Clerk. They also passed a resolution that required eleven conditions of capitulation to be addressed before the question of self-government would be considered.

It was during the sitting of the committee of twenty five a few days later, that Mr. Joseph Orpen, one of the delegates from Harrismith, made an observation that would take the committee in a whole new direction, and me with it.

"You know, gentlemen," said Orpen, "as you are aware, the word 'abandonment' does not occur in the Decree. I happened to bump into Mr. Stuart after our meeting yesterday, and he alerted me to the fact that this whole exercise could be one of abandonment by stealth."

"I agree," said Henry Halse of Smithfield. "From what I am able to ascertain, no Act of Parliament has been passed regarding this matter. And once we have formed a government of our own, the present administration will pull out at a moment's notice and leave us with the problems they've created. The Colonial Secretary can then claim that the withdrawal is a fait accompli."

"Well, good riddance," said Frederik Senekal, one of the pro-republican Boers from Winburg. "Withdrawal is exactly what we desire."

"Do you really, old chap?" said Halse, indicating by 'the old chap' that he was about to niggle Senekal with a morsel of information not to his liking. "Well let me enlighten you: Without an Act of Parliament you'll still be British."

"Halse is right," said Adolph Coqui. "An informal withdrawal will mean we'll have to maintain our allegiance to the Crown without receiving anything in return, except, perhaps, unwanted interference. It's my firm opinion that if the British are going to pull out, it has to be done legally."

"Not only that," said Frederik Linde, who was one of the representatives for Bloemfontein, "we also need to be assured of our independence and rights."

There was a chorus of agreement that came from the Boer contingent around the table. Some, however, looked thoughtful and undecided.

Josias Hoffman now indicated that he wanted to express a view. Being both deputy chairman as well as representing the pro-Moshesh party, his opinion carried weight.

"What disturbs me about an abandonment by stealth is that we Boers will still be regarded as British subjects. In other words, we won't be able to enjoy the same rights as were granted to our Transvaal compatriots. With this in mind, we need to ensure that the British withdrawal is done legally so we can claim our independence and self-determination."

I observed that the settler delegates were exchanging concerned glances. A legal abandonment was not what they had in mind. On the contrary, they wanted to halt the withdrawal by proving that it had not been sanctioned by Parliament.

Joseph Orpen, a skillful debater, now tried to steer the meeting in the direction the settler delegates wanted it to go.

"Let's review the situation as it stands at present," he said. "Russell Clerk asserts that he will be receiving the legal authority to oversee an abandonment at any moment. But why wasn't this authority given in the first place? And why no Act of Parliament? I put it to this meeting that there's something amiss here. I don't trust Russell Clerk nor Cathcart, for that matter. It's obvious that they're in league. I say we go over their heads and send two delegates to London to put forward our concerns."

After everyone had voiced an opinion, Orpen's motion was formally passed. It was then suggested that Dr. Fraser and I be nominated as delegates.

"But I'm not a member of this committee, gentlemen," I said. "I'm only the interpreter. An elected delegate needs to be chosen."

"We can't have two English delegates," said Jacobus Groenendaal, the Dutch teacher from Fauresmith. "One delegate has to represent the Dutch community. And as none of the Boers on this committee speaks English fluently—least of all me—it has to be you, *Dominee*."

"In that case, I request a few weeks to give this matter prayerful consideration."

After a short pause, Fraser turned to me and said, "I think we'll need to know by Friday, 23 September, Mr. Murray. This will give us enough time to choose another delegate in case you decline."

"That's very considerate of you," I said.

Fraser nodded then turned to address the meeting once more. "Now what about Sir George Russell Clerk? How long should we give him to respond?"

"Exactly a month from today," Adolph Coqui said. "That's more than fair. But I can already tell you what his response will be. He'll say that he has to wait to hear from Sir George Cathcart. And because we're requesting to view the abandonment legislation, Cathcart will say that he has to wait for a response from the Colonial Secretary."

"But if legislation already exists," said Orpen, "then Governor Cathcart should already possess it. And if it doesn't, he is sure to tell Russell Clerk to stall or try to fob us off. Then we'll know that this is indeed an abandonment by stealth."

After further discussion, it was decided that if Sir George Russell Clerk failed to respond positively to our demands by 10 October, then the two delegates should proceed to England in November.

I was walking home with Dr. Fraser after the meeting when he said, "You know, Mr. Murray, a trip to England and back will serve the same purpose as taking three months' leave of absence to improve your health. In fact, the sea air will do you the world of good. I therefore strongly advise that you go."

"The problem I have with such a trip, Dr. Fraser, is that it presents too attractive a prospect. And then there's Russell Clerk's accusation against me.[9] Apparently, he didn't like the fact that I discussed the Griqua question with the Boers of Fauresmith when I was there in August. And according to Owen, he went so far as to accuse me of interference."

Fraser stopped abruptly in the middle of the road. I was taken aback when I noticed that this mild-mannered man was looking positively livid.

"Let's just set aside Russell Clerk's unwarranted accusation for a moment. What I want to know is how you can possibly equate the chance for rest and sea air with too attractive a prospect? And since when does one isolate the spiritual from national events that pertain to a whole population? And how do you propose to look after the spiritual welfare of your people when you are ill? More to the point . . . what is the use of thinking of their spiritual welfare in the short term, when you'll be too weak to serve them in the long term, or at all? Believe me, Mr. Murray, those painful tingles in your arms and hands, not to speak of your back pains, point directly to the possibility of a complete physical breakdown if you do not get the rest I've prescribed."

I did not answer, but took his comments on the chin. If only I could explain my predicament to him. But I feared that, unlike Dr. Drury, he wouldn't understand. The crux of the matter was that all major decisions thus far had been made for me by my parents. The Transvaal was a case in point. I had thought that the Lord was calling me there, but it was obvious now that I had been following my own desires and deluding myself about the state of my health. The problem I'd faced then was that I hadn't been able to discern God's will. I now wanted the opportunity this new decision presented to learn how to hear His voice for myself.

We proceeded along the path in silence. We were nearing Fraser's home, when he said, "While I do not count myself as being in the same spiritual league as Dr. Drury, I can nevertheless say with certainty that God would want you well again. So seize the opportunity that He is handing you on a platter."

I thanked him for his concern, but didn't commit myself. I still needed to receive God's peace in my heart.

26

Dirk Van Velden to the Rescue

21 September 1853

It was Wednesday afternoon, 21 September, and I was still in recovery mode after delivering the quarterly communion services over the weekend. I was sitting in my wicker chair on the *stoep* enjoying the stillness of a perfect spring day, when I saw a Cape Cart approaching. On the box seat sat an African driver, which in these parts meant that the cart had come from a considerable distance. Because it was slowing down, I sat upright and stretched my neck to see who the occupant was. He, in turn, was leaning forward, pointing in the direction of the parsonage.

To my surprise, it was none other than Dirk van Velden. Knowing that he hated to travel any distance unless it was absolutely necessary, I knew there would have to be some news of import that would compel him to travel overnight from Winburg.

I waved to him from the *stoep*, then rushed through to the kitchen to open the back door. That done, I immediately set about preparing a fresh pot of coffee. Fortunately, a couple of women from our congregation had replenished my larder over the weekend. So I selected some cookies from the tin in the kitchen trunk, placed them on a plate, grabbed two mugs, then dived back to the *stoep*, where I arranged them on the rough-hewn table. I then doubled back to the kitchen door, ready to greet Van Velden and to invite him to follow me to the *stoep*, where he could smoke to his heart's content.

"You're probably wondering why I'm here," he said, seating himself in the wicker chair alongside mine. "A number of people urged me to come, not least your father's friend, *Meneer* Theron. When I agreed, he insisted that I use his Cape Cart along with his personal driver. Most generous of him."

"So, why are you here, *Meneer* Van Velden? Your arrival has certainly piqued my curiosity."

"Well it might, because there're a few important issues we need to discuss. To be honest, I first dithered about coming. I was even in two minds about it until I visited your elder, Willem Pretorius, on my way here. Fortunately, my conversation with him was an endorsement of my decision. I'm convinced now that I'm doing the Lord's will by playing envoy."

I leant forward and turned my head sideways to study him for a moment. He was looking up and down the street, seemingly taking in the spread of the town before him. Despite his relaxed demeanor, I noted his determined expression and the fact that he had made no move to smoke his pipe—a sure sign that what he was about to say was important. I recalled, when visiting his home, how he had always put his pipe or cigar down before reprimanding the children or broaching a serious matter with an elder or visitor. It was his way of stressing the importance of what he was about to say. So I waited for him to continue.

"Willem Pretorius tells me that you are far from well and have requested three months' leave of absence over summer."

"I'm afraid so. Dr. Fraser told me that I'm facing a complete physical breakdown if I don't get a period of prolonged rest."

"I also heard from the Winburg delegates on the committee of twenty-five that you have been nominated with Dr. Fraser to go to Britain. Apparently, you have until this Friday to accept or reject this nomination."

"Yes, but surely you haven't come all this way to discuss that with me?"

"It's vital that you accept, *Meneer* Murray, and not just for the reasons stipulated by the committee."

"Well, aside from my health, what other reason could there possibly be?"

"Several, as it turns out, and all to do with the well-being of our people and our Church. So listen closely."

He rose and swung his wicker chair around to face mine. Eyeing an iced cookie on the table between us, he popped it in his mouth, licked a finger, then began to explain. "When our delegates on the committee arrived back in Winburg and showed me the eleven conditions of capitulation, I was taken aback. They all have to do with treaties, boundary disputes, and compensation issues. There was no vision for the future—no requests to further the well-being of the Church or to initiate special education programs for our youth."

"So what are you suggesting *Meneer* Van Velden?"

"For starters, we need a pastor for Fauresmith. Seeing Cathcart has agreed to continue paying our stipends, it wouldn't be too much to ask—in the interests of promoting Christianity and stable government, you understand—if he could provide the salary of a fourth pastor for Fauresmith. If you agree to go to London, you'll be able to put forward this suggestion while you're in Cape Town. The British are leaving no legacy behind for posterity. You could remind Cathcart of that."

"A valid point. But a letter from here would do equally well, don't you think? And then there's the matter of not knowing whether a withdrawal will actually take place."

Van Velden let out a high-pitched snort. He then lent forward, eyeing me from close quarters. "Well, let's get down to specifics. In relation to pastors, who will be returning from Utrecht next year? Surely there will be an Afrikaner who could fill the position at Fauresmith?"

"The only one I know of is my brother Willie's friend, Andreas Louw. I believe he'll be returning in November this year."

"Do you know anything about him?"

"Only that he was called to the ministry through my Uncle Stegmann's preaching during a revival at the mission church of St. Stephen's." After a moment's thought, I said, "Come to think of it, he'll probably make an excellent pastor."

"Right. So now that we have a potential candidate, our next step is to persuade the consistory of Fauresmith to present him with a letter of call."

"Hmm, I suppose we can do that during our first Presbytery meeting here in a few weeks' time. But the question still remains as to whether Cathcart will agree to fund the position."

"Personally, I have every confidence in your ability to persuade him to come to the party. After all, in the scheme of things, it's a miserly amount."

"You're jumping the gun, *Meneer* van Velden. You seem to forget that I haven't made a final decision to go to England yet."

"*Ach*," he said, waving his hand, "by the time I'm finished, you will have seen the light. And the reason why I say this is because the Lord will present you with an assignment that only you, as a pastor, can accomplish."

I chuckled. "Now I'm really intrigued. Please tell me more."

"My next suggestion relates to our dire need for more teachers. During the Synod last year, I made friends with *Dominee* Gottlieb van der Lingen of Paarl. Now there's a man with a vision! He's established primary schools for both White and Colored students in every ward of his congregation. He also told me that he plans to build a gymnasium, or public school— as they call it in Britain—in a few years' time. This will be a boarding school for secondary students who wish to attend university in Holland or the Theological Seminary that both he and your father would like to see established at the Cape. I'm sure you would agree that we need funding for a similar-type boarding school here."

He waited for me to answer, but his mention of the Theological Seminary had channeled my thoughts in a different direction.

"What is it, *Meneer* Murray? I note that you have donned that far-away look that tells me that you've had some revelation or other."

"I've just seen the light, *Meneer* Van Velden. That's what."

He favored me with a broad grin. "Fancy that! And I haven't even finished yet. What, may I ask, ignited it?"

"The Theological Seminary. You see, the Synodical Committee has been searching for two professors for our would-be Seminary for some time now. But each candidate they have approached has declined their offer. It dawned on me that if I were to accept the nomination of Boer delegate, I could personally visit these candidates to discuss any concerns preventing them from accepting the call. I know them personally, you see."

Van Velden frowned. "I'm not quite with you, *Meneer* Murray. From what I understand, the Theological Seminary will be housed at Stellenbosch in the Western Cape."

"I understand that. But if I manage to persuade two professorial candidates to come to the Cape, it would mean that lectures could be in Dutch instead of Latin. This fact alone would swing the doors of the Seminary open to interested young men whose families are not able to afford a Latin teacher, let alone raise the necessary funds to send then to Utrecht. And more students would mean more pastors to fill the empty positions around our country, including those in the Transvaal."

Van Velden eyed me with amusement. "It seems that you are trying to persuade *me* now."

He opened his jacket and withdrew a cigar from his inside pocket. Holding it aloft he said, "I take it then that I may smoke a celebratory cigar while you fetch the coffee?"

"By all means, *Meneer* Van Velden. You've certainly earned it."

"By the way," he said as I got up to go, "I still need to report on the happenings in the Transvaal."

Not batting an eyelid, I said, "It goes without saying that your report will prove most interesting."

As I made my way to the kitchen, I realized that even six months before, a similar statement would have stopped me in my tracks. I would have begged to know more on the spot. But at that moment, my focus was on the coming trip to London and all the possibilities it held.

I sent up an arrow prayer of thanks to the Lord for His confirmation that I should accept the role of delegate. Van Velden was right. As pastor, I was the only one in the Sovereignty who could fill the dual roles of Boer representative and Church envoy.

When I returned with the coffee a few minutes later, we sat in silence, taking our time to sip our drinks and think our thoughts. After a decent interval, Van Velden broached the topic of the Transvaal.

"That scenario you described in your note to me has proved correct. As you surmised, both the *Volksraad* and the people's assembly arrived at a decision to sever all ties with the Dutch Reformed Church in the Cape."

"Their decision pierces my heart, *Meneer* Van Velden. You may not be aware of this, but I went on tour to the Transvaal at the end of 1849 to dissuade them from taking this action. You see, a group in the Rustenburg and Marico districts had concocted a story that Sir Harry Smith had sent Drs. Faure and Robertson on a preaching tour to spy on the Boers. And because this rumor had spread and was causing some consternation at the time, my consistory here in Bloemfontein decided to send me there in order to calm things down. It was my first tour to the Transvaal, and the one that led to the ruin of my health. And what did it achieve? They've just turned their back on everything I've told them. But worst of all, I didn't see it coming. I was too busy congratulating myself that the Lord was using my preaching to change their hearts. I'm afraid there was far too much of me in it."

I was doing my best to suppress my tears. But now that I was verbalizing what had happened, my emotions were bubbling to the surface like the waters of a spring that had been cleared of silt.

Van Velden sighed. "I'm afraid to say that the same group you've just spoken of has been causing problems again. Shortly after Van der Hoff arrived in Potchefstroom at the end of May, Andries Pretorius went to welcome him to the Transvaal. While on this visit, he told Van der Hoff of the opposition by the Rustenburg group to joining the Synod."

Van Velden drew deeply on his cigar and watched my reaction through hooded lids. I knew he would be thinking exactly what I was.

"I would never have thought it! So it was Pretorius who was behind this move on account of the rebellion within his ranks."

"It would certainly seem so. He told Van der Hoff that the Natal Party—which is his own party, of course—was against joining the Cape Synod because of English influences and the fact that they did not want to submit to its authority."

My tears were rolling freely down my cheeks now. I brushed them aside with the back of my hand, then asked, "Do you know what reasons the Natal Party gave for not wanting to submit to the Synod?"

"Apparently, the argument Pretorius offered was based on Romans 13. He said that they feared the 'spiritual sword' of the Synod if they didn't keep all the requirements. And as some of those were tinged with political motives, they could never adhere to them all."

Speak about the pot calling the kettle black, I thought. Fancy accusing the Cape Synod of political motives when they themselves wanted the *Krijgsraad* and *Volksraad* to have the right to wield the sword of authority over the church!

"We both know that their arguments don't add up, *Meneer* Murray. But what disturbs me more is the readiness of Van der Hoff to fall in with Pretorius's plan, instead of standing firm on what he knows to be true and right."

"What about Wolmarans? He's no pushover."

"According to my elders, Wolmarans and the Potchefstroom consistory are following Van der Hoff's lead in this matter. Perhaps Pretorius also had a hand in it. In any case, the decision to support this about-turn was made as early as 6 June when the consistory met."

I leant on my knees while holding my face in my hands. Through my tears, I said, "I can't believe that Pretorius, Wolmarans and Gert Kruger would allow themselves to be swayed by the political views of a few. It can only be that they feared conflict in the church, and wanted all to be calm at the start of Van der Hoff's ministry."

"That may be so, but why the lack of integrity? Van der Hoff has not only hidden the truth from you, but he has also written a curt and unbrotherly letter that can't be easily excused."

I tried to put myself in Van der Hoff's shoes. Being new to the Transvaal and also to the ministry, he would have been no match for someone like Pretorius. His aim would have been to please and even inveigle himself into Pretorius's good books. Oh, the wiles of Satan for which we fall!

Van Velden, who had been puffing away, now placed his half-smoked cigar on the lip of the astray, ready once more to have his say. "It might ease your hurt to know that my consistory is as incensed as I am about the decisions taken across the Vaal. I told them that despite what had occurred at Rustenburg, Van der Hoff still needed to be inducted. I added that I was quite prepared to accompany you there, or even to go alone to perform the ceremony."

I blew my nose then offered Van Velden a wan smile. "I can imagine how that went down across the Vaal. It must have spread like wildfire."

"Ha! That's an understatement. By the time it crossed the Vaal, it had accumulated the ire of the Sovereignty Boers who consider you outrageously treated. To convey their indignation, they claimed that both of us would be coming, invited or not."

Van Velden fumbled again with his shoulder bag. He undid the clasp and withdrew a wad of writing paper that he carefully unfolded and placed before me.

"The top sheet is a letter I received from them. It's dated 8 September. The other sheets comprise the letter I wrote in reply. As you may notice, it is tantamount to a small booklet. My wife kindly wrote out several copies. This one is yours."

I peered at the address given at the top of the Transvaal letter, and then at the signatories at the end. Unlike the note I'd received from Van der Hoff, where all the men mentioned were from Rustenburg, the signatories to this letter were all from Potchefstroom.

"I notice, *Meneer* Van Velden, that it's been signed by A. Smit, G.V. Schoeman, and Landdrost H.H Lombard. They're not even on the church council."

"*Ja*, I noticed that as well."

Van Velden took up his cigar again and blew a ring of smoke towards the *stoep* ceiling. "Note the reason they gave for not wanting us to venture across the Vaal. It's given in the last six lines."

I located the spot and began to read:

We must advise you to refrain from such a journey, which will be in vain, since the highest church body and the highest political authority in these territories have decided that the induction shall not take place. Being a legally ordained minister of the Dutch Reformed Church, Dominee Van der Hoff's presentation or induction is unnecessary."

"Unnecessary! But every pastor of the Dutch Reformed Church is inducted, both here and in Holland. Why doesn't Van der Hoff explain that to them?"

"Because he's compromised his integrity. There's also something else I need to tell you. When he agreed to fall in with Pretorius's plan, he also promised Pretorius that he'd bypass being inducted by you."

I stared at Van Velden in disbelief.

"Yes, *Meneer* Murray. Pretorius asked him not to invite you. And when he agreed, Pretorius clasped his hand and thanked him profusely, his eyes apparently welling with tears."

"But why?"

"Don't you think the answer is obvious? He feared your holy boldness and integrity. And being aware of the people's love for you, he knew that neither the *Krijgsraad*, the *Volksraad*, nor Van der Hoff would be able to counter the truth of what you would have to say."

"Well I certainly wouldn't pull my punches. But the question remains: Where does Wolmarans stand in relation to Van der Hoff's induction?"

"He may not have known about this letter at the time it was written. But he certainly knows about it now. Just before setting out to travel here, I heard that he was insisting upon Van der Hoff's induction."

"By us?"

"No. He's obviously been forced to compromise on that score."

"Who then?"

"Who do you think, *Meneer* Murray?"

I puzzled over this question for a moment, then comprehension dawned. I threw back my head and laughed. "Wolmarans himself, of course. He's the only one who would have the spiritual standing to enforce church law."

Van Velden chuckled along with me.

"Even so, it won't count in the eyes of the Cape Synod."

"But in the eyes of God?—surely it will, *Meneer* Van Velden."

27
Cape Town
November 1853 – January 1854

D r. Fraser and I arrived in Cape Town at the end of
November. I had looked forward to staying with my
mother's brother, Uncle William, in Schotsche Kloof,
where my health would have benefited from the sea breezes
wafting up from Table Bay. But this was not to be. Just before
leaving Bloemfontein, he had written to say that he had moved
to a home named *Craig Cottage* in Kloof Street. He described
it as being situated directly below Table Mountain, and only a
few streets away from the Dutch Reformed parsonage where
Dr. Abraham Faure lived.

Although he expressed sadness at having to leave behind
the magnificent views of the ocean and Robben Island in the
distance, he wrote that he had felt compelled to relocate to
the Kloof Street district on account of my cousin George's
education. He explained that the district there was home
to many families whose home language was Dutch. And as
several of these families had recently clubbed together to
employ a secondary-school Dutch teacher for their sons,
Uncle William had wanted George to benefit from this opportunity.

It was apparently around that time that a certain Mr. Craig, who lived in the district, had decided to follow his sons to the gold diggings in Australia, prompting Uncle William to seize the opportunity to purchase his home.

As it happened, his move to Kloof Street proved most convenient for Dr. Fraser and myself during our first two weeks in Cape Town. I, for one, was able to schedule evening meetings with Dr. Abraham Faure as well as Andreas Louw, who'd arrived back from Utrecht earlier that month. As Andreas was living with family in walking distance of Craig Cottage, I took the opportunity of meeting with him on a regular basis.

We took to each other from the start. What I liked most about this striking Afrikaner with hazel eyes and hair that dipped in front to form a forelock was his enthusiasm for the ministry that was rooted in reality. He told me how he'd experienced a quickening of the Holy Spirit during the revival at St. Stephen's under the preaching of Uncle William. He went on to say that since that time, he had cherished the hope of being able to serve the Boers beyond the borders of the Cape.

At one of these meetings, he looked me in the eye and said, "I have to be honest with you, Andrew. Being born and bred in the Western Cape, I realize that I have much to learn about the frontier Boers and the issues that concern them."

"I'm well aware of that, Andreas. And so is my father. That is why he's extended an invitation for you to spend a month or two in Graaff-Reinet under his tutelage. It makes no difference if you accept the call to Fauresmith or not."

I withdrew the small envelope containing my father's invitation and handed it to him. His face lit up in appreciation. "Tell your father that his invitation is most generous, and that

I gladly accept. I'll be writing to him myself, of course, once all the details are finalized."

Andreas's readiness to accept the call to Fauresmith was ratified when Sir George Cathcart agreed to fund the position. Unfortunately, Cathcart was not as positive about our intended trip to England.

"I'm hoping to receive the final orders in relation to the abandonment any day now," he said. "So I doubt whether you'll be able to proceed to England as planned. But if no dispatch regarding this matter arrives by mid-January, you may book yourselves on the steamer *The Queen of the South*. It is due to leave for England on 21 January."

As this meant a lengthy stay in Cape Town, Dr. Fraser insisted that we find lodgings at a boarding house in Green Point. I readily consented because I was already feeling the strain that came from all the excitement of being amongst family and friends again.

It was shortly after our move to Green Point that I received a letter that had been addressed care of Abraham Faure. He duly handed it to me after church one Sunday.

"Here's a little surprise for you," he said, while arching his brow.

By the tone of his voice and facial expression, I guessed that he knew exactly who'd penned it and the message it contained.

"Glancing at the handwriting, I recognized it immediately. "It's from Dirk van Velden, the pastor of Winburg," I told Andreas Louw, with whom I was conversing at the time. "He would never write unless it were urgent. So I'd better read it immediately as it could have a bearing on Fauresmith."

I tore the envelope open, unfolded the letter, and began to read:

Beste Mnr. Murray,

I have no idea where you'll be when this reaches you, but I owe it to you to let you know that I've accepted a call to Ladismith. It's not the Ladysmith in Natal, but the Ladismith spelt with an "i" that is in the Little Karoo of the Cape. To be more specific, it is situated in an outlying corner of Dr. William Robertson's parish of Swellendam. From what he tells me, the people there are very caring and have a zeal for the Gospel. He thinks my family will be both happy and healthy there. I'm due to be inducted on 9 April.

Please pay me a visit on your return journey. It's on the same route as Prins Albert where your sister Maria and Jan Neethling live. I'm afraid Winburg became too demanding for me. . . ."

I sighed as I handed the letter to Andreas. "Dirk van Velden has just accepted a call to Ladismith in the Cape, so I'm afraid there will only be you and Piet Roux left in the Sovereignty while I'm away."

Andreas straightened his back and donned a determined look. "*Ach*, that shouldn't prove a problem. After all, you coped for several years there alone."

I nodded and flashed him an encouraging smile. If only he knew, I thought.

28

London

February–April 1854

As no dispatch from the Colonial Secretary in England had arrived by mid-January, we left for England as planned on *The Queen of the South*, arriving there at the end of February. Unfortunately, we had to wait two weeks before we were granted an audience with the Duke of Newcastle. It took place on 16 March.

Newcastle was a striking-looking man with large brown eyes and long sideburns that merged into a jawline beard that stopped short of his chin.

He greeted us warmly, then ushered us into his office where he invited us to sit on two upright chairs in front of his desk. I couldn't help noticing that he had bypassed the lounge area with its comfortable chesterfield sofas. It was obvious, that as colonials, we were way down in the pecking order.

"I'm afraid gentlemen, you've come too late," Newcastle said. "The final orders for abandonment were dispatched at the end of November. The mail steamer must have passed your ship on the high seas."

Our facial expressions must have portrayed our dismay, because he softened his tone and hastily added, "I realize that our withdrawal could be of major concern to some residents in the Sovereignty, but let's call a spade a spade. It's time to let the locals do things their way."

Quick off the mark, Fraser asked, "Could you tell us, sir, if your office consulted Parliament regarding this matter?"

"Not necessary," answered Newcastle, with a flick of the hand. "The Law Officers of the Crown have taken great pains to research this matter. That's why it took so long for the final orders of abandonment to be dispatched."

Law Officers or no, he was not going to fob us off that quickly, I thought.

"But what about the Letters Patent, sir? From my understanding, they establish the Sovereignty into a separate State with its own constitution. Surely there needs to be an Act of Parliament to rescind them?"

After a slight pause, he said, "Well, seeing you have come all this way, I dare say you're entitled to the truth. I'm afraid that the Letters Patent were never promulgated."

Still looking my way, he swished his tongue across his upper teeth in typical schoolboy fashion to indicate that what he was about to say was rather amusing.

"You see, when the Letters Patent were sent to the Cape in March 1851, Sir Harry Smith's attention was focused on the Frontier War. So the Letters Patent were placed in a pigeon hole and promptly forgotten."

Observing my expression of incredulity, he said, "I agree, Mr. Murray. Sir Harry's governorship wasn't exactly covered in glory. But in this case, his lack of attention to detail has enabled Britain to withdraw in exactly the same way as Sir Harry annexed the Sovereignty—simply by proclamation. Of course, we've also had to issue new Letters Patent to that effect."

I was about to enquire about the legal status of the Boers, when I noticed Fraser extracting an envelope from his satchel. As I did not want to hog the discussion, I decided to wait to ask my question until after he'd presented the Conditions of Capitulation.

Newcastle opened the envelope and withdrew the papers. He scanned them quickly, then looked up. "Fortunately, I'm already au fait with these Conditions. I've also given Sir George Russell Clerk wide ranging powers to deal with them. Furthermore, I'm expecting a dispatch from him later this week telling me that the withdrawal has taken place. But having said that, are there any questions you would like to ask while you are here?"

Fraser glanced my way, indicating that I should go first. As the focus was now on the Conditions, the first question of import that came to mind concerned the various treaties with the Griqua and Moshesh.

"Could you tell us, sir, if Sir George Russell Clerk has been given the necessary authority to amend the Maitland Treaty with the Griqua as well as the boundary question with Moshesh?"

Newcastle favored me with an unexpected smile that seemed to indicate that I'd be favorably disposed to his answer. "Although I've left both questions to Russell Clerk's discretion, I've nevertheless recommended that the Griqua be allowed to sell their land to the Boers in the Griqua Reserve. After all, the Griqua have already violated the treaty. And as for the land north of the Reserve, I've instructed Sir George Cathcart to withdraw a sum of £10 000 as a one-off payment to compensate them for that land. And because they've never farmed it, I happen to agree with Sir Harry Smith's previous decision that it should revert to freehold. I'm sure the Boers will be happy with this decision. Fortunately for them, you alerted Russell Clerk to this question early on so that we could make these timely decisions."

I'd actually done nothing of the sort. What had probably happened was that Russell Clerk had been alerted to the problem because of my request to see the Treaties together with my subsequent visit to Fauresmith.

"Well of course," continued Newcastle, "dealing with Moshesh is another matter altogether. Nevertheless, the Boers will be pleased to know that due to the Battle of Berea, all former treaties with Moshesh have been cancelled."

Without waiting for me to comment, Newcastle started to shuffle the sheets and glance through more of the Conditions. I looked sideways at Fraser to indicate that he had the floor, but he shook his head and lowered his eyes to indicate that it was useless to prod Newcastle further. Having got to know similar cues from Fraser during the abandonment meetings in Bloemfontein, I was certain he must have another option up his sleeve.

Newcastle cleared his throat and began to speak. "I'm sure Russell Clerk will deal with most of these Conditions in a satisfactory way. I see here that your committee also requests a share in the custom dues levied at Cape and Natal ports. Well, that would be an issue for the incoming government to negotiate with the Cape Administration. As for the question of compensation, you have to realize that there is a major war on in the Crimea. So funds are scarce."

He lay the sheets down and regarded us across his desk. I had wanted to ask how much compensation the Sovereignty could expect, and had even opened my mouth to do so, when he indicated that he had not finished speaking.

"You'll be interested to know that the citizens of the Cape are now taking on greater responsibility for ruling their colony.

A new Legislative Council has just been formed with elected members. I'm sure they'll be interested in deciding upon questions such as custom dues and what not."

He slipped the sheets into a folder, pressed his outspread hands on the desk, and rose from his chair. "I'm afraid that's all I can comment on at this juncture, gentlemen."

A moment later he had rounded his desk and was shaking our hands. The interview was over, and we had come all the way to England only to realize that our journey had been a waste of money and time.

After stepping out of his office, we decided to walk along the Thames to take advantage of the isolated surrounds to consider our options.

"This whole business has given me a sad insight into political proceedings, Dr. Fraser. The abandonment has been solely about political expediency."

"Perhaps so," Fraser said. "But the impression I got was that it had more to do with lack of funds. That's why I'm pleased you didn't come back at him over the compensation issue, or mention the building of that teachers' college-cum-school you're so keen on. It wasn't the time for that, especially with the Crimean war on the go. You see, I didn't want him to dismiss them out of hand."

"So when and where should we mention them?"

"Well, first we need to try our best to get the abandonment issue raised in Parliament. If nothing else, it might lead to a decent amount of compensation. As for your boarding school idea, that will keep until you return to Cape Town. There's a reasonable chance that this new Legislative Council will support your cause, especially now that its members are elected."

I noticed that Fraser had selected his words carefully. They had implied that he might not be returning. If so, it was only fair that I be kept abreast of his plans.

"I notice that you make no mention of yourself, Dr. Fraser."

He didn't reply, but stared across the murky waters of the Thames as though mesmerized by the reflections of the grey clouds above. When he finally spoke, he did so with conviction.

"I feel it my duty to help out in the Crimea, Mr. Murray. I intend to enlist as an army surgeon once we have explored all options related to the abandonment. The plight of those soldiers weighs heavily on my heart. Over the last few years, I've been chasing money. But I have come to realize that it doesn't satisfy."

I greeted this announcement with equanimity, knowing I would have done the same had I been in his shoes. After expressing my thoughts in favor of his decision, our discussion returned to the predicament at hand. We decided that we had to try to do more to discover if the abandonment had taken place legally. It was, after all, one of the main reasons why we had come.

As we reviewed our conversation with Newcastle, it struck me that I had forgotten to inquire about the Boers' legal status. After sharing this thought with Fraser, he said, "Let it lie, Mr. Murray. Don't even mention the issue around here. Leave it to the incoming government to raise with Britain. Hopefully, they will have forgotten the issue before long. What Boer and Brit need to do now is focus on what unites them, rather than on what divides. Besides, some citizens might like to be thought of as both Boer and Brit—if you understand my meaning."

I certainly did. And with this insight came a seed of an idea for my school. Why couldn't it cater for both English and Dutch-speaking students? I knew that nothing along these lines had ever been tried at the Cape before, but there was always a first time.

Fraser jolted me back into the present with the comment, "Our job now is to get the abandonment question raised in Parliament."

After kicking various options around, we decided to approach Mr. Adderley. He was the obvious choice on account of his efforts in 1848 to overturn the decision to send convicts to the Cape. To commemorate this achievement, the City of Cape Town had renamed the top half of its main thoroughfare *Adderley Street* in his honor.

"It's a long shot, and may not succeed," Fraser said, "but no one will be able to criticize us for not trying."

On Tuesday of the following week, we were able to obtain an interview with Mr. Adderley.

"I advise you to do the following," he said. "Consult a few legal minds regarding the power of the Crown to be able to abandon the Sovereignty without consulting Parliament. If there is even a smidgen of a doubt concerning the legality of the British withdrawal, I'll raise the question in Parliament."

We thanked him for his advice, and left his offices feeling buoyed.

Once outside, Fraser turned to me and said, "Why don't I seek out some legal firms while you go to the London Missionary Society offices to fetch our mail. I'm expecting a few letters from Scotland, while you will probably be receiving a few from Holland. I couldn't help noticing that you've been writing to all and sundry there."

His eyes danced with mirth as he observed my enthusiastic nod. "I know you love walking down the Strand and then visiting the Christian societies that have their headquarters at Exeter Hall. So enjoy the rest of the day. I'll be home in time for dinner this evening."

His words were like heavenly music to my ears. On other occasions, we had always gone together to collect our mail, giving me little time to chat with the officials there. But now that I was alone, I intended to become acquainted with as many as possible.

I never dreamt, though, that this visit would become a stepping stone to the fulfilment of my most erstwhile dreams.

When I arrived at the offices of the London Missionary Society, the door was standing ajar and two men were conferring next to a bulletin board attached to the right-hand wall. One was the clerk, Mr. Moss, but I did not know the other.

When I knocked, they ceased their discussion and looked towards the door. On recognizing me, Mr. Moss beamed a welcome, while nudging the other man. "The Lord has provided the answer, Dr. Morison. Didn't I tell you He would. This young gentleman is none other than Rev. Andrew Murray Jr., pastor extraordinaire of the Boers in the Orange River Sovereignty. He's here on official business related to that part of the world. But before we get sidetracked on that topic, I'd better welcome him and share our little conundrum."

He stepped forward and pumped my hand with enthusiasm. "You have no idea how pleased I am to see you, Mr. Murray. Let me introduce you to Dr. Morison who is a fellow board member of the London Missionary Society. Unfortunately, Dr. Morison is coming down with influenza and will not be able to preach at Surrey Chapel this coming Sunday evening. Because I'm an elder there, he decided he'd better inform me of this fact before he was laid low. You see, our pastor Rev. James Sherman is leaving us this Sunday, and Rev. Newman Hall, who will be taking his place does not arrive until July. So dear Dr. Morison, here, agreed to fill in. But by the looks of him, it might take several weeks before he is able to do so."

I glanced at the ageing Dr. Morison who had a high color and was gravelling a series of coughs. I watched as he buffed his nose, then turned to me with pleading eyes. The last thing I wished to do was discuss my own health problems at a time like this. So I knew I had no option but to accept.

"I'd be much obliged to you, Mr. Murray, if you could preach in my stead next Sunday evening as well as on April the second. I'm afraid that at my age throat problems take much longer to heal."

"Think no more of it, sir," I answered. "I count it an honor to be asked."

In actual fact, just the opposite was true. I had to steel myself to accept this invitation, especially at a renowned church like Surrey Chapel with its huge congregation. But what was I to do? It would have been churlish in the extreme to have declined the request.

To my surprise, the turnout on Sunday evening was far greater that I'd expected, considering the farewell service for Mr. Sherman that morning. I judged the number to have been around a thousand souls. On 2 April, the number had increased to well over two thousand. This had prompted Mr. Moss to request that I take charge of Surrey Chapel during the months of May and June.

"You'll receive a full stipend as well as the use of the parsonage," he said.

Fortunately, I was ready for such a request with a genuine excuse. During the intervening weeks, Dr. Fraser and I had sought various opinions concerning the legality of the British withdrawal. And as doubts about its validity had been expressed, Mr. Adderley had agreed to raise the matter in Parliament on Tuesday, 9 May. Because I had several free weeks up my sleeve, I had decided to pay a quick visit to Charles in Utrecht. I also knew that this trip would give me the necessary excuse to decline any further preaching offers.

"I'm afraid I'm due to leave for Utrecht on 12 April, Mr. Moss."

"What a pity! Everyone's been appreciating your sermons so much. But as you'll still be here this coming Sunday, which is the ninth, I don't suppose you would consider preaching for us again? One of the readings is from Revelation chapter 5—a most edifying passage, and quite a challenging one, I should imagine. Are you up for it, Mr. Murray?"

I had expected a request of this sort, so I replied without hesitation: "Yes, I'm up for it, Mr. Moss."

"Well in that case, my dear fellow, the text we elders would like you to preach on is from Revelation 5 verse 5: '*And I beheld, and, lo, in the midst of the throne . . . stood a Lamb as it had been slain.*'

"Ah, a challenge indeed," I said. "May the Lord grant me the spiritual insights to do it justice."

"Just so, Mr. Murray. We'll be upholding you in prayer throughout the week, as is our custom. It's a fail-safe system that the Lord always honors."

29
Preaching on Revelation at Surrey Chapel

9 April 1854

S urrey Chapel was full to overflowing on Sunday evening, 9 April, with at least three thousand or more in attendance. At the end of the service, I made my way to the main door which led into a small vestibule that helped to protect the circular auditorium from undue drafts wafting in from outside. As I shook the hands of the departing parishioners, one and all commented favorably on the sermon.

After the last of the parishioners had dribbled past, Mr. Moss came over to shake my hand. I noticed that he had been standing to one side with a family of five.

"Well done, Mr. Murray. That was certainly an excellent exposition of the passage. Our guests from your homeland thought so too. Let me introduce you to the Rutherfoord family from Cape Town.[10] Mr. Rutherfoord has just heard that he's been elected to the new Legislative Council."

Rutherfoord stepped forward and shook my hand, while the rest of the family waited to take their turn. He was dressed in a dark overcoat with a silk white scarf tucked in underneath. His brown hair, which brushed the top of his scarf, was streaked with grey. But it was his kind face and intelligent eyes that attracted me to him. His smile lit up his face and crinkled the lines around his eyes.

"I'm pleased to be able to make your acquaintance, Mr. Murray."

"Likewise, Mr. Rutherfoord."

"I'd also like to add a word to that already expressed by Mr. Moss: A most splendid sermon, sir, and one that will lift my spirits for some time to come."

"Thank you for your kind words. And now it's my turn to congratulate you on your election to the new Legislative Council. As a Christian, I'm sure your presence there will prove to be salt and light."

"I certainly hope so, Mr. Murray." He paused, then said, "I know this is not the time nor place to discuss the political situation in the Orange River Sovereignty, but I'd like to help out in that respect. Mr. Moss, here, has explained the current situation to me. But as things stand, I'm afraid the withdrawal has probably taken place. Needless to say, I feel strongly that the Cape Administration should be doing their bit to compensate the Sovereignty for the dishonorable way in which this abandonment has been handled. After all, it was the Cape Administration under Sir Harry Smith that sparked this whole debacle."

He withdrew a filigree card case from his pocket, flipped out his card, and handed it to me.

"I'll probably be back in Cape Town before you will, Mr. Murray. So please look me up when you arrive. I run a shipping agency with my brother and son. My office is at 3 Burg Street. If I'm not there, my son, Frederic, will be."

He now turned to his wife and daughters, indicating that they should come closer. They looked a picture in their woolen dresses, dark capes and fancy straw bonnets. As Maria had been asking me about the fashions in London, I couldn't help noticing that they were fetchingly lined with blonde[II], and trimmed with white ribbon.

Rutherfoord presented me to Mrs. Rutherfoord first and then to his daughters Emma, Ellen and Lucy. I shook hands with each in turn, then waited for Mrs. Rutherfoord to finish complimenting me on my sermon before turning my attention to her daughters. I decided it was best to address them as a group.

"I dare say this is your first trip to London, ladies—a most exciting experience to be sure."

Emma, as the eldest, spoke first. "Actually, I'm missing the dear old Cape. There's less artificiality of thought there. And that's also where my sphere of usefulness lies. I teach Sunday school and also go on door-knocks with Mama to hand out tracts, you see. But here I find that the minds of the ladies are mostly bent on trifles and frivolities. It's almost impossible to converse with them on any topic of substance. And when I try to initiate such a conversation, they look at me askance."

Her honest assessment of society ladies in London had taken me by surprise. What a self-possessed young lady she was! And now that I was focusing my attention solely on her, I liked what I saw. In fact, I felt inexplicably drawn to her. I couldn't help admiring the little kiss curls dangling down her forehead, her generous mouth that was at that moment twitching at the corners, and her deep brown eyes that matched her chocolate-colored bonnet. What lovely eyes, I thought. They simply exuded intelligence.

Unfortunately, I had to peel my gaze away to focus on her sister Ellen, who was now expressing her thoughts on London. From her vivacious chatter, she seemed just the opposite to

Emma in both personality and interests. She was also prettier, with rosy cheeks and glossy fair hair that glistened in the lamp light. Her most outstanding feature was her dark eyelashes that framed her blue eyes. When she spoke, she batted them from time to time, obviously wanting to be admired. I judged her to be a year or so younger than Emma.

"I simply love London," she gushed. "It's so exciting being able to catch a train and go on an orgy of shopping. There's so much to do and see, whereas in the dear old Cape I have to be satisfied with the odd church bazaar to break the monotony of embroidering collars and cuffs each afternoon. We do a lot of pedestrianism, of course, but much depends upon the person accompanying one."

"I think the word is walking," butted in Emma, with a twitch of her brow directed at me.

"Everyone in London society employs that term, Emma, so it's quite in keeping for me to do so too."

I exchanged a knowing glance with Emma, comprehending now what she had meant by the phrase "artificiality of thought."

"I'm afraid I'm not at all like Emma," continued Ellen. "At home she keeps to a seven-hour schedule on week days. She's quite the intellectual of the family, you know. Before we left Cape Town she was taking German lessons and reading Hallan's History of the Middle Ages. She also sings and plays beautifully. Her new interest since arriving in London is German poetry and *lieder*. It's all the rage since the Prince Consort introduced it to Queen Victoria. But while I don't mind joining Emma in singing Italian operetta, I certainly draw the line at *lieder*."

During the pause that followed, I was able to turn my attention to Lucy, who looked to be about eleven or twelve. Her coloring and looks were much like Emma's, except for the odd freckle on her nose and cheeks. She was also blessed with thick, wavy hair that made her bonnet sit awkwardly on her head. She looked up at me with serious eyes, and said, "I like both the Cape and London. But I think London has more to offer by way of service to others—that is, if you're a lady. If you want to be a missionary, like Emma, then of course Africa or India is best suited for that purpose. But I don't think that's for me. If I were a bit older, I'd join the ladies going out to the Crimea to nurse the soldiers. Yes, something like that is what I'd prefer to do."

"Most interesting," was all I could muster in response to her serious statement.

"Oh, don't mind Lucy, Mr. Murray," said Ellen. "She's always serious. And knowing what a determined head she has on those shoulders of hers, I'm sure that's exactly the type of thing she'll choose to do one day."

Lucy appeared to have ignored Ellen's remark. Her focus was now drawn to the circular design of Surrey Chapel. I followed her gaze to the dome above. During the day, it let in a stream of glorious light, but now it took on a gloomy appearance because of the shadows cast by the lamps below. They hung from hooks attached to a balcony that circled the dome. Just below, were two half-moon mezzanine floors situated on either side of the pulpit.

"Mr. Murray, why is this church built like a theatre?" asked Lucy.

"Well, from what I know, it was designed by the famous preacher Rev. Rowland Hill. He was particularly interested in church music, and felt that a round design would improve the acoustics for church music as well as preaching. One of his favorite sayings was: 'Why should the devil have all the good tunes.' He also used to joke that a round chapel prevented the devil from hiding in corners."

Lucy's face brightened, "He must have been a funny man."

"Quick witted, I believe. The story goes that on a particular Sunday some people came into the chapel during the service to escape the rain. In the middle of the sermon, Rowland Hill announced that he had heard of people using religion as a cloak, but never as an umbrella."

I watched amused as Lucy broke into a broad grin. Emma, who'd been watching her closely, seemed thrilled that I had managed to elicit this reaction from her. Meanwhile, Ellen was giggling nervously, peering this way and that at every shadow in view.

It was at this juncture that Mrs. Rutherfoord reappeared in the vestibule. She had apparently slipped out with Mr. Moss and her husband while I was talking with her daughters.

"Excuse me, Mr. Murray," she said." I'm so sorry to interrupt, but we have just managed to hire a cab—no easy matter after a church service around these parts. Thank you so much for keeping the girls entertained. From their smiles, they have obviously enjoyed chatting with you."

Turning to her daughters she said, "Come along, girls. You can continue this conversation with Mr. Murray when he visits us in Cape Town. I'm sure there'll be plenty of mutual experiences to share then."

She favored me with a broad smile, then led the way outside. Lucy and Ellen said their goodbyes and traipsed after her. Emma, who was bringing up the rear, stopped to shake my hand again.

"I'm sure we'll have a great deal to discuss on your return, Mr. Murray. I look forward to some scintillating conversations."

I watched her go with a quickened heartbeat and the realization that her deep brown eyes would be haunting me for the duration of my stay.

❦

30
News from Bloemfontein

April–May 1854

I left London for Utrecht on Wednesday the twelfth as planned. My short stay in Holland proved far more hectic than I had bargained for. From Rotterdam I rushed to Amsterdam, where I spent the night before proceeding to Utrecht to visit Charles. A few days after arriving there, I was introduced to the theological students from the Cape, or *Kaapenaren*—as everyone liked to call them.

I then busied myself visiting old friends and acquaintances, especially Van den Ham and Beets, who had been called to be the first two professors of our proposed Theological Seminary at the Cape. Both had declined their calls due to pressure exerted by parents.

After that, it became a whirl of activity, which included a host of meetings, a ministers' conference in Amsterdam, plus visits to former professors.

The conference presented a wonderful opportunity to meet up with former students from Utrecht. When I broached the topic of professors for our Theological Seminary, I was surprised that the prevailing thought was that the Cape should choose two professors from amongst her own pastors. And the name that came up time and time again was that of my brother John.

My stay in Amsterdam provided another opportunity for a round of visits that included the Amsterdam Seminary. My discussions with the professors there raised my hopes of obtaining some good men as pastors for both the Transvaal and the Sovereignty.

On Monday, I was back again in Rotterdam meeting with more friends. Then on Tuesday, I started out for Middelburg to visit Taats and Toorenberg, who had also declined their respective calls to be professors of our proposed Seminary. As with the others, they too had indicated pressure from ageing parents.

The sad reality of the situation was that God seemed to have closed the door to the Cape obtaining orthodox professors from Holland. At the same time, the overwhelming opinion seemed to point to the Cape having to choose professors from among her own pastors. The more I thought about it, the more appealing this option became. After all, it wouldn't be difficult to find men at the Cape who were both evangelical and mission oriented. I just prayed that the Synod would see it that way as well.

I arrived back in London on Friday, 5 May, feeling utterly exhausted. After entering the front door of the home where Dr. Fraser and I had hired rooms, I spied Fraser sitting in the lounge reading a book next to a roaring fire in the hearth. Instead of proceeding directly to my room, I took off my overcoat and hat, hung them on the hallstand, then went into the lounge to join him. He'd obviously been waiting for me there, because his first action was to present me with a pile of letters.

"Any news about the situation in the Sovereignty?" I asked, going to stand with my back to the hearth while shuffling my letters. I noted one from Willem Pretorius, which I immediately placed on top of my pile. He would provide a Boer perspective on the situation, whereas Fraser's feedback would be from the English-speaking delegates.

"It's as we expected, Mr. Murray. The abandonment has already taken place. I received a full account of events from Joseph Orpen. He said that as soon as Russell Clerk had received the authorization to proceed with the abandonment, he went on tour to all the centers to let the Boers know that he was now able to deal with the Conditions of Capitulation."

"I see. So that is what happened."

"Yes, but that's not the full story. Following closely on Clerk's heels was Commandant Adriaan Stander, who took it upon himself to persuade the Boers to accept Clerk's offer of independence."

"But he lives in the Transvaal."

"Not any more. According to Orpen, he's just bought a farm in the Vaal District."

"So what happened to the committee of twenty-five, then?"

"Well, Josias Hoffman, and his supporters decided to secede from the committee of twenty-five. As a result, only thirteen of the twenty-five delegates remained. While that number was sufficient to constitute a quorum, Russell Clerk thought otherwise, and dissolved the original committee. He then proceeded to hold secret meetings with Hoffman and those willing to take over the reins of government. These meetings resulted in the Convention of Bloemfontein that was held on 23 February."

"But that's before we even landed here."

"Just so. And exactly what Russell Clerk was hoping."

I took a moment to digest this news.

All that mattered now was the hope that a *Volksraad* would make a better fist of it than the British administration had done.

Anxious to find out more, I said, "I suppose Josias Hoffman is President?"

"You suppose correctly. He's formed a provisional government until a plebiscite can be held this month."

I could hardly believe my ears. Unlike the Transvaal, the Boers in the Sovereignty had certainly got their act together.

"I suppose Adderley will no longer be raising the issue in Parliament?"

"As a matter of fact, he still intends to go ahead with it on Tuesday."

"But whatever for? It's too late for that now."

"He knows that full well, Mr. Murray, but the aim is now to improve the Sovereignty's chances of obtaining compensation."

"Well, that's very honorable of him, but how does he propose to do that?"

I noticed a glint of amusement in Fraser's eye that indicated that Adderley must have something up his sleeve.

"He'll present a robust description of the events leading up to the abandonment. I showed him Joseph Orpen's letter, you see."

In my mind's eye I could see Adderley delivering arrowed barbs at the Government. But being a realist, I could also imagine their dismissal of his arguments.

Dr. Fraser appeared to undergo a mood change to match mine. "Adderley thinks that our chances of obtaining compensation are slim at the moment. Nevertheless, he is also of the view that once Parliament knows what has transpired, the Sovereignty could expect to receive a small amount. But it will be up to us to exert pressure on the Duke of Newcastle after Adderley has delivered his speech."

I grimaced, dreading the thought.

Observing this, Fraser continued, "We'll compose a well-argued letter, Mr. Murray. That way, our request will be on the Government books. If no amount is forthcoming, you can exert pressure on the new Governor and the Legislative Council when you arrive back at the Cape."

"New Governor, did you say? Is Cathcart being recalled?"

Fraser smiled, obviously amused by my unabashed surprise. "I believe so. They want him to go to the Crimea. And that, of course, means that there'll be a new Governor who will be anxious to endear himself to the people."

"Ha! We can only hope."

In the silence that followed, I opened the letter from Willem Pretorius and began to scan the contents. I couldn't help chuckling while reading the first few paragraphs.

"You won't believe this, but there's a gold rush on near Smithfield."

Fraser snorted. "Don't say the English farmers have concocted that story as a ruse to try and persuade the British to stay?"

"According to Elder Pretorius, one of the farmers was taking aim at a jackal while he was digging his burrow. To his astonishment, the jackal kicked out a nugget that weighed about eight ounces. He also found an additional 115 grains. But the hubbub it caused soon died down when nothing further was found."

"Thank goodness for that. What else does he have to say?"

"Oh, you'll love this titbit. I wish I'd been a fly on the wall when it occurred."

"Well, don't leave a man in suspense," said Fraser. "What happened?"

"Apparently, just before Russell Clerk left Bloemfontein, Josias Hoffman arranged for a subscription dinner to be held in the school hall to honor him. Hoffman had just risen to propose a toast, when Joseph Orpen beat him to the post. Holding his glass on high, Orpen looked Russell Clerk in the eye and called out: 'To Sir George Russell Clerk, the instrument of the greatest injustice ever perpetrated on a people. May we never see him here again!'"

Fraser roared with laughter. After calming down he commented, "I can't get over the fact that Orpen had the gumption to say that to Russell Clerk's face, especially at a packed dinner. Quite undignified really. Nevertheless, I would have loved to have heard the gossip afterwards. It must have been the talk of the town."

"I'm sure it was."

My light-hearted mood changed to one of concern when I read the next few paragraphs. "I'm afraid the following items are rather disturbing. A few of the Boers north of Winburg want to join up with the Transvaal. But Willem Pretorius assures me that that is unlikely to happen because the majority don't want to be a part of the bickering that goes on in the *Volksraad* there. They also want our church to remain with the Cape Synod."

I paused while reading the next few lines. "He also says that a rumor is doing the rounds that Marthinus Pretorius, who has taken over from his father in the Transvaal, has declared that if the British grant the Sovereignty compensation, then he intends to claim a large proportion of it to cover the cost of ammunition that was used during the Battle of Boomplaats."

"Oh dear! By the sounds of it, that rumor could be true."

I observed the worried expression on Fraser's face and decided that some reassurance was needed.

"But like Willem Pretorius says, the Sovereignty Boers want Marthinus to keep his nose out of Sovereignty affairs. And if compensation is granted, then he will have to lodge his claim along with everyone else."

"Hmm, your elder is obviously a sensible man. What else does he have to say?"

"Only that both Boer and Brit are determined to pull together and make a go of governing the people wisely. He also mentions that the English land jobber, Henry Halse of Smithfield, is sure to gain a seat in the *Volksraad*, and that Major Warden's son, Charles, is likely to become landdrost of Bloemfontein. It is also muted that Mr. Ford will become landdrost of Smithfield, and Joseph Orpen landdrost of Winburg and Harrismith."

Fraser arched a brow in surprise. "Well, that certainly sounds reassuring. There must be an amazing atmosphere of goodwill and cooperation between the two language groups. It's now up to us to put our best foot forward to gain some compensation."

I folded the letter and stuffed it back into its envelope. I heaved a sigh, and said, "Elder Pretorius also asks when I'll be returning."

"Not for a while, by the looks of you."

"This time I plead guilty, Dr. Fraser. I'm afraid I overexerted myself while in Holland."

Fraser bent forward, switching easily into doctor mode. "One of your problems is that you don't seem to realize the seriousness of your illness. As I'll be leaving for the Crimea within a few weeks, I would like you to consult a good physician before I leave."

He bent sideways and withdrew a folded note from the side pocket of his tweed jacket. "Here are a few names I was given by a medical friend of mine. The sooner you're able to make an appointment with one of them, the better."

The doctor I consulted the following week delivered a similar prognosis to that of Dr. Fraser, except that his was even more dire, if that were possible.

"I want you to visit the water-cure establishment in Ben Rhydding, Yorkshire," he said. "You'll need at least four weeks there to be able to notice any positive results. After that, you'll need at least six months complete rest. Do not even contemplate returning to the Cape before the end of the year."

Although I decided to obey his advice, I felt that I required some form of stimulation to steer my thoughts away from being preoccupied with myself. So after my spell at Ben Rhydding, I made a rush trip to Scotland before a planned visit to Charles again.

It was while I was back in London, making preparations for my trip to Utrecht, that I was able to catch up with the backlog of letters that had been accumulating during my extended absence. While they were always brimming with accounts of family doings and church affairs, I was certainly not expecting the surprise news that literally gushed from my father's pen— not to speak of Maria's embellishment of events.

I was astounded to hear that my brother Willie, who had only been back at the Cape for little over a year, was getting married in January to Ellie Gie, a distant cousin from Stellenbosch. And if that weren't surprising enough, the next announcement made my jaw drop. My eighteen-year-old sister, Jemima, had just become engaged to Andreas Louw.

According to Maria, he had fallen in love with her while spending a few months in Graaff-Reinet prior to his induction at Fauresmith. But because of his extra duties during my absence from the Orange Free State—as it was now called—they would only be getting married in September next year.

While on one level, I was overjoyed to hear the news of these impending marriages, on another, it only served to dampen my spirits. A sense of loneliness overwhelmed me, and the pains in my arms and hands flared up accordingly. As per usual, they were an index of my emotional state. I was determined not to give in to them, for surely the Lord would give me Emma Rutherfoord as a wife. She was the only girl I'd ever been drawn to. And although we'd only exchanged a few sentences, I just knew in my heart that she was the one for me.

I sat there and reviewed my situation. I realized that I had to make every effort to improve my health. After all, how could I get married when I was always feeling fatigued? I decided that during my visit to Holland, I would not career around. Instead, I would avail myself of the theological library at Utrecht, catch up with my reading, and spend time with the Lord in prayer.

I bowed my head there and then, and prayed fervently that the Lord would give me the staying power to adhere to my resolutions.

31
Gaining Spiritual Insights

September 1854 – February 1855

When I arrived in Utrecht in early September, I was still so weak and incapable of the least exertion that I felt compelled to consult a well-known physician there. I was particularly worried about the pains in my arms and hands. I found that even an hour's lively conversation or earnest study would result in pain in these regions.

It came as no surprise when his prognosis was exactly the same as that of the London doctor. He likewise advised a cold-water cure, this time at Boppard on the Rhine. He was also adamant that I should stay in Europe over winter.

Because I knew I'd find the cold water trying, especially during a German autumn, I decided to boost my spirits by visiting Professors Krafft and Bleek in Bonn on my way to Boppard. John and I had met them while on a walking tour in Germany during our student years.

As it turned out, my visit to Professor Krafft proved most interesting. When I enquired about the advisability of obtaining German professors for our Theological Seminary, his interest was such that he immediately sprang into action to search in his clutter of files for the list of Reformed ministers and professors serving in Germany.

We spent an age poring over the list and making pencil crosses against men who didn't match my orthodox requirements. In the end, we could only find one whom Krafft could unreservedly recommend. Once more, this brought home to me the necessity of choosing a professor from amongst our own pastors at the Cape.

It was also in Bonn that I came across a work by Johann Tobias Beck in the university bookshop that fired my interest. It was titled *Umriss der Biblischen Seelenlehre (Outlines of Biblical Psychology)*. In it, Beck questioned the dichotomous view of man, where the soul and spirit are interpreted as being synonymous in the Bible. He then went on to propose a trichotomous view that distinguished between body, soul and spirit. To my surprise, he argued that the trichotomous view had been the orthodox interpretation in the first three centuries, and that the two-fold division had only come into prominence with St. Augustine. He also postulated that Augustine's two-fold view was based on the Greek dichotomy of matter and spirit.

While the theology was interesting, I wondered whether it really mattered. What were the implications of believing that the soul and spirit were synonymous, as against the three-fold distinction of body, soul and spirit? That was what I wanted to know. And as Beck's book had initially been published in 1843, with several later editions, I assumed that he was still alive. And if so, I planned to pay him a visit after my cold-water cure.

It was while visiting the plump and squinting Professor Bleek the following day that I learnt that Beck was Professor of Theology at Tübingen University. I was also interested to discover that Bleek considered Beck to be an excellent preacher and one of the few orthodox professors left in Germany. He nevertheless questioned his trichotomous view of man as well as his pietistic leanings.

After leaving Professor Bleek, I made my way to the university library where I requested a map of Germany. The helpful librarian pointed out Tübingen on the River Neckar, a major tributary of the Rhine. He suggested that I could easily get there by barge from Boppard, passing though Heidelberg, Heilbronn and Stuttgart on the way. I didn't hesitate to make a decision. In fact, I couldn't think of a more relaxing way to take in the delightful autumn scenery for which the Rhine and Neckar Rivers were known. Yes, to Tübingen I would go.

I found a seat at one of the library tables and hastily wrote a short note to Professor Beck. I introduced myself, explaining that I was from the Cape, and that I sought an interview to discuss his book. I intimated the dates I was likely to be in Tübingen, and followed this up by asking him to leave a reply with the faculty clerk. Not for a minute did I doubt that he wouldn't see me. I knew from experience that an introduction saying I was from the Cape always secured a warm welcome and opened every professorial door to me.

When I arrived in Tübingen several weeks later, I was feeling both physically and spiritually refreshed. As I disembarked from the barge, the vista that met my eyes made me feel that I was stepping into the Reformation era of the sixteenth century. The picturesque multi-storied homes and narrow cobbled streets were reminiscent of that era, even more so than Amsterdam. My spirits soared as I joined a throng of boisterous students who kindly pointed the way to a lodging house reserved for visitors passing through town.

On the following day, I was thrilled to discover that Professor Beck was available to see me that afternoon. When I entered his office several hours later, I had to stop myself from chuckling. There before me was the spitting image of *Sinterklaas*, a character beloved by the Dutch, and who was based upon Saint Nicholas, the Greek bishop of Myra who had lived in the third century.

While browsing in a bookshop in Utrecht, I'd purchased a children's book for my brother Georgie titled *St. Nikolaas en zijn knecht* (Saint Nicholas and his servant). And as I shook hands with Professor Beck, I couldn't help thinking that the illustration of St. Nikolaas in that book must have been based on this man standing there before me. The white hair and cotton-wool-like beard were exactly the same. Even his facial features were similar, although Beck's cheeks were a little plumper.

After a brief conversation about my ministry in the Orange Free State, we got down to discussing the query uppermost in my mind. Fortunately he had decided early in the piece that it was best to conduct our discussions in Dutch, seeing that his competency in that language was better than my German.

"What I'd like to know, Professor Beck, is this: What are the implications for my walk with the Lord if I believe in the three-fold view of man as against the two-fold view where the spirit and soul are regarded as synonymous?"

"For me, young man, the three-fold distinction is vital because it clearly explains what is happening within our hidden parts when we grow spiritually. We can liken it to the courts of the Temple. The body represents the outer court and the external life. The soul represents the inner life of the mind, feeling, will, and consciousness, and is essentially the man. In a born-again Christian, this can be likened to the Holy Place. The renewed spirit nature, on the other hand, is deeper than the soul, and is linked to the Holy Spirit in the Holy of Holies. The soul now has a choice. It can either follow after the desires of the flesh, or it can be governed by the Holy Spirit through daily communion with God."

Beck fell silent to give me the opportunity to take this in and to pose another question.

"So what happens in your schema when someone becomes a Christian?"

"Ah, now we are getting to the crux of the matter. In Ezekiel, God says, '*I will put a new spirit within you.*' By that He means that our own spirit is to be renewed and quickened by the Holy Spirit. Then He follows this up by saying, '*I will put My Spirit within you.*'"

"True, but do you think this happens simultaneously or successively?"

"From God's side the twofold gift is simultaneous because the Holy Spirit cannot be divided. But for the believer, much depends on how the Word is preached and whether the indwelling of the Holy Spirit is distinctly proclaimed. If it is not, then I'm afraid the Holy Spirit as an indwelling presence remains a mystery."

I felt I needed to repeat what he had just said to clarify it in my mind. "Let me just go back to your three-fold distinction for a moment, Professor Beck. What you are saying is that the soul is essentially the man, and that it finds itself between the body and the spirit. It can either follow after the body and the world, on the one hand, or it can follow the promptings of the Holy Spirit speaking through its renewed spirit, on the other."

"Quite right, *Meneer* Murray. The soul is therefore in a position to choose between the voice of God, speaking to the spirit, or the voice of the world, speaking through the senses."

"So where do you think the Holy Spirit resides?"

"Well, Scripture says, '*That which is born of the Spirit is spirit*'—John 3:6. It also says, '*The Spirit Himself bears witness with our spirit that we are the children of God*'—Romans 8:16. In other words, our spirit is the renewed spirit that the Holy Spirit gives when we are born again. At the same time, He comes to dwell within our spirit, but can nevertheless be distinguished from it."

I nodded to show that I agreed.

Beck continued: "This is what John Calvin calls the mystical union with God. It is similar to grafting a branch onto a vine. It is only a structural union. From this point on, the sap has to flow through the branch. In other words, the union now needs to become vital. In a similar way, we have to become filled with the Spirit. Through daily fellowship with God, we have to give the Holy Spirit time to penetrate every part of our being. And the more time we spend with the Lord, the more sanctified we'll become. We cannot strive to become sanctified, *Meneer* Murray. It is a gift of God. We have to surrender our lives to let Him do it."

This was the part I'd never fully understood—in theory yes, but not through personal experience. I leant forward, knowing that this was my golden opportunity to speak to this man of God about my own struggles. I lifted my eyes to meet his.

"My father has been telling me since the beginning of my ministry that I should allow the Spirit to accompany my preaching. But I've never fully understood that concept."

"It seems that you have yet to learn the great things you are entitled to as a Christian, *Meneer* Murray. Christ has done it all, and you cannot add a single thing to His finished work. All you can do is walk by faith and appropriate what He is offering you."

I donned a skeptical expression to indicate my lack of comprehension.

"See here, *Meneer* Murray, although you are complete in the Lord, you still have to grow spiritually. The new birth is like a seed planted in the earth. It is whole, but now it has to grow to maturity. And what will ensure that? The best conditions for growth, of course. And in a similar way, we have to place ourselves under the conditions most favorable for growth. If we try to do so by effort, we will fail. God has to do it."

He sighed heavily, his bottom lip quivering as he did so. "I'm afraid I don't have time to go into more detail. So I will point you to some authors who have found the secret to sanctification by faith. The first is the Puritan Walter Marshall who wrote *The Gospel Mystery of Sanctification* in 1692. He has much to say about squeezing holiness out of the efforts of the flesh."

I stooped down to grab my notebook from my shoulder bag. I had a feeling he was about to give me a long reading list.

"The second writer," he continued, "is one of the great Fathers of the church and my hero of the faith. He is St. Bernard of Clairvaux."

I looked up puzzled. "But he was a monk living in a cloister who was trying to gain sanctification for personal spiritual gain."

"Bah, *Meneer* Murray! Your ignorance is showing. He was the most active of monks and a Spirit-filled preacher. It is recorded that when he preached at the University of Paris, more than half the students there gave their lives to the Lord. As a result they left for the cloisters."

He paused, while tipping his head from side to side. "Well, that is what you did in the Middle Ages when you wanted to follow the Lord. If I remember correctly, St. Bernard lived between 1090 and 1153."

The look on my face must have shown my skepticism, because Beck continued to sing his praises.

"It's a historical fact that he drew thousands into the cloisters through his preaching. It is said that when he came to town, mothers hid their sons, and wives tried to stop their husbands from going to hear him preach. He was also sent as an envoy to negotiate peace between warring rulers as well as to handle disputes between Papal hopefuls. And when one of his monks became Pope, he didn't hesitate to send him a letter describing how he should conduct himself. Luther later sent the same letter to the Pope of his day. We can therefore justly say that Bernard of Clairvaux was *the* Father and leader of Christendom during the first half of the twelfth century."

"That may be so, Professor Beck, but the fact still remains that he was a monk of an erring Church."

Beck rolled his eyes and blew out an audible sigh. "Let me tell you a little secret about the cloisters of that time. Later they were different, but not then. Besides the early works of the great Fathers, they essentially had one text, and one text only: the Holy Scriptures. And they knew whole screeds of it off by heart."

I realized that I couldn't voice an opinion because I knew next to nothing about the history of the Church around that time. Even the works of the early Fathers were a mystery to me. So I waited for Beck to continue.

"By the way," he said, "even John Calvin considered Bernard to be the last of the Patristic Fathers. As such, he belongs to Christendom as a whole. And look how many times Calvin quotes him over the years. If I'm not mistaken, it's forty-one times. But more to the point, he also quotes him in relation to justification by faith alone."

I vaguely remembered something of the kind, but before I could gather my thoughts, he was leaning forward and pointing a forefinger at me.

"And another thing," he said, "there is evidence to suggest that Luther learnt about justification by grace through faith alone via an old priest who pointed him to the works of Bernard."

I couldn't help smirking at the thought that I was like a fish he was trying to reel in. I laid my pencil along the fold of my notebook and waited for the next barrage of words.

"And while I'm on this topic," he continued, "let's for a moment look at the Dutch Reformed theologians and pastors of that wonderful seventeenth century movement in the Netherlands known as the *Nadere Reformatie*. As you may know, it coincided with the Puritan movement in England, and overlapped with German pietism here. But let's focus on the Dutch Reformed movement for a moment."

He halted in mid thought and raised a questioning brow. "Help me out here *Meneer* Murray. I've always wanted to know how the English translate *Nadere Reformatie*. There doesn't seem to be a direct translation, does there?"

I racked my brain to recall what my father had named it. "I think the Puritans called it the Dutch Further Reformation. But my father prefers to call it the Dutch Continuing Reformation."

"Equally good," said Beck, leaning back in his chair and looking more relaxed. "He's probably based it on the favorite saying of the members of this movement: '*Ecclesia semper reformada quia reformata est*' (The Church Reformed should continuously be reforming)."

"I suspect so. My father particularly held Herman Witsius in high regard, and made me promise to read his book on the Covenants. It was the second book I ever read at Utrecht."

Beck looked into the distance as if viewing a scene from another age. "Ah, Witsius, one of the great theological professors at Utrecht. And a lover of St. Bernard, I might add. Do you know offhand when he was appointed to the Theological Academy there?"

"Around 1680," I said, feeling relieved that I could remember that much. At least Beck wouldn't consider me a complete ignoramus.

"Now listen carefully, *Meneer* Murray. When you return to Utrecht, read his book *Practicale Godgeleerdheid* (Practical Godliness). In it he tells us how to focus on being admitted into the precincts of the Heavenly Academy, where we shall be instructed by seeing and tasting the secret manna when we draw nigh to God."

"The Heavenly Academy?"

"It's a term used by the mystic Puritan Francis Rous. What on earth did they teach you at Utrecht?"

"I'm afraid my professors poured scorn on the adherents of the Continuing Reformation, so we tended to avoid their works."

"Well, now is the time to make up for that, *Meneer* Murray. Herman Witsius also devised a motto that is well worth embracing. It says: *In necessariis unitatem custodiant, in non necessariis libertatem, in utrisque prudentiam et charitatem* (In essentials unity, in non-essentials liberty, in both wisdom and love)."

He waited for me to scribble the motto down, repeating it again for my benefit before continuing.

"Witsius was a mystic, yet Reformed through and through. What he did—what all of them did, including theologians like Gisbertus Voetius and preachers like Jodocus van Lodenstein and Wilhelmus à Brakel, as well as forty other representatives of this movement—was to integrate the spirituality of the great Fathers of the Church within the bounds of their Reformed theology. So when you read the great works of the Fathers, that is what you also need to do."

Beck was taking far too much for granted, I thought. I hadn't given any indication that I was interested in following in the path of the Continuing Reformation. Yet here he was, forever trying to reel me in.

"A quick question for you, *Meneer* Murray. Have you read the works of Jodocus van Lodenstein?"

"I know my father has. He particularly admires his hymns, and has included them in a hymnal for the congregations at the Cape."

"How splendid! But it's *you* I'm interested in, not your father. Have you read any of his works?"

I shook my head.

"Did you know that he was very critical of the Reformation and called it a deformation? You see, for him it hadn't achieved its true goal of fostering self-denial and sanctification."

"Sounds an interesting man."

"And a member of the Utrecht Circle within the Continuing Reformation, no less. And whose works did he draw upon? None other than those of Bernard of Clairvaux. And like Bernard, he wanted members of his congregation to enter into the inner sanctuary of the Holy of Holies, which he called the inner chamber of God's love. It would be there, he said, that they would experience an intimate communion with God. And it would be there that they would be emptied of self and filled with Christ. And it would be there that they would be equipped with the power to serve."

Like all good preachers, he paused for effect. I suspected that he sensed my growing interest in wanting to know more about being filled with the Spirit. I decided to be candid about my lack of experience in this regard.

"To be honest, Professor Beck, I know nothing by experience of what Lodenstein is speaking of here. What you have just described has triggered my interest in his writings. I'll make a point of reading his works when I get back to Utrecht."

"Quite so. But I also think you need to go back to the source that opened up the Scriptures to him. You see, he learnt a great deal about the inner chamber and the love that God bestows on the believer there from Bernard's eighty-six sermons on the Song of Solomon."

"Eighty-six!"

"Ah, *Meneer* Murray, there's a great treat in store for you when you read the works of that sweet-as-honey preacher. He's a wonderful exegete of Scripture whom Luther says causes the Spirit to flow from the text. After all, it was Bernard who wrote that 'Christ died for our sins and rose from the dead for our justification.'"

"Where did he write that, Professor Beck?"

"In his treatise *On Loving God*, section seven, following."

He waited for me to write this reference down, then continued.

"What I like best about Bernard is his sense of humor. In his tract on the *Steps of Humility and Pride,* he takes St. Benedict's ladder of humility and reconfigures it so that the steps leading up the ladder describe our progress in humility, and the steps leading down, our descent into self and pride. He was also honest enough to admit that he was always coming down the ladder by falling into pride because of his light-headedness and stupidity. But then he goes on to correct himself as follows: 'Did I say *come* down? *Crash down*, would be more like it.'"

Beck had accompanied the words 'crash down' with a slight bow from the waist and a twinkle in his eye.

"I have to admit I have the same problem, Professor Beck. Like Bernard implies, you don't just descend the ladder of pride one rung at a time, you usually crash down because you are focusing on self instead of Jesus."

Beck heaved a sigh. "Don't I know it, *Meneer* Murray. Nevertheless, Bernard says that we can ascend the ladder of humility, not by our own efforts, but by depending upon God's grace to do it for us. Our task is to let the life of Jesus infiltrate our whole being so that His life can caste out self and pride in a natural way. Walter Marshall discovered this secret as well."

"I think I'm beginning to like this Bernard of Clairvaux."

"In that case, *Meneer* Murray, why don't you tootle across to the Catholic faculty. All Bernard's works are there—in Latin, of course. But as you were at Utrecht not so long ago, your competency in that language should still be good. The Utrecht library should also hold most of his works."

He had finally reeled me in. I observed his smile of satisfaction as he stood to indicate that the interview was over. After laying a hand on my shoulder and raising the other in blessing, he prayed for my spiritual growth and a safe return to the Cape.

His parting words to me were: "Make a point of reading the early Church Fathers. See what they have to say about the three-fold division of body, soul and spirit. Discern for yourself how easily the way of sanctification fits into that model. For me, at least, it helps explain why the flesh is always there to niggle us to the very end."

I left his office with an inner conviction that I should regard his advice as guidance for my spiritual growth and wellbeing. And so began my exploration of the writings of the early Fathers, particularly those of Bernard of Clairvaux. As I dipped into his works that very afternoon, I felt certain they would open up the Scriptures to me and shine a light on the world of the Spirit, just as they had done for the theologians and pastors of the *Nadere Reformatie.* And like them, I would take the pearls from these works and incorporate them into my Reformed theology.[12]

32
Joyful Days at Herschel

March–June 1855

I sailed from England on 9 March and arrived back in Cape Town on Thursday, 31 May. The sea air plus the fine weather between the Tropics of Cancer and Capricorn made for an enjoyable and restful voyage. By the time we sailed into Cape Town harbor, I was feeling relaxed and well.

Just before arriving, I penned a letter to my consistory explaining the need to remain in Cape Town for an extra few weeks in order to meet the new Governor, Sir George Grey. I went on to explain that I intended to negotiate funds for a combined teachers' college and senior school for boys. In the same letter, I also indicated my pleasure on hearing the news that the British Government had paid out a sum of £50 000[13] to compensate the new Orange Free State for Britain's hasty withdrawal. I added, by way of a reminder, that I hoped Dr. Fraser's and my efforts had made a small contribution to this payout.

Shortly after our ship docked, I took a cab into town to post the wad of letters I had written aboard ship. I then made my way to Uncle William's abode in Kloof Street, where I spent the next few days catching up with family and friends. With these commitments behind me, I was now ready to visit Howson Rutherfoord at his offices on Tuesday morning.

Fortunately, I was able to get a lift into town with Dr. Abraham Faure. He hadn't changed a bit since I'd first met him after returning from Utrecht in 1848. His white, bushy eyebrows were still a wonder to behold, as were his sideburns and full beard. The only difference I noted was that he had put on weight and was now sporting a protruding paunch.

During our short drive into town, I described my plans for a teachers' college-cum-school.

"If you can persuade the Governor to fund this venture," he said, "it'll be a great coup for the new Orange Free State. Besides the South African College here in Cape Town, it will be the only other college in the country."

"I'm well aware of that, Dr. Faure. That's why I need to speak to the Governor about it face to face."

"Hmm," he said, "you are certainly setting your sights high. I just hope your powers of persuasion are up to the task."

"Thankfully I have a powerful supporter in Mr. Howson Rutherfoord, a member of the Legislative Council. I met him while in London."

Faure arched a surprised brow. "Well you certainly move in exalted circles. Rutherfoord's a good man and knows his way around the political scene. He's also a member of our Commercial Exchange, and was its chairman a few years back. It might also interest you to know that he's just been appointed to the council of the South African College."

"My goodness, Dr. Faure. You certainly have your finger on the pulse of what's happening in town."

He waved a hand to dismiss my statement. "*Ach*, I only know all this because my daughter, Geertruide, is a friend of his two daughters Emma and Ellen. She used to visit them regularly when they lived in Green Point. I've since heard that he's bought the Herschel Estate in Claremont. Quite impressive, I believe."

"He appears to be an impressive man all round, Dr. Faure."

"By the way, Andrew, I hope you have written to advise your consistory that you'll be staying on in Cape Town."

"You'll be pleased to know that I posted my letter to them as soon as I landed. I didn't want them to hear of my arrival from another source."

"Good thinking. I'll write to them as well, saying that I approve of your plans. And if Rutherfoord invites you to spend time at his estate—which he's bound to do—you can let me know on Sunday how matters are progressing. And that reminds me, you'd better spend the weekends with your Uncle Stegmann so that you can show your face at church, otherwise tongues will wag."

When we arrived at the back entrance to the *Groote Kerk*, I parted company with Abraham Faure, and made my way to 3 Burg Street with a spring in my step. As Faure had surmised, Rutherfoord extended an open invitation to spend time at his estate, expressing the desire to acquaint himself with all matters related to the Orange Free State.

"There's a well-appointed cottage just behind my home," he said, "so you'll be able to come and go as you please. The omnibus, which I sometimes catch, passes our home at 9.00 and 10.00 a.m. each weekday morning, and leaves Cape Town at 4.00 and 5.00 p.m. each afternoon. At the moment, my friend, Mr. Beauchamp, from Bombay is staying at the cottage. So another occupant there will prove no burden."

I readily agreed, and promised to meet him back at his offices the following day at 2.00 p.m., as arranged. He was apparently keen for me to meet his family over afternoon tea, and to show me around the estate before sunset.

When we drove up the avenue of oaks leading to his home the next day, I knew why he had insisted on my seeing it in daylight. From my seat in his Cape Cart, I was able to catch a glimpse of an imposing two-storey home set against the wooded lower slopes of Table Mountain. The scene was made even more memorable by a cascade of autumn leaves fluttering down on us as we drove past.

As the house came fully into view, I noticed that it had been built in the Cape Dutch style, with a central gable in front, and one to match around the side. But unlike the classical Cape Dutch homes in-and-around the town of Stellenbosch, where the front *stoeps* were open to the elements, here the *stoep* was under cover, and extended from the front of the building half-way around the side. Besides being framed by Table Mountain at its rear, the house was beautifully set off by a large expanse of lawn at the front, and two enormous oaks that flanked the front steps.

After feasting my eyes on this scene, I turned to Rutherfoord and said, "I'm reticent to say how impressed I am with your home, because I fear it would be an understatement. It looks enormous. How many rooms are there?"

"Eleven on the ground floor and five bedrooms upstairs. But before I invite you to look around, let's first deposit your luggage in the guest cottage."

As we drove up the side path toward the rear of the house, I noticed an extensive array of outbuildings. Behind them was a well-established orchard as well as a vineyard.

"How much land comes with the home?" I asked.

"About nine acres all up. Fortunately there's a spring that the former owner utilized to lay on water and indoor sanitation throughout the house. We are also blessed to have a picturesque stream in the woods nearby. It's just off the main avenue. Emma has taken charge of that section of the estate and has been developing a water garden there with an ornamental pond. She also plans to have a rustic bridge built over it. I'm sure she'll be delighted to show it to you after tea."

I made a mental note to ask her to do just that. It would hopefully give me the opportunity to speak with her alone.

After being shown around the cottage, we proceeded to the front entrance of the main house, where a female servant opened the door to us. She was followed by a beaming Mrs. Rutherfoord, who extended a warm welcome to me.

"Please make yourself at home, Mr. Murray, and consider yourself one of the family. Everyone is looking forward to all the tales you have to tell."

Being able to observe her without coat and bonnet, I realized that she was slim and willowy in physique, with fair hair and blue eyes that matched those of her daughter, Ellen. Emma, by contrast, had deep brown eyes, which I had since come to realize, matched those of her father's.

When I had first met Mrs. Rutherfoord at Surrey Chapel, she had conveyed the impression of an English lady very much in charge of those around her. I now noticed a softer, more motherly side, which I instinctively warmed to. She also struck me as an outgoing woman who could take the lead in any social enterprise.

Rutherfoord excused himself, leaving me in the capable hands of his wife. From the parlor, she led the way through a large, formal lounge into an interleading room with folding doors that she referred to as the drawing room. The first thing I noticed upon entering was the afternoon sun streaming through the windows. The room was further enhanced by a view out onto the rose garden.

I was also struck by the length of the room. It was divided into two distinct sections by a large piano that had been placed strategically off-center in the middle, thus creating a pathway by which one could pass from one side of the room to the other.

On closer inspection, I realized that this room had once been two on account of the inside wall housing two fireplaces. On the near end was a low table set for tea, with an eclectic array of chairs and side tables surrounding it. And judging from the sewing baskets below several side tables, it also appeared to be utilized for close needlework.

On the far side of the room, facing the fireplace, were a few stylish couches with high-backed easy chairs interspersed between. It was obviously a homely spot for conversation and reading.

"We basically live in here," said Mrs. Rutherfoord, interrupting my appraisal of the room. "And because it faces due north, we get the full benefit of the sun in winter, and virtually none during the heat of summer."

She paused to favor me with a broad smile, before turning to face a middle-aged man who had been viewing the rose garden from one of the windows.

"Let me introduce you to our dear friend Mr. Beauchamp from Bombay. He was on his way back to England, when he decided to stay over to enjoy the sunny Cape for a while."

My eyes came to rest on a stocky man with receding hair and unremarkable features. But what he lacked in looks, he certainly made up for in dress. He was beautifully attired in bone-colored pants with matching frockcoat that was set off by a maroon-patterned breast coat and bow tie.

Beauchamp extended a hand with a listless grip. "Pleased to meet you, Mr. Murray. From what Rutherfoord tells me, you are serving the Dutch Reformed Church in the wilds of Africa."

"Just so, Mr. Beauchamp."

"I should imagine that it must be a strain working amongst those uncivilized Boers?"

"Uncivilized! By what measure do you judge, Mr. Beauchamp? They are uneducated, for sure, but uncivilized—certainly not. They are honest, God-fearing people who do not abscond, like the British, in a dishonorable fashion at the slightest inconvenience. But to answer your question. I find the work most fulfilling."

Beauchamp looked confused and began to splutter a reply. Mrs. Rutherfoord gave him a warning look, then hastily snatched the handle of the little tea bell nearby and rang it vigorously.

"Where are those girls? They should have been here by now. I do apologize for our disorganized household, Mr. Murray."

Realizing that she was still standing, and so were we, she hastily sat down and beckoned to us to do the same.

I studied Beauchamp sitting across from me. Judging from his manner and dress, he seemed to be a high-society gentleman of some means. Nevertheless, he struck me as a bit of a fop, lacking in both discernment and mental vigor. It would not have surprised me if he had left India on account of the heat or some other situation not to his liking. If this were the case, my retort would have hit home, even embarrassed him in front of Mrs. Rutherfoord. I decided he was not up to the usual repartee or educated discussion that was customary amongst gentlemen of his class. I therefore decided to temper my retorts in future.

I offered him a smile in an attempt to clear the air between us, but his pokerfaced response made me realize that I had just made an enemy. Fortunately, the maid arrived with our tea, followed by Lucy and a breathless Ellen. Lucy looked very pretty in a blue pinafore frock, while Ellen was dressed in deep maroon that highlighted her fair complexion and sleek blond hair.

"I'm afraid Emma snagged her dress in the woods," said Ellen, "So she's asked me to say that she would be down shortly."

"No need," said a flushed Emma, entering the room. "I had no idea it was so late." Turning to me she said, "I sincerely apologize for not being here to welcome you, Mr. Murray."

I stood to greet both her and her sisters. "Not at all, Miss Rutherfoord. I believe your father and I arrived earlier than expected."

I didn't want to stare, but she looked a picture in her ivory dress with brown trimmings. I noticed that her hairstyle matched that of Queen Victoria's. It was parted in the center and rolled stylishly at the back. The only difference was that Emma favored wearing a series of little kiss-curls at the front. They both softened her face and added to her allure.

"By the way," she said, still addressing me, "Papa asked me to apologize on his behalf for missing tea. He has a few things to discuss with the workers as well as with Joseph, his driver. He said to tell you that he'll see you at dinner this evening."

I greeted this news with relief because it would probably allow me more time alone with Emma. I sensed that it might also have been the real reason for Rutherfoord's absence. So I felt that a short explanation was due.

"We spoke at length in the cart coming here, so I'm pleased your father has been able to take this opportunity to catch up with other matters."

"He also made a splendid suggestion, Mr. Murray. Apparently you'll be free the whole of tomorrow, so he thought it would be an ideal opportunity to go out riding with Ellen and me. There's a most picturesque ride between Constantia and Muizenberg that skirts along the farms. I hope this plan meets with your approval?"

"It sounds delightful. But do you have enough horses for the cart as well as for three riders—perhaps even four if Mr. Beauchamp would like to join us."

"You can count me out," said Beauchamp. "I'm not feeling too well."

"I'll opt out as well," Ellen said. "Emma is the horsy person in this family. And unfortunately, Papa won't let her go riding unless Joseph is available, or she has a male companion. So you'll be doing Emma a great favor by escorting her on her rides."

At this point, Mrs. Rutherfoord butted in." To answer your question about the horses, Mr. Murray, my husband will probably take the omnibus to work tomorrow. He often does."

"Even Judge Bell takes the omnibus these days," Ellen said. "I overheard him complaining to Sir George Grey the other Sunday that his salary was not adequate enough to make it possible for him to send his sons to university in England as well as travel to work in a carriage every day."

"I think he was trying to make a point about the lack of educational opportunities here at the Cape, Ellen," said Emma. "I also heard him say that if he had to make drastic economies for the education of his sons, what hope was there for deserving youths from poorer households."

It struck me that if the Rutherfoords moved in the same circles as the Governor, then the chances of my obtaining funding for my college project had just risen considerably. It also seemed that Judge Bell had been making a similar request for Cape Town.

"Do you know Sir George socially, then?" I asked.

"Well, sought of," Emma said. "He attends Claremont Church like we do. But it wouldn't be considered proper to speak to him unless he spoke to us first."

"But Emma," said Lucy, "He spoke to you for ages at Mordaunt's birthday party."

"It was just chit-chat," Emma said. "Nothing more."

"Hardly," said Ellen. "He asked us lots of questions, and wanted to know all about our trip to England."

"Let me enlighten you, Mr. Murray," said Mrs. Rutherfoord. "My girls, here, were asked by Mrs. Boyle, the wife of Sir George's aide-de-camp, to arrange a birthday party for her four-year-old son, Mordaunt. And because it was approaching Christmas, my clever girls thought they'd introduce the idea of a Christmas tree to the Cape. While we were in England, we'd seen a few decorated ones—still a novelty there by the way—so they decided to try the idea out at the birthday party."

"I also helped," Lucy said, brimming with pride. "We fixed tapers, sugar plums, and flowers to the tree, and everyone said '*ahhh!*' when we opened the door to the dining room to let them in."

"But Lucy," said Ellen, "it wasn't only the tree they were admiring, it was also Emma's beautiful flower arrangements around the room." Turning to me she said, "Sir George and Lady Grey told us that it was the first time they'd seen cut flowers in a vase. Lady Grey was particularly taken by the idea."

I glanced around the room and noticed some lovely wild-flower arrangements. I turned to Emma and said, "So you're the one who's arranged the flowers in this room. The variety is astounding. Come to think of it, I never came across cut flower arrangements in England, Holland, or Germany while I was there."

"You were in Germany!" exclaimed Emma, her eyes lighting up with excitement. "So you must speak German?"

"Conversational German only, I'm afraid. But I also read it, of course."

"How splendid! I'll be able to practice my German on you. I'm taking conversation lessons at the moment as well as studying *Lieder* and German poetry. I'm most taken by the poetry. In addition to them being both romantic as well as heart-wrenching at times, they depict great depth of insight into the human condition."

I noted a roll of the eyes from Ellen, an amused look from Mr. Beauchamp, and a rather stricken one from Mrs. Rutherfoord, who hastily laid her cake fork down despite it containing a bite-size piece of cake.

"Tell me, Mr. Murray, what took you to Germany?"

"Well, to cut a long story short, I contracted malaria while on a tour through the Transvaal in 1849. Unfortunately, it undermined my constitution in a serious way. So on the advice of a good physician in Holland, I undertook a cold-water cure in Boppard on the Rhine."

It was the briefest of answers that I hoped would suffice. In fact, I was pleased that the question had arisen early in my stay, because if I were to court Emma, the Rutherfoords needed to be aware of my health problems.

"And did the cold-water cure prove helpful?" asked Mrs. Rutherfoord, her expression a picture of genuine concern.

"I'm certain it did. But I still need to take great care of my health in order to preserve the progress I've gained."

"Well, you've come to the right place, Mr. Murray. Please regard this home and its beautiful surrounds as an extension of your time for rest and relaxation. Stay as long as you please. It would be far better for your health to be out here than in claustrophobic Cape Town."

"You are most generous, Mrs. Rutherfoord. I'm inclined to accept your kind offer."

I noted that everyone else was beaming with delight, all except Beauchamp, who looked positively out of sorts.

As teatime was drawing to a close, and Lucy and Ellen had already hauled out their sewing baskets, I was about to suggest that Emma take me on a tour of the grounds, when Mrs. Rutherfoord beat me to it.

"It's such a beautiful afternoon, Emma. Why don't you show Mr. Murray that lovely rock pool you've designed. I'm sure he will enjoy the stroll."

"An excellent idea," I said. "But I wouldn't want to keep you from your sewing, Miss Rutherfoord."

"Not at all. I'd rather be going for a walk by far."

As soon as we were outside, she began to describe her passion for German poetry.

"I have to be careful not to mention it in company because I go on about it so. Mama becomes quite irritated when I do. But seeing that you've been to Germany and can speak the language, I was certain you wouldn't mind."

"And I don't, I assure you. So with this in mind, I'd like to make a special request: Would you be so kind as to sing a few *Lieder* this evening?"

She thought for a moment, then favored me with a cheeky grin. "You have no idea how shy I am about singing in public, Mr. Murray. So you've caught me out. Mama will undoubtedly laugh and say it's poetic justice. But if I do, will you please ask Ellen to accompany me in singing a few Italian duets. She draws the line at *Lieder*, you see. By the way, I don't suppose you sing?"

"Completely tone deaf, I'm afraid—or so my brother, John, tells me."

I then went on to relate how annoyed John had become when I had joined junior officer Angus Ross in singing the chorus: *Will Your Anchor Hold* when we had arrived back in Cape Town from Utrecht in 1848. I even described how unruly my hair had become after washing it in sea water, and how John had described it as 'a floating bunch of kelp.'"

She loved the story, and giggled uncontrollably at John's description. The ice was well and truly broken, so that by the time we reached the path that led off from the main avenue into the woods, our conversation was flowing freely. It was as if we had known each other for ages. We chatted about this and that and everything in between. When we finally reached the rock pool, we had just embarked on the topic of books.

"I suppose most of your reading is of a theological nature, Mr. Murray?"

"I'm afraid so. While I was in Utrecht, my aim was to catch up on all the reading I hadn't had time for while a student. But what about you? Have you read any good devotional works lately?"

"To be honest, the only one that comes to mind is the *Inner Man* by Winslow. I thought it rather good. But other than that, they've all been of a secular nature." She heaved a little sigh, then said, "We'll just have to be contented with discussing whatever comes to mind."

She led the way to the bench overlooking the pond, and indicated that I should follow. I had barely joined her there when she said, "Oh yes, there was a book that Mama read to us just before we left for England. It was such a best-seller there that it even reached the Cape. But I'm sure it wouldn't be the type of book you would choose to read. It was the *Life of Madame Guyon*."

I broke into a mischievous smile. Bulls eye, I thought.

Noticing my playful expression, she said, "You've read it, haven't you? Mama used to read it to us at a pretty spot during our walks in the mornings. But there was a great deal I didn't understand. Now I have you to explain it to me."

I uttered a wry chuckle. "What an amazing coincidence. My sister, Maria, and I used to read it on our morning walks as well. We even used to take a picnic basket and an old bedspread with us to sit on."

Her eyes sparkled as they looked into mine. "Perhaps we can read select portions of Madame Guyon's autobiography again, especially the sections I didn't understand. Then you can explain them to me. What do you think?"

"It will be my pleasure."

33
My Meeting with Sir George Grey

June 1855

Emma and I had got off to a flying start, and by the end of the week it was clear that I needed to place my interest in Emma on an official footing. As Rutherfoord had managed to organize an interview with Sir George Grey on Friday morning, I broached the topic while we were driving into town. As I had hoped, he didn't hesitate to express his pleasure at my interest in Emma. He'd also added that Mrs. Rutherfoord was bound to do the same. I was naturally overjoyed with this positive response.

My spirits were still soaring when I entered Sir George Grey's office. And if Grey was surprised by my over exuberance, I was certainly surprised by his youthful looks. He was a slim and athletic-looking man in his early forties. His most prominent feature was his drooping moustache that descended well below his bottom lip and was perfectly aligned in length on both sides. Following closely behind was his unruly-looking hair that bunched to one side at the top. Unlike Governor Cathcart, who had treated Fraser and myself in an offhanded fashion, Grey was warm and willing to give me a hearing. I'm afraid I hardly gave him the opportunity to get a word in edgeways.

"What the Orange Free State desperately needs now, Sir George, is a college that will not only instruct senior-school boys, but also train young men for the teaching profession. It will also need to house at least thirty boarders. In my opinion, the best way forward is for the Trust Deeds to stipulate that the Presbytery of the Dutch Reformed Church should act as board of management."

I noticed Grey's lips twitch when I pronounced the last requirement, but I decided not to be put off. Before he could say a word, I plunged ahead. "My vision for this college, sir, is that it be bilingual, with both English and Dutch as mediums of instruction. This is crucial to the success of the college. You see, if it were single-medium only, it would founder on the rocks of opposition from the other language group."

"Hmm, a novel experiment, to be sure, Mr. Murray. And one that I'll follow with great interest."

"We'll name it Grey College in acknowledgement of your generous donation. It will be a memorial to you in years to come."

I halted there, realizing that I may have overstepped the mark. He'd been listening while sitting with his elbows on the table and his chin resting on his hands. He now sat upright, his eyes lifting to meet mine. They were crinkled round the edges and dancing with mirth.

"Well, I suppose the name does have a certain ring to it. Anything else you wish to bring to my attention about this college idea of yours?"

Encouraged by his interest, I decided I had nothing to lose. "I'd be most obliged if the plans could be designed by a Cape Town architect. It will help avoid the usual bickering that goes on when people want their ideas incorporated into the design."

"Yes, I can certainly help out there. The architects will need to know your budget of course."

He took up his pen and began to write, speaking while he did so. "I'll donate £1500 towards your college, Mr. Murray. As it happens, I have a meeting with our architects on Monday morning. So if you can be here to see them directly afterwards, you could let them know your requirements. Just let my clerk, Mr. Boyle, know."

I was still in the throes of thanking him, when he made another suggestion. "Come to think of it, please make an appointment with Boyle to go through the draft of the Trust Deeds next week. You might also like to meet with the architects again to view the rough plans."

Grey rose from his desk, and with a twinkle in his eye said, "Anything else?"

I knew I would be overplaying my hand with a further request, but decided that nothing ventured was nothing gained. So mirroring Grey's mirthful approach, I said, "As a matter of fact, sir, we will need a good principal."

Grey accepted my request with good humor. Then turning to Rutherfoord, he said, "These Scottish Boers love to chance their arms, don't they?"

He was about to usher us to the door, when he changed his mind and started to flip through his diary. "If you don't mind, Mr. Murray, I would like to sound you out about the Boers in the Orange Free State. What if I make an appointment to see you again in two weeks' time? We'll make it for Thursday, 10 o'clock sharp."

I naturally agreed, counting it an honor to be asked. It also struck me that this interview would enable me to spend an extra two weeks in Cape Town. Furthermore, I was fairly certain that Rutherfoord would invite me to remain at Herschel for the duration of that period.

Blessing upon blessing was coming my way. I was indeed a fortunate man. Not only would I be given extra time to get to know Emma, but I would also be able to return to Bloemfontein bearing a gift of a school building.

What I hadn't bargained upon was the opposition I'd be facing from Beauchamp and Ellen.

34

Opposition

Weeks Two and Three at Herschel

I noted a distinct cooling in Ellen's attitude towards me when I arrived back at Herschel after spending the weekend and most of Monday in town. I was helping myself to breakfast at the sideboard on Tuesday morning, when Ellen sidled up beside me to do the same.

In an undertone that only I could hear, she said, "I don't understand Emma's ridiculous notion of wanting to become a missionary. She was born and bred to be a lady and not to slave away in some far-flung part of Africa."

She then turned tail and went to sit opposite Beauchamp, with whom she exchanged a meaningful glance. It was obvious that he had put her up to it. But little did the two realize that Ellen's remark would have the opposite effect. Because I now knew what Emma was thinking, it encouraged me to pursue my courtship with renewed vigor.

Each day after that, I prayed that nothing Ellen nor Beauchamp would say behind my back would cause a wedge to come between Emma and me. I consoled myself with the thought that Emma was spirited enough to counter their arguments with reasoned replies of her own.

While I was ever conscious of their opposition, it was not until my third week at Herschel that it flared into open hostility. It happened on Wednesday afternoon when Mrs. Rutherfoord and Lucy were absent from afternoon tea on account of dress fittings for Lucy.

I entered the drawing room in high spirits. My meetings with Boyle and the architects had gone well, and I was therefore looking forward to being handed the Trust Deeds and note for £1500 from the Cape Treasury the next morning. During the past two weeks, I had been careful not to discuss the content of my meetings with the rest of the family. The reason was that Rutherfoord had warned me that Ellen was unable to keep a secret, and would probably let my negotiations with Grey slip before matters were finalized.

But now that I had read the draft agreement, and was satisfied with the design concept for the building, I could explain what my meetings at the Government offices had been all about. This I proceeded to do with a little more self-satisfaction and swagger than I had intended. But instead of receiving congratulatory comments from Beauchamp and Ellen, it afforded them the golden opportunity to put a dampener on my educational vision for the Orange Free State.

"But Mr. Murray," said Beauchamp, "what are these people supposed to do with a decent education? How are they supposed to use it out there in the bundoo. It will be lost on them. If you ask me, your concept is a waste of time and money."

"Well, Sir George doesn't seem to think so," I shot back.

"I wouldn't be surprised if he does, but feels that his gift might help placate the feelings of the English settlers who are still smarting over the abandonment."

He spooned some sugar into his tea, then looking my way with a condescending smirk, said, "But mark you, I'm one of those who think the British have done the right thing by de-annexing the Sovereignty. I'm all for pulling out if one can see the writing on the wall and can't make headway with a rough and ignorant population."

I couldn't believe that he'd just made a statement that would enable me to trump him. Keeping my tone even, I said, "But Mr. Beauchamp, they wouldn't be ignorant if they were given access to a decent education, now would they?"

Quick off the mark, Ellen came to his defense by saying, "Even you have to admit, Mr. Murray, that the situation in the Orange Free State is potentially dangerous. And if the British couldn't control Moshesh with over 2000 troops, what hope is there for a Boer administration?"

Emma straightened her back and looked disapprovingly at Ellen. "That's not quite true, Ellen, and you know it. The British lost the Battle of Berea because Cathcart was arrogant and didn't plan his battle strategy well. Papa made a point of telling us about it."

"That may be so, Emma, but it's dangerous out there, and the terrain is rough. Remember what Gertrude told us about it."

"But that was four years ago. In any case, she was describing the conditions in Natal while attending her brother Hendrik's induction."

"So? Nothing much has changed since then. And the travel conditions are bound to be similar."

Ellen turned to address me, her cheeks aflame from her altercation with Emma. "The Gertrude to whom I was referring, Mr. Murray, is Dr. Faure's daughter. Oh, I forgot. You know her by her Dutch name GGG---, GGG---

Ellen had grasped her neck in dramatic fashion while trying to pronounce the Dutch guttural "g" which the English despair of doing. On any other occasion I would have laughed out loud, but not on this one. I was too aware that she was bent on jeopardizing my relationship with Emma.

With a shrug of her shoulders she said, "I'm afraid I can't pronounce that gargle "g" in Gertrude's Dutch name, Mr. Murray."

"It's Geertruide," said Emma, making a passable stab at it.

"Anyway, as I was saying," continued Ellen, "Gertrude told us that she actually cried while riding in an ox-wagon because it bounced around so much."

"Well, I'm sure I shan't," said Emma. "You have to realize, Ellen, that Gertrude is not the most stoic of persons."

As if to accentuate this point, Emma helped herself to a biscuit and bit off a sizable piece with a snap. Ellen, by contrast, took a sip of her tea and then placed her teacup daintily down. She then folded her hands in her lap ready to tell all. As my travels in an ox-wagon had always been in the company of men, I was intrigued to hear the female point of view.

"You know, Emma," she said, "stoic or not, Gertrude's description of the frontier Boer was rather telling. She was absolutely appalled at having to conduct conversations through a continual haze of pipe smoke. She even told us that the *Dominee* who had inducted Hendrik was a pipe smoker. In fact, she claimed that he was the worst of the lot. He'd even blown smoke into the face of Hendriks' little baby. And when she'd asked him to desist, he'd simply ignored her."

Knowing that Dirk van Velden had inducted Hendrik Faure, I sighed at the thought that the news of his chain smoking had even reached the Cape.

"And you should hear what Gertrude had to say about the ignorance of the people. You have never heard the like. They met this magistrate named Captain Struben in Ladysmith who told them about a group of Boers who were going to Jerusalem."[14]

Emma rolled her eyes in frustration and said, "I'm sure Mr. Murray doesn't want to hear such nonsense, Ellen."

"On the contrary, I'm very interested." I said. And I was, because Captain Struben was a magistrate in Natal. And presumably he was discussing the Boers of that area. I was therefore concerned to know if the movement had spread from the Marico District to there.

Ellen seemed taken aback at my keenness to hear this story, so turning my way, she said, "Apparently this Captain Struben was on an official tour through Natal when he happened to visit a farm where the Boer family was preparing their wagon for the journey to Jerusalem. They told him that a prophetess had told them to go."

My ears pricked up at the word prophetess. It seemed that an unscrupulous person was attempting to start up a similar movement to that of the Marico District to get their hands on the farm of those poor people.

"Well everything worked out well in the end because Captain Struben took a piece of charcoal and drew a map on their table to illustrate how far they had to travel. About six months later, he visited them again. Fortunately, by then, they had decided to remain. They told him that they had seen a similar map to his in an old Bible on a neighbor's farm that had convinced them that he had been telling the truth. They also told him that the prophetess had confessed to cheating and unscrupulous behavior on her deathbed."

"A happy ending indeed," I said. "Fortunately for them, they were able to receive a basic geography lesson that saved them from losing their farm."

I watched Ellen's upright posture sag. Although she was apt to say anything that came into her head, she was nevertheless quick-witted enough to know that she had painted herself into a corner.

"Tell me, Ellen," I said. "Why do you think these people were ignorant?"

She didn't look up, but gazed into her lap. "I suppose it was because they hadn't received any schooling."

"Exactly. And that is why it is so important for the Orange Free State to have a senior school and teachers' college."

"And Ellen," said Emma in a soothing tone, "That is the reason why Hendrik Faure and his wife, Marianna, decided to go to Natal. And it's obvious that Marianna must be a woman of gumption and resourcefulness to have left the comforts of home in Holland to accompany him there. It's such a pity that some English are lacking in these qualities."

She now turned to me and smiled. "Well, on that note, Mr. Murray, it's time for us to do a little pedestrianism. Come, let's go."

She was still giggling when we let ourselves out via the side door leading to the rose garden. While we had won that round, I couldn't help wondering what arguments awaited us during the next—for I was certain there would be one. What I didn't foresee, was that the next round would be between Emma and me.

35
An Untimely Request

Thursday, 21 June 1855

I swaggered into the office of Sir George Grey the next morning feeling on top of the world. Not only was my relationship with Emma blossoming, but I would now be presented with the Title Deeds and draft plans of Grey College.

"Please take a seat, Mr. Murray." Grey said. "This won't take long. I've requested this meeting to ask you to deliver a message to Mr. Boshoff, the President-elect of the Orange Free State. He is due to be sworn in sometime in August, so I can't very well send him an official missive. This one will be unofficial and therefore hush, hush, you understand."

I returned his smile with a nod, while hoping desperately that he wouldn't be expecting me to leave for Bloemfontein within the next few days. I needed at least another week to cement my relationship with Emma.

"Let me fill you in," Grey said. "According to my informants, matters have taken a dive in the Free State's relationship with Paramount Chief Moshesh since President Josias Hoffman was deposed."

Grey stared vacantly across the room, then heaved a sigh. "I feel sorry for the chap because to my mind he did the right thing. Moshesh asked for a keg of gunpowder to compensate him for firing off salutes when dignitaries paid a visit. And to retain peaceful relations with him, Hoffman agreed. But he didn't tell the *Volksraad* about it. So the end result was that he was forced to resign."

Because I'd already read about this in the Dutch newspapers, I let my thoughts wander to Grey's request for me to deliver his note to Boshoff. It had just put me in a state of agitation that I was doing my best to hide. For one thing, I couldn't just rush back to Bloemfontein. I'd need to have several stopovers on the way. I'd promised to visit Dirk van Velden in Ladismith, Maria and Jan in Prins Albert, my parents in Graaff-Reinet, John and Maria-Anna in Burghersdorp, and Andreas Louw in Fauresmith to congratulate him on his engagement to my sister Jemima. And the journey, along with adequate breaks, would take at least eight weeks, especially during the short days of winter. And it was no trumped-up excuse that I actually needed these breaks to retain the gains in health that I'd made while away.

Despite my disquiet, I forced myself to focus on what Grey was saying. "So now that Josias Hoffman is no longer president, Moshesh is instigating trouble on all fronts. In the Orange Free State, he is doing so through his sons, and in Natal, he is whipping up unrest amongst the Zulus. I won't have it, Mr. Murray. I simply won't have it!"

After a short silence during which I willed myself to look interested, he said, "I intend to go on tour to Natal in October. On my way there, I'd like to visit President Boshoff to show my support. This will send a clear message to Moshesh that the Cape and the Free State are allies.

He leant forward, his expression serious. "What I'd like you to do, Mr. Murray, is to convey my best wishes to Boshoff, report this conversation, and ask him to set aside 4 to 6 October for my visit. Tell him that I'd be most obliged if he could arrange a meeting with Moshesh."

Observing my frown, he said. "Do you perceive a problem with this plan, Mr. Murray?"

"It's just that I may not be back in Bloemfontein in time for Boshoff's induction, sir."

Grey donned his now familiar smirk. "I'm sure you will be because my informants tell me that Mr. Boshoff intends to have no one else but you swear him in. I believe the Presidential command is on its way."

Before I could catch myself, I blurted out, "But why me, sir? There are two other pastors who could do the honors."

Grey observed my consternation with open amusement. "I believe Mr. Boshoff was visiting Graaff-Reinet when he was asked to stand for President. He's also an elder of the Dutch Reformed Church and a friend of your father's. There's also the small matter of doing the right thing by you as chairman of the Presbytery beyond the Orange River. From what I hear, he was appalled by the way the Transvaal—or should I say the South African Republic—treated you in relation to Mr. Van der Hoff's induction. So seeing he wants to endorse you as the pre-eminent pastor of the Orange Free State, don't let him down."

Still smiling broadly, he rounded his desk and presented me with the draft plans of the college.

"As I'll now be visiting the Free State, I've decided that it would be an appropriate gesture if I presented Mr. Boshoff with the Trust Deeds along with my gift of £1500. Then as soon as the Presbytery has purchased the land, the architects can get to work on your design. It will also enable you, in consultation with others, to make any last minute adjustments."

This was yet another blow, for *I* had hoped to present Grey's generous gift to Boshoff myself.

He must have sensed my disappointment, because he tapped me lightly on the arm while flashing a broad smile. "Make the most of your last day at Herschel, Mr. Murray. I await the outcome in that quarter with great interest."

Grey's parting statement led me to focus on my predicament. I knew I wouldn't be able to rest until I'd discovered if Boshoff's summons had arrived from Bloemfontein. And the only person to whom this letter would have been sent was Dr. Abraham Faure.

Because I knew he would be putting the final touches to his sermon in his home office, there was nothing for it but to step it out to Faure Street where his parsonage was.

When I arrived at Faure's home, he appeared relieved to see me. And before I could even explain what my errand was about, he handed me an official looking letter.

"It came with a covering note," he said. "It's time to leave, Andrew. You've accomplished all you have set out to do here. So there's no excuse for extending your stay."

"That's not quite true, Dr. Faure. I still have one more objective left, and I desperately need another few days at Herschel to achieve it."

He gazed through his study window while considering my request. Although I'd never mentioned my courtship with Emma, I knew he had guessed as much.

He heaved a sigh, then shook his head to convey the hopelessness of my request. "Boshoff has set the swearing in date for

Monday, 27 August. As it is, you'll barely make it there in time if you're going to take several rest stops en route. And it's only fair to spend at least a week with your parents. No Andrew, you will have to leave Herschel tomorrow, and depart for Bloemfontein on Tuesday or Wednesday at the latest. You will also have to come to some understanding with Emma Rutherfoord before you leave. Have you thought of proposing?"

"It's too early for that Dr. Faure. The English are very conservative in these matters. We do not even address each other by our Christian names yet."

"You seem a bit slow to me."

After a short interval, his face lit up. "I have an idea. Ask Rutherfoord to tell his driver to drop your cases off at my office at the *Groote Kerk* tomorrow morning. I'll then take them to your Uncle Stegmann's place in the afternoon. That will leave you free to spend the day with Emma and to return to town by omnibus. I believe there's one that passes that way in the late afternoon. Geertruide always takes it when she visits Herschel."

Although it was a sound plan, my whole being was opposed to cutting short my stay. And the idea of proposing to Emma before our relationship was ready, seemed like an insurmountable hurdle.

"Well, there you are then," Faure said. "Now it's up to you. As I see it, you can't leave a lady dangling. So your only option is to propose."

36
Crashing down the Ladder of Self

22 June 1855

I left Faure knowing in my heart that Emma wasn't ready to take this mammoth step. And although she'd expressed the desire to become a missionary on a few occasions, I knew her desire to be a romantic one fashioned more by the idea of it rather than reality.

And if the truth be known, Ellen's attempts to make her face facts by describing the jolts of an ox-wagon ride and the ignorance of the Jerusalem Pilgrims were not really problematic areas for Emma. She was athletic and an excellent rider. She also loved to teach Sunday school and give Scripture classes at the local mission school.

More to the point, it was that she was used to being waited on hand and foot, not to speak of her deficiency in Dutch and lack of domestic skills. I also suspected that her close needlework was more of a decorative type, rather than stemming from the need to make her own bonnets and clothes.

Nevertheless, as far as I was concerned, these foreseen difficulties could always be overcome. What I wanted in a wife was a friend and confidante. And Emma fitted those requirements perfectly. Furthermore, I was in love with her.

At breakfast the next morning, I couldn't help noticing how lovely Emma looked. She was wearing a green frock with a waist-length jacket in brown that set off her brown eyes beautifully. Although I was far from the nervous type, I found myself taking in deep breaths to ease the tension within. I knew that Emma was attracted to me and felt at home in my company, but I'd never broached the topic of our feelings for one another. I had intended to do so the following week. But now I was forced to propose.

The first step was to get her out of the breakfast room. Despite the nip in the air, she was delighted at my suggestion that we should walk to the rock pool in the woods.

"I hope it won't be too cool for this time in the morning?" I said.

"Of course not," she countered. "I have a woolen shawl hanging on the hall stand for early morning walks."

That's what I loved about her. When it came to stiff walks and climbs up Lion's Head, nothing was too daunting for her. And even when a challenge proved too great for others, she was always game to try.

I watched her with renewed admiration as she swung a bone-colored shawl around her shoulders, and donned an old bonnet. "I must say, Miss Rutherfoord, you do look fetching."

Her eyes sparkled with mirth as they met mine. "Well now, Mr. Murray, I didn't take you for a tease."

As she led the way outside, I wanted to place my arm around her to keep her warm, but knew this would only be allowed once we were engaged. It struck me while walking down the avenue and then along the pathway into the woods that Emma was aware of my intentions. She appeared to be as nervous as I was.

At last we entered the picturesque clearing where the dappled light created sparkles off the rock pool and highlighted odd ferns and rocks around the edge. This was it, I thought. The sooner I could get my proposal over and done with, the sooner I could hold Emma in my arms. It was an intoxicating thought. In fact, the idea held such allure that it prodded me on to plunge headlong into unchartered waters in a clumsy fashion reminiscent of an over-eager youth, rather than a loving and refined gentleman of twenty-seven.

We had just sat down on the bench overlooking the pool, when I turned to Emma, not sure where to begin. "I simply love it here at Herschel, Miss Rutherfoord—Emma. As you can probably detect, my heart is heavy because I'm compelled by circumstances to leave you and this lovely home this afternoon."

"From what I understand, Mr. Murray, you are only leaving Herschel. So when do you actually depart for Bloemfontein?"

"On Tuesday or Wednesday. It will depend on when a Cape Cart with driver is available to take me as far as Graaff-Reinet. From there I'll make other arrangements."

I looked into her eyes, and knew she was egging me on. In fact, I persuaded myself that her "yes" was a foregone conclusion. So I put my diffidence aside and ploughed ahead.

"I've so appreciated being able to spend these weeks with you and your family. You have no idea how stimulating it's been. And although I love the work in Bloemfontein, and know that God has called me to it, I'll truly miss your companionship. What I need most in Bloemfontein is someone to share my dreams and schemes with. It's lonely out there,

Emma, even more so now that my friend, Mr. Stuart, is married. I've prayed so long and earnestly for a helpmate. And then I met you."

I paused to take her hand in mine. "Dearest Emma, would you do me the honor of becoming my wife?"

She snatched her hand away and clasped it with her free one as if she had received a sting. She then began to sway ever so slightly while gazing into her lap. When she looked up, her eyes were brimming with tears and her expression one of deep hurt. What had I said to elicit such a response, I thought.

"Emma, what on earth is the matter?"

She took a few shallow breaths and straightened her back. "You didn't ask me what *I* thought and what *my* feelings were. You just went on about your own needs and what you wanted, as if you were at a negotiating table, putting forward arguments to persuade me to marry you. I'm not that cabinet minister in London, Mr. Murray, nor Sir George Grey, for that matter. I'm me, Emma."

She paused to wipe her nose, her tears beginning to flow. "There was no heart in it—no expressions of love. There has to be heart, don't you see. I won't marry anyone who doesn't have heart."

She got up and dabbed her tears with her shawl. I was so taken aback by her negative response that I was glued to the spot. What could I say to make her change her mind?

"But I do love you Emma. I really do. Please listen! I'm afraid I blurted things out because I was agitated and nervous."

"That's the whole problem. Your proposal lacked refinement. Not only that, you didn't give a single thought to how I would be feeling. It was all about YOU. You were heartless, Mr. Murray."

She stood there looking down at me, the tears pouring down her cheeks, her hurt palpable. "You have to leave right now.

There's still time to catch the 10 o'clock omnibus. And don't say goodbye to Mama. I simply forbid it. It will make you late."

She lifted up her skirts and ran along the pathway. I followed behind, my anguish making itself felt in my stomach. "Emma . . . Please hear me out!"

But all that met my ears were her sobs. When I reached the avenue, Emma was already racing towards the house. And to my utter dismay, there was Beauchamp walking along the *stoep* on his way to breakfast. I saw him stop for a moment to take in the scene, then hastily avert his gaze while he proceeded to the front door.

While I knew he'd be exalting in my humiliation, I didn't care a hoot about him at that moment. It was Emma I was thinking of. Why, oh why, didn't I tell her that I loved her! What was wrong with me!

As I walked slowly up the avenue and watched her enter the house, her words kept reverberating in my ears: "It was all about YOU."

She was absolutely right, and like Maria, had detected my besetting sin of self-focus. My proposal had been all about me. Worse still, the two-edged sword of the Spirit—the Word of God—was now convicting my inner spirit. And the pain was unbearable.

When I walked down the avenue to catch the omnibus a little later, I was a broken man.[15]

37
Smarting from My Wound

June–July 1855

The next morning, I forced myself to pay a visit to Rutherfoord at his offices in the city. I felt I owed him an explanation, and Emma an apology. From Rutherfoord's response, it became clear that Emma had given her parents only the sketchiest of explanations. While he didn't say anything, it was clear by his frown that he seemed baffled by the whole affair.

I then made my way to the Parade, where I hired a Cape Cart with horses and a driver to take me as far as Graaff-Reinet. This done, I paid a visit to Dr. Faure. He only had to take one look at me to discern the outcome of my proposal. I hung my head in shame, letting him do the talking.

"All is not lost, Andrew. Regard it as a lover's tiff. You'll be far better prepared next time."

"There won't be a next time, Dr. Faure. And I doubt whether I'll even return for the Synod in October 1857."

Faure rolled his eyes, not caring if I saw his look of frustration or not. "Don't be ridiculous! Speak to your sister, Maria, about it. She will give you advice from a woman's perspective."

Fortunately, my stay with Dirk van Velden in Ladismith helped me focus on other matters besides my own short-comings. For the duration of my stay, we discussed the people and places I'd visited in Holland and Germany.

When I arrived in Prins Albert, the situation was completely different. Maria wanted to know every dot and tittle about my proposal. "What did she actually say, Andrew? If you don't tell me, I can't help you."

I was sitting with my elbows on my knees, my hands covering my face. Maria had drawn up a chair close to mine so that our knees were almost touching. I couldn't help thinking how well marriage suited her. She was wearing her favorite turquoise frock that highlighted her dark hair. It was still tightly drawn back into a bun at the nape of her neck. Despite the severity of the style, I had to admit that it suited both her features and her personality.

I was weighing up whether to tell her the whole story, knowing that she was bound to go off the deep end. But be that as it may, I needed to know her perspective on events. So I took the plunge: "Emma said that my proposal lacked heart and that it was all about me."

Peering through spread fingers, I noticed her raising a questioning brow before understanding dawned. "You didn't patter on about how lonely you were and how desperately you needed a wife, did you?"

I nodded.

"Oh Andrew! How could you! I can't believe you did that, especially after your self-focused response to my engagement. It was all about you then. And now you're telling me that your proposal was all about your needs as well. What were you thinking?"

She stood up and placed the palm of her hand against her

forehead, tapping it several times while she walked up and down, stopping only to berate me.

"Do you honestly think I sat at my desk, all dignified, when composing that reply to you? No! I filled my wastepaper basket with crumpled notes. You stole my happiness and delight at being engaged, Andrew. And now you've stolen the enchantment Emma should have felt by a loving proposal. And all because of self-focus. You'll have to put it right!"

While I was conscious that Maria was giving the flamenco performance of a lifetime for my benefit, I knew there was truth in what she said. And it hurt.

"Believe me, Andrew," she said. "Emma will be suffering at the moment. I hope you realize that your proposal will have been like a slap in the face."

"Well, what do you think I should do?"

Maria sat down on the chair opposite, her anger having abated as quickly as it had flared up. "The person who helped me most during my crisis was Ma. I'm sure it will be the same with Emma. You will have to write to Mrs. Rutherfoord to ask her permission to resume your courtship." She paused, then asked, "Do you think she likes you, Andrew?"

"I'm sure she does. She couldn't have been more considerate or caring."

"Well then, if her reply is positive, you already have a foot in the door. The next step is obviously to write to Emma. After apologizing, you'll have to touch on something that is of interest to her, something dear to her heart."

I groaned aloud. "It's German *Lieder* and poetry. And I'm afraid, I have little knowledge of either."

"Then acquire some. Surely there's an educated German missionary somewhere in the Orange Free State. Come to think of it, what about Mr. Wuras?"

"But he lives at Bethany on the Riet river, about sixty miles south of Bloemfontein."

Maria gave me a withering look. "Fine! Shelve that idea and Emma with it. You obviously don't think she's worth the effort. Well, do you or don't you?"

I raised my eyes to meet hers. "She's worth it alright."

The next day, Maria encouraged me to write to Mrs. Rutherfoord. As she pointed out, I couldn't afford to wait until I reached Bloemfontein. As it was, it would take a month before I received her reply. As I anticipated that Emma would get to read the letter, I was careful to include statements that described us as being kindred spirits and soul mates. I only hoped that Emma perceived it that way too.

But despite Maria's encouragement, Emma's rejection had triggered a marked decline in my health—so much so—that by the time I reached Graaff-Reinet, I was seriously ill.

My father took one look at me and declared that he would accompany me back to Bloemfontein. Unlike Maria, he was most solicitous. Putting an arm around my shoulder, he said, "While you are ill and in pain now, you must admit that Emma's rejection has taught you much about yourself and your spiritual walk. And although you've come crashing down the ladder of self and pride, as you so descriptively put it, the Lord can now help you climb the ladder of humility again."

There was a twinkle in his eye as he added, "I haven't read any of St. Bernard's works, but from what you've told me, he seems to depict our spiritual walk in a most realistic fashion. Calvin learnt much from his writings too, so I advise you to read more of him. The two of you obviously have a lot in common."

I let my father make all the arrangements for our journey to Bloemfontein. He also arranged for Andreas Louw to help out with the communion services prior to the swearing in ceremony. The plan was then for Andreas to accompany him back to Graaff-Reinet, where he would marry my sister Jemima a week later.

I marveled at the perfect timing that would allow my father to enjoy the company of his future son-in-law on his return journey. I also praised God for a father who was understanding enough to show his support when it really counted.

I can't recall much of my first week back in Bloemfontein, except that Mr. Stuart was the first to visit us. He'd also arranged for the parsonage to be cleaned and stocked with provisions. On the following day, he and my father went out with the purpose of buying me a horse and acquiring an African servant to look after it. They returned with an excellent horse and a wide-eyed, twelve-year old African boy named Cupid in tow.

Later that day we paid our respects to President-elect, Jacobus Boshoff, who was thrilled to see my father as well as make my acquaintance. As we were near neighbors, he would visit the parsonage whenever he felt the urge to get away during the days leading up to his swearing in. As expected, he found the message of support from Sir George Grey most reassuring.

I was also pleased to note that he had a good sense of humor. On hearing that the Presbytery would be acting as Board of Management of Grey College, he laughed heartily. "You've obviously learnt a thing or two about politics while you've been away, *Dominee*. I'm afraid, there are bound to be those on the *Volksraad* who will be against your bilingual concept. So it's just as well that it will be written into the Trust Deeds. In fact, any opposition from the pro-Dutch quarter will have to deal with me. You see, as a sitting elder of the church—albeit in Natal—I propose to be chairman of the Trustee Committee, with you and Elder Griesel as co-members."

Sick as I was, I couldn't help chuckling along with my father at this news. After all, what could I say when the President of the Orange Free State decided to pull rank as well as adopt my school project as his own?

38
Playing the Waiting Game

August 1855 – April 1856

A fter the departure of my father and Andreas Louw a few
days after the inauguration ceremony, it had taken me
a full two weeks to feel well enough to begin my ministry. And to my mind, there was no better way than by reading
my correspondence. As there was a substantial pile, I decided
to sort them on the dining room table.

Steeling myself to set aside the letters from family and friends,
I turned my attention to the correspondence from persons unknown to me—all except one, which I knew to be from Mrs.
Rutherfoord. Slitting the envelope open with feverish haste, I
scanned the contents quickly for what I wanted to know, then
returned to the beginning to savor every word.

Like the lady herself, her letter was warm and filled with
news. But although she intimated that she welcomed my interest in Emma, she also made it clear that it was up to Emma
whether she would accept my renewed proposal or not.

I said a prayer of thanks, and placed her letter to one side. At
least I had a foot in the door.

The next letter I opened was from Hendrik Faure in Pietermaritzburg. To my surprise, it was accompanied by an official

call to Ladysmith. While it lifted my spirits, I knew this call was not for me.

The third letter was an even greater surprise than the previous one. It was a joint invitation to Jan Neethling and me to pay a pastoral visit to Lijdenburg and Rustenburg. From its contents, it was clear that all was not well in relation to church affairs across the Vaal. Lijdenburg had given Van der Hoff his marching orders as their *consulent*, and had established their own little republic.

I sighed and read on. Elder Bothma of Lijdenburg, who seemed to have been the letter writer, also described a clash between Smellekamp and Van der Hoff at a people's assembly at Rustenburg. During their heated exchange, Smellekamp was reprimanded for interfering in local church affairs, and issued with a fine for £37 10s. This, in turn, led to two Dutch teachers handing in their resignations.[16]

I groaned as I read what had happened. Although Lijdenburg was now back in the fold, Elder Bothma still wanted the Presbytery to answer a series of questions related to the issues Van der Hoff had raised. He was particularly concerned over the question of a pastor having to swear allegiance to the Queen.

Apparently, Van der Hoff had told Lijdenburg that this was compulsory, while both Jan Neethling and I had said that it wasn't. I, for one, hadn't done so, nor Jan Neethling, nor Andreas Louw, nor Van Velden. I also knew that Van der Hoff hadn't done so either. So he'd lied. And if he could lie about one issue, perhaps he had also lied about Pretorius's request that I not induct him. Unfortunately, I would never know.

I'd have to call a Presbytery meeting as soon as possible, I thought. And while I doubted whether Van der Hoff would make an appearance, especially if he had lied and Elder Bothma were present, I'd invite him anyway.

I was still penciling in the dates of 18 and 19 October for the Presbytery session, when I heard a voice calling my name at the front door. There to my utter amazement stood a jovial-looking man wearing a typical Swiss hat with side feather.

I must have been staring at him open-mouthed, because he said, "No, you are not in Switzerland or Germany, *Dominee*, but fortunately—or unfortunately, as the case may be—in Bloemfontein. I'm Willem Krause, the new doctor."

Remembering my manners, I jumped up and pulled out a dining room chair, the words "*Lieder*" and "German poetry" flashing through my mind as I did so. I was also conscious of a profound peace enveloping me. And strange as it may sound, I just knew at that moment that all would be well between Emma and me.

"I've come to ask you a favor," he said, turning serious. "There are a number of Germans now in town, and we would like our children baptized. The problem is that we find it difficult to say yes to the question that demands that we bring our children up in the Reformed faith. I was therefore wondering, *Dominee*, if you would be prepared to baptize our children in a private room, and substitute the term Christian for Reformed?"

I thought back to my first two years in the Sovereignty when I had acted as Colonial Chaplain to Presbyterians, Anglicans, Methodists as well as four Dutch Reformed congregations. Conscious of the various denominations present in my English services, I had not hesitated to substitute Christian for Reformed during the baptismal services. So I couldn't see why I couldn't do the same for the Lutherans who spoke Dutch.

I smiled across at Krause, and said, "That shouldn't be a problem."

Krause's relief was palpable. "Then I take it that you wouldn't mind dispensing the Lord's Supper to us in a private room as well, *Dominee*?" You see, if we partake with the Dutch, it will be seen as a virtual confession of the Reformed faith."

Again, I couldn't foresee any problem, especially if I used the Reformed formulary. I'd simply leave it to the Lutherans to interpret the words as their consciences dictated.

Favoring Krause with another smile, I said, "In that case, I'll combine both services at the same time, Dr. Krause."

He thanked me profusely, then got up to go. It was now or never, I thought. I had to grasp this opportunity while it presented itself.

"Dr. Krause? Just before you go, I would like to ask *you* a favor."

"Of course, how rude of me. You've been ill, so you would like me to examine you?"

"Yes that too. But this request has nothing to do with my health. It has to do with German *Lieder* and poetry. You see, I'm hoping to court a young lady who's interested in these art forms. And I have to do so via correspondence."

He looked at me quizzically, then burst out laughing while slapping his thigh in delight. "You've asked the right person, *Dominee*. I love poetry, and so does my little wife. I'll teach you exactly what to say to win your young lady's heart. I'm quite an expert at it you know. After all, I was able to persuade my little wife to leave home and accompany me all the way to Africa."

In the weeks that followed, I became firm friends with Krause. And despite my resistance to becoming a poetry-sprouting Romeo, albeit in German, I was assured that young ladies of tender sensibilities loved to be wooed this way.[17]

Sir George Grey arrived to great fanfare on 4 October. At a private family reception given by Boshoff at which I was present, Grey presented us with the Title Deeds and promised gift of £1500 for the college. During the course of the evening, I again mentioned our desperate need for a good headmaster.

"Leave it with me, Mr. Murray," he said. "If there are no other projects requiring urgent funding, I'll give your request due consideration."

This, I'm proud to say, he did. In a promissory note to Boshoff just prior to his departure, he raised the amount to £4500. So not only would his gift cover the cost of the building, but also the ongoing salary of a headmaster from interest accrued.[18]

While the extra funds for my Grey College project had helped to boost my sense of wellbeing, the Presbytery meetings in Winburg on 18 and 19 October had just the opposite effect. As expected, Van der Hoff did not attend. What was particularly disturbing was his disapproval of Elder Bothma's attendance. In a protest note addressed to the Presbytery, he made it clear that it was against the law of the Transvaal for Bothma to be present.

"He's the one who should be censured," said Bothma. "It's his job to let the *Volksraad* know that it is not their business to oversee the consistories. But instead, he's acting as their agent by merging church affairs and politics in a way never countenanced in the Transvaal before. And because the consistories are now directly beholden to the *Krijgsraad* and *Volksraad*, they can no longer make their own decisions."

"The same thing happened with us," said Elder du Plessis from the small Republic of Utrecht in Zululand. "That's why we are now an independent republic. We had been incorporated into the Transvaal at our own request, but because of Van der Hoff's arrogance, we decided to join up with Lijdenburg instead. You see, earlier this year when Van der Hoff came to visit us, he wrote a directive saying that we would no longer be known as Utrecht, but Dordrecht. He also reminded us that it was against Transvaal law to associate with churches linked to the Synod. We were naturally shocked by his high-handed approach. So we let him know that we had no knowledge of a district named Dordrecht, and that he was no longer welcome as *consulent* in our congregation."

Turning to me, Bothma asked, "So how do we censure him, *Dominee*?"

"We don't, *Meneer* Bothma. He has chosen to break off relations with the Synod, so all we can do now is leave him and the Transvaal to God. I fear that his uncompromising stance and distortions of the truth will follow him to the grave. In the meantime, we'll arrange for a deputation to visit Lijdenburg next year. Fortunately Dr. Hendrik Faure, here, has agreed to be *consulent* of Utrecht."

Amidst heavy sighs, we bowed our heads and prayed for Van der Hoff.

Emma's reply to my letter arrived on Tuesday, 13 November. It was short and business-like, but I had expected nothing less. In it, she explained that I would have to return to the Cape to resume our relationship before she could answer my renewed proposal of marriage.

The fact that she had even written was enough to make me feel elated. In my reply to her the following day, I agreed to her stipulation, saying that I'd return as soon as I was able. Although I had May in mind, I was loath to stipulate a date until

I was certain that she was over her fit of pique and comfortable with the idea of becoming my wife.

Quite unexpectedly, the thirteenth turned out to be one of those days I'll never forget. My heart was singing in gratitude one moment, then drowning in sorrow the next. If it hadn't been for Emma's reply that would buoy me through my time of grieving, I might have succumbed to another bout of illness.

I was still busy with my pile of correspondence, when Dr. Krause made an appearance at the door. As it was open to let in the breeze, he called my name, then came in while fingering his hat in an uncharacteristic manner. I took one look at him, and knew that something was wrong.

"I have sad news for you, *Dominee*. Your friend, Charles Stuart, has just passed away."

He waited for me to digest the news.

"When? How? He's too young to die. He's only forty-seven."

"He died on the way to the Circuit Court at Fauresmith. He pulled in at *Meneer* Visser's farm this morning feeling unwell, and died there a few hours later. It seems he may have succumbed to a bout of that recurring tropical fever he suffers from."

I sat there stunned. I wanted to howl and throw the ink pot at the wall, but knew I had to stay strong for others. I'd have time to mourn later.

"Mrs. Stuart doesn't know yet," said Krause. "And being his closest friend, we thought you'd be the best person to tell her. In the meantime, can you suggest where we should lay his body? Fortunately, he's already been placed in a rough box that Visser hammered together."

"In the church," I said without hesitation. "That's where he deserves to lie. He placed the promised Government funds in the church account so that the building could be completed, and was subsequently sacked for doing so. It will be a great comfort to Emily to know that he is there. Let's do it now."

The next few hours, which were spent comforting Emily, planning the funeral, and composing what I'd say, helped me mourn his passing. And I knew that over the years when his memory came to mind, I'd recall his much loved phrase: "*The Lord is able to save to the uttermost, so why should we then despair.*"

As the months passed, I discerned an increasing warmth in Emma's letters. This prompted me to make arrangements to return to Cape Town on horseback during May. My plan was to change horses at regular intervals en route, and so shorten the time it would take to reach my destination.

I was fortunate enough to be able to embark upon this plan, because my "Herschel" suitcases were still at Uncle William's place at Craig Cottage. Uncle William—bless his heart—had insisted on taking them off the cart, declaring that it was already far too heavy with my trunk full of books.

"You'll be back next year, Andrew. I'm convinced of that. So leave them here. They contain your lay clothes that you'll never get to wear in Bloemfontein. Besides, not having to return to Cape Town with cases will allow you to travel on horseback, and so save time and money."

With his words still ringing in my ears, I made the necessary plans, including a request for him to purchase a Cape Cart that I could use on arrival.

My decision to go in May was endorsed when I received a letter from Emma in mid-April asking me to write an essay on the peculiar trials of missionary life. I knew for certain then that she was ready to replace her romantic notions of being a *Dominee's* wife with more realistic ones.

The only problem I could foresee was that she would only have four weeks to prepare for her wedding. Nevertheless, the alternative of having to wait another sixteen months before I returned to attend the 1857 Synod, was unthinkable.

39
Ellen Helps Out

31 May – 2 June 1856

I arrived back in Cape Town on Saturday, 31 May, and literally fell into bed at my uncle's place in Kloof Street. I had managed to cover the huge distance to Cape Town in just thirteen days, instead of the usual three weeks. To my amazement, my horseback journey had left me no worse for wear. Come Sunday morning, I was feeling refreshed and ready to go. But because I was without my black tail suit, which was a requirement to sit in the pews allocated to the elders at the *Groote Kerk*, I was forced to miss church. But I reasoned that a prolonged rest would do me good. To address the issue of acquiring a tail suit, I planned to visit Uncle William's tailor the next morning to have one made. It could then double as both my church and wedding attire.

On Monday morning, my aunt and uncle were on hand to wish me well as I harnessed my horse and stowed my "Herschel" suitcases between the box and front seats of the cart.

"Your shirts have all been fleshly laundered and your suits aired," said my aunt before pecking me on the cheek.

"Now remember, it's all about her," said my uncle with a twinkle in his eye.

I just smiled at each in turn, then flicked the reins. How different I felt from that fateful Friday a year before. For one thing, I was a much humbler man.

The oak avenue at Herschel was aflame with autumn leaves as I drove beneath its fluttering canopy around 11 o' clock that morning. As I knew the way to the guest cottage with its own wagon house and stables, I made my way directly there. This time I'd have the cottage to myself without having to endure Beauchamp's derogatory comments and haughty demeanor.

I had barely led the horse into the stable, when Ellen came running up on tiptoe, beckoning me to open the adjacent stall. Although I knew her to be twenty-one, or thereabouts, her actions were more like those of a young girl. What added to this impression was her floral day dress with its tiny blue flowers and frilled bodice. And as she was obviously not expecting visitors that morning, her sleek blond hair was loosely rolled in a net at the back.

"I've come to apologize for my unconscionable behavior while you were here, Mr. Murray. All I wanted was for Emma to be happy. But I see now that I was the one choosing for her, instead of letting her choose for herself. Both Mama and Lucy pointed that out to me after you left. So please forgive me and tell me we can be friends."

Before I could answer, she rushed on. "I've also come to have a serious chat with you about Emma. You see, she has refused to get her trousseau ready in case you didn't come and people started to talk. So she hasn't done a thing—not a single thing—about getting twelve dozen of everything ready."

"Twelve dozen of everything?"

"You know . . . tablecloths, napkins, bed linen, towels—that sort of thing."

Ellen paused, her blue eyes opening wide as she pondered this fact. I dismissed it as a gross exaggeration, but little did I know.

"She has also set her heart upon a summer wedding, arguing that you'll return for Christmas. But both Mama and Papa know you are unlikely to do so."

I nodded. "It's out of the question, I'm afraid."

"Frederic thought so too. He'll be on your side because he'd like to be here for the wedding. You see he's off to England early in July. And even though Mama will virtually be losing two children at the same time, she would like to please Frederic. But I'm afraid you will still need to help Emma see sense. She claims that it's always the bride who sets the date."

I hadn't foreseen this problem. But at least I'd have her parents as well as Frederic on side. And as Emma was one of the most thoughtful persons I knew, I hoped she would relent once she understood my circumstances. In any case, I had no intention of leaving without her.

My thoughts were cut short when Ellen said, "I know you think I'm a scatterbrain, but when it comes to these types of matters, I have my feet firmly on the ground, I can assure you."

"So where is Emma now?"

"She's reading a book at her rock pool—where else?"

"But wouldn't she have heard the cart arrive?"

"Yes, but she would have thought it was Mama returning with Miss Hollsworth, the dressmaker. They went to purchase material for Frederic's shirts. You see, Mama is at her wits' end because Emma has no practical skills. So she's come up with this idea that Emma and I should make a few shirts for Frederic before he sails for England. And Miss Hollsworth is supposed to give us a lesson on cutting out material after lunch. The thing is, if they arrive back in the next few minutes, then Emma will know it's either you or another visitor who's arrived. So she's bound to come rushing out to see who it is. So I'd better be quick."

In the short time we'd been speaking, Ellen had already conveyed a great deal of information. I decided that despite her penchant for the dramatic, I had better listen to what she had to say. As time was obviously of the essence, I invited her into the stall, while I fetched two veld stools that were last minute gifts from Uncle William.

Ellen eyed her stool with some misgiving, then sat down gingerly, her blue dress with its flounces ballooning around her like a huge pumpkin.

"So what else do you want to tell me, Ellen?"

She grasped her pinkie and said, "Number one: Take Emma back to the rock pool so that you're out of sight of prying eyes when you propose. Two: Propose on bended knee. She's expecting it and will be upset if you don't. Three: Make sure you give her an appropriate wedding gift—something personal, just for her."

I thought back to the tea set my father had bought my mother. It was her pride and joy, and sat on the sideboard, never to be used. She had seen it on the Cape Parade shortly after her engagement, and had mentioned it in my father's presence one evening. Without letting her know, he had gone to purchase it the next day, but had decided not to tell her until they were in Graaff-Reinet. She had thought it a wonderful surprise, and had treasured it ever since.

But judging from what Ellen had to say, I couldn't very well buy Emma a tea set. So what could I get her? Then it came to me. "Of course!" I said out loud.

Ellen, who had been pattering on about a friend of Frederic's who had given his bride an inappropriate gift, stopped mid-sentence. "I see you've already decided what it's to be. Do tell."

Keeping my voice light, I said, "None of your business, Ellen. What's number four?"

Not at all put out, she clutched her index finger to tick off the fourth point. "Assure her that she's there to help you in the ministry and not to cook or clean. You see, she's assured my sister Mary in India that she wouldn't have to do any housework or slave in the kitchen because she would be your co-worker in the ministry."

"Did you read that in her private letter, Ellen?"

"Well, how else was I to know what Emma was thinking? If she could tell Mary, I couldn't see why she couldn't tell me."

I stood up to show my disapproval. "I'm not sure I should be listening to this."

"Oh, but you must," she said, while struggling to rise from her low position on the stool. I helped her up and was about to usher her out the stable, when she barred my way.

"Mama is beside herself with worry, so she's giving you Mrs. Henly as a wedding present. She's one of the best cooks in Cape Town, and has agreed to work for you until you return to attend the Synod next year. Mama is also insisting that you sign a contract to ensure that there are always two servants to help Emma."

I thought of Cupid, and hoped he would count. And although I had misgivings about Ellen reading Emma's letters, I knew that being forewarned was forearmed.

"What else do I need to know, Ellen?"

"Well, if all else fails, stress that Frederic would like to attend the wedding. And if that doesn't work, mention Catherine Cloete. That will definitely do the trick."

"Who on earth is Catherine Cloete?"

"Believe me, she was the talk of the town a few years ago. Her fiancé, Capt. Shuckborough, left for India without taking her with him. He said he would be back on the *Mauritius*, but then let her know that he couldn't return for three years. She was in such a state . . ."

Ellen stopped abruptly, and turned her head towards the open stable door. "That's the cart. Oh drat! I haven't finished yet."

"You'd better run."

"No, hear me out first. This is the most important point of all. You see, the society gossipmongers said that Catherine should have gone with Capt. Shuckborough to India in the first place."

As soon as she was sure that the penny had dropped, she turned to go.

"Thank you Ellen. You'd better hurry now."

She scurried on tiptoe to the back entrance of the house, waving to me as she entered. I listened as the cart came to a halt before the front door, and waited until it had pulled off again. I slipped out of the stable and walked rapidly towards the avenue, hoping to reach the track before Emma emerged. But I was too late. There she was racing towards the house for all she was worth. She stopped when she saw me, and pointed back to the track, a broad smile lighting her face. She and I were obviously of the same mind.

I noticed that she was wearing the same green dress and waste jacket in brown that she had worn on that fateful day. Her brown hair was also styled in the same fashion with little kiss curls framing her face. It was as if all the delightful aspects of that day were the same as before, and that I'd been given the opportunity to expunge the negative and the unpleasant. I only hoped that her smile would still be there when I explained that she had only four weeks to prepare for her wedding.

40
My Second Try

2 June – 2 July 1856

After a lively exchange of greetings and a comment on how beautiful she looked, we ambled arm in arm to the rock pool with its lush ferns and picturesque bridge. She took her seat on the bench while I laid my handkerchief on the ground and proceeded to kneel.

"Not yet, Mr. Murray—I mean Andrew. Let's wait a few days to become reacquainted. That's all I ask."

I got up off my knee and went to sit beside her again. I spoke gently, being mindful that the information I was about to impart would not be to her liking.

"There's no time for that Emma. I have to return in a month's time, and I'm determined to take you with me. I love you dearly, you see, and wouldn't be able to cope a another sixteen months without you."

"Don't be silly," she said, "You're just pulling my leg."

"I'm afraid not. The next time I'll be in Cape Town is for the Synod sitting in October next year."

"But what about Christmas? You told me that you always got six weeks leave around that time."

"I've taken that leave now, don't you see. And it will amount to far more than six weeks if we factor in travel."

Her mouth fell open while she looked at me with pleading eyes. "Four weeks! FOUR WEEKS! It's impossible, Andrew! No girl can get ready for her wedding in four weeks."

She scrutinized my face to observe my response, but I was a different man from the one who had proposed before. And studying her keenly now, as she was me, I was sure her intuition told her so.

She turned to look at the little bridge across the rock pool and, as if speaking to herself, began to voice her objections. But the way she conveyed them sounded too pat—too rehearsed. It struck me that if Ellen were aware of her parents' thoughts regarding the wedding, Emma might be too.

"You see, I haven't got a thing for my trousseau ready yet. I didn't want to be like Catherine Cloete, who even had her wedding dress made in case her fiancé turned up from India unexpectedly. In the end, she had to wait three years before he came.

"So why didn't she go with him in the first place?"

Emma didn't answer, but hastily focused on the next objection. "You don't understand the predicament I'm in, Andrew. I have to get twelve dozen of everything ready."

"But who would know if you haven't done so? You could simply take the material for the tablecloths and napkins with you to sew in Bloemfontein."

She paused to think this through. "I suppose so. But besides that, Mr. Murray—I mean, Andrew—it's a most inconvenient time for the family because Frederic is preparing to move to England in early July."

"But wouldn't you want him to attend your wedding? I was hoping to ask him to be best man. I'm sure he'd be most disappointed if he were to miss it."

She lowered her eyes and nodded.

"And what will you tell your friends when they ask why you've decided to have such a long engagement? You can't very well say that it was because you had to finish your twelve dozen of everything—now can you?"

Emma covered her eyes with her hands and began to giggle. "I'd be the laughing stock of Cape Town."

Keeping my tone level, I said, "Seriously Emma, why don't we show Cape Town society how our type of situation should be tackled. We'll demonstrate by our four-week engagement exactly what Catherine Cloete and her fiancé should have done. It may also help other couples facing similar situations."

"That's a thought," she said looking at me again. "I definitely like it. In fact, I think it's brilliant. But a short engagement is not why I'm wavering, My problem is whether I'll be up to it. I don't want to undertake duties and responsibilities for which I might prove unequal. To tell you the truth, being a pastor's wife in Bloemfontein scares me, Andrew."

I put my arms around her and pressed her close. "Of course you'll be up to it. With your education and teaching background, you'll be more than equal to the task. In any case, you're looking at this challenge the wrong way. You have to make a decision, then say: 'With the Lord's help, I have every intention of meeting this challenge.' I'm sure that's what Frederic is saying to himself now, and what Marianna Faure said when she agreed to leave Holland to go to Natal with Hendrik."

Still holding her close, I rubbed her arm gently, giving her time to make her decision. "In any case," I added, "we will be facing the challenges of life together. And from where I'm sitting, I cannot see myself growing into the man I should be without you."

I knew she was ready, so I gently released her from my embrace. I placed my handkerchief once more on the ground, and knelt before her while clasping both her hands in mine. "My dearest Emma, I love you dearly and want to spend the rest of my life with you. I would love you to be my co-worker in the ministry—someone with whom I can discuss my dreams and schemes; someone with whom I can meet the challenges of life; and above all, someone with whom I can pray and walk the path that the Lord has set before us. Dearest Emma, will you consent to be my wife and marry me within four weeks?"

She withdrew a hand and wiped away a tear, smiling as she did so. "Of course I will."

I got up and held her close again, kissing first her hands, then her lips. I wanted to savor the moment and capture it forever in my memory. But then life intervened: The lunch gong went.

Emma rose off the bench looking panic-stricken. "Four weeks, Andrew! Just four weeks! I have to take my piano, my chest of drawers, and my little table. I hope all my things will fit into the wagon. And what about my wedding dress and those of the bridesmaids? We'll have to tell Miss Hollsworth straight away. There's not a minute to lose. She'll have to live in at Herschel for the whole month."

She grabbed my hand and tugged me along the track leading to the avenue.

"Emma wait! We have to set the date. It can't be later than a month because the wagon will be heavy and we'll need to travel slowly. We'll be riding in the Cape Cart, of course, but we won't be able to travel faster than the wagon."

Her face was glowing with excitement as she asked, "So what's the date today?

"June the second."

"So it will have to be July the second, then. Do you know what day that is?"

"A Wednesday."

"Perfect, So come on! We'll be late for lunch."

I tugged her gently back. "I'll have to ask your father first. It's the right thing to do."

Emma stopped to think. "I tell you what. We'll go into town this afternoon and take Miss Hollsworth with us. You can visit Papa at his offices, while Miss Hollsworth and I shop for materials. Mama will have to come too, of course."

I nodded, although it was on the tip of my tongue to protest. I so wanted to spend the afternoon alone with her.

"We have to run, Andrew. They only sound the gong when they think I haven't heard the bell. And now that Mama knows you are here, they'll all be sitting at table itching to know what has gone on between us, but not being able to say a word on account of Miss Hollsworth's presence."

When she noticed my downcast expression, she raised an amused brow. "I'm far more practical than you think, you know. One thing I'm really good at is planning events. So if you want me to marry you on 2 July, this is the way it has to be."

I heaved a loud sigh because I'd seen the same look on the faces of Maria and Jemima. Emma was in wedding mode.

To say it wasn't a rush, or even a merry-go-round, would be telling a lie. From my side, I had to purchase a wagon, a team of horses, hire suitable drivers, as well as see to the feed. The horses alone cost the princely sum of £140. But because good horses were in short supply in Bloemfontein, I knew I would be able to sell them easily, and perhaps even make a profit. This went for the wagon and Cape Cart as well.

While making all these arrangements, I bought Emma's wedding gift. It was a beautiful Dutch Bible with the Dutch hymnal at the back. The print was clear, the paper fine and trimmed with gold, and it was bound in high-quality calfskin. My hope was that it would last a lifetime.

The actual arrangements for the wedding proved quite simple. To cater for everyone, it was agreed my Uncle Stegmann, a Lutheran pastor, would conduct the service in English in the Dutch Reformed Church in Wynberg.

On the evening that I introduced Emma to his family, Emma kindly invited my fourteen year old cousin, Maggie, to be the fourth bridesmaid. This caused quite a flurry, as another dressmaker had to be hired.

Miss Hollsworth was now a permanent fixture at Herschel, and was being given every consideration. Besides making Emma's wedding dress and going-away outfit, she was also coordinating the clutch of dressmakers and milliners who had been especially hired to make the bridesmaids' dresses and bonnets. Apparently they had to be made to exact specifications.

Emma's first realization that she was actually leaving home came when I started to pack the wagon. She soon discovered that she had to drastically reduce what she intended to take. For one thing, one of the wickerwork benches, or *katels,* as they called it in Dutch, had to serve as Mrs. Henly's seat by day and bed by night when we travelled through the Karoo. So space in the wagon was limited, especially with Emma's piano there.

Thankfully, we'd be sleeping on the turned-down seats in the Cape Cart. It would be freezing in the mornings and rough going at times. But knowing Emma, she wouldn't want to be outdone by Marianna Faure, who reportedly took the ox-wagon and horse rides in her stride.

The wedding itself was a simple but elegant occasion, just as I dreamed it would be. Emma walked down the aisle on her father's arm looking radiant. She wore a plain white muslin dress with a waterfall of ruched flounces, or so Maggie described them later to me. Her attractive face was obscured by a veil that flowed from a wreath of flowers on the crown of her head. But once the veil had been lifted, there stood my Emma with her fetching little kiss curls dangling over her forehead.

I'm afraid I didn't notice the bridesmaids until much later. They also wore white, with white bonnets to match. Their silk shawls, however, added a splash of color. Two wore blue, and two, pink.[19]

After the service, which was at eleven, we returned to Herschel where we enjoyed a sumptuous lunch with close family and friends. Directly afterwards, we changed into our going-away clothes in readiness for the first stage of our journey to Stellenbosch, where my mother's family was expecting us.

The leave-taking of family and friends was a bitter-sweet moment for Emma. Everyone lined up on the *stoep* to bid us farewell, all except Mrs. Rutherfoord and Ellen, who were crying copious tears in the drawing room. The sight of their distress, made Emma shed a tear as well.

Putting on a brave face, she said, "Please don't cry, Mama. I'll write every week. And before you know it, I'll be back."

Thankfully, Emma didn't prolong the leave-taking. As the cart pulled off, her tears soon gave way to smiles. Our grand adventure had begun—me, with my soulmate at my side, she, determined to face the challenges that lay ahead.

Epilogue
Clairvaux, Wellington

July 1915

D r. Murray was still smiling to himself when I rose to place a few logs on the fire. I then proceeded to stoke the dying embers until the flames crackled and popped in harmony with his joyous mood. When I returned to my seat, he was back in the present moment.

Looking across at me, he said, "Emma turned out to be a wonderful wife you know, Johan."

"So I believe, Dr. Murray. But I can't help thinking that it must have been a daunting prospect for her to leave family and friends after such a short courtship. How long did it take her to adapt to Bloemfontein?"

"Not long at all. You see, for the first few months, she regarded the cultural and language challenges as a great adventure. And after the settling-in period was over, she found herself too busy with pastoral visits, letter-writing, gardening, and Dutch lessons to dwell on the life she had left behind in Cape Town. In fact, she soon realized that she was equal to any challenge."

While I pondered this fact, I couldn't help wondering whether there were any memorable upsets along the way. I decided to do a little prodding to discover more.

"Can you recall any specific challenges that *Mevrou* Murray found difficult to deal with during her first few months in Bloemfontein?"

He thought for a moment, then started to chuckle. "Oh yes, there were several. But one particular one stands out: It was knowing how to manage my sister Maria."

He paused for effect, knowing that at the mention of Maria my curiosity was bound to be aroused.

"At the time of our arrival in Bloemfontein, Maria happened to be keeping Jemima company in Fauresmith while Andreas and Jan were on tour in the Transvaal. So in her eagerness to help Emma settle in, she arrived in Bloemfontein only a few days after our own arrival. And within half an hour, she had broken every social rule in the book—that is from an English perspective. You can imagine my inward groan when she started to tell Emma how she should keep house and how important it was to learn to bake bread."

"Oh dear! So what happened next?"

"Well, during our pillow talk that night, a great deal of pacifying and scheming took place. I tried to make a game of it by thinking up ways of how Emma could manage Maria's enthusiasm for wanting to transform her into a good little housewife. Emma would then report back the next night, often giggling happily, while congratulating herself on the outcome. Thankfully, before Maria left, they were the best of friends."

I could tell that Dr. Murray was eager to end the interview. Nevertheless, I couldn't leave without posing a final question: "What about your spiritual walk, Dr. Murray? Did the lessons you learnt leading up to your marriage serve as a turning point?"

"Only important stepping stones, Johan. I'm afraid a great deal of water still had to flow under the bridge before I really understood what my spiritual walk with the Lord could be."

Perceiving my puzzled frown, he began to explain: "It was during the 1860s revival that I first experienced the almost palpable presence of the Lord each day. But then came the backlash from the Liberals who took the Synod to court. By then, I was moderator of the Synod, and due to my heavy workload, was beginning to strive in my own strength again. It was only during the early 1880s, when I was unable to preach for two years because of a serious throat complaint, that the Lord was able to use that trial to slow me down and teach me how to worship and pray."

Like everyone else, I was only aware of the bare bones of that story. So like a typical student, I thought a prod would encourage him to tell more.

"I believe God healed you in a miraculous way, Dr. Murray."

"That He did, Johan. But now you are jumping the gun. I'd like to leave that story for our next interview."

I reluctantly closed my notebook and placed it in my briefcase. As I did so, I was mindful of the privilege I'd been given of recording this godly man's struggles as well as the spiritual stepping stones that would lead him to enjoy a victorious Christian life. I just hoped I could do it justice.

If you enjoyed this book, and think it worth sharing, please take a moment to write a short reader's review on Amazon. It will go a long way in helping to make Andrew Murray's story known to a new generation who may be inspired to read his insightful books.

Free download of the booklet:

What Emma Thought

Would you like to learn Emma's side of this story?

If so, you can download this free accompanying booklet to *Andrew Murray Destined to Win* from my website at: http://www.onandrewmurray.com. It contains snippets from her letters to her sister in India. They also cover her first three months in Bloemfontein.

(NB This booklet is a spoiler, so please read *Andrew Murray Destined to Win* **first.)**

Notes

1. Some historians have suggested that Major Warden sent Andrew Murray to Potchefstroom to stop Andries Pretorius from entering the Sovereignty, but this is not the case. In a letter to his brother John, Andrew says, *"It will be very difficult to get horses, and I trust that my plans may be thwarted if it be not the Lord's will that I go"* Fortunately, the Lord did open the way via Adolph Coqui (Johannes du Plessis p. 130).

2. George McCall Theal, is the only historian who mentions that Charles Stuart misapplied funds. Andrew Murray doesn't mention it, nor does William W. Collins, whom we shall meet later in this story. As the Sovereignty was not paying its way at the time, the only way funds could magically have appeared in the church building account would have been if Stuart had placed them there. Around the same time, Hogge released the fund. Of note is the fact that Stuart was highly esteemed amongst the Boers after this event, so much so that a few years later the Volksraad employed him to manage the £50,000 in compensation they had received from the British Government.

3. Reading Madame Guyon was an important stepping stone in Andrew Murray's life. In 1914, when Andrew Murray was 85, he visited Bloemfontein by train. His daughter Annie recalls that on a drive around Bloemfontein by car, Murray pointed to a *kopje* (hillock) where he and Maria had read Madame Guyon. Years earlier, in a letter to his father on 26 May 1864, he wrote: *"I cannot say that I agree in everything with Upham and Madame Guyon. I approve of their books and recommend them, because I think they put our high privileges more clearly before us than is generally done, and thereby stir us to rise higher"* (Johannes du Plessis pp. 496 & 238.).

4. Paul Kruger tells us in his memoirs that he was made Field Cornet just prior to his departure for Sand River. Unfortunately, he doesn't record what occurred there. What we do know, however, is that he became very friendly with Andrew Murray after this event. During Andrew Murray's fourth tour of the Transvaal with Jan Neethling a short while later, Kruger accompanied them from Rustenburg to Potchefstroom (Du Plessis p.133). In 1864, when Andrew Murray returned to the Transvaal on a short visit in relation to missions, he stayed with Paul Kruger. Of particular interest is the fact that Kruger sold one of his farms to the Cape Synod so that they could establish a mission farm there.

5. The description of what occurred at Sand River is based on information supplied by the historians George McCall Theal, Robin Binckes, and H.J. Hofstede. With regard to Van der Kolff's escape, it appears that it could have been orchestrated. Unfortunately, it is not known whose horse just happened to be saddled and tied up near to where Van der Kolff was sitting. For all we know, it could have been Venter's. Although the planning scenes prior to Van der Kolff's escape is a figment of my imagination, it is more than likely that something of the kind would have taken place. Be that as it may, Andrew Murray would have been in the thick of it.

6. While the dates for Potgieter's invitation went ahead as described, and were duly linked to the services Andrew Murray was to take at Rustenburg, it appears that Andrew had a change of mind about conducting services with an undecided Potgieter present. So he made alternative arrangements, which will be described in a later chapter.

7. Andrew fell from his pedestal in Maria's eyes after his unwarranted response to her engagement. A few years later, she told another family member (still to be introduced in this novel) what had happened. This person, obviously referring to Andrew, writes: *"I think she (Maria) idolizes people, and then is so dreadfully disappointed if they fall short of her expectations"* (Joyce Murray, 1954 p. 25).Years later, when Maria was in her seventies, she was still going on about what had happened, declaring that God had chosen for her. She writes the following in the third person: *"Her love and admiration for her two eldest brothers were unbounded. For three months she was with her brother Andrew at Bloemfontein; but her promise to remain with him always was broken when she accepted the offer of marriage made by her brother's friend, the Rev. J. H. Neethling! The many happy years of married life that followed, showed that God had chosen for her"* (MN, p. 94).

8. Events leading up to the Battle of Berea, as well as the aftermath, were religiously recorded in many Australian and New Zealand newspapers. I was amazed to find a description of this battle in the *Littelton Times* (1853) in Haratua, New Zealand. This paper had copied it from the *Sydney Herald*, which had in turn copied it from the Cape Town Mail of 25 January. In the latter article, mention is made of the Boer Commando that had turned out *"to protect the border in the rear of the Governor's operations"*.

9. After Andrew had left Bloemfontein for Fauresmith, where he was due to conduct the usual set of services in relation to Holy Communion, Russell Clerk wrote the following to the Duke of Newcastle on 25 August, 1853: *"Mr. Murray, a clergyman of the Scottish Presbyterian Church here, is now out in the district actively engaged in denouncing the purposes*

of my mission" (Cory p. 97). Interestingly enough, the date of this missive was before the general meeting of delegates on 5 September. And as Russell Clerk had only been in Bloemfontein for a week, he would have not known much about the Griqua question, if anything at all. Needless to say, Andrew would have definitely discussed the issues related to the Griqua treaties with the Fauresmith congregation.

10. Johannes du Plessis states that it was Dr. John Phillip, Secretary of the London Missionary Society, who introduced Andrew to the Rutherfoord home in Cape Town on his return journey from Europe in 1855 (p. 168). The problem with this story—which was an educated guess on the part of Du Plessis—is that Dr. Philip had died in 1851 at Hankey, near Port Elizabeth. The true story, as told by Maria Murray Neethling, is that Andrew had met the Rutherfoords briefly while in England (MN, p. 80).

11. *Blonde* is a type of material that was often used to sew puffy sleeves and line bonnets.

12. Andrew would embrace Beck's trichotomous view of body, soul and spirit. You can find a description of Andrew's view in the *Indwelling Spirit*, p. 220 (first published as *The Spirit of Christ* (1888), and in Healing Secrets p. 38. With regard to Bernard of Clairvaux, Du Plessis tells us that he was *"a favorite historical character with Andrew Murray"* (Du Plessis p. 451). In a similar vein, Andrew's friend, Rev. Walter Searle, tells us that Professor Beck was *"a favorite author with Andrew Murray"* (Douglas p. 257).

13. This is the amount John Galbraith quotes.

14. The stories about Geertruide Faure and *Dominee* Van Velden's smoking, plus the Jerusalem Pilgrims in Natal, are told by Marianne Faure, the Dutch wife of Hendrik Faure, in her booklet: *My First African Excursion.*

15. According to Joyce Murray in her book: *In Mid-Victorian Cape Town*, Andrew proposed to Emma in the afternoon of 21 June, after she and her sisters had returned from preparing the decorations for Mordaunt's fifth birthday party, which would be attended by Sir George Grey. I purposely introduced the birthday party earlier in the story so that the description of the Christmas tree and Emma's cut flower arrangements could be described and discussed by the family. It allowed me to introduce the fact that the Rutherfoord's moved in the same circles as the Governor. I judged that this rearrangement of the information would also allow me to focus solely on Andrew's proposal without cluttering the telling beforehand with a non-essential side issue.

16. It appears, from what Elder Bothma had to say, that Van der Hoff had persuaded Lijdenburg to break off their connection with the Synod

by presenting them with false information. Van der Hoff had apparently said that the Cape Synod stood under the supervision of the British Government, and that it was compulsory for ministers of the Cape Church to swear allegiance to the Queen. He had also stated that the Cape ecclesiastic laws placed whites and blacks on an equal social footing. The slanging match between Van der Hoff and the Dutch envoy Smellekamp had come about because Smellekamp had wanted to call a pastor for Lijdenburg, but Van der Hoff had been against it on account that his stipend and travel costs had not been finalized by the combined Volksraad. At that stage only Potchefstroom and Rustenburg were probably contributing to his stipend. What Van der Hoff obviously wanted was for Lijdenburg and Zoutpansberg to contribute as well. If he remained their consulent, this requirement could be expected. But if they chose to remain with the Cape Synod and call their own pastors, then he would lose their respective contributions. So sadly, he was doing everything in his power to stop Lijdenburg from calling their own pastor.

To bypass Van der Hoff's opposition, Smellekamp wanted the issue discussed at a combined consistory and Volksraad meeting at Rustenburg in June 1854. At this meeting Smellekamp was accused of sweeping up trouble in the Transvaal, and was placed under censure for a year.

17. It would seem that Andrew did all in his power to woo Emma with romantic comments about German poetry. She writes the following about him in a letter: *"He is very romantic and German in his disposition. All sorts of things that in reading German poetry and plays I had put down to German mystery and romance, I find he fully sympathises in. I thought no one in this matter-of-fact age did; that it was only the philosophy of poets"* (Joyce Murray, 1953, p. 139).

18. While President Boshoff appears to be the one these days who is lauded for establishing Grey College, the whole idea came from Andrew Murray. It was also Andrew who asked for extra funds for a headmaster. In a letter to his brother John, Andrew tells him about his request. "Your idea with regard to getting a headmaster for our school is exactly what I have proposed to the Governor" (Du Plessis p. 167).

19. Fortunately, we have a lovely description of the wedding in a letter that Maggie Stegmann wrote to Kitty Murray in Graaff-Reinet. My description is based on her letter (Joyce Murray, 1953, pp. 152-153.

Glossary of Terms

Ach!: (*Ag* in Afrikaans): An interjection used by Dutch and Afrikaans speakers.

Afrikaner: Those who were born in South Africa and spoke Cape Dutch (Afrikaans today).

Boer: A farmer. Also used to denote those who spoke Dutch.

Boerbeskuit: A rusk used for dunking in coffee or tea.

Consistory: Church Council of elders and deacons. Also used to denote the vestry.

Consulent: A minister from a neighboring congregation who administered Holy Communion.

Dominee: The Dutch equivalent of Reverend in English.

Drostdy: Magistrate's court and administrative center. Could double as home of the landdrost.

Field Cornet: A civilian official with the authority of a military officer. In peacetime, he was responsible for maintaining law and order. It also denoted a military rank equivalent to a lieutenant.

Krijgsraad: War Council.

Groote Kerk: Great Church of the Dutch Reformed tradition situated at the top of Adderley Street, Cape Town.

Juffrou: Miss.

Holland: This name was always used to denote the *Netherlands* amongst Afrikaners during Andrew Murray's day.

Impi: Zulu regiment.

Inspan: To harness horses or yoke oxen in a team to a vehicle.

Katel: A bed or backless bench made of wood and wickerwork. There were usually two to a wagon.

Kleinbaas: Small or deputy boss. Used by servants to address sons in the family.

Koeksisters: A syrup-coated doughnut that is plaited.

Kopje (Dutch) / *Koppie* (Afrikaans): hillock.

Laager: A circle of wagons protecting an encampment.

Landdrost: Equivalent to a magistrate.

Liefie: Lovey.

Liefling: My love.

Melktert: South African milk tart.

Meneer: Mr.

Mevrou: Mrs.

Môre: Good morning.

Oom: Uncle. Also used as an honorific when addressing an older person.

Ouma: Grandma.

Oupa: Grandpa.

Outspan: To unharness horses or unyoke oxen from a vehicle.

Predikant: Minister.

The Resident: A British commanding officer of a territory.

Schoft: The distance travelled before horses or oxen were out-spanned. The duration was usually three hours, covering fifteen to eighteen miles for a horse-wagon, and nine to ten miles for an ox-wagon.

Stoep: Veranda.

Transgariep: The vast area of land across the Orange and Vaal Rivers.

Volksraad: People's council.

Bibliography

Badenhorst, W.T. *Ladismith `n Eeu Oud, 1851-1951: Gedenkskrif by die Eeufees van die Gemeente Ladismith.* Ladismith: Kerkraad, 1951.

Beck, J.T. *Outlines in Biblical Psychology.* Translated from the third Enlarged and Corrected German Edition. Edinburgh: T. and T. Clark, 1877.

Binckes, Robin. *The Great Trek Uncut: Escape From British Rule.* Pinetown, SA: 30° South Publishers, 2013.

Collins, WM. W. *Free Statia or Reminiscences of a Lifetime in the Orange Free State, South Africa from 1852 to End of 1875: 23 Years.* Bloemfontein: The Friend, 1907.

Cory, Geo E. *The Rise of South Africa: A History of the Origin of South African Colonisation and Its Development Towards the East From the Earliest Times to 1857.* Vol. VI, Chap. 1-6. Cape Town: Archives of the Union of South Africa, 1940.

Douglas, W.M. *Andrew Murray and His Message: One of God's Choice Saints.* Fort Washington: Christian Literature Crusade, 1926

Dreyer, A. *Die Kaapse Kerk en die Groot Trek: Amptelike en ander stukke versamel, van aantekeninge voorsien en uitgegee.* Kaapstad: Van de Sandt de Villiers, 1929.

—. *Die Voortrekkers en hul Kerk: Sketse Uit die Kerklike Geskiedenis van die Groot Trek.* Kaapstad: Nasionale Pers, 1932.

—. *Korte Levensschets van Ds. Andrew Murray, M.A., D.D. Predikant te Wellington.* Kaapstad: P & P Co., 1900.

Du Plessis, Johannes Christiaan. *The Life of Andrew Murray of South Africa.* London: Marshall Brothers, 1919.

Erasmus, H.J. "Land 'Jobbing' by British Officials in the Orange River Sovereignty, 1848-1854." *Fundamina* 17, no. 2 (2011): 56-69. http://bit.ly/1CU6rM3

Faure, Marianne. "My First African Excursion." *Natalia* 36-37 (2007). http://bit.ly/1frvAm3

Galbraith, John S. *Reluctant Empire: British Policy on the South African Frontier 1834-1854.* Berkeley: University of California Press, 1963.

Gerdener, G.B.A. *Ons Kerk in die Transgariep: Geskiedenis van die Ned. Geref. Kerke in Natal, Vrystaat en Transvaal.* Kaapstad: Suid-Afrikaanse Bybelvereeniging, 1934.

Giliomee, Hermann. *The Afrikaners: Bibliography of a People.* Charlottesville: University of Virginia Press, 2003.

Hofstede, H.J. Jr. *Geschiedenis van den Oranje Vrijstaat:* In Verband met *Eene Korte Geschiedenis der Aangrenzende Kolonien, Vooral der Kaapkolonie.* London: Bibliolife, 2014.

James, Nancy C. *The Complete Madame Guyon.* Massachusetts: Paraclete Press, 2011.

Keegan, Timothy. *Colonial South Africa and the Origins of the Racial Order.* Cape Town: David Philip Publishers, 1996.

Kruger, Paul. *The Memoirs of Paul Kruger Four Times President of the South African Republic: Told by Himself.* Toronto: George A. Morang, 1902.

M.N. [Maria Neethling]. *Unto Children's Children.* London: T.H. Hopkins & Son, ca. 1909.

Madame Jeanne Guyon. *Experiencing Union With God through Inner Prayer & The Way and Results of Union with God.* Revised in Modern English by Harold J. Chadwick. Orlando, FL.: Bridge-Logos, 1982.

—. *A Short Method of Prayer and Other Writings.* Massachusetts: Hendrickson, 2005.

Murray, Andrew. *The Indwelling Spirit.* (Previously titled: *The Spirit of Christ,* 1888). Minneapolis: Bethany House, 2006.

—. *Healing Secrets.* (Previously titled: *Divine Healing,* 1900). USA: Whittaker House, 1982.

Murray, Joyce. *Claremont Album.* Cape Town: A.A. Balkema, 1958.

Murray, Joyce, ed. *In Mid-Victorian Cape Town: Letters from Miss Rutherfoord*. Cape Town: A.A. Balkema, 1953.

—. *Young Mrs. Murray goes to Bloemfontein, 1856-1860: Letters.* Cape Town: A.A. Balkema, 1954.

Nel, Olea. *Andrew Murray Destined to Serve: A Biographical Novel.* Canberra: Clairvaux House, 2014.

—. *South Africa's Forgotten Revival: The Story of the Cape's Great Awakening in 1860.* USA: Xulon Press, 2008.

Oliver, E and A.D. Pont. "Dirk van der Hoff: Skeurmaker?" *HTS* 46/3 (1990).

Papers Past. "The Cape of Good Hope." Wellington Independent [New Zealand], Vol VIII, Issue 786, 23 April, 1853.

Saks, D.Y. "Botched orders or Subordination? The Battle of Berea Revisited." *Military History Journal* 9, no. 6 (1994). http://samilitaryhistory.org/vol096ds.html

Smith, Harry George Wakelyn, ed. "Sir Harry Smith and the Orange River Sovereignty." Chap 50 in *The Autobiography of Lieutenant-General Sir Harry Smith, Baronet of Aliwal on the Sutlej, G.C.B.* London: J. Murray, 1903.

Templin, J. Alton. *Ideology on a Frontier: the Theological Foundation of Afrikaner Nationalism, 1652-1910.* London: Greenwood Press, 1984.

Theal, George McCall. *History of the Emigrant Boers in South Africa.* London: Swan Sonneschein Lowrey, 1888.

Williams, D. "Sir George Russel Clerk and the Abandonment of the Orange River Sovereignty, 1853-54: Room for Another View." *Historia* 36, no. 1 (1991): 30-42. http://bit.ly/1enAUWO

www.ingramcontent.com/pod-product-compliance
Lightning Source LLC
Chambersburg PA
CBHW051129030726
47504CB00004B/776